LIKE A LADY

He raised his head. "Is something wrong?"

She swallowed, opening her eyes. His blue eyes were fixed anxiously on her. What had she done? Why wasn't he touching her anymore? "Why would something be wrong?"

"Well, did that feel good, when I did that?"

She flushed. "Yes."

"It's just you're being awfully still and quiet."

"Aren't I supposed to be?"

He sat up. "Why on earth would you be supposed to be?"

"I—I don't know," she said, mortified. "I didn't want to give you a disgust of me. Ladies don't give in to their base urges."

"They don't?"

Despite her embarrassment, she wanted to laugh at his confounded expression. "I don't know. Do they?"

"I don't know either. I've never done this with a *lady* before." Nev thought for a moment. "Did you *feel* like moving, or making any noise?"

Penelope held herself very still. "Well . . . yes."

He sighed in relief. "I'd really rather you did then. It lets me know I'm doing it right. Otherwise I start to worry." He started over . . .

CALGAR'

DE

P9-DWD-536

_____ PUBLIC LIBRARY

In for a Penny

Rose Lerner

Dorchester
Publishing

DORCHESTER PUBLISHING

September 2011

Published by

Dorchester Publishing Co., Inc.
200 Madison Avenue
New York, NY 10016

Copyright © 2010 by Susan Roth

All rights reserved. No part of this book may be reproduced or transmitted in any form or by any electronic or mechanical means, without the written permission of the publisher, except where permitted by law. The scanning, uploading, and distribution of this book via the Internet or via any other means without the permission of the publisher is illegal and punishable by law. Please purchase only authorized electronic editions, and do not participate in or encourage electronic piracy of copyrighted materials. Your support of the author's rights is appreciated.

This is a work of fiction. Names, characters, places, and incidents are either the product of the author's imagination or are used fictitiously. Any resemblance to actual persons, living or dead, events, or locales is entirely coincidental.

ISBN 13: 978-1-4285-1456-0
E-ISBN: 978-1-4285-0820-0

The "DP" logo is the property of Dorchester Publishing Co., Inc.

Printed in the United States of America.

Visit us online at www.dorchesterpub.com.

To my mother.
I wrote this book for you.
I wish you could have read it.

Acknowledgments

I would like to thank my editor, Leah Hultenschmidt, and my agent, Kevan Lyon, for liking this book and for all their guidance and support.

I'd like to thank the members of the Demimonde: Karen Dobbins, Alyssa Fernandez, Vonnie Hughes, and especially Susan Wilbanks. Without you, I would never even have finished my first draft, let alone turned it into a book. Your encouragement, understanding, and thoughtful feedback have meant more to me than you can know.

I'd like to thank all my friends who listened to me ramble on about this book, helped me brainstorm, and gave me their thoughts on earlier drafts. There's too many of you to mention, but you know who you are. I'd also like to thank my online reading and writing friends—you guys are amazing!

And finally, thanks go to my family, who told me that "writer" was a perfectly reasonable career goal.

One

June, 1819

"Thirkell, you know what happened the *last* time we went to one of the Ambersleighs' do's." Lord Nevinstoke winced at the sound of a badly tuned piano from inside the town house. How had he let Thirkell talk him into this? "Can't we go to Amy's instead? She's laid in some lovely French brandy, just for us."

Thirkell rolled his eyes and shoved Nev up the steps. "After you've danced with my cousin, lent her some countenance, *then* we can go to Amy's and get as drunk as you like."

"But, Thirkell," Percy said, "I don't think we *have* any countenance to lend Harriet. We're disreputable, remember? And as Nev has so accurately reminded us, the last time we attended one of Lady Ambersleigh's little gatherings, the orchestra fled in hysterics."

"Well, if she wouldn't hire such bloody incompetent musicians," Nev grumbled, "I wouldn't have had to—"

"I'm sure she's forgotten about that by now! Besides, Nev, your father's an earl, and Percy here is—" Thirkell broke off.

"Yes?" Percy inquired poisonously. "What am I?"

"A very good dancer?" Nev suggested.

Thirkell shot him a grateful look. "Exactly what I was going to say. And we're all bachelors. Lady Ambersleigh will be delighted."

Lady Ambersleigh did not *look* delighted when the three young men were announced. Nev tried to avoid the eye of a young matron on whose new settee he had accidentally upended a punch bowl the month before, and that of an earl from whose son Percy had won almost two hundred pounds at piquet the week before, and that of a lady whom—oh, hell, he tried not to meet anyone's eye.

"There." Thirkell pointed to a mousy girl in the corner. "That's my cousin Harriet. Come on, I'll introduce you."

A few minutes later, Thirkell was dancing with his cousin, and Percy and Nev had engaged her for the following two sets.

"What say we investigate the buffet table?" Nev asked Percy. "I think I might have seen blackberry tarts."

"You didn't. Where would anyone get blackberries this early in the summer? Oh, look, it's Louisa."

The two young men were standing next to a line of wallflowers. Nev's sister Louisa was not one of those unfortunate girls. Despite her undistinguished brown hair and blue eyes, so similar to his own coloring, she was laughing and flirting with six gentlemen at once on the other side of the room.

Nev was struck by a sudden troubling recollection. "Oh, seven hells! My mother isn't here, is she? I was supposed to dine in Berkeley Square tonight."

"I don't see her anywhere," Percy said, and abandoned his friend to his own devices. Nev was unsurprised to see him leading Louisa out onto the floor a minute or two later. After all, none of the other gentlemen present had made Louisa her first wooden sword. Besides, Louisa was a minx; it was like her to use an old friend to make her beaux jealous.

A violin screeched painfully. Behind him, someone groaned. Nev turned. A slender, dark-haired young lady tricked out in orange silk was grimacing and whispering in an older lady's ear.

He liked orange, he liked slender girls, and he liked people who disliked bad music. Of course, it was improper to approach her without an introduction; and the older lady, swathed in appallingly purple satin, looked a bit of a mushroom. Nev didn't let that stop him. Unused to worrying over-much about the niceties at the best of times, the bottle of claret he had shared with his friends before coming to the ball made him even less worried now.

"Good evening," he said to the girl. "It's awful, isn't it? I won't ask you to dance to this, but perhaps you might take a turn about the room with me? The hors d'oeuvres looked lovely."

Dark eyebrows arched. "Excuse me, sir, but I don't believe we have been properly introduced."

"How rude of me. I ought to have said straight off. Nathaniel Arthur Delaval Ambrey, Viscount Nevinstoke, at your service." He seized the hand that was not resting on her mama's waist and bowed over it with a flourish that usually made girls giggle.

She didn't giggle, but a corner of her mouth quirked up. "I said *properly* introduced."

"Oh, Penny, don't be so stuffy," her mama said. He was taken aback for a moment by her accent; it was pure Cockney.

It must have shown on his face, because Penny stiffened. "I'm not being stuffy, Mama. I'm merely trying to avoid complete impropriety. I'm sorry, my lord, but I'm afraid I must decline your offer."

"Don't listen to 'er, my lord. I'm Mrs. Brown, and this is my daughter, Miss Brown. We're very pleased to make your acquaintance, I'm sure."

"Mama!" Miss Brown hissed.

Mrs. Brown's eyes twinkled. "Bring me some lobster salad when you come back, love."

Miss Brown's jaw set, but she put one kid-gloved hand on Nev's arm. "Well, my lord, shall we walk?"

Nev smiled.

They walked for a minute or two without speaking. Nev was surprised when Miss Brown broke the silence. "You wouldn't, by any chance, be the same Lord Nevinstoke who broke into Almack's at midnight last month?"

"The very same. I can't take all the credit, though—Percy and Thirkell were with me. And it was Percy's idea to wear trousers. Were you there?"

Her mouth twisted. "I have not received vouchers."

"It's overrated. Your father's a Cit, I suppose."

She didn't answer.

Nev repeated the last few sentences in his head and panicked a little. "Oh, the devil—I mean, the deuce—I mean—" He collected himself. "I'm awfully sorry, I really shouldn't have said that. I've had a bit of claret, you know. Please forgive me."

For the first time, she smiled at him. "It's all right. I know it's obvious I'm not old money."

"Doesn't matter. I think it's terribly clever, you know, making money. My father only knows how to spend it." He paused, considering. "And gamble with it, of course."

Miss Brown didn't answer, but she took his arm a little more tightly.

Nev decided to be daring, and covered her hand with his. She looked at him and quirked a brow, but she didn't take her hand away. It was small and warm under his, and she was really very pretty, with fine dark eyes, a straight little nose, and a girlish mouth, thin and expressive. Her complexion, framed by straight dark hair, was almost translucent. He suspected she would freckle in the sun.

"Would you like to step out on the terrace?" he asked hopefully.

She laughed outright. "I hope I'm not such a green girl as that. But I will allow you to select some hors d'oeuvres for me."

"A task! My lady has set me a task! But first I beg a token of your favor."

"I'm afraid my red sleeve embroidered with great pearls is

pinned to my other evening gown, my lord," she said with ironic courtesy.

His eyes lit up. "You like Malory!"

She flushed, as if it were something to be ashamed of. "I've always been fond of the *Morte d'Arthur*. I hope my taste in *modern* literature is rather more elevated."

Nev grinned. "Says you! I'll wager a pony you're hiding *The Mysteries of Udolpho* in your reticule even as we speak!"

She wrinkled her nose at him, and Nev wished very much that she were not a young lady, or that he were not a gentleman. He turned hastily to the buffet table. "Well, I shall now perform the momentous task of choosing your hors d'oeuvres. Hmm, this one seems a little lopsided, doesn't it? And this one's rather too brown. Aha! Here we have a perfect specimen!"

"Nev!" Percy gasped behind him.

Nev nearly dropped the plate on Miss Brown's skirts. "What *is* it, Percy?"

"Retreat, man, retreat! Your mother's got Thirkell!"

Nev started, and turned. Sure enough, Lady Bedlow had poor Thirkell at bay, her gilded curls bobbing indignantly as she shook her vinaigrette at him. Thirkell was sending Nev pleading stares in a manner that would soon betray his location. Then would follow recriminations, accusations of heartlessness, and probably some pointed jabs at poor Percy, who, Lady Bedlow was convinced, was Low Company and also Leading Her Precious Boy Astray.

"Where did she spring from?" Nev railed inwardly against the unfairness of the universe. Turning to Miss Brown, he shoved the plate at her. "Terribly sorry, I must be off." He met Thirkell's eyes and jerked his head at the door.

Thirkell took off for the exit, Percy and Nev close on his heels. At the door, Nev glanced back once. He caught a glimpse of Miss Brown loading some lobster salad onto her plate and shrugging ruefully across the room at her mother.

Then he was out the door and under the stars, running down South Audley Street with his friends.

"Shhhh!" Nev hissed. "I'm trying to listen!"

Thirkell cheerily ignored him—and the soprano singing her heart out across the clearing. "Pass the ham."

"Oh, yes, will you serve me some too?" Amy asked.

"If I buy you rapacious eaters another ham, will you hush?" Nev speared a few slices of paper-thin Vauxhall ham as the plate went by.

"I should very much doubt it," Percy said. "Hand of piquet, Thirkell?"

"Not bloody likely. Not after watching how masterfully you fleeced Salksbury last night."

Percy smiled. "I'm wounded. You know I never fleece my friends."

"What are the stakes, then?" Thirkell asked.

"No stakes; I play for practice. My sister's sweet on the apothecary and if I'm to dower her before the Season ends and all my partners remove to the country, I need to be at the top of my game."

"Well, that's no fun. Penny points?"

"Oh, do be quiet and listen to the concert." Amy gave Thirkell a friendly shove. "You know how fond Nev is of Arne."

Nev raised his head to thank her, and his attention was wrenched away from Arne's aria by the sight of a slender, dark-haired girl in the box opposite, clearly shushing her companions. She looked across at the same moment, and their eyes met. The champagne seemed to go to Nev's head all at once.

"I say, who's Nev staring at?"

As if she could hear Thirkell, Miss Brown turned her attention firmly back to the orchestra.

Percy glanced across the lawn. "It's that girl he was talking to at the Ambersleighs' last week."

"Miss Brown," Nev supplied. "She likes music."

Amy leaned out to peer across. The movement knocked a yellow curl out from behind her ear to fall distractingly over her cheek. "She's pretty. Just your type too."

Nev felt a rush of affection for Amy. She really was a great gun, and never jealous. He tucked the lock back behind her ear. "Mmm. Too bad she's respectable."

She swatted his arm. "She's a deal more than respectable, you nodcock! She's rich as the Golden Ball!"

"What?" Nev glanced back at the box opposite. Miss Brown, her eyes closed, looked to be entirely focused on Arne; but somehow his fingertips burned where they still touched Amy's shoulder.

"Her dowry's a hundred and seventy-five thousand pounds." Amy was always better informed about these sorts of things than he was. "If you think she's taken a fancy to you, you'd best snap her up before someone gets in ahead of you."

"You don't say," Percy said. "What's her father do?"

"He's a brewer. Mrs. Brown used to be a friend of my mother's, back when they were girls." Amy sounded wistful, suddenly. "Wouldn't me mum have liked to lord it in a fine house in Russell Square!"

Nev put an arm around her waist. "But then we would all be deprived of your note-perfect performance in *Twelfth Night*."

Amy laughed, but she nestled closer. "Oh, you just like seeing me in breeches!"

"We all like seeing you in breeches," Percy said, "but I think Nev here actually listens to the words."

"*You* only listen to the words when no one else can understand them," Thirkell grumbled. "Remember when he dragged us to Reading Hall for that ancient Greek stuff? It was bizarre."

"It was *authentic*," Percy said. "My trick, Thirkell."

"It's *always* your trick."

Miss Brown was forgotten; Nev called for another bottle of champagne and another ham; and what with one thing and another, it was six in the morning before they left Vauxhall and stumbled back to Amy's, singing a naughty ballad that had been popular during their school days at Trinity.

One of his mother's footmen was waiting on the steps. Nev took one look at his face and had an abrupt, chilling suspicion that he was far too drunk to deal with whatever was about to happen. "What is it, Tom?"

"It's James, my lord," the footman corrected distractedly. "I've been waiting—I've got bad news—I'm that sorry, your lordship—"

"For God's sake, out with it before you scare him to death!" Amy snapped.

James looked as if he would rather be anywhere than where he was. Nev felt pretty much the same.

"It's your father, my lord. He's dead."

Two

It was past noon before Nev, feeling as though an entire orchestra was pounding out a discordant symphony in his skull, left Amy's house for Berkeley Square. He remembered little of the previous night—or rather, earlier that morning—after James's dreadful announcement, aside from confused impressions of vomiting in Amy's roses and, to his surprise, sobbing drunkenly in Amy's arms.

His eyes were dry now. He had loved his father, of course. As a little boy he had even idolized him, but that idolatry was long dead. Lord Bedlow had had a great deal of charm and been carelessly generous with his affection, yet he could never quite remember how old his children were or that strawberries made Louisa sick or that he had promised to take them to the fair that summer.

Nev would miss him, and he supposed he would have to spend more time with his family now that he was the head of it. And there was sitting in Parliament and talking to the steward and a good deal of bother like that, but really it seemed that in a month or two things would be almost back to normal.

Amy had seen him out and was standing on her porch wearing nothing but one of his own silk dressing gowns. It was too large for her and had already slipped half off one shoulder. Her eyes were shadowed. "I know you'll have a lot on your mind for the next while. You've got your people to look after now. Don't worry about me. I'll be here when you want me."

"I want you now. Or I would, if I didn't have such a cursed

head." Her curls were tumbling over her freckled shoulders, and he reached out and wrapped one around his finger. "Thanks, Amy. You're a Trojan."

She stood on tiptoe and kissed him. "Don't forget it."

"Are you all right for money?"

She smiled. "Yes, you're all paid up. I told you, don't worry about me. I'm sorry about your father."

He tugged on her yellow curl. "I'll be back before you know it, I promise."

When he was shown into his mother's presence, he saw that it would be longer than a month or two before things were back to normal. Lady Bedlow was pale and red-eyed; two furious spots of color burned in her cheeks; and, worst of all, her blonde hair was a bird's nest.

Louisa sat on the settee beside their mother, looking rather worn herself—but mostly uncomfortable, darting helpless glances at Lady Bedlow and twisting a handkerchief in her hands. When Nev came in, she started up with a grateful look. "Oh, Nate—"

Nev opened his arms and she flew into them.

"Oh, Nate!" Louisa clung fiercely to his lapels. It steadied the pounding in his head, a little. "What took you so long?"

Nev flushed and let go of her. "I came as soon as I was able. Bear up, Louisa, we'll be all right. I promise."

She smiled at him.

"You can't promise it," Lady Bedlow said in a dull voice. "Nothing will ever be all right again. I could *kill* your father— if he weren't already—" Her face contorted, and she controlled herself with an effort. "Did James tell you what happened?"

James had told Amy, actually. Amy had told Nev the details—quietly, to spare his head—when he had awoken from his three hours of rest. "Indeed he did, Mama. You needn't—"

She ignored him. "Well, your papa was in a duel. A duel! And him with children grown. He would never have done such a thing if he had been sober. He is always excessively foolish when in his cups, though I have never known him to be violent—indeed, he is generally very affectionate at those times—" For a moment Lady Bedlow could not go on.

Louisa made a pleading gesture. "Mama, pray do not distress yourself."

But Lady Bedlow spoke as if by compulsion. "Well, he quarreled with Lord Chilcote last night, and a meeting was arranged for early this morning, and what happened is Chilcote shot him. I never liked Chilcote. He jilted your Aunt Hareton, you know. Alex's brains were all over the carriage—and they wouldn't even tell me what the quarrel was about—"

Louisa's hand quivered on Nev's arm.

"Mama, don't." He tried to conquer his own rush of nausea.

"It was something about money, I daresay!" she said with sudden energy.

"Money?"

His mother avoided his gaze. "He owed Chilcote money, I gathered. But Chilcote will not dare try to collect it now."

"Mama—"

"And when Bunbury woke me I knew—I saw her face and I knew it was *someone*, and I thought, *Don't let it be Nate!* Your father's body lying below with half his face away and I thought 'Please not Nate'—" Lady Bedlow pressed her fist to her mouth and turned away.

Nev could not help being touched beyond measure. "Mama, don't torment yourself." He went to her at last and drew her close. From this angle, the light from the front windows hurt his eyes. "Please."

"I didn't want to marry him, you know. But after twenty-five years . . ." She turned her face up to his, blindly, and smiled a little. "Here, Nate. This is yours now." She drew his father's signet ring off her thumb—Nev hadn't noticed it before—and laid it in his palm and curled his fingers round it. It felt heavy and unfamiliar, and Nev wished like anything he could give it back.

When he at last took his leave to go and discuss various arrangements for the funeral, the reading of the will, and the like with Lord Bedlow's solicitor, Louisa followed him into the hall.

"Will you be all right?" he asked her.

She gave him a tired smile. "Oh, yes. Lucky beast! I wish I had my own lodgings."

"Mama oughtn't to speak like that in front of you."

"You mean about Papa's brains and all that? It doesn't matter, I'd already seen them." She noticed his face, and said, "I'll be all *right*, Nev. It's you I'm worried about."

Every word she said made him feel worse. "Me? Why would you worry about me? Last night while *you* were looking at Papa's brains I was merely drunk and singing too loud."

She bit her lip. "Oh, poor Nate! You must have a terrible head. I only meant you'll have to deal with business and everything, and sort out Papa's finances."

"What do you mean?"

"Nate, you know Papa was—well, dipped, don't you?"

Nev relaxed. "Oh, is that all? He always bled a little too freely." He wished he had chosen a different expression. "That is, I expect I'll have a few thousand pounds to settle with his creditors, but surely they can wait, and I'll pay them something down on quarter day—"

Louisa was shaking her head. "I don't know for certain, but—when's the last time you were at Loweston?"

"A couple of years ago, I should think."

"Well—it doesn't look quite the same anymore. I don't think the harvests have been very good. And—a man was here this morning, already, from the grocer's, asking to be paid."

The cleansing wave of anger was a relief. "Someone *dunned* you? This morning? With Papa's body still warm? I'll *kill* him!"

"That isn't the point, Nate." The poor girl really did look worried.

"It's nothing, Louisa. The grocer is a vulture, that's all, and you know Papa always liked town better than Loweston. I'm not surprised it's been a trifle neglected. I'll go see Papa's man of business tomorrow and straighten it all out."

"But—"

"Don't *worry*." He smiled at her. "I daresay we shall contrive to keep out of the poorhouse, provided you don't buy another of those outrageously large bonnets you're so fond of. Wax cherries, Louisa? What were you thinking of?"

The corners of her mouth turned up reluctantly.

"Don't let Mama nag you too much. I'll take care of everything. I promise."

Nev needed a drink. There were arrangements to be made for the funeral, black coats to be ordered, and a million other things to look after; but for now Nev went to his lodgings and poured himself a glass of claret.

He'd only drunk half of it when a knock came at the door. It was Percy, his dark eyes somber. "I came to see how you were doing."

Nev shrugged. "I'm all right. Claret?"

Percy took a glass and sat. "Just—I know it's not pleasant, the funeral, and your grieving mother clinging to you and all that."

He looked at Percy in surprise, but of course Percy knew. Mr. Garrett had died several years ago. Percy hadn't said much about it at the time—all the details Nev knew, he had learned from Lord Bedlow, who had been quite put out at the

difficulties of finding a new steward who would suit him as
well as Percy's father.

"She kept talking about his brains." Nev tried not to picture it and found that the image of his mother's red-rimmed
eyes was not much better. "I suppose I shall have to tip whoever got stuck cleaning the carriage." Was it wrong, to think
about that at a time like this?

"At least you know it was quick," Percy said quietly. "My
father was ill for months, and my mother kept sending for
new doctors—but it'll get better. Honestly. There's still things
I wish I could tell him, but . . ." He sighed.

Nev could have nodded sympathetically and pretended
that was comforting, pretended that he felt just as he ought,
but he found he couldn't. Not to Percy. He shrugged. "You
knew my father. Remember Louisa's sixth birthday?"

"I'm afraid you'll have to be more precise."

"She'd been telling everyone in sight for months that she
wanted a pirate sword, and—"

"Oh, Lord, and your father bought her that enormous doll
in a pink satin dress. I never saw a child look more forlorn in
her life."

"He had no idea what was wrong."

"I can picture that doll perfectly to this day." Percy smiled
reminiscently. "As I recall, I was betrothed to it for a time.
Louisa used to commandeer its ship as it sailed to England to
be my bride, and I had to duel her for it."

"Bloodthirsty little creature, wasn't she?"

Percy chuckled and nodded. "Poor girl. How's she taking it?"

"You know Louisa, she's a brick." Nev thrust away the
memory of her anxious face. "She'll do all right. Percy, do you
know what my father and Chilcote quarreled about?"

Percy rubbed at his temple. "It's not a pretty story, Nev."

"It's all over town, isn't it?"

Percy nodded. "I suppose I'd better tell you, for there'll be ghouls enough eager to discuss every detail with you." He drew in a breath. "Here is it then. Having already lost a considerable sum at faro, your father was playing piquet with Chilcote at White's. He was losing—I collect he had a run of bad luck recently—and the long and short of it is, he hinted that perhaps Chilcote was cheating."

Nev groaned. "As if he needed to. My father couldn't possibly beat Chilcote at piquet."

Percy's lips quirked in acknowledgment. "Even I find Chilcote to be more trouble than he's worth. But Bedlow was only half-serious, from what I can tell, as well as three sheets to the wind, and Chilcote could have played it off. But he was foxed too and responded with something to the effect that even if, as a gentleman, he were capable of cheating, there would be no point cheating your father because—" Percy looked deeply uncomfortable.

"Come on, out with it. I know *you* didn't say whatever it was."

"He said Bedlow was certain not to honor his vowels." Percy would not meet Nev's eyes. "Your father—well, from what I could glean, he nearly went crazy. He would be satisfied with nothing but a duel."

"Chilcote said *what?*"

Percy was silent.

"Percy, are you saying you think Chilcote was *right?*"

"I knew Lord Bedlow," Percy said slowly, "and I think that he would never fail to discharge a debt of honor if it were in his power to do so."

Nev stared at him, an unpleasant chill creeping up his spine. His mother had avoided his eyes when she said *It was something about money*, and Louisa had said, *Loweston looks different now.* "You think it might not have been in his power?"

Percy shifted in his chair. "I've heard rumors he was badly dipped, Nev. We all did. But there wasn't anything you could do, so—we thought you must know, and if you didn't—we didn't want to worry you."

Nev stood. "I—I think I'd better visit my father's solicitor." He looked at his half-drunk glass of claret. Had there still been liquor on his father's breath when they carried him into the hall with his head half away? His mother's voice echoed in his ears—*He would never have done it if he were sober.* He pushed the glass away, queasy.

Percy hesitated. "I've never much of the ready, but if you need, I could probably scrape together a couple of hundred pounds." His shoulders were tense. Two hundred pounds would not go far toward any debts Lord Bedlow had amassed, and they both knew it. But it was a lot of money to Percy, who was saving for his sister's dowry.

Nev tried to smile. "I expect it's a tempest in a teapot. Don't go dooming your sister to a life of spinsterhood just yet."

Percy let out his breath. "But if you should need any help—"

"I promise you, if I should need anything, you and Thirkell would be the first I'd turn to, as always."

At the solicitor's, Nev discovered that his father had been living beyond his means for years.

He and his family were utterly ruined.

Three

Nev climbed the Bedlow House stairs, pushing past the duns who clustered before the door. He felt years older, though it had only been two weeks since his father's death. He had spent most of that time closeted with his father's man of business, trying to understand the extent of his difficulties and selling everything he could think of. He had worked far into the night adding columns of figures and trying to organize the stacks of bills in his father's desk into some semblance of order—then worrying at the cost of the candle, and all too aware that he was like a schoolboy practicing the piano, plunking out the same five notes over and over and entirely failing to turn them into a tune.

And every day, as the news spread around London that Lord Bedlow was dead, more bills arrived—duns from the tailor, the stables, the milliner, the bootmaker, the stationer, the wine seller, the butcher, the jeweler, the glover, and a thousand other tradesmen whose existence had previously been merely theoretical to Nev. There was even a polite request for repayment of a generous loan from a Mr. Mendoza of the City.

And still there were this week's expenses to be paid—food for his mother and sister, his father's funeral, oats for the horses, wages for the servants, mourning clothes. Every day, every hour that Nev found no solution put them deeper in debt; and Nev knew very well he could not find a solution. The quarter's rents had been spent long since—probably years ago. He had come to tell his mother that the town house must be sold.

Lady Bedlow went very pale. She darted a few glances around the room, allowing her eyes to rest for a long moment on the portrait of herself and Lord Bedlow that hung over the mantel. Then she turned her face to the window, presenting Nev with a sorrowing profile. "Will that put us out of debt?"

Nev was unsure how to deal with this display of regal suffering. "Er, I'm afraid not. But it will make up what Papa spent of your jointure. I haven't quite worked out how to get us out of debt yet. I was thinking of selling the oaks on the drive to Loweston—Papa cut down nearly everything else already."

Lady Bedlow's head snapped around at this. "Sell the oaks at Loweston? Those oaks have given your forefathers shade for centuries!"

"But, Mama—" Nev subsided at her glare. "Well, but I don't know what else is to be done! I've already sold the hunting box in Essex and most of the horses and—" He realized that listing everything he had sold to his mother would be an unsurpassed act of folly, and stopped.

Lady Bedlow turned back to the window. "Your father and I honeymooned in Essex."

"You didn't sell Blackbeard, did you?" Louisa asked.

Nev smiled for what felt like the first time in months. "No, I didn't sell Blackbeard."

She straightened her spine. "I see how it is."

"Er—how is it, Louisa?"

"You must marry me to some horrid old merchant. That will bring us to rights, won't it?"

Lady Bedlow was speechless.

Nev tried not to laugh. "Must it be an *old* merchant, Louisa?"

"I'm not pretty enough to get a young one, I know that. It's all right. I'm prepared to make sacrifices for the family."

Nev was abruptly appalled. "Louisa, you goose, you're pretty enough to have a hundred young merchants eating out of your hand, but if you think I'm going to consent to any such scheme you're all about in the head." In fact, their neighbor Sir Jasper Montagu had already offered to buy Loweston for a generous sum and settle the land on Louisa's children if Louisa would marry him. Nev had refused without consulting her. In his late thirties, Sir Jasper was old enough to be her father; and Louisa, Nev recalled vaguely, had been frightened of the baronet as a child.

Lady Bedlow nodded. "As if I could feel a moment's happiness living in the lap of luxury, knowing that my child had been sold to some wretched Cit!"

Suddenly, Nev remembered a small warm hand and a sweep of brown hair. His eyes widened. "You know, I think I may have a chance to get us out of debt after all."

And he bounded out the door and down the steps before his mother could say another word.

Her thoughts were silently fixed on the irreparable injury which too early an independence—and its consequent habits of idleness, dissipation, and luxury—had made in the mind, the character, the happiness, of a man who, to every advantage of person and talents, united a disposition naturally open and honest, and a feeling, affectionate temper.

Penelope looked up from her well-thumbed copy of *Sense and Sensibility* when she heard the great front door swing open. But as no one came to announce a visitor, she decided that it must be one of her father's business acquaintances. Or perhaps it might be the post; she was hoping for another letter from Edward. She had reread the last one this morning, but somehow it had not told her anything new.

Poor Edward! He sounded lonely in Paris, and always busy working and learning the French that would help him sell his employer's woolen goods on the Continent. She wished he had been sent to France the following year, so that she might have gone with him—for surely by then Mama would have given over hoping for a lord for her. Mama could be romantical and talk of noble lords and Grand Passions and ancestral art collections all she liked, but Penelope didn't care for any of that. Mutual esteem and warm affection were good enough for her.

She had to admit it was partly Edward's own fault. Her parents might have been willing to consider the match if Edward hadn't left the brewery to work for a northern industrialist. She herself had wished that Edward would stay in her father's company; she had little desire to live so far from town.

But she was willing to make the sacrifice for Edward's sake. In the meantime, she would wait patiently, and if Mama wanted her to accept the invitations to *ton* affairs that Penelope still sometimes received from old schoolfellows, well, there was no real harm in it.

She wished her mother could be made aware of how very out of place they were at the *ton*'s social occasions—or rather, made to *care* how out of place they were, for her mother *was* aware of it. Dear Mama; she thought it a great joke how everyone looked at her, and with true maternal loyalty refused to see that everyone looked at her darling Penny in exactly the same way.

Mrs. Brown had nearly burst with pride when Penelope attracted the attention of a *viscount* a few weeks ago—waving away Penelope's most forceful representations that Lord Nevinstoke had merely walked with her for a few moments before sprinting out of the house as if the hounds of Hell were after him. Penelope had not had the heart to tell her mother of the improper way he had looked at her—at least, she was sure from the way it had made her feel that it must have been improper.

Nor had she had the heart to mention that she had seen

him a week later at Vauxhall, well on his way to being drunk as a wheelbarrow, and with a woman Penelope would have wagered a hundred guineas was his mistress. A very pretty woman. Penelope had seen her in a production of *Twelfth Night* the previous month, and she had been a charming and talented actress.

There was no use her mother feeling the pain of disillusion that must follow.

His image rose again before her eyes. There was, to be sure, nothing out of the common way about him. *A perfectly ordinary-looking young man*, Penelope insisted to herself. He was of middling height, his shoulders neither slim nor broad. His hands were not aristocratically slender—there was nothing to set them apart from the hands of any other gentleman of her acquaintance.

His hair was a little too long, and she thought its tousled appearance more the result of inattention than any attempt at fashion; it was neither dark nor fair, but merely brown—utterly nondescript save for a hint of cinnamon. His face too would have been unmemorable if it were not for a slight crookedness in his nose, suggesting it had been broken. His eyes were an ordinary blue, of an ordinary shape and size.

So why could she picture him so clearly, and why did the memory of his smile still make her feel—hot, and strange inside?

But it was his voice that stayed with her the strongest; the timbre of it was imprinted on her ear, and there was nothing ordinary about it. It was rich and mellow, and there was something graceful in the careless rhythm of his speech.

So strongly had she conjured up Lord Nevinstoke's image that when the door opened, Evans spoke, and that same gentleman entered the room, it was a moment before she was quite convinced he was real.

He was in every particular as she remembered him, save

that he was dressed from head to toe in black, and his blue eyes were anxious and grave. She realized that Evans had not announced him as Lord Nevinstoke, but as Lord Bedlow.

She stood without thinking, and her book fell to the floor. In an instant he had stepped forward, bent down, and returned it to her. She was conscious that her fingers closed too tightly on the book; he was very close, an odd expression in his eyes. His nearness affected her, alas, just as she remembered.

"Has something happened to your father, my lord?"

He looked away and stepped back. "You are very perceptive. My father was killed Wednesday before last."

"You mean—the day after I saw you at Vauxhall?"

He smiled. "You remembered me."

She had been so shocked by his news that at first she had forgotten to listen to his voice. Now she experienced the full effect of the pure vowels and husky overtones; her pulse sped up. "I am so sorry to hear about your father."

"Thank you," he said, then stood silent. "Dash it, this is awkward."

"I own I am a little surprised to see you."

"I suppose I had better out with it. My father had run into debt before he died. A great deal of debt."

Penelope's heart plummeted into her boots. She struggled for composure. "I see."

"The long and short of it is, I've come to ask you to marry me."

Four

Though she had been half expecting it, the world seemed to stand still a moment; then it started again, with a stutter. "I beg your pardon?"

"You heard me correctly, I assure you." He ran a hand through his hair, confirming her impression that its disorder was unfeigned, then took a few steps back. "Do you—do you think we might be seated?"

She chastised herself for a poor hostess. "Of course." Resuming her seat, she gestured to him to do the same.

She had meant for him to take the chair placed conveniently a few feet off, but he, misreading her gesture, seated himself beside her on the window seat. He leaned forward, his elbows on his spread knees and his hands clasped.

"I've no intention of offering you Spanish coin. I need your money, very much—oh, how much! I don't know how I'm to manage without it." His mouth twisted. "I never thought about money till I hadn't got it, you know. And now there's candles and black gloves and ink and my sister's dowry"—he had begun to tick these off on his fingers as he went; it had the air of a familiar pattern of thought. But he caught himself and shook his hands, ending with, "oh, and a thousand other things I never gave a moment's thought to! How do people contrive who haven't money?"

Penelope had never had to contrive without money; she had still been a babe when her father began to make his fortune. But she knew how it was done. "With tallow and small dowries, I'm afraid."

He flushed. "I daresay I look a regular wastrel to you."

He did, and Penelope hated insincerity. Nevertheless, the words flew to her lips without her thinking them. "Oh, no!"

He gave her a rueful smile. She tried to ignore its effect on her. "You're a sweet girl. And that was what I meant to say. I can't deny I need your money, but I still wouldn't offer for you if I didn't feel we could rub along tolerably well together."

His words warmed her more than they should, but that didn't mean she had lost all sense. "We've spoken together for all of five minutes in our lives, my lord. How can you possibly know we could rub along well together?"

"I can tell." He hesitated for a moment; then he slid closer to her on the window seat, tilted up her face to his, and kissed her.

Penelope had been kissed before, once or twice. (Not by Edward, of course. He had always been all that was respectful, never given her more than a chaste kiss on the brow or the cheek.) She had found it awkward, wet, and extremely unwelcome. But Lord Bedlow's mouth was warm and coaxing against hers. It was not really one kiss, but several in quick succession, and she found herself instinctively responding. It was clear that Lord Bedlow knew what he was about. Her eyelids fluttered closed, and a feeling that was unfamiliar and hot and uncomfortable—at least, she *thought* it was uncomfortable, but she wasn't sure—began to stir in the depths of her body. She ached in places it wasn't ladylike to think about. And for all she still hadn't decided if the new feeling was uncomfortable or not, she was sure she wanted more.

When he raised his head and let go of her chin, she half expected him to smirk or look triumphant. But he only looked pleased and flushed; his blue eyes, when he opened them, sparkled a little. "And you like Arne's arias."

Penelope liked Arne a great deal. She suspected she had liked the kiss a great deal too, but it was civil of him not to point that out. "Still, that is hardly a basis to be considering matrimony," she said, as severely as she could when her pulse was racing and she knew she was blushing all over.

The pleased light died out of his eyes; turning, he stared out the bow window. "I know it. But I've tried everything else."

She pitied him sincerely. "Have you no other way of making money? Surely you needn't rush into a marriage that— that cannot be what you wish." She looked away, conscious of her folly in fishing for a compliment when he would have had to be an idiot to contradict her. "I know it isn't done, for a gentleman of your class to engage in business, but—I remember you told me that you thought it was clever, making money."

"Well, I am not particularly clever." His crooked profile was bleak.

She wanted—she hardly knew what, but to touch him, to comfort him.

"And I need money right away, a great deal of it. I've sold off my mother's favorite estate and my father's guns. I've sold half the silver and most of the horses and all the jewels my mother hasn't hidden under her mattress. I'm putting the town house up for sale tomorrow—but it won't cover a tenth of the debts. I've sold everything I can think of, and it isn't enough. The only thing I have left is myself." His self-mocking smile was out of place on his boyish face. "I know it's not a very good bargain."

She opened her mouth to tell him that she was very sorry, but it would be the height of imprudence even to consider, etc., etc.—and heard herself say, "All right then."

"You mean you'll marry me?" He turned back to her, his face lighting up.

Again her tongue moved without consultation with her brain. "Well—yes." Even in the midst of her consternation, his smile was contagious; she found herself smiling foolishly back.

"Oh, this is wonderful! Thank you!" With an effort he looked more grave. "I hope I am sensible of—you won't regret it."

She regretted it already. Had she really consented? Had she lost her mind? Faintly she said, "Thank you, my lord." She ought to back out—to tell him she'd made a mistake, that she hadn't considered—but she knew she wouldn't. Some part of her didn't want to.

She squared her shoulders. "I shall do my best to be a good wife to you, even if I'm not the wife of your choosing. I see no reason why two people of good sense and amiable dispositions should not find a tolerable measure of conjugal felicity, even if they are not, perhaps, united by those bonds of affection and familiarity which one might wish."

He looked a little bewildered by this speech, but he said, "Precisely my sentiments."

She was still caught in the grip of a sense of unreality. "You have already spoken to my father, I presume."

"Of course. He said he would let me ask you myself, but— to be honest, I don't think he had any expectation of your agreeing."

Penelope's eyes widened, the scene to come already clearly before her eyes. "Here—I shall undertake to make him keep his word, but perhaps you had better not talk it over with him now. I know speed is important to you, but can you come back tomorrow to arrange all the details?"

His eyebrows rose, but he answered, "Certainly."

"Will eleven o'clock answer?"

"Very well. He *will* agree, won't he?"

"I believe he will." Privately, Penelope wasn't sure. "Only— you'd better bring a statement of your debts with you. Have you got one?"

He looked abruptly frustrated. "Not a good one, no. New bills come every day, and—I've no head for numbers, Miss

Brown. I've added it all up enough to make my eyes ache and come up with a different answer every time."

Here at least she was on sure ground, and the sudden sense of her own competence bolstered her. She smiled at him. "Well, I cannot help you with your other problems until we are wed, but that one I can help you with now. Has anyone ever taught you to cast out nines?"

"What is that?"

"It's a method for verifying sums. Here, come over to the writing desk." She scribbled a short column of numbers and totted them up. "This won't catch all mistakes, but it'll catch most." She showed him what to do. ". . . Now when you add up all the one-digit numbers—again ignoring any nines—they ought to be the same as your sum. Do you understand?"

His eyes were narrowed in concentration. "Do it once more?"

His evident amazement that the trick worked a second time made her want to laugh. "Here, let me try," he said, scrawling an example of his own in a sloping Italian hand. "Jupiter! That's astonishing! However did you come to know such a thing?"

She looked down. "I sometimes help my father with his books." Keeping the books of a brewery was not a proper occupation for a young lady. It was a moment before she could raise her eyes to his, knowing she could not but be lowered in his esteem.

His eyes were filled with such azure wonder that she caught her breath. "I knew you were just what I needed!"

She laughed. "Perhaps you had better bring your man of business with you tomorrow."

But all laughter was at an end when Evans arrived to show him out. Any moment now her mother or father would come in, and she would have to admit what she had done. She would have to admit that she had agreed to spend the rest of

her life with a man of whose character she knew nothing—
or worse than nothing! A man, in fact, of whom she knew
only that he had a spendthrift father, a taste for strong drink,
and a very pretty mistress.

He likes music, an insidious voice whispered inside her.
And he kisses well. She flushed with mortification. She had
always prided herself on her self-command, her firmness of
purpose. Yet she had staked her future on one throw of the
die; she had agreed to give herself, body and soul, to a handsome young man on the strength of a kiss. She was a weak-
willed, foolish girl, indeed. Her eyes ran listlessly over the
desk—and lighted on Edward's letter.

She had forgotten Edward! Her eye dwelt in horror on his
familiar neat script. *This weekend, an associate insisted on taking me on a tour of Paris's most picturesque Gothick churches,
though I assured him I have no part in the great fad for all things
Gothick that ensnares so many of my countrymen. But I think
you would have enjoyed hearing the organ of Notre Dame de
Paris—it is larger than anything you can imagine, and though I
could not judge myself I am told that the organist is prodigious
talented.*

What was she going to tell Edward?

Penelope was still staring at the letter when her father walked
in a few minutes later. "My, you got rid of that Bedlow fellow
quick, didn't you? I told him it were a waste of time, but he
seemed awful set on talking to you, and I knew you'd be able
to send him about his business with a sight more tact than
I could." He noticed her dazed face. "He didn't insult you,
did he?"

She took a deep breath. "I accepted his offer, Papa."

"What?"

She nodded.

"But—but—call him back and refuse it, then! The black-
guard's a fortune hunter. I thought you would *know* that."

Though she had been longing to do that very thing when her father had walked in, she stiffened. "I did know it, Papa. He was very honest with me. He is coming tomorrow at eleven to discuss the settlements with you."

Mr. Brown turned very red. "I shall certainly not receive him! A wastrel and spendthrift if I ever saw one! He showed me a pathetic calculation he had made of his debts. An illegible scrawl. The boy can barely add!"

"Yes, Papa," Penelope said more strongly, angry with her father for being so unfair to Lord Bedlow, who was doing the best he could. "That is why he wishes to marry me. He was not brought up to understand money."

"Your dowry was to set you and your husband up in life and make you comfortable, not to redeem the mortgages of some profligate lordling!"

"You never wanted Edward to have it either." She knew that it was childish to be so contrary, but the more her father stormed, the more she clung to her rash decision. "His father's profligacy is not Lord Bedlow's fault. Anyway, it is too late now to repine. I have given him my word."

"Much his lordship will care for the word of a Brown!"

"That is no reason to cheapen it! How many times have you told me that once you've shaken hands on a deal, you cannot shrink from it?"

As Penelope was finishing this fine speech, her mother entered the room. Mr. Brown's face seemed to cave in a little. Turning on his wife, he said, "This is all your doing! Filling her head with notions of lords and family seats! I hope you will be happy, Mrs. Brown, when your daughter is the countess of a run-down, drafty, out-of-the-way place with holes in the upholstery."

Mrs. Brown stared. "George, whatever are you talking about?"

"She's said yes to that Nevinstoke you've been yammering on about, that's what! His father's got himself killed and now he's bound for the *Gazette* unless he can marry an heiress, and your daughter was fool enough to accept him."

"Oh, George, you're in a taking for nothing. Penny wouldn't be so foolish, would you, Penny?"

Penelope's face heated. "I am not foolish. But—but I did agree to marry Lord Bedlow."

Her mother stared at her in incomprehension. "*Why?*"

Penelope was conscious that she did not know; embarrassment made her stubborn. She tilted up her chin. "You ought to be pleased, Mama. It's what you've always wanted, isn't it?"

Mrs. Brown's eyes narrowed. "George, may I talk to Penny alone for a moment?"

Mr. Brown grumbled, but he left the room.

"Penny, what on earth has come over you?" Mrs. Brown asked. "Are you angry with us for something?"

"My decision had nothing to do with you!" Perhaps if her mother had come in first, Penelope might have yielded to her persuasions and sent an apologetic refusal after Lord Bedlow. But now it was too late. "You seemed to like him well enough when you met him. *You* introduced us to him. *You* looked him up in *Debrett's* the moment we arrived home. What was your purpose, if not exactly what has transpired?"

"I meant you to know him a bit longer first! You needn't make me out to be some kind of heartless schemer. Why shouldn't you marry a man with a university education? A man who's seen something of the world? Who'll take you to Venice?"

"Edward's traveling!"

"Pooh, Paris," Mrs. Brown said, who had loved Paris the one time she had managed to convince Mr. Brown to take her there. "What *are* you going to tell Edward?"

Penelope's face crumpled. "Oh, Mama, I don't know! I didn't even *think* of it until Lord Bedlow had gone, and then—"

Mrs. Brown frowned. "Lord Bedlow must have been very persuasive."

Penelope blushed. "I felt sorry for him."

A corner of Mrs. Brown's mouth twitched. "Is that what the young folk are calling it nowadays? When I was a girl we said we was sweet on a boy."

"Mama," Penelope snapped, "I am not sweet on Lord Bedlow."

"Then why are you blushing like a bonfire? I never saw you look like that after half an hour in Edward's company."

Penelope raised a hand to her flaming cheeks. "I'm merely a touch discomposed."

"He didn't do anything he oughtn't, did he?"

"Of course not," Penelope said reflexively. And then, because she hated lying to her mother, "He did kiss me."

Mrs. Brown was silent a moment. "And did you like it?"

"Mama!"

Mrs. Brown folded her arms. "Don't you 'Mama' me. You're asking me to let my baby girl marry a man she's spoken to twice, who's only after her money, and I am not going to even *think* about it if you didn't like the way he kissed you."

"Mama!" But her mother was implacably silent. "I liked it," she said very, very quietly.

Mrs. Brown nodded.

"And—and he isn't *only* after my money." Penelope hoped it was the truth. "That is—he was *mainly* after it, and he wouldn't have offered for me without it, of course, but—he said he wouldn't have asked me if he didn't think we could rub along tolerably well together. And he likes Arne."

Mrs. Brown's face softened—a little. "That composer you're always on about? What a coincidence." She sighed. "He did seem a nice boy." After a few more moments' frowning thought, she said, heavily, "I'll speak to your father. We shan't be too hasty, but there's no harm in talking to the boy, I suppose."

* * *

Nev's heart was pounding as he and his father's man of business waited on the Browns' steps at five to eleven the following morning. He was sure, perfectly sure, that Miss Brown would have thought it all over and realized what a poor bargain she was getting.

He did not feel much reassured when they were ushered into Mr. Brown's study and found the brewer and a dapper young clerk in earnest consultation over a ledger so heavy it made Nev's eyes ache just looking at it.

The face Mr. Brown turned on him was not particularly friendly. "Well, you've ensnared my daughter, so I suppose there's nothing I can do about that." He put his hands in his pockets and rocked back on his heels. "If I refused the dowry you'd skip off readily enough, but the girl says to me, 'Didn't you teach me that once you've shaken hands on a deal, there's no turning back?' And bless me if I didn't. Has your man here got an accounting of your debts?"

Nev breathed an inward sigh of relief. Miss Brown had kept her word. "Yes, sir, and the mortgage papers too."

Mr. Brown looked them over with an expert eye. "Well, the list's honest, at least," he said with some surprise.

Nev stiffened. "Certainly. Wait a moment—how the deuce did you know that?"

For the first time, Mr. Brown's eyes twinkled a bit. "I asked a few questions. Do you think a man gets to be as rich as I am without being able to do a little thing like investigate a fellow's debts?"

Nev had never considered the matter. "I suppose not, sir."

Mr. Brown was looking at the total again. "Do you know, considering how much it's going to cost me to dig you out of this hole you've got yourself into, I wonder if I ought not to ask you to change your name."

"Er—change my name, sir?"

Mr. Brown nodded. "When my friend Lewis married his

daughter to an impoverished nob like yourself, he made the fellow change his name to Lewis. And *he* was a dook." Mr. Brown looked at his clerk. "The Browns of Loweston. It has a nice ring, don't it?"

Nev stared.

"Indeed, sir. But I believe the fad these days is for hyphenation." The clerk turned to Nev, eyes glowing with enthusiasm. "Which do you like better, my lord? Brown-Ambrey or Ambrey-Brown? I should think Ambrey-Brown, myself. Very euphonious."

Nev tried to imagine his mother's face if he told her he was changing his name to Ambrey-Brown.

Mr. Brown and his clerk burst out laughing. "Naw, I'm only teasing you, m'boy." Mr. Brown clapped Nev on the back, almost knocking him over. "Imagine an earl named Brown!" The brewer laughed harder. The clerk grinned at Nev.

Nev knew a good prank when he saw one. He grinned good-naturedly back. "My congratulations. I was utterly taken in." He laughed. "My mother would have had *spasms*." He laughed harder.

Mr. Brown looked approving.

At the end of it he was ushered in to see Miss Brown again. She did not look as if she had slept well, but her expression was composed as she invited him to sit. "Have you and my father arranged everything to your satisfaction?"

"Indeed," he said. "I have copies of the settlements right here. They aren't signed yet—he said he and your mother want to get to know me a little better before they make their decision, and I'm invited to dinner this evening—"

"Yes, I know. Can I see them?"

He didn't know how to refuse her, so he handed them over. To his surprise, she sat down at the little writing desk and began reading them methodically.

She was only on the third page when she gave a little cry of distress. "Oh, you have let Papa tie up over half the money in my jointure! I'm sure you could have talked him down to seventy-five thousand if you'd tried."

He frowned at her. "It seemed fair. The money is his, after all."

"Yes, but that is what you are marrying me for, and it seems a deal too bad if you must go to all the trouble and not get what you need!" She looked daggers at the contract. "And see here, if I die without heirs that whole portion reverts to my parents! Oh, I *knew* I should have insisted on being there when you drew these up!"

Unexpectedly, Nev felt a surge of protectiveness, mingled unpleasantly with guilt. Miss Brown deserved better than to be married for her money. "Morbid little thing, ain't you? But I've no intention of letting you die without heirs." He favored her with a lascivious smile. Nev's lascivious smile had been known to attract Cyprians from as far as fifty feet away.

Miss Brown smiled back distractedly. "How on earth did your seat come to be mortgaged? Aren't those usually tied up in a settlement of some sort?"

"Entails have to be renewed every other generation." Damn it to Hell, she was sure to think him the worst sort of fool. "And they can be broken. When I turned twenty-one, my father told me he wanted to sell a tract of land we had no need for, to fund an annuity for me until I inherited and a portion for my younger sister. We would break the old entail and draw up a new one that didn't include that land." He looked away. "As you have collected, I'm not much good with documents."

Miss Brown's jaw dropped. "He told you that you were merely breaking the entail to sell a small piece of land—and then he mortgaged the family seat without your knowledge?"

"I know it sounds fantastic. I know I ought to have read

the new entail more closely. But there were pages and pages, with the most dashed tiny printing you ever saw, and I—" *I was in a hurry to meet my friends, get roaring drunk, and gamble away some money,* he didn't say. Her pitying expression made him feel faintly ill.

She straightened her shoulders. "No matter. In the future you shall have me to read over such things for you."

That odd combination of protectiveness and guilt rose in him again. "I really will try to make you happy," he said, not knowing what else he could offer her.

To his surprise, she flushed. "Actually, I—I made a list. Of—of terms. I thought some things were best agreed on right away, while you can still change your mind."

Fat chance of me changing my mind, he thought with a flash of resentment. He needed that money. But—"you made a *list?*"

She flushed harder. "It's a habit of mine. So that I am sure not to forget things."

"All right," he said blankly.

She pulled a sheet of paper out of a desk drawer, with a column of neat writing down the side. She frowned at it. Her blush was working its way under the neckline of her gown. Nev wondered how far it extended. He pictured it sweeping over the curve of her breasts and darkening her nipples . . .

He struggled to focus on her voice.

"I suppose there is but one," she was saying. "I am very fond of my parents, my lord. I could not be mistress in a home in which they were not welcome. I don't mean you must entertain them with your friends, but just that they might visit me, and perhaps have dinner with us every so often when we dine *en famille.*" Miss Brown met his gaze squarely. "I won't have my mother hurt. I know she drops her h's, but if she should ever get so much as a hint that you despise her for it—"

Nev's eyes widened. "Gad no! A petty rogue I should be, to take her money and condescend to her. I can't answer for my family, I'm afraid. My mother can be—difficult."

She bit her lip. "I understand that one cannot choose one's relations or always control their behavior as one would like. But I must have, at least, your word that you will do your best to make her civil."

"You have it." He was relieved to have got off so lightly. Then it dawned on him that there was a whole column of writing on that sheet. "Wait a moment! That can't be all you've got there."

She glanced at him, and with a jerky movement crumpled the paper. "Never mind. It was very late when I wrote this. I wasn't thinking clearly."

Now Nev was dying of curiosity. "Oh, no you don't." He made a grab for the paper. She snatched it back quick enough, but didn't recognize the gesture for the feint it was. His other arm snaked around her and seized the fist that held the scrap of paper. Unfortunately, this brought her breasts in contact with his waistcoat, distracting him for the crucial moment it took her to spin round and try for escape. Nev narrowed his eyes and lunged.

A few seconds later she was pinned to his chest, his arm across her arms and stomach, and he was uncurling each clenched finger from around the note.

"Let me go!" she said in a low voice. That was a good sign. She didn't want to call the house down upon him. Yes, that was good, because Nev didn't want to let go of her. She was warm and small and fit beautifully against him, and besides, he had a very good view of her neckline from this angle. And she was breathing hard. Mmm. Unable to resist, he let his grip on her body relax and slid a hand up to cup her breast.

She drew in a sharp, startled breath and let go of the note. Catching it, Nev bent to kiss her neck. If he had calculated right, she would tilt her head back and arch her body, and that would press her breast more firmly against his palm . . .

But Nev had calculated wrong, as usual. She jerked away from him as if he had the plague. "Of all the low-down, dirty tricks! Give it back!"

Nev sighed. "I don't think I shall." He straightened out the sheet of paper. She made one last attempt to snatch it back, but he held it over his head, and she was apparently too dignified—or too afraid for her virtue—to tussle for it.

Retreating to the window seat, she sat with her face averted. "You needn't consider them binding. I told you I had reconsidered." Her mouth was set in a cold little line.

For a moment he almost gave in. Then he realized what she was doing. "Oh, no. No feminine wiles. Trying to make me feel guilty, are you? Well, I won't stand for it." He held the paper in the light and read it. *1. No leaving me in the country while he gallivants about town.* His stomach clenched. That had been one of his father's favorite tricks, leaving his wife and children in the country while he went up to town for a few days on business—and came back two weeks later. But he and Miss Brown would both be rusticating for a while. From what his solicitor had told him, Loweston was a wreck. He didn't think Miss Brown would find that comforting.

2. Do not overspend our income. "I assure you, I'm just as eager as you are to stay out of debt."

Her eyes narrowed. "I know, my lord, but I am also aware you have been used to every luxury. Old habits are hard to break."

In twenty-three years, he could not once remember refusing a dare—old habits were, indeed, hard to break. He straightened. "I can do it!"

A hint of a smile curved her lips. "If you say so."

She would see. He could be a miser if he wished to. And yet . . . he was not sure how. He had always been a spendthrift; he had only ever pursued amusements that cost money.

3. Don't be ashamed of my parents. They'd discussed that.
4. Don't be ashamed of me. He frowned. "Suspicious little thing, aren't you? Do you imagine I'll pretend I don't know you at parties and make you walk ten paces behind me in the street?"

She paled a little, and he was startled to see he was near the truth. "I hardly know what I imagined, my lord. I asked you not to read that, but if my doubts were unworthy of you, I apologize."

"I don't know what you're so worried about. You're hardly vulgar."

Her lips tightened. "They say what is bred in the bone will come out in the flesh."

Nev wished he knew who "they" were, so that he could wring the vipers' necks. He didn't know how to convince her. "The behavior of a gentleman's wife reflects on him," he tried at last. "Her honor is his honor. I cannot be ashamed of you without being ashamed of myself."

"Have you never been ashamed of yourself, my lord?"

That drew him up short. Her list made it plain what she thought of him—that he was a rake and a ne'er-do-well with no more self-restraint or capacity for self-reflection than a newborn infant, who would spend her money on himself and despise her. Why would she think anything else? "Of course I have. Knowing what you do of me, can you doubt it?"

"The mere fact of wrongdoing does not in itself produce repentance. After all, you have done no more than a hundred young men of your rank—though with rather more imagination, which naturally produced more notoriety."

He did not know what compelled him to continue, when it could hardly help his case. "You yourself saw me carousing the night of my own father's death! Every feeling revolts—"

She started, and took a step toward him. "But you didn't know he was dead!"

Nev's father wouldn't be dead for hours yet when Nev had seen Miss Brown, but somehow that wasn't the point. "No. But I would have known sooner if I had been home. My little sister knew. She saw them bring in his shattered body."

Miss Brown's lips parted in a silent exclamation. "I hadn't thought—"

He didn't want to hear it. He turned back to the list. *5. Do not resent me. We have made an honest bargain, from which you benefit as much as I do.* He shrank from the cold statement of it, in that neat clerk's hand. How like a merchant she sounded, there! But he knew very well how she would react to that sentiment—or rather, he thought she would react unpredictably, but badly.

6. Allow me to still correspond with Edward. "Why the devil would you ask me who you can correspond with?"

She blinked. "You'll be my husband."

His brow wrinkled. "I can't remember m'mother ever asking my father who to write to. She'd be in the morning room half the day scribbling away and he never came near her. So long as you don't bed the fellow—"

She looked away.

He frowned. Could Edward possibly be—but no, she was a virgin, he would stake his life on it. And then he forgot all about Edward as item #7 burned into his eyes. "No *mistresses?*"

Five

The black words stood out accusingly from the crisp white paper she had used. *7. No mistresses.* Nev remembered his fingertips burning on Amy's shoulder as he watched Miss Brown. He felt overheated. "You saw me at Vauxhall, didn't you?"

"I told you, I changed my mind!" She would not meet his eyes. "You mustn't suppose that I think I have bought you, and will try to control your every movement. I know it's nothing to do with me if I—if you occasionally find yourself in need of more than I can provide." Her voice trembled a little. "So long as you're discreet and don't give me the pox."

He had a sudden image of Miss Brown, raving, her pretty features rotting away. He shuddered. It didn't matter; he had known in the back of his mind that he would have to give Amy her *congé* anyway. She was too expensive.

"I promise you"—he drew a deep breath and didn't think about Amy—"I promise you that the connection you witnessed will be at an end immediately, and that your sensibilities will never hereafter be wounded by hearing of another."

Her eyes flew to his face. Then she smiled, shyly. "It would, perhaps, be nobler to insist on letting you go your own way, but I won't. You are very generous. Thank you."

He knew very well he wasn't generous in the least. But he let himself smile back and say with mock solemnity, "No mistresses."

By rights, Penelope ought to have been hoping her parents would take a dislike to Lord Bedlow at dinner; then she could say that she had done her best and be free of the whole matter. But when he showed up with his cinnamon hair combed rigidly into place and a nervous smile on his lips, she felt it would be hideously unjust if they rejected him. Couldn't they see he was *trying?*

She found herself relieved and a little disconcerted when both her parents showed signs of succumbing to his charm. He complimented the food, Mrs. Brown's embarrassingly large pearls, and Penelope's gown—all with apparent sincerity.

When her father, who did not drink, offered to have a bottle of claret opened, Penelope held her breath. One of the things her father had never forgiven Edward for was that he had once, years ago, got himself foxed at a Brown Jug Brewery Christmas party. Mr. Brown had made some terrible remarks about Papists. And Penelope knew that Lord Bedlow drank.

To her surprise, the earl hesitated for only a moment before saying, "No, thank you." Mr. Brown commended him and launched into one of his sermons on the value of sobriety. And her father owned a brewery! But Lord Bedlow didn't even point out the inconsistency. Penelope flushed in mortification and sighed in relief all at once.

She was on tenterhooks for the half hour the gentlemen remained at table with their watered-down wine. She played snatches of Scotch airs on the piano and replied to her mother's conversation in monosyllables.

She heard her father's uproarious laughter first. Then she caught the sound of footsteps, and they entered the room, her father's arm slung about Lord Bedlow's taller shoulders.

"That's a good one! Mrs. Brown, do you know what his lordship said when I told him how many obscure musical instruments Penny would insist on bringing with her to his house? 'In for a Penny, in for a pound,' he says!" Mr. Brown laughed again.

Penelope flushed. She knew it was contrary, but the more her parents were won over, the more she resented how easily they were taken in. It was so obvious that a gentleman like

Lord Bedlow would not have found anything to admire in a prosaic parvenue like her if he had not needed her money, or anything to flatter in her parents—so patently clear that he was too good for them, and too good for her.

But Lord Bedlow, though he had to slouch to fit under Mr. Brown's arm, just smiled sheepishly at her and winked. If he was disgusted, he hid it well.

It was as though he had the Midas touch. He went straight to her mother's wall of sentimental engravings and old book illustrations in gilt frames, and pointed to a garishly colored old engraving of Venice that her mother loved. "It's the Bridge of Sighs! Have you been to Venice, Miss Brown?"

"No," Penelope said. "I have never been out of England."

Mrs. Brown smiled. "Oh, those old pictures are all mine. Penny is much too elegant for such trifles! I hope very much to go to Venice with Mr. Brown someday."

"Oh, you must!" Lord Bedlow said. "It's splendid! I wish the gondoliers still sang Tasso, but it *looks* just the same as always! My grandfather bought some sketches when he was there half a century ago, you know, and a Canaletto, and—"

A familiar gleam came into Mrs. Brown's eye. "Oh, yes, your grandfather's art collection is very fine, isn't it?"

Lord Bedlow shrugged. "I've been told it is. People come rather often to view it."

Mrs. Brown looked anxious. "You haven't sold any of it, have you?"

Penelope winced at her mother's lack of tact, but Lord Bedlow did not seem to take offense. "No. Fortunately my father allowed all of it to remain entailed, or I might have been tempted. I had offers from all over the country for the Holbein."

Lord Bedlow could not have known that those words would advance his suit more than any amount of touching rhetoric. Mrs. Brown's eyes took on an almost fanatical glow. "You have a Holbein?"

Lord Bedlow nodded. "There are over a hundred paintings. You ought to come out for a few days and look it over. They're all over the house, and I think there are some boxes of sketches and things in the attic that no one's looked at in years."

Penelope grinned outright at the expression on her mother's face—the face of a woman trying to remain honest when offered an overwhelming bribe.

Mrs. Brown returned to a safer subject. "So Venice really looks like it does in the paintings?"

"Exactly like. It is just as Childe Harold says, you know: 'I saw from out the wave her structures rise / As from the stroke of the enchanter's wand . . .'"

Penelope was torn between laughing and gaping in astonishment. The Midas Touch indeed—her mother adored that passage.

"Really?" Mrs. Brown breathed.

"Oh, yes. I only wish the fourth canto had been published when Percy and Thirkell and I went, so that we might have read it to each other in St. Mark's Square."

"Will you read it to me?" Mrs. Brown asked. "Poetry isn't the same unless you can hear it aloud, I find. But Mr. Brown doesn't care for poetry, and Penny turns up her nose at Byron—"

Lord Bedlow shot a nervous glance at Penelope.

Penelope rolled her eyes. "Naturally I don't insist that we agree on everything. If I did, it would only be an incentive to falsehood."

He didn't answer that; instead he said to Mrs. Brown, "Sometimes I read poetry aloud to myself, if there's nobody about. But it does somewhat puzzle the servants, I find." He gave her a smile that was like candlelight—bright yet somehow soft and friendly—and Penelope, for one insane moment, was jealous of her mother.

Mrs. Brown was clearly charmed—how could she help it?

"I do that too. But you know—I haven't got the voice for it, not really."

"What do you mean?" Lord Bedlow sounded genuinely puzzled, and if Penelope hadn't already been thinking of kissing him, she would have for that. "You have a perfectly pleasant voice."

"Well," Mrs. Brown said, nonplussed, "thank you, but what I mean is, it don't sound quite like Lord Byron intended it, do it? With my accent, I mean. It doesn't flow all crisp consonants and perfect vowels like yours."

Lord Bedlow looked self-conscious. "All right. I'll read you the fourth canto, but only if you promise to read me something by Mr. Keats."

Penelope considered Keats a radical hothead. And she doubted the poet would be flattered by the notion that his verse might be best appreciated by hearing it read in Mrs. Brown's motherly Cockney voice. But Mrs. Brown *was* flattered, so Penelope could not help being pleased.

Mrs. Brown fetched out the volume of Lord Byron, and Penelope prepared to feign interest; but she found herself rapidly enthralled. Lord Bedlow was a sensitive and engaging reader, and, what made him all the more dangerously appealing, it was evident that he read so well because he loved to do it—because he loved the poetry and wanted to share it. She was reminded disloyally of Edward, who was a charming conversationalist but could not read aloud at all. He had no gift for mimicry; he read everything as if it were a treatise on philosophy. Penelope had always thought it rather sweet. But she heard the music in Lord Bedlow's voice, and something inside her echoed it.

No sooner had he finished than she impulsively asked, "Do you sing?" She was sure he must.

"What about Keats?"

She was impressed that he remembered and ashamed that she had forgotten. "Oh, of course, Mama—"

Mrs. Brown's knowing smile made Penelope blush. "No, no, you children sing. I would love to hear that. Lord Bedlow can listen to me butcher the English language another time."

Nev thought he had been doing all right; the Browns were less intimidating than he had expected and less different from himself. But Miss Brown had barely spoken all evening, and it worried him. So he was inordinately relieved when she asked if he sang—and asked with real interest. And he was, he admitted to himself, very eager to hear her sing.

She rose and went to the piano. She looked perfectly composed, but her movements were a little clumsy. She glanced at him while she was getting out the music and blushed when their eyes met. He smiled and went to her side.

She was leafing through Arne's settings of Shakespearean songs and stopped at "Under the Greenwood Tree," glancing up at him for approval. He nodded, though the choice was an awkward one; it was a song he had sung often with Amy. She played the opening notes and began to sing in a clear, sweet contralto. After a few bars he joined in.

She was no opera singer, of course—neither was he. But, Nev realized, their voices fit together somehow. They seemed instinctively to know when to rise and when to fall in harmony, when to soften and when to strengthen. When the duet was over, he found himself wanting to sing another, and another. Instead he shook himself and turned to her parents. "I don't wish to overstay my welcome. I thank you for a very pleasant evening."

Mrs. Brown smiled at him and opened her mouth, but she was forestalled by Mr. Brown, who cleared his throat. "If you'd wait in the other room for a moment, my lord, I'd be much obliged to you."

He was taken aback, and Miss Brown said, "Papa, you can't mean to ask the earl—"

But it was Nev's role tonight to be obliging, so he said, "It's no bother, honestly," and let a servant show him into a room across the hall, where half a dozen fine wax candles were already lit. Nev looked at that sign of wealth and plenty, and prayed he had been charming and obliging enough. Or had he been *too* charming and obliging? What if they all thought him an even more inconsequential fellow than before?

He had begun to fidget when Miss Brown came in, sooner than he expected. He stood at once, waiting for her parents to follow her, but instead she was accompanied by a maid who took up a seat in the far corner of the room. Miss Brown came up to him, looking very awkward and pressing her hands together.

"If it's a no," he said, "just tell me straight out."

She glanced up at him. "It isn't a no." He couldn't tell whether she was pleased. "You have my father's leave to purchase a license."

He knew he should thank her and go before any of them could change their minds. "Are you quite sure? If you wish, I can wait a few days before I send the notice to the *Gazette*."

She hesitated, but she shook her head. "I'm sure. Besides, the sooner you announce our engagement the better. Once the word is out, your creditors will stop hounding you."

That would be nice for his family. "Thank you."

She tried to smile. "You were very kind to my parents— thank you."

"I like them." It would horrify his mother, but it was the truth. He wasn't sure she believed him, but her smile was real this time.

An hour after Nev announced his engagement to his family, his mother was still crying in her room. At last Louisa came soberly down the stairs.

"Has she turned off the waterworks yet?"

Louisa shook her head. "She blames herself, Nate. She

thinks if she had been able to control Papa, you wouldn't have to make this tragic sacrifice." She looked at him sorrowfully. "You should have let me do it, Nate. I was prepared."

"Louisa, don't be a goose. We aren't living in a Minerva Press novel. I'm just glad you gave me the idea. I might not have thought of Miss Brown otherwise."

Her eyes flew wide. "*I* gave you the idea? Oh, my wretched, wretched tongue! Oh, poor Nate!" She flung herself on him.

"Don't take on so." He tried to fend her off. "I daresay you'll like Miss Brown."

"Never!" Louisa said fiercely. "I shall detest her eternally!"

"You *won't*. Wait till you meet her. She likes music."

"Oh, Nate, you're so brave!"

He threw up his hands and left the house.

Nev would have preferred to take a few days to screw his courage to the sticking point before going to see Amy. But he had sent the notice to the *Gazette*, and a gentleman did not let a woman find out a thing like that from the *Gazette*.

He walked slowly up the stairs to Amy's house, as he had hundreds of times. He didn't even make it all the way to the top before the door opened and Amy looked out. He looked at her, but he didn't see her brown eyes or the mischievous tilt of her mouth or even the small, creamy breasts that curved into the clean white muslin of her frock. He didn't remember the year of laughter and sex and casual affection they had shared. He looked at Amy and all he could see were the thousands of pounds she had cost.

She smiled. "Hullo, Nev."

He tried to smile back, but he felt a little sick. "Hello, Amy."

She stood on tiptoe and kissed him. "I was about to have lunch. Will you join me, or would you rather go straight to bed?"

"Actually, I—I need to talk to you."

She frowned, but she took him into her salon and sat down on the settee, leaving plenty of room for him. He took a chair. Her face changed a little, but she didn't say anything.

"I reckon you've heard my father left us just about ruined."

She nodded. "I'd heard, but I hoped the rumors were exaggerated." She paused and looked down. "Nev, my friends would laugh at me if they heard this, but—I've been saving. I could loan you as much as five hundred pounds, if you needed it."

"I owe tens of thousands."

"Oh."

"That's not the problem." He waved his hands about, as if maybe they could say this for him. They couldn't. "I'm fixing that. That's what I came here to tell you. Amy, I—I'm getting married."

For a second her face was blank—and then, to his surprise, it flooded with relief. "Oh, Nev! You frightened me for nothing! Did you think I would scream or throw the gravy boat at your head?" She smiled at him. "I don't say I won't be sorry not to have you all to myself anymore, but I know I'm spoiled. Don't worry about it any longer."

Nev knew it was unreasonable and unfair, but he felt an instinctive revulsion, a delicacy he would have sworn he did not possess, at the idea of leaving Miss Brown quietly sleeping at home and sneaking off to see Amy. He shook his head. "I'm sorry, Amy. I can't do that. This is good-bye."

She stared at him. "Why?"

He couldn't tell her she was too expensive. So he told her the other reason. "I promised her. No mistresses."

Amy's eyes narrowed. "She made you promise that, did she? The slave trade's been abolished, or hadn't you heard? She's bought your title, Nev, but she doesn't own you. What's it to her if you get a bit on the side?"

"That's not fair, Amy. The poor girl's getting a bad enough bargain."

Amy raised her eyebrows. "Oh, is she? Who is it?"

Nev looked away. "Miss Brown."

He heard Amy draw in a sharp breath. "Oh. Well, I said she was your type, didn't I?"

Nev nodded.

"I daresay she's thrilled. A brewer's daughter generally has to settle for the old, ugly earls, never mind how pretty she is, and instead she gets you, handsome and young and charming and foolish enough to believe you're a bad bargain."

Nev looked up at Amy, remembering her wistfulness when she'd said *Wouldn't me mum have liked to lord it in a fine house in Russell Square?* It was in her voice again. He didn't understand it at first, but she thought he had, and she answered the question she thought he was asking.

"No, I never thought for a second you'd marry me, Nev. I wasn't dropped on my head as a baby. But a girl can't stop herself wishing it every so often, can she?" She smiled ruefully at him. "Even if you wanted me, I wouldn't have you now you're penniless. Don't worry about me, Nev. I'll be fine. I do hope you'll be happy."

"I hope so too." Nev was relieved that the awkwardness seemed to be over. "Listen, Amy, I wanted to buy you a pretty diamond bracelet or something for a good-bye present, but I thought—well, I thought maybe the money would be more useful. Your rent's paid to the end of the quarter, and—I brought you a hundred and fifty pounds."

She looked at the money as he counted it out of his pocket. "How very practical of you," she said with a smile. "I suppose you've learned this week how hard it is to sell pretty diamond bracelets for what you paid for them. Thank you, Nev."

He smiled back at her.

"Did her father give you an advance?"

He shook his head. "I sold Tristram."

Her mouth flew open. "Oh, Nev! Not Tristram! He was your favorite horse!"

"Second favorite. I kept Palomides."

She sighed. "I can't believe you sold Tristram to pay my rent. But I suppose you couldn't soil the future Countess of Bedlow by using her money to pay off a girl like me." She looked at him. "I did make you happy, Nev, didn't I?"

He nodded.

She swallowed hard. "Well, thank you, Nev. It's been a good year. Would you like to stay to lunch?"

He shook his head.

She stood and held out her hand—not palm-down to be kissed, but sideways to be shaken, just as Mr. Brown had at the conclusion of their negotiations. He shook her hand; she showed him to the door. "Good-bye, Nev. Look me up if you change your mind."

Thirkell beamed. "Congratulations! Bring on the champagne! Who's the lucky girl?"

"No champagne," Nev said.

Percy looked as if he understood a little better. "An heiress?"

Nev nodded. "Miss Brown."

"Brandy, then." Percy strode to the decanter and took out the stopper. Nev could smell the brandy, and he wanted it; he wanted something that would burn as it went down, burn away the worry and the confusion and the sad look on Amy's face. It smelled like a sickly sweet promise of heaven.

"No brandy either," he said with difficulty.

Percy raised his eyebrows. "Nev, you've done nothing but mope since Lord Bedlow died. You're wound tight as a spring, and you need to relax. Now have a glass of brandy and then we'll go out and have some fun, forget about all this for a few hours, and in the morning things won't seem so bad."

Percy was right, Nev thought. What could it hurt? A few

glasses of brandy, a few games of cards, a few hours when he wasn't thinking about Louisa turning shabby-genteel or the look of politely hidden disapproval on Miss Brown's face. He deserved that, didn't he, after the past few weeks? Percy was already pouring the glass; Nev held out his hand.

"Yes, come on, Nev," Thirkell said. "Perhaps you'll have a run of luck and you can call the whole thing off!"

Nev plucked the decanter out of Percy's hand and stoppered it. "Yes." He hardly recognized his own voice. "I suppose that's what my father kept telling himself too."

Percy gave Thirkell a sharp glance. "Thirkell didn't mean that, Nev. Stop being so melodramatic. A glass of brandy won't send you to the graveyard. Now drink it, and then we'll go to the theater and have a good time. We'll even go the opera if you like."

"I sold the box," Nev said. "All of them."

Percy sighed. "All right, we'll stand in the pit. Amy won't mind. You'll be married soon enough, and then you can buy them all back."

Nev was suddenly furious. "No. I can't. And I gave Amy her *congé*."

Thirkell gaped. "You did *what*? Nev, how could you?"

"I'm getting married!"

Percy gave Nev the severe look that meant he was about to read Nev a lecture in which common sense featured prominently. It reminded him of Miss Brown a little. "It's not as if it's a love match, Nev. You're mad about Amy. You deserve to keep something fun in your life. I think sobriety has unbalanced your brain. *Pan métron áriston*, you know."

"Don't quote Greek at me!" Moderation in all things—that was exactly what Nev was trying to do. He was trying to curb the excess that had led his father to ruin. "And anyway, Miss Brown asked me to be faithful. What was I to say? 'Thank you for your money and your future, but I'll do as I please'?"

Percy's jaw set. "How dare she? Trying to get you under the cat's paw already and not even married! What business is it of hers if you keep a mistress? She'll be Lady Bedlow, isn't that what she wants? That's the problem with Cits, they think everything can be bought, even affection—"

Nev snatched the glass of brandy out of Percy's hand and splashed the liquor into the fire, aware that it had been expensive and feeling guilty and furious. Moderation had never been his forte. "Stop it. That's not fair. She's—" He stopped. He did not know how to explain Miss Brown.

Besides, part of him was touched by Percy's anger on his behalf. And, worse still, there was a small shameful part of him that agreed with Percy. He had looked at Miss Brown's neat little list and thought, *Merchant*. In a minute he would give in; in a minute he would apologize and let Percy pour another glass.

Nev looked at his two oldest friends and hated his father. But that wasn't fair either. It was his own fault, his fault for being too weak. His fault for wanting that glass of brandy and a night at the theater with Amy more than anything else in the world.

He had lived like this for the past six years: drinking the night away with Percy and Thirkell at a never-ending stream of gaming hells and Cyprian's Balls, curricle-racing, attending the theater, spending as little time as possible at Loweston except when the three of them had a mind to do a little fishing. Just like his father. He could scarcely imagine any other way of living. That was why he had to do this. "I think that you two need to leave."

Percy threw up his hands. "Fine. We'll see you tomorrow. Maybe by then you'll have come to your senses and begged Amy to take you back."

"No. I—oh, Christ." Nev's voice was still firm, but on the inside he could feel himself cracking. He was weak and miserable and nothing could ever make this right, but he *had* to do it. "Percy, Thirkell, you can't come back. I'm sorry, but you can't."

"What—*ever?*" Thirkell asked.

Nev couldn't look at his round, hurt face. Instead he thought about Miss Brown, clutching her list. "I'm sorry, Thirkell, but I've got responsibilities now. I'm going to—I'm going to have a wife. I can't live like a bachelor anymore."

Percy folded his arms. "So you're going to give us up just like you've given up claret?"

"I don't want to. But I can. What I can't do is keep you and still do what I have to do."

"Nev—" Thirkell sounded bewildered.

"I'm not Nev anymore, Thirkell," Nev snapped. "I'm Lord Bedlow now."

Percy's eyes flashed. "And shall we call you 'my lord' now? We've been calling you Nev your whole life! For God's sake—"

"I'm sorry," Nev said again, knowing it wasn't enough. "But I've got to be respectable now, and I can't do that with you two."

"Fine. If we're not good enough to associate with the Earl of Bedlow, we'll take ourselves off." Percy turned to go, but Thirkell just stood there, looking like a kicked puppy. "Come along, Thirkell," Percy said gently. Thirkell hesitated, but Percy nodded his head at the door, and he went. Percy gave Nev a deep, ironical bow and slammed the door behind them.

Nev fell into a chair and stared longingly at the decanter.

"Here, put a forget-me-not there, just above her ear." Mrs. Brown pointed.

"Mama, I'm already wearing about fifty forget-me-nots."

"And you look lovely! Lord Bedlow won't be able to take his eyes off you."

"Yes, because he will be staring at all the forget-me-nots in horrified fascination."

Mrs. Brown laughed. "I don't think so. Blue is a good color for you."

Penelope smiled at her mother. "Oh, you think everything is a good color for me."

"That's because everything is," Mrs. Brown said. Penelope felt tears pricking at her eyes, but she forced them back.

As the wedding had neared over the last three weeks, she had become more and more certain she was making a terrible mistake; she couldn't have explained what streak of stubborn perversity kept her clinging to her bad decision. She'd even started again with the nervous fits she'd thought were left behind in the schoolroom: as the wedding approached, she woke each day with her stomach tangled and sick, and spent breakfast fighting not to vomit in the eggs.

It had been bad enough her first year at Miss Mardling's, when Penelope had no idea what was wrong with her and feared an exotic illness. Her roommates, of course, had suspected her of a shocking illicit pregnancy, and spread the rumor all over the school. The sick feeling had faded after a few weeks, and only when it had started up again the first day of every term, regular as clockwork, had she realized it was nerves.

It was worse now. Now she had to hide it from her mother's watchful eye, or the wedding might still be canceled.

"Let us hope Lord Bedlow agrees with you."

Mrs. Brown tweaked one of Penelope's silk forget-me-nots. "He will. I've seen the way he looks at you."

Penelope knew what her mother must mean, but she wanted to ask anyway, so she would know that at least one person thought she hadn't been imagining those looks, the few times she'd seen her betrothed since that dinner with her parents—the looks that said there was hope, that he didn't just think of her as the strip of brown paper that held together a stack of freshly minted banknotes.

Mrs. Brown placed one last flower in Penelope's hair and stepped back with a satisfied air. "Perfect. Let me fetch my pearl earrings." She bustled out the door.

A minute later, one of the footmen poked his head in. "This came for you, miss. We've opened it, but where do you want it?" He pushed the door open wider and Penelope could see the crate in his arms. On the side it read DUPRÈS ET FILS. Below, in smaller letters, was GRAVURES, AQUARELLES, DESSEINS, LITHOGRAPHIES, &C. 22 RUE DE RIVOLI, PARIS.

Paris. Her heart began to pound. Edward had sent one letter after he got the news, pleading with her to change her mind, reminding her of all their plans. Her reply had been too short—she didn't know how to explain herself, or what to say but no, she would not be changing her mind. He hadn't written again. "Just set it on the floor by the bed."

The second he was out the door she was kneeling by the crate—but carefully. She didn't want to rip her dress, even though Molly, her lady's maid, had said it would be good luck. With hands that shook a little, she took out one of the flat packages, ripping away the careful wrapping to reveal the expected picture frame. She turned it over, saw the engraving—and froze.

It was Plate 2 of Wm. Hogarth's *Marriage à la Mode* series.

Penelope opened the other five packages, but she knew already what they would contain. Plate 1, of course—"The Marriage Settlement"—showed Lord Squanderfield displaying his mortgages and his ancient family tree to the stooped, myopic merchant while their two bored children sat in the corner, the young nobleman preening in the mirror and the merchant's daughter flirting with another man. The next three plates showed in lovingly gruesome detail the young couple's idle, unchaste life, chiefly spent apart from each other.

In the fifth plate the bride knelt beside her dying husband as her lover escaped out the window, leaving his bloody sword behind him. In Plate 6—Penelope felt sick—in Plate 6 the widow, back in her father's house, had taken an overdose of laudanum on hearing of her lover's execution. A nurse held her syphilitic child as the merchant himself slipped the gold ring off his dying daughter's finger with an appraising eye.

Penelope picked up the neatly written note in the bottom of the crate and read it. *Lady Bedlow—I hope you will accept this small token of my esteem on the occasion of your marriage. I saw them and thought of you at once. I hope you will be very happy as a countess. Fondest regards, Edward Macaulay.*

The door opened, and Penelope crumpled the paper in her fist.

"Penny, what's wrong?" Mrs. Brown asked in dismay.

Penelope straightened. "It's nothing, Mama." Her voice quavered. "Only a tasteless joke. A wedding present, you see."

Mrs. Brown came closer. "Hogarth!" Then she saw which engravings they were. Her smile faded. "Who sent those to you?"

"I don't know," Penelope lied. "There was no note."

"What kind of devil would *do* such a thing? It's bad luck! And on your wedding day too."

"Don't be superstitious, Mama."

Mrs. Brown knotted her fingers together. "But—but who could hate you so much?"

Penelope would not cry. "It's just someone's idea of a joke," she repeated mechanically.

Mrs. Brown's gaze lingered on the crate, clearly marked PARIS. Her eyes narrowed, but she made no comment. "Here, come help me choose my pelisse. I bought some new ones."

"Won't we be late?"

Mrs. Brown looked at the clock. "We have time. Come

on. After today, there will be no one to laugh and tell me they become me abominably."

Penelope smiled around the lump in her throat. "All right, Mama. You go on. I'll be there in a moment."

The minister's voice droned on and on. Nev looked at his bride. She looked adorable—her shining brown hair was braided and curled and adorned with about fifty silk forget-me-nots that fluttered and bobbed with every movement of her head. Her light-blue muslin dress was embroidered with more of the small flowers. Yes, she looked adorable—but she had been crying. Nev was sure of it. He had not the faintest idea what to do.

This was not how he had imagined his wedding. Not that he sat around dreaming of it like a *girl*; but yes, he'd thought of it once or twice, and he'd always planned a last glorious night of bachelor debauchery, a bride with an indistinct but joyful countenance, and—and Percy or Thirkell at his side, or the two of them grinning at him from the front row and miming toasts and the key turning in a leg shackle.

Instead, he had spent his last night of freedom sitting in his rooms, sober as a judge, gazing at the empty decanter and thinking about Amy. He had gone to bed early. Now, his friends weren't in the church at all, his mother was sobbing brokenheartedly, and his sister was sitting furiously straight and refusing to look at him. And his bride had been crying.

He couldn't blame her. Tomorrow night they would be at Loweston. *Loweston doesn't look quite the same anymore.*

Trapped in the country on a run-down estate. Far away from London and the comfortable life she knew. Without her friends. About to bed a stranger. Nev gulped.

Poor Miss Brown must be terrified.

"Therefore if any man can show any just cause why they may not lawfully be joined together, let him speak now or

forever hold his peace," the minister finally intoned. Nev felt
a flash of panic. He glanced suspiciously at his mother, but
she showed no signs of emerging from her handkerchief with
an impediment.

Nev was so relieved that when the minister said "forsaking all other, keep thee only unto her," he winked at Miss
Brown. *No mistresses*, he mouthed. Preoccupied with the sudden blossoming of a smile on her face, he almost missed his
cue to say, "I will."

"Wilt thou have this man to thy wedded husband, to live
together after God's ordinance in the holy estate of Matrimony? Wilt thou obey him, and serve him, love, honor, and
keep him in sickness and in health; and, forsaking all other,
keep thee only unto him, so long as ye both shall live?"

Miss Brown turned to look at him, her smile still in her
eyes. Her clear voice reached effortlessly to the far corners of
the church. "I will."

Nev couldn't explain why he suddenly felt a thousand
times better. He just did.

But when it came time for the ring, the unthinkable happened. He took it carefully from his pocket. It wasn't the
Ambrey ring—his mother had refused to take that off—but
it was another of the entailed family heirlooms. In fact, the
ring he was giving Miss Brown was bigger than the Ambrey
ring, because he knew that would annoy his mother, and besides, he had always liked women in heavy jewelry. It was a
square agate intaglio face, ringed with—well, he was fairly
sure the large clear stones were paste, but they were pretty.
The thick band was gold, at any rate. It had been cleaned and
fitted to Miss Brown's finger the week before.

She had made no demur when he showed it to her, but he
was suddenly uncomfortably aware that he had never seen
her wear anything but a tiny gold locket or, once, an amber
cross on a chain. Was she eying the ring with distaste?

He took her hand and began, "With this ring I thee wed,

with my body I thee worship, and with all my worldly goods I thee endow—"

Someone, somewhere in the church, laughed. "Rather the other way round, isn't it?"

Nev dropped the ring.

Six

It hit the stone floor with a heavy thunk. Mrs. Brown's shocked gasp was probably audible all over the church. She muttered something in which the words "bad luck" were clearly discernible.

Frozen in horror, Nev stared at Miss Brown. The girl gave a minatory glance to the congregation, then knelt and retrieved the ring. "I don't believe in bad luck." She smiled encouragingly and handed it back to him.

This time he got it on.

It was done, then. By her own hand and with her own voice Penelope had given herself to Lord Bedlow, to obey and serve him, as long as they both should live.

For the rest of her life was a long time.

Her father drew her aside. "Penny—I wish you very happy, but I want you to know—your mother and I discussed this, and if he's not good to you, we'll get you a divorce. Never mind the scandal."

Penelope laughed. So much for *as long as you both shall live.* "Whom God hath joined together let no man put asunder."

Mr. Brown scowled. "Never mind that. For twelve thousand pounds Parliament will sunder you well enough. We want our little ha'penny to be happy."

Penelope felt tears pricking again. Her Nonconformist father was strictly opposed to divorce. "I won't need a divorce, Papa," she said, and kissed him.

* * *

Six hours later, a divorce sounded pretty tempting. Her new husband did nothing but fidget, stare out the window, and complain about how slowly they traveled. "Loweston is only a day's journey from London by post," he said for perhaps the twentieth time.

"How much extra is it to hire post-horses? Surely we might have afforded it."

Lord Bedlow waved a hand airily. "Oh, post-horses are no good. My father used to keep our own horses at every coaching inn on the Norwich Road . . ." He trailed off.

"What does an extra day matter?" Penelope asked gently, although a moment before she had felt like snapping at him. After all, she would have liked to lessen their journey too. She was tired and jostled, the relentless rhythm of hoofbeats and carriage wheels was giving her a headache, and Lord Bedlow had already eaten most of the food her mother had packed for them—but *she* wasn't complaining.

He slumped back against the seat cushions. "It doesn't, I suppose."

"Are you very eager to be home?"

It was painfully easy to tell when Lord Bedlow was being evasive. He fidgeted like a guilty schoolboy.

She hid a smile. "Not very eager, then?"

He shook his head. "I—I suppose I ought to warn you. I haven't been there in over a year. I don't quite know what to expect. My father's solicitor assured me it could be put to rights with a little money."

"But you're worried?"

"My sister told me it wouldn't look like I remembered. She didn't think the harvests had been very good." He looked at her. "But—it couldn't have got too bad, could it? In a few years?"

Penelope had no idea how bad it could have got. She had never been out of the city for more than a few days before. "I don't know anything about farming."

Lord Bedlow sighed and resumed staring moodily out the window. She wanted to ask more, to ask if he trusted his father's solicitor and what kind of accounting system the steward used and if he'd looked at the books. But she doubted he would have useful answers to any of her questions, and she didn't want to make him feel worse.

She wondered what it would have been like to make her wedding journey with Edward. There would have been no uncomfortable silences, of that she was sure.

She watched her husband surreptitiously. It was getting dark. In a few hours they would have to stop and take rooms for the night.

Would Lord Bedlow find it tiresome to have to tutor a virgin? Would he expect her to know things she didn't? What if she turned out to be a poor study?

And yet, he had seemed happy with her response, the one time he had kissed her. She closed her eyes and replayed the moment for the thousandth time—his lips descending on hers, his body warm and close. Again, that uncomfortably tantalizing ache started in her—well, *down there*—and moved throughout her body. His hand on her breast had burned through her dress, her corset, and her shift. What would it feel like on her skin?

It was getting too dark for Nev to see much out the window. He turned his gaze to Miss Brown, who was leaning back in her seat with her eyes closed. Since she couldn't see him, he let himself ogle the swell of her bosom above the black muslin of her gown. He remembered the feel of her breast in his hand. Soon Miss Brown wouldn't be obliged to wrench herself away when he touched her.

He recalled abruptly that she wasn't Miss Brown any longer; she was Lady Bedlow now. That sounded deuced odd. Lady Bedlow was his *mother*. "Can I call you Penelope?"

Her eyes flew open. She flushed and shifted in her seat. Was there something improper about his request? "Um—yes, of course."

"Is everything all right?"

"Yes, of course," she repeated quickly. "Why wouldn't it be?"

Nev could think of only too many reasons.

"What shall I call you? Bedlow?"

"I suppose so." He grimaced. "I haven't got used to it yet."

"Your friend called you Nev at Lady Ambersleigh's."

"You remember that?"

She smiled. "It isn't every day the heir to an earldom offers to choose my hors d'oeuvres," she teased.

"Really? Even with a hundred and seventy-five thousand pounds?"

Her face fell.

"Oh, Lord, how tactless of me! I didn't find out about your dowry until later, truly."

She shrugged. "It's quite all right. It is irrational to object to the truth. I should rather thank you for not feeding me Spanish coin."

She really had a way of making him feel small. "I never feed anyone Spanish coin. I'm not clever enough."

One of her brows arched in delicate skepticism, but she smiled. "I don't know quite how these titles work. Would it be improper for me to call you Nev, still?"

Nev had been determined to leave every scrap of his old life behind and start anew, but—his nickname sounded so right on her lips. It sounded comfortable, and intimate. "I don't see why. No one new will be Lord Nevinstoke until—until we have a son."

"Nev it is, then." She sighed. "I'm ashamed of being so frivolous, but—there is something about a title, isn't there?"

He felt faintly self-conscious. "In my experience, girls prefer a scarlet coat."

Her eyes narrowed. "It would put you in your place if I agreed with you."

Nev smiled. "It would, but I suspect you would rather die than be suspected of being officer-mad."

"I hope I am not so immoderate. However, I have always felt that choosing a pleasing form, easy address, or an attractive costume over sense and character is unpardonably foolish."

"But can't one choose both?"

"Surely a good, sensible man must always be pleasing."

Nev was opening his mouth to scoff when he realized he could not do so without sounding like the worst kind of cad. The full extent of her innocence crashed down on him. It really had never occurred to her that there might be a good and sensible man whom she did not wish to take to her bed. Apparently she never thought of taking men to her bed at all.

And tonight he had planned to deflower her. He had never been with any woman who did not know exactly what she was doing. How painful was it, the first time? He knew there was often blood, but how much? What if he hurt her? What if she found the whole business unsanitary and repulsive? What if she cried?

Worse yet, what if she endured his lovemaking with the same expression of patient forbearance she sometimes wore when he talked? What if she said, *Never mind, I expect it will not be so very bad when I am used to it?*

Nev wished that he were a man of good sense and character. Then he would know what the devil to do.

When they finally pulled into an inn yard for the night, Penelope was starving and exhausted. And there was another whole day of this to endure on the morrow! Her remark that a good, sensible man must always be pleasing had effectively silenced her husband. He had looked very doubtful, but refrained from contradicting her. How did he contrive to make her feel a puritanical schoolgirl, when she knew that it was he whose too-lively mind had been led astray by bad company and worldliness?

She sighed. She could hardly give herself airs of superiority when she herself had chosen a pleasing form over every dictate of reason.

Feeling penitent, she said nothing when he left her standing in the hall while he saw to the stabling of his horses. By the time he came back, she had fallen half-asleep leaning against the wall.

She opened her eyes to find her husband regarding her with an unreadable expression. "How much did you sleep last night?"

"Not very much," she admitted, then realized that might not be politic.

He gave her a crooked smile. "Come along, I've engaged a room and a private parlor. Supper should be along at any moment."

Supper! She gazed at him gratefully.

Supper was a silent affair. The food was good, but as the meal drew to a close, Penelope's nervousness increased. She could hear her abigail in the next room, laying out her night things. In an hour, or perhaps two, she would no longer be a maiden.

She glanced at her husband, but he was not looking at her. He hadn't been looking at her any of the admittedly hundreds of times she had glanced at him throughout the last half hour. That didn't seem to bode well. Several times he'd been eying the decanter of wine with a peculiar expression on his face, but he drank only tea, as he had done at her parents' home. Was it for her benefit, or had he really given up drinking since his father's death? Penelope was not sure whether to approve or to think the gesture theatrical. She didn't let herself look at him again until she had finished the last of her apple tart.

This time, his eyes were on her face. She was reminded, somehow, of the way he had looked at the wine.

"I—I think I'll get ready for bed," she said, and went into the next room.

Molly was waiting, looking distressingly energetic. Penelope was sore and tired, but she let Molly help her into her nightdress. Then she got her copy of *Mansfield Park* out of her trunk and sat down in bed to read.

This would be the way to Fanny's heart. She was not to be won by all that gallantry and wit and good-nature together could do; or, at least, she would not be won by them nearly so soon, without the assistance of sentiment and feeling, and seriousness on serious subjects. . . .

But she must not have been as absorbed in her reading as she thought, because when her husband put his hand on the doorknob, she heard it immediately.

Nev looked her over. Penelope felt her soreness and weariness fading. Now—now, he would—

"You look tired out," he said.

"Not too tired."

"I've been thinking."

For some reason Penelope really, really didn't like the sound of that.

"Do—do you know what goes on between a husband and wife?"

Penelope's lips went dry. "My mother explained it to me."

He nodded. "What did she say it was like?"

"She said it could be uncomfortable and awkward the first time, but that it got better with practice."

He blanched.

"Was—was that not right?"

He seemed at a loss for words.

"Surely it cannot be so very bad. I had hoped it might even

be—pleasant. When you kissed me—" She stopped, blushing. A lady did not speak of such things.

"When it's done properly, it's very pleasant."

"For women too?" she blurted out.

He nodded. "For women too. Only—perhaps not the first time, as your mother said." He licked his lips. Penelope's gaze was riveted on his tongue. "I think we ought to wait until we know each other a little better. Then perhaps you will be more comfortable helping me find out what you like."

Penelope could not tell if she was disappointed or relieved. It hardly mattered; such decisions naturally belonged to him. "If you think it best." Her voice sounded small.

She had not realized how tense he was, until he relaxed. "I do think it best." He looked at her for a moment, and then he came and sat on the edge of the bed, grinning at her. "This is deuced awkward, isn't it?"

Some of her own tension eased. She nodded.

"That is why it will be better to wait. Now turn around like a good girl while I put my nightshirt on."

It was a little chilly; she didn't want to get out from under the blankets. Instead she snuggled down on her side of the bed, facing the wall and closing her eyes. She heard one boot hit the floor, then the other. Then a chair rattled—she conjectured that he had thrown his jacket over it. After that there was nothing definitive, only a series of rustlings and footsteps.

She tried not to think about it, but her imagination was out of her control. Candlelight would glint on his naked shoulders, his torso, his—but here her mind skittered away. She had seen paintings and statues of naked men before, of course—Greek athletes and etchings of Michelangelo's David. But a wide gulf lay between that and what she would see if she turned around, and she was not capable of bridging it.

The bed bounced as he jumped into it. The darkness behind her eyelids became darker; he had extinguished the candle. There was silence for a moment. "Good night, Penelope."

"Good night, Nev."

The mattress shifted as he lay down and pulled the blankets over him. Penelope lay perfectly still, not daring to move. But soon enough everything faded into exhausted sleep.

Now that Nev had done the generous—or was it cowardly?—thing and given his bride time to accustom herself to him, he couldn't think about anything but bedding her. She sat across from him in the carriage, not a shining brown hair out of place, turning the pages of some appallingly proper novel—and he was imagining ripping the book from her hands, getting her out of that depressing black, and exercising his conjugal rights in all the deliciously improper ways the cramped confines of the carriage would necessitate.

Of course, there was nothing else *to* think about, except what awaited him at Loweston, and Nev did not want to think about that. Unlike his bride, he had not brought a book. He was bored, bored, bored. He longed to be out in the open air, spelling the coachman with the horses—but that would be rude to his wife, and besides, he could not drive the horses as fast as he would like, because they weren't changing them at the next stage. Every time his restless mind began to search for a new topic, it brought up unwelcome, all-too-pleasant images of Amy or his friends or even a damned game of solitaire. Nev had sworn off cards along with liquor and horse racing and women of easy virtue, and so all that was left was mentally undressing his wife, over and over again.

To make matters worse, the interior of the carriage, even with the windows open to their fullest extent, had become unbearably hot. The day before had been cloudy, but this afternoon there was no such shelter from the elements. Nev's black coat, pantaloons, and boots were suffocating him, and even Penelope in her short-sleeved carriage dress was starting to wilt. July was a poor time for long journeys in full mourning. Nev was well aware that in a few minutes he would be indulging in thoughts of the most unfilial kind—viz, if only Papa had had the decency to die in the winter, when it was not so damned hot!

Then, as he watched, a trickle of sweat ran down Penelope's collarbone and into the space between her breasts, and Nev had had enough. "What are you reading?"

She laid down the book readily enough. "*Mansfield Park*, by Miss Austen."

"Are you enjoying it?"

She looked away. "Not quite as much as I did the first time. I don't think—" She licked her lip. "I don't think she likes music very much," she finished awkwardly.

He could have sworn that wasn't what she'd been planning to say. "She doesn't?"

"Well . . ." She flipped through the book. "In this scene she talks of Miss Crawford playing—here it is—'with an expression and taste which were peculiarly becoming.' Not pleasing or inspiring, *becoming*. And it is not even her playing that ensnares Edmund, but rather the elegant picture she makes with the harp."

Suddenly Nev found he was in complete harmony with her. "Plenty of young ladies make a dashed elegant picture with their harp! But most of them don't practice sufficiently, or haven't the feeling for it. Even if they are proficient enough, one grows bored after a very few minutes. One certainly doesn't fall in love with them."

She gave him an approving smile; he tried not to feel as proud as if he'd slain a dragon for her.

"This is too bad," he said. "I'd been planning to read Miss Austen's work, for Sir Walter Scott gave one of her books a most favorable review in the *Quarterly*—"

Penelope raised an eyebrow. "You have been planning it a long time, then. That review was three years ago." Her eyes glinted with amusement.

"I've been busy. Besides, now I am thinking of changing my mind.

'The man that hath no music in himself,
Nor is not moved with concord of sweet sounds,
Is fit for treasons, stratagems and spoils;
The motions of his spirit are dull as night
And his affections dark as Erebus:
Let no such man be trusted.'"

"*Merchant of Venice*," she said. Damn her, she looked startled. It wasn't even an obscure quote.

"I'm not quite a dullard, even if I can't audit a banker's books."

"I'm sorry. I should have known better. You took a first at Cambridge, didn't you?"

It was his turn to be startled. "How the dev—how on earth did you know that?"

She bit her lip and gave him a mirthful sidelong glance. "My mother looked you up in *Debrett's*."

"Really," he said, fascinated. "What else do you know about me?"

She considered, a smile playing around her mouth. "I think I shall keep the strategic advantage best by not telling you. I don't think that quote is quite fair, anyway. Edward is tone-deaf, and he—" She stopped, looking stricken.

"Ah, yes, Edward," Nev said cautiously. "He is like a brother to you, is he not? You correspond." Then why did she look guilty as sin every time his name came up?

"Not very often."

"Well, that is only to be expected, isn't it?" Nev was startled at the undercurrent of anger in his own voice, but he couldn't stop. "Brothers are notoriously bad correspondents. But sisters are rather different creatures. And you, presumably, are like a sister to Edward—"

She shot him a furious, cornered glance. "Stop it! We quarreled, all right?"

Well, he had wanted to know, and now he did. Penelope and Edward had quarreled between Penelope's betrothal and her wedding. What else could it be about? He wanted desperately to inquire further, but something stopped him. *It's none of my affair*, he thought. Well, that was patently ridiculous. Of course it was his affair; Penelope was his wife. But he felt, nonetheless, that he had no right to demand confidences. She had married him; he was sure she would not betray him. That would have to suffice.

Penelope was staring out the window. He did not think she was seeing the landscape.

"I'm sorry," he said, clumsily. "Surely—surely he'll come around, in time."

She shrugged. Then, with an effort, she turned and smiled at him. "Maybe so. I do recommend Miss Austen's work. As Sir Walter wrote, her writing is astonishingly entertaining and lifelike. There are none of the constant swoons and desperate duels amidst Gothic ruins that one sees so often in the work of other novelists."

"But they are novels," Nev said with some surprise. "I never imagined they were supposed to be lifelike. That is not their purpose."

"But they *can* be. They *ought* to be. Have you ever *read* a horrid novel?"

In fact, Nev's shameful fondness for the Minerva Press had been an open secret among his peers since Lower Shell at school. But he found he had not the heart to admit it, not when Penelope's eyes were flashing scornfully. "I prefer poetry, myself," he said, "but my sister is uncommonly fond of *The Castle of Otranto*." Damn. He would have to inform Louisa of that as soon as possible, before she let slip that she generally read nothing but tales of knights and accounts of the doings of pirates, the bloodier the better. Oh, and Byron's poems, but only because he was so handsome, and *The Corsair* was about a pirate, after all.

"Much may be forgiven the enthusiasm of youth, but *I* could never read that book without a shudder—not at the horror or pathos of the material, but at the woodenness of the prose, the improbability of the action, and the flatness of the characters! It and its ilk never taught us to know ourselves or our fellows better; it never inspired the spark of recognition that Miss Austen achieves so effortlessly. I never felt, while reading, that here was *myself.*"

"Perhaps so," Nev said, stung, "but one doesn't always wish to be oneself. Sometimes it can be pleasant to imagine oneself as a dark hero tormented by his sinful past, or a noble knight capable of saving a fainting female with one blow of his lance."

She leaned forward, her cheeks flushed. Nev tried not to look at her bosom. "Do you have any notion how galling it is to see oneself everywhere portrayed as a fainthearted creature incapable of a single coherent speech or thought? Existing merely to be abused by one's guardian or abducted by an unprincipled rake? I never fainted in my life, and I am quite as capable of self-exertion and rational thought as Sir Horace Walpole."

Nev, prey to the lowering suspicion that his wife was a good deal more capable of self-exertion and rational thought than he was himself, turned the subject. "If you are so hot on the subject of Gothic ruins, you won't be best pleased when you see Loweston."

"Is there a ruin? Surely Mama would have mentioned that."

"Oh, there's a ruin, all right. A ruined corner of a medieval Ambrey fortress, on a hill near the house."

She nodded sagely. "I expect most of the stones were carried away for reuse. Papa took Mama and me to Canterbury once, and all the old abbeys were nearly down to the foundations."

"I'm afraid most of the stones were never there at all. It was built by my grandfather."

She stared for a moment, then started to laugh. "Oh, dear."

"You should have read *Debrett's* more carefully. We haven't been at Loweston long enough to have family ruins. If you were hoping we dated to the Conquest, you've been most cruelly deceived. The first earl was one of Charles the Second's by-blows."

"Alas, Mama only read me the parts about your Cambridge career and your grandfather's art collection."

He tsked.

She shook her head regretfully. "If only I had thought of it, I might have refused you and waited for an earl with a genuine ruin!"

He realized all at once how little she *had* sought to find out about him. She had not asked or investigated anything—she had accepted him on the spot, on an acquaintance of a few minutes. Would she have accepted any peer with full use of his limbs?

He had assumed he understood the nature of their bargain: he got her money, while she got his title and his position. After all, the idea of a Cit's daughter *not* wishing to marry an earl had been utterly foreign to him. Everyone knew that was a self-made man's goal in life. First he made his millions; then he bought a noble name for his grandchildren; then he sold his business and purchased a house in the country.

But she had never suggested, by word or sign, that she cared a straw for his title or his position. She could not even say that "there was something about a title" without blushing for her frivolity. Her parents had not pushed her into it; they had been against the match. If he read matters aright, this Edward, no doubt a "good, sensible man," had wanted to marry her.

What then? Why had she married him?

And was she satisfied with her mysterious side of the deal, or did she regret her choice?

Seven

Penelope awoke in an unfamiliar bed, in an unfamiliar room, with unfamiliar sounds leaking in from outside. It took a moment to recall that she was married and at her husband's seat of Loweston. Yes, now she remembered; the last hour, after they diverged from the highway, had been over terrible country roads. They had stumbled into her new home travel-stained and weary, and Nev had simply taken her to "the countess's room" and given her privacy. After Molly had undressed her, Penelope had gone straight to bed and fallen into a deep sleep. Too deep, evidently, for nerves—her stomach had not troubled her in the mornings since the wedding, for which she was profoundly grateful. Casting up her accounts in front of Nev would have been the worst possible start to a marriage.

Now she sat up and looked about her with interest. The room showed no signs of neglect, even in the bright sunlight streaming in through the enormous picture windows. The furnishings and wallpaper were modern and fashionable. The bureau was cluttered with an array of expensive perfume bottles, rouge jars, and silver brushes and combs that Penelope realized must be the dowager countess's. She moved to the window—it was late morning, and the room was already close and hot. Opening the casement was not a large improvement and made the cheeping of birds even louder, but at least there was a warm breeze.

The air, though, was clearer and purer than in London. Penelope had forgotten how much. And the view was lovely—a rolling lawn with picturesque stands of trees, winding paths, and even a narrow, sparkling brook. It did not look in the least neglected or impoverished. For a mad moment, Penelope wondered if Nev could have been mistaken about his financial situation—if he had, in fact, married her for nothing.

A moment's reflection convinced her of the folly of this notion. She did not know the countess well, nor had she ever met the late earl; but she was not surprised to learn that little economy had been practiced in the park itself. She would have to look over the books to find out where, exactly, it *had* been practiced—if at all.

Yes, Penelope decided, she would have a quick breakfast before asking the steward if she might see the books; it was the only thing here in the country that she still knew how to do. She called for Molly, and when she was dressed asked a passing maid to direct her to the breakfast room.

"Do you know where Lord Bedlow is?" she added.

"He's in the steward's room, my lady."

Penelope decided breakfast could wait.

"Oh, Penelope!" Nev stood up so fast he nearly knocked the chair over. "Perhaps you can make some sense of this."

She couldn't help smiling at his obvious relief at seeing her. "I can certainly try."

She looked about the room—and felt a pang of dismay. Her father would have fired on the spot any agent of his who kept his office in so sorry a state. Open ledgers were everywhere, as were dirty wineglasses, small piles of pipe ash, and broken pens. A bottle of ink had spilled in one corner and been left to dry where it lay.

"Lady Bedlow, may I present Captain Trelawney?" Nev said.

"How do you do?" Penelope said, trying to hide her consternation. The steward looked more promising than his office. He was an upright, well-built man in perhaps his late forties, with a military mustache and a ruddy complexion.

"At your service, my lady." His smile struck her as too friendly. "I'm honored. Please, sit down."

Nev took his seat again once she was settled. "My wife is going to be helping me with the business end of things. She understands these things better than I do."

Penelope could not help blushing under the captain's speculative gaze. "What were you discussing with Lord Bedlow?"

"I was explaining the nature of the estate's expenses and how difficult any new economy would be." His patronizing tone raised Penelope's hackles. "As you can see, my lord, Loweston will not run itself, and the harvest is close by."

Nev nodded uncertainly. It was perfectly clear to Penelope—and, she was sure, to Captain Trelawney—that he could not make heads or tails of the accounts. "May I see?" she asked.

"Certainly, my lady." The captain smiled and passed the ledger across the table.

Penelope stared. No wonder Nev had been baffled. The accounts were in a largely illegible scrawl—the captain's, she assumed. She squinted at the page. It appeared to be nothing more than a long tally of expenses, all jumbled together, and every so often a gain from the sale of—she squinted closer—"4 grate oaks" or the like. The last several pages appeared mostly to record the sale of various horses: "Prometheus, a prime goer, to Sir J," and so on.

"How are the books organized?" she asked at last. "Have you separate accounts for the house and the farm? Surely economies might be most easily made here."

"Separate accounts?" the captain said in some amusement. "I don't know how it's done in London, but I've never met a steward who kept separate accounts. Estate books merely show charge and discharge."

"But then, how can you tell if you've made money on a particular venture or if your expenses are rising?" She looked at the expenses more carefully, but it seemed he was right. She saw an outlay for candles cheek-by-jowl with one for feed for the workhorses, and there a record of wages paid to have the lawn scythed.

"Either you've a balance or you haven't, I'm afraid," he said, confirming her worst fears. It would be next to impossible to make any kind of systematic analysis of where money might best be saved. She thought of her father's shelves of ledgers, all so clear and neat. All showing a profit.

She glanced at Nev, who had been counting on her to make sense of these chaotic, unreadable books. He was staring longingly out the window at the morning sun. "Is the principal income from the home farm or from rents?" she asked.

The captain chuckled. "Oh, rents, certainly. Fortunately all your tenants are upstanding men who paid even through the recent bad harvests."

"How many tenants have we?" Penelope asked.

"Four, and good men all."

Nev turned his head sharply. "Only four? But I thought we had dozens of tenants."

"Not during my tenure here," the captain said. "I daresay you mean before your father enclosed the commons, four or five years ago. The majority of your former tenants chose to avoid the expense of the hedges by selling to larger farmers."

"Oh." Nev was plainly disconcerted. "Who's left?"

"Thomas Kedge, John Claxton, Henry Larwood, and William Shreeves. Mr. Kedge has by far the largest part. He pays us almost three thousand pounds per annum in rents and does very well for himself with what remains. The others amount to less than a thousand pounds each."

"So our income at New Year's will be . . . ?" Penelope asked.

"Very nearly two thousand pounds and three-quarters."

She sat appalled. Only a few thousand pounds left of her dowry to last them through the year, and then only a few thousand more to be gained! And Nev thought the estate had been abused; where was the money to refurbish it to come from?

"Will there be much profit on the home farm's harvest?" Nev asked.

The captain stroked his mustache. "Five hundred pounds at the most. Very likely less. It has not been a good year, though nowhere near so disastrous as '16, of course. With more funds, perhaps, we might have made more of it, but—" He shrugged, without the least embarrassment at this reference to his late employer's prodigality, nor with the least consciousness, Penelope thought angrily, of Nev's stricken look.

"How much of an outlay will we need to make the farm more profitable next year?" Nev said. It had to be asked, but Penelope suspected the answer would not comfort him.

The captain made an airy gesture. "Oh, two thousand pounds at the least."

Nev stared out the window again, shoulders slumped.

"Why don't you assemble the last five years' ledgers and receipts for me to look over? I'll get them from you this evening," Penelope said. "Perhaps going over the home farm and visiting our tenants will help us understand what needs to be done. Lord Bedlow, what is your opinion?"

Nev started, then looked hopeful. "Oh, yes. Jolly good idea. I'll have two horses saddled directly."

Penelope would have liked to tell him when Captain Trelawney was not by, but then he would have the horses already saddled and he would want to know why she hadn't said anything, and she would look a fool. "I don't ride."

Nev stared at her. "You don't—you don't *ride?*"

Penelope could not help glancing at the captain. Sure

enough, his eyebrows had shot up nearly to his graying hair-
line.

"No," she said shortly.

Nev's disappointed look smoothed away into probably
false cheer. "No matter. We'll take the cart."

They plodded down the tree-lined avenue in silence. Nev
had wanted to be on horseback for this, able to gallop off and
lose himself in the wind on his face and the ground flashing
away beneath him if things got too bad. He would have to
teach his wife to ride soon. It wasn't an unpleasant thought.
He glanced at Penelope, sitting quietly beside him in the cart.
Her face was hidden by the brim of her bonnet as she gazed
out over the lawn. But he could see the rest of her just fine,
and she would look nice in a riding habit.

"If we cut down these trees, we might be able to get almost
a thousand pounds for them," she said.

Nev turned to look at her.

A wash of crimson covered her cheeks before she looked
away. "I'm sorry," she said in a small voice. "That was mercan-
tile of me. Of course we can't cut down the trees, they've been
here for generations and—"

Nev grinned at her. "I wanted to cut them down myself,
but my mother threw a fit."

She relaxed and smiled at him. He wondered what would
happen if he leaned over and kissed her. He probably couldn't,
because of the bonnet. He was calculating his angle when
the gardener came into view and the opportunity was lost.

Nev had been encouraged by the appearance of the park
when he had looked at it out of his window this morning.
Although he knew it couldn't be true, he had almost hoped
for a moment that it was all a sham, that when he looked over
Loweston later he would find it as prosperous and flourishing
as ever.

He had known it couldn't be true, and it wasn't.

Things began to deteriorate as soon as they passed out of sight of the house. Nothing dramatic, at first. The grass was less well-kept, and there were stumps where Nev remembered inviting stands of elms and beeches. Then the path curved through a small wood of trees not valuable enough to be cut down, and they came out in view of the home farm.

There seemed to be fewer people working than Nev remembered from previous years this close to harvest—not that he had ever paid much attention. Indeed, Nev wasn't sure he would even notice if there were anything wrong with the fields or the equipment. The swaying, ripening wheat ran in thick, crooked rows just as it always had. Was it a little thinner, or was that his imagination? He had no idea. In the distance he could see pastures where sheep grazed, but it was too far off to judge the size or health of the herd.

No, what struck Nev were the men. As a child he had known them all, by sight if not by name. Now he recognized a few faces, but the majority were unfamiliar. They seemed thinner than he remembered, thinner and harsher, somehow. As a child he would ride past them, waving and shouting, and they would wave and shout back. Now they tugged their forelocks or touched their caps in sullen silence.

Nev glanced at his wife. She was shrinking back against the seat, but when she caught his eye she straightened. "I'm sure they will be friendlier when they've got to know us better." Her voice barely shook at all. "They are just unsure of what kind of master you will be."

Nev was not sure what kind of master he would be either.

"Have you met Mr. Kedge before?" Penelope asked her husband.

"Tom Kedge? A hundred times. A stout man with dirt under his fingernails, a roly-poly wife, and a loud voice. His cottage is half a mile up ahead. His laborers live with him until they marry, so there are always a dozen folk in and out.

Every time I've seen Mrs. Kedge she's been passing someone a mug of ale in one hand and swatting someone with a rolling pin with the other. She used to give me fresh rolls."

Penelope smiled.

He bit his lip. "I haven't seen them in years, though." Then they rounded a bend, and Thomas Kedge's cottage was visible. It was larger than Penelope had expected, the largest house they had seen along the road—although, of course, on nowhere near the same scale as Loweston Grange itself. Nev whistled. But it was not until they got closer that Penelope realized why; it was larger than he had expected too. The whole left part of the cottage was visibly newer, as were the shingles on the roof. Honeysuckle and roses, along with a local plant she didn't recognize, were just beginning to creep up a new trellis on the older side of the house.

"Tom Kedge never had glazed windows before!" Nev pulled up the horses in front of a neat drive. "I don't understand—I thought things had been going poorly here."

Surely this was a good sign, but Penelope could not appreciate it. She was seized with nervousness. She did not want to meet Nev's tenants. What if she could find nothing to say to them? What if they disliked her? What if they only gazed at her blankly like the laborers in the field?

Nev looked as uncertain as she felt. He had pulled the cart to a stop, but now merely sat holding the reins. They exchanged rueful smiles. She wished there were something she could do, but she was as out of her depth here as he was; more so, probably. He, at least, was used to the idea of having tenants. Mrs. Kedge had given him fresh rolls.

After half a minute or so, a scrawny boy ran out from behind the house to take the horses. As Nev and Penelope walked up the path, the front door opened and a round woman of middle years stuck her head out the door. "Come in, come in!" As they got nearer, Penelope saw that her blue muslin gown was nearly new. So was the lace on her cap, though it looked machine-made to Penelope. Her graying hair was inexpertly teased into ringlets around her ears. "I haven't seen you in so long, Lord Bedlow! Look at you, handsomer than ever! Is this Lady Bedlow?"

Nev introduced them as Mrs. Kedge led the way into a whitewashed parlor. Freshly cut roses in an earthenware jug stood on the table. The wooden floor gleamed, and the mantelpiece and end tables were crowded with porcelain figurines.

"Betsey!" Mrs. Kedge called shrilly. "Bring tea for his lordship! And some rolls!" She turned to Nev. "Those were always your favorite. How have you been? We were all so sorry to hear about your father. He was such a wonderful man!"

Penelope didn't think Mrs. Kedge noticed the skepticism that flashed across Nev's face. "Thank you," he said easily. "I've been well. It looks like you have too—you were never so fine the last time I begged rolls from you!"

Mrs. Kedge smiled at him. "Yes, we had a couple of bad years, but Tom works very hard and he turned us right around. And he tells me there's so much less waste now that the fields aren't divided in that ridiculous way. Here, do sit down, please."

They sat on sturdy wooden chairs around the table. "Is Tom by?" Nev asked. "I was hoping to discuss with him what needs to be done to—" He trailed off, then repeated, "What needs to be done."

"Oh, yes, he's talking Poor Authority business with the vicar in his counting room. Dear," she hollered, and Penelope jumped. "Come meet her ladyship! We've all been half dying to meet you," she added more quietly, smiling at Penelope.

A rather dirty maid came in at that moment, ostentatiously carrying a great silver tea tray. A plate of rolls and half a seedcake sat in the center. "Just set it down on the table and

go, Betsey," Mrs. Kedge told her. "And wash your face! Aren't
you ashamed for his lordship and her ladyship to see you?"
Betsey set down the tray with a rattle and fled, red-faced.

"She's a good girl." Mrs. Kedge poured the tea and pre-
sented it in a manner she clearly thought very grand. "I do
worry she'll break the china, though."

"You have quite a collection." Nev gave every evidence of
admiration for the china shepherdesses and monkeys dressed
as fine lords and ladies that littered the room. "Aren't you
afraid the boys will knock them over? I remember you were
forever telling me how all your nice things were broken."

"Oh, the boys don't live here anymore," someone said from
the doorway, and Penelope turned. This must be Tom Kedge.
His sunburnt, genial face and massive body seemed too big
for the house, as did his stentorian voice; it was probably just
the right volume for directing men in a wheat field.

"It's not like the old days." Kedge shook his head. "People
used to be content with their lot, and now—new men in and
out of the district every year, and half the population up and
emigrating to America. And the soldiers—I hate to speak ill
of men who fought for their country, but it seems like a lot of
them came back wrong. Couldn't have 'em in the house anymore! Not safe for my Sally." He smiled and winked at his
wife.

Mrs. Kedge smiled back at her husband. "I do miss the
racket sometimes. It's so quiet in the house. But that's progress, isn't it? Things change. We shouldn't like to live in the
Dark Ages!"

Penelope looked around at the comfort and the cleanli-
ness and pictured again the sullen, lean faces of the workers,
even the boys. No, it would not do to have them tramping in
and out and getting mud on Mrs. Kedge's nice floor or breaking her fine china. Mrs. Kedge was too good for that now.

She thought of her father's managers and foremen. Her
father was friendly enough with them at the brewery, but he

certainly did not invite them to dinner in Russell Square. Penelope tried to imagine those men drinking a glass of brandy at the mahogany dining table, but it was impossible; and they would hardly have wanted to. Yet her father had known some of those men from boyhood. So had her mother. Penelope remembered meeting a Mrs. Raeburn, who worked at the brewery affixing labels to kegs, bottles, and casks. The woman had pinched her cheek and told her that she and Mrs. Brown used to steal pies off a cart together.

Penelope knew that people found her mother distasteful; now she looked at Mrs. Kedge sticking out her pinky as she drank from a teacup painted with fat little Chinese boys and understood how they felt. She hated herself for it.

Kedge stepped out of the doorway. A much smaller man entered the room in his wake. An unprepossessing fellow in his middle thirties, his dirty linen and pompous air made him look even plainer than he would have without it. He waited, a small smirk on his face, until Mr. Kedge said, "The head of our flock, Mr. Snively."

"How charming it is to see you again, Lord Bedlow, even under such sad circumstances," the vicar said. "Your father will be severely missed by all true souls at Loweston. I am deeply pleased to meet your ladyship. It is an honor, truly, Lady Bedlow." He took her hand and bowed, a little too low, in a way that made Penelope wonder if he were not trying to show up the Kedges as ill-bred.

"Thank you, Mr. Snively," she said. "I—"

"He's right about Lord Bedlow," Kedge interrupted. "A real gentleman. If he'd raised the rents any higher in '16, we'd all have lost our holdings to the bank."

Nev nodded. "He would never have wanted that." Penelope didn't think anyone else caught the way his mouth twisted over the words. "You old-timers are the backbone of this place. You've lived here since before I was born, haven't you?"

Penelope was amazed how well he did this. She was nearly paralyzed with shyness and distaste, but Nev sat easily at the Kedges' table, looking not at all out of place, the sun from the window glinting on his cinnamon hair and candor shining in his blue eyes. Tom Kedge would be eating out of his hand.

Kedge puffed out his chest a little. "I have indeed. Why, I remember when you was that big, running about wanting to play with the workhorses!"

Nev smiled at him. "I was hoping you might advise me on what is best to be done to get things back in shape."

"I am so glad you asked," Mr. Snively began. "I've been keeping a list—"

Penelope grimaced, and Nev flashed her a laughing look. "That is wonderful. My wife is fond of lists as well. But I should like Mr. Kedge's opinions on agricultural matters first."

Kedge chewed on his lower lip. "It's going to take work. Unless you've got a lot of the ready at your disposal, it could take a long time too."

Penelope thought wistfully of the hundred thousand pounds in trust for their children.

"The soil just isn't up to snuff," Kedge said. "If you could afford a few head of cattle, that would help quite a bit."

"Cattle?" Nev asked. Penelope was equally at a loss.

Kedge roared with laughter. "You know what they say in these parts. Muck is the mother of money!"

Mr. Snively wrinkled his nose in distaste. Penelope, seeing it, hastily smoothed out her own features.

"Mr. Kedge—" Penelope was unsure if it were wise to ask, but she was desperate for an answer of some kind and foresaw a long conversation full of manure and farming implements if she did not. "We drove past the fields on the way here, and—the men did not look happy."

Kedge chuckled. "You should have seen them in '16! Lucky

for us, the worst have been transported. Poachers and mal-
contents, the lot of 'em."

Mr. Snively sniffed. "I cannot agree. The threat of revolt
is as real today as it was in '16. Indeed, if I may just drop a
word in your lordship's ear—I worry that certain of your tenants are far too lenient with their men."

Penelope frowned. "What do you mean by 'too lenient'?"

"Allow me to warn you, my lady, against the tales of hardship you will surely hear. I see you are delicately bred with
tender sensibilities"—Penelope tried not to stare in disbelief—"and these sneaking folk will seek to impose upon you
in hopes of money."

"And which of my tenants are you accusing of overle-
niency?" There was a slight edge in Nev's voice. "Not Mr.
Kedge, I presume."

"I hope not!" Kedge laughed loudly.

Mr. Snively permitted himself a dry chuckle. "Certainly
not. Tom's laborers come to church on Sunday, every one, if
they know on which side their bread is buttered, and afterward they work a half day."

Well, that explained the vicar's enthusiasm, Penelope
thought.

"He had the idea from Mr. Coke," Mrs. Kedge said.

Mr. Snively raised his eyes to Heaven as if Mr. Coke were
to be found there. "That man is the benefactor of Norfolk,
and it would be a great thing if everyone who held the souls
of these rough folk in their hands would do as much. The rest
of your tenants' men spend the Lord's day in drunken idleness, and you know they say the devil finds work for idle
hands." He looked at Nev significantly. "*Poaching.*"

Kedge shrugged. "I'd rather have them poaching than
burning the barns."

Mr. Snively folded his hands together with a very grave
air. "I am afraid I cannot agree. I know Sir Jasper is most con-

cerned. Nothing discourages the blackguards, not even the increased severity of the laws. Even Sir Jasper's spring guns do nothing to deter them."

"Spring guns?" Penelope asked. "What are those?"

"They are dangerous and criminal," Nev snapped. "They are designed to shoot anyone who sets off a trip wire, and they will maim or kill a dog or a—a passerby as often as a poacher. Does Sir Jasper really still use them?"

Mr. Snively changed tack impressively. "Unfortunately, he does, though I have urged him against them many and many a time. They are, alas, not in the tradition of Christian forbearance. It is not easy for sinful men to turn the other cheek, but so we must strive to do, else our own souls shall become as black as the pitch-smeared faces of these poachers. I see your lordship is a true follower of our Lord."

They had been traveling along the road to Loweston Grange for less than a minute when Nev said fiercely, "I should have told you before. Never, under any circumstances, set foot on Greygloss land if I am not with you. If you are in our woods, and you come to a fence, do not go over it. Sir Jasper uses mantraps and spring guns to catch poachers. It isn't safe."

Penelope was touched. He needed her alive, of course, to keep the interest on the hundred thousand pounds that remained, and even if he wished for his freedom she hardly imagined him capable of arranging her death; but there was surely a measure of real concern in his looks. "I never heard of such a thing," she said. "It seems barbaric."

"It is. If a man is poaching, he must take his chances. But a spring gun doesn't look before it shoots. I cannot credit that Sir Jasper has not taken them down, after what happened."

"What do you mean?"

Nev's profile was grim. "Sir Jasper's wife was killed by one of the guns, two years ago. She ought to have known better than to go walking in Sir Jasper's coverts, but—well, no one knows what happened. She was found with a bullet through her head."

Penelope shuddered. "How awful!"

Nev shook his head. "I still cannot believe the guns haven't been taken down."

"And yet, it appears that Sir Jasper has put a deal of energy into improving the district. Perhaps he is a good man, with simply this one mania against poachers."

"The district does not seem much improved to me."

Penelope could not argue with this. "Maybe it would have been even worse without the changes," she said uncertainly. "Nev, what exactly happened in '16?"

"It was a bad summer. It rained a lot. The harvest failed in a lot of places. There were riots all over East Anglia—didn't you hear about them?"

She felt her cheeks heating. "Oh! I suppose I did. There were riots at Loweston?"

"Nothing big. They smashed up some things. It was worse in other places, I think. I remember at Cambridge, there was talk of arming the students to put down the riots."

Penelope couldn't help a smile. "That sounds rather . . . ill-judged."

Nev smiled ruefully back, and something warm unfurled inside her. "I didn't think so at the time, but yes, it probably would have been."

Eight

Nev missed the city. It was dark now, and in London he would have been out with his friends or spending the evening with Amy. The sounds of bustle and life and other people would have been outside the window. If he'd liked, he could have gone to a concert. He wanted music with a pain like homesickness. Even the songs of the nightingales, which he had loved as a boy, did not comfort him.

The only sounds of real, human life were the rustlings from the next room. Nev was ashamed to see Penelope; ashamed that he had brought her here to face a thousand impossible burdens he was totally unequipped to bear. And he was tired of making polite conversation with a stranger who was somehow also his wife and who had already witnessed some of the least proud moments of his life.

But anything was better than standing alone in his father's room, looking into his father's mirror, and wishing there were some of his father's brandy in the decanter. He knocked at the connecting door, and at her soft invitation, he opened it.

He was unprepared for the wave of longing that went through him at the sight of her. She was sitting cross-legged in bed, a stack of heavy ledgers in front of her and a branch of candles on the night table. She looked up and smiled at him. Her night rail enveloped her almost completely, but she had rolled up the sleeves to reveal slender forearms and hands, and he could see one bare foot peeking out from under her crossed legs. Her hair was not yet braided for the night, but it was out of its daytime knot and tied back with a black satin ribbon. The end of the ribbon was almost, but not quite, disappearing into her night rail's prim neckline. Nev swallowed. The month since he had last slept with a woman seemed like a very, very long time.

Damnation, she was his wife! Why did it seem so wrong to untie the ribbon, lay her back on the bed, and make love to her?

She looked so young, and he had seen her frowning worriedly in the brief instant before she looked up at him. A worry caused by the sorry state of his affairs.

As his silence stretched, her smile grew uncertain. "Is everything all right?"

"Yes, of course," he lied. "How are the books?"

"It's too early to tell." She turned back to the books and absentmindedly ran the end of her quill over her mouth in a way that might have been designed to drive Nev crazy, but in reality had nothing to do with him. "Can you look at something for me?"

He wasn't sure what useful knowledge he could possibly impart, but at the moment he was willing to seize any excuse to cross the room and sit on the edge of her bed. "Yes?"

"There are several different handwritings in these. This one"—she pointed to an illegible scrawl—"is Captain Trelawney's. There are two before that, though, and they alternate. It's generally this one, but every so often, this one shows up."

She pushed the ledger toward him. He looked where she pointed, at the two neat hands—and recognition slammed into him like a runaway horse. "The more frequent one is our late steward, Mr. Garrett's," he said slowly. "The other is his son Percy's." It was Percy's bookkeeping hand, fine and precise as an accountant's. His ordinary hand was larger, more slanting, and much, much harder to read.

Her brow wrinkled. "Percy Garrett. That name sounds familiar."

He reached out and took the pen from her. She gave it up without a struggle, but when he began to tickle her ear with it, she shrieked and leaped sideways.

"Ticklish, are you?" He had intended to distract her and himself, and he succeeded. A few moments later he could think of nothing but Penelope, wriggling and giggling and showing intriguing flashes of limb as she struggled to escape. Finally she went on the attack, seizing his hand and trying to wrest the quill away. He leaned back, misjudged, and fell sideways onto the bed. Penelope overbalanced and sprawled on top of him.

They both stilled. Nev could plainly feel the soft give of her breasts and the curve of her hip through her night rail. She shifted, letting go of the pen. Nev didn't dare move for fear she would feel his erection. Her hair had come loose; it brushed his face as she pushed herself upright. He sat up, and she edged away, laughing, holding up her hands as if she thought he would start tickling her again.

He put the pen down. It would be so easy to slide after her and kiss her. He knew she would let him. And then he would take off that oversized night rail, and then—then he would take her virginity. What if he hurt her? There would be no more tickling and giggling then. She would shy away when he touched her.

"Good night, Penelope." And then, because he couldn't help himself, he reached out and ran a lock of her hair through his fingers. It was smooth and warm and silky, and he almost gave in to his desire after all.

"Good night, Nev." She smiled shyly at him. He let go of her hair and went back to his own room.

Lying in bed, he listened to the *scritch-scritch-scritch* of Penelope's quill. There was something comforting about it.

The following day Nev rode over to pay a call on Sir Jasper. He would have liked to bring Penelope, but he couldn't think of an excuse, and it would have looked odd anyway. Sir Jasper had not bothered inviting a female relative to be his hostess since his wife's death. If Nev had dragged Penelope along, Sir Jasper would have known at once that it was because Nev didn't know what he was doing on his own.

As an adult Nev had seen Sir Jasper only rarely, in town; he had never been impressed by him. But here in Greygloss's beautiful, well-kept entrance hall, after a ride through Greygloss's prosperous home farm and rich, sweeping lawns, it was different. The baronet even *looked* different, the very picture of a country landowner in well-cut riding clothes, his dark hair graying at the temples. He wrung Nev's hand in a very friendly way, though, and Nev tried to feel heartened.

"I'm glad to see you," Sir Jasper said. "There are a number of things I've been meaning to speak to you about. But it would be a shame to waste such a fine day indoors, and I daresay Lady Bedlow would like a fine quail for dinner."

Nev had never done much shooting. Percy wasn't legally eligible to hunt game, and leaving him behind, or worse yet asking him to beat the bushes like a servant, had been unthinkable. Wandering about with Sir Jasper killing birds and talking about the estate sounded unutterably dreary, but he plastered on a smile and agreed.

It turned out that Sir Jasper did, in fact, have a number of things he'd been meaning to speak to Nev about: the insidiousness of poachers, the importance of a firm hand, various people in the district who were not to be trusted, and details of crop rotations and planting potatoes and drainage that Nev knew he would have forgotten by the afternoon. It didn't help Nev's mood that, unpracticed with the long fowling pieces, he failed to shoot a single bird.

"Have you thought about becoming a justice of the peace?" The baronet seemed to be slowing down after an hour of solid advice. "There are a number of offenses that cannot be tried by one magistrate sitting alone, and it would be invaluable to have two in the district. Your father was considering it, but alas he never found the time before his death . . .”

Nev doubted that his father had seriously been considering anything which sounded like so very much work. He didn't relish the idea himself. “I hadn't thought about it,” he said honestly. “But I will think about it now.”

Sir Jasper looked at his face and laughed. “But enough of business! Is your family returning to the neighborhood soon?”

“Any day now.”

Sir Jasper smiled. “Wonderful. It will be a pleasure to see your charming mother again—and of course Lady Louisa.” He paused meaningfully.

Nev's refusal of Sir Jasper's suit hung awkwardly in the air between them. Trying to think what to say, Nev tramped ahead, searching the underbrush for signs of movement.

“*Stop!* For the love of God, stop at once!”

Nev froze, and saw the tripwire two inches from his thigh.

Sir Jasper pounded up. “Oh, thank God. I thought I warned you about the spring guns in this area.”

He had, and Nev felt the worst sort of fool. If he hadn't stopped in time—if he had been shot—what would have become of his family? Of Loweston? Of Penelope?

Penelope would probably be better off as a widow. A hundred thousand pounds, no one to answer to, no Loweston to worry about. He shoved that thought aside.

If he had accepted Sir Jasper's offer to buy, the baronet might have put up spring guns at Loweston. The idea repulsed Nev more than he had expected.

At the end of the day, he still hadn't managed to shoot anything. Sir Jasper gave him two quails anyway. Nev had to struggle to accept the birds gracefully.

* * *

Nev and Penelope were eating breakfast. At least, it had started out that way. Somewhere along the line, it had shifted into Nev watching Penelope eat breakfast. She ate a good deal, but very neatly. She cut everything up into ladylike bites, chewed slowly, and washed it all down with ladylike sips of tea. It was refined, sensible, and a little too careful, like everything about her. Just now she was spreading a thin layer of jam on her toast, with an adorable frown of concentration.

"Are you going to cut your toast into tiny pieces too?" he teased.

She flushed. "Of course not. Whoever heard of cutting up toast?"

"I just wondered."

She looked away. "When my parents sent me to finishing school, the girls made fun of me for how I ate. I suppose I overcompensated."

Nev felt guilty suddenly, and angry. "Wretched cats. You ought to have eaten with your elbows on the table and your fingers in the food. That would have shown them."

"Perhaps, but it wouldn't have been very attractive."

"Who cares?"

"I rather think you would. You'll have to sit across the breakfast table from me for the rest of your life."

A life sentence. Penelope only, always, forever. Nev thought of all the times he had eaten breakfast with Amy. They would rise late and make their way to the breakfast room, and Amy's cook would make them buttered eggs and crumpets. Amy hadn't had good table manners—she ate quickly and used her fingers sometimes. But Nev had never minded; it just meant he could eat as messily as he wanted too. They would always laugh and talk and read each other things from the morning paper, and sometimes he would feed her strawberries. Of course, he and Amy would have just risen from a night of lovemaking. He and Penelope hadn't even kissed since his proposal.

Penelope began to take a bite of her toast, then pushed it away, with a blush and a little laugh. "I can't eat it now, you've made me embarrassed!"

Nev wondered if he would ever know the right thing to say again.

"I suppose I'll have more tea." She poured herself a cup and reached for the jar of honey. But as she opened it, she glanced up at Nev. She fumbled with the spoon, and honey flew all over her fingers.

Nev stared at the sticky molten gold sliding down his wife's ink-stained fingers.

Penelope saw his fixed look and misinterpreted it. "Don't look at me like that! I know I'm hopeless!"

"That's not it," Nev said with utmost sincerity. "That . . . looks like it tastes good."

"Well, it's wasted now. Unless you want to lick it off?" She spoke sarcastically, as if she were proposing an obviously implausible alternative.

"Of course I want to lick it off. But I said I wouldn't touch you till we knew each other better, and—"

Penelope looked at him in perplexity, then laughed. "A few weeks of celibacy, and this is what men descend to!"

"It's not that," Nev told her with sudden conviction. "It's you. You're driving me mad. Just watching you eat breakfast is enough to make me want to—"

"Really?" A mischievous light came into Penelope's eyes, and she raised her honey-spattered fingers to her mouth. She sucked lightly on her index finger, then withdrew it, letting her mouth drag open. Then she licked a drop of honey off her lip.

She was teasing him, he realized—to her, this was no different than the tickling or the fighting over that absurd list. It was only a game. She felt nothing.

Nev's eyes narrowed. He was fairly sure he could do something about that.

He rose from his seat and bent over her, one hand flat on the table. Grasping her wrist, he pulled her honeyed hand toward him; she only resisted for a moment. He took the same finger into his mouth and sucked it gently. Penelope's eyes widened. He slowly pulled the finger in and out of his mouth and watched her eyes glaze over. He moved on to the next finger, and the next. Then he kissed her.

She gave a startled gasp and let him. He began gently, coaxingly, and she melted like honey, her mouth soft and pliant beneath his. He nipped at her lower lip, and when he teased with his tongue her mouth opened under his. She did not know what to do, that was clear, but she followed his lead willingly enough, sending her tongue forth to touch his lightly.

Nev was disarmed by the utter honesty of her response. She had never done this before; she wasn't letting him kiss her because she wanted anything from him. She was his, his to teach. She had never known passion, he was sure of it. Nev could scarcely wait to show it to her.

His hand still around her wrist, he drew her out of her seat and set her on the edge of the table, the teapot and the rolls forgotten beside her. When he stepped between her legs, she murmured a little in satisfaction, and he felt it everywhere.

He pulled her closer, pressing his erection against her heat. There were too damn many layers of black fabric in the way, but he ran his hands up along the bones of her corset and closed one hand over her breast. She sighed and relaxed as though she had been waiting for it—but only for a moment. When he brushed a thumb over her nipple, she tensed like a bowstring. He drew back to watch her. She kept her eyes closed, but her whole body was waiting—it was as if she were listening very carefully for the opening strains of an overture. Her face was flushed, and her hair was coming down, and she seemed aware of nothing but his hands. He drew a finger across her nipple again, watching, mesmerized, as her breath came faster. She made no sound—it was as if she did not know how to react to pleasure. He squeezed her breast, and she shifted restlessly. Nev groaned in pleasure and frustration at the friction against his cock.

She shivered at the sound, pressing up against him. Nev pushed back, and she opened her thighs wider and took a shuddering breath—

"I'm just up from town, Nate. I told Hathick there was no need to announce me, I—*oh!*"

He turned around, sure this was all a horrid dream, but it wasn't. His mother was standing there, immaculate, her golden hair piled on her head.

He stepped frantically in front of Penelope. "God *damn* it, Mother, do you never knock?"

"Nate! Such language! You ought to know better how to behave to a *lady*! I saw no need to knock. I am sure it never occurred to me that you would be mauling your wife at breakfast as if she were a common trollop." His mother sniffed, and for one furious, unfilial moment Nev would have liked to break her neck.

Penelope was tugging her skirts into place, bright red all over. Her eyes were open and full of horror.

"Go and wait in the parlor, Mother. I'll be out in a moment."

"You're going to make your mother wait in the parlor?" Lady Bedlow asked. "I've had nothing to eat, and—"

"Go," Nev said, with a firmness that surprised him. It surprised him even more when his mother actually left the room in a huff.

He turned. Penelope had mostly righted her clothes, and her hair was back in place, but she looked utterly wretched. His mother was right; he had no notion of how to behave to a lady. He had let his desire overcome what little sense he had, and he had exposed Penelope to ridicule. Of course one could not treat one's wife as one might treat one's mistress. No matter how enticing she was or how much honey she spilled on her fingers.

"I'm so sorry," he said. "I should have been more careful."

She shook her head. "I ought not to have allowed it, I know that very well. I suppose she is right. I am common at heart. I must be."

"You are uncommon generous. She shouldn't have said that. I really am sorry—this hasn't been a good time for her." Lady Bedlow had never stood up well to strain. When seven-year-old Nev had broken his nose falling out of a tree and, frightened by the amount of blood, had gone crying to his mother, she'd fainted dead away. You couldn't blame her; she couldn't help it. It had been Lord Bedlow who had stanched the bleeding and called the doctor, he remembered; and who had told him, not unkindly, that a gentleman didn't cry, no matter how bad the pain. For a moment he missed his father.

Penelope's eyes filled with sympathy. Thinking of someone else seemed to ease her discomfort. She smoothed her skirts, straightened, looked competent and reassuring again. Penelope, Nev thought, was naturally responsible. "Of course it hasn't, poor lady. I promise you, I shan't regard it in the least. Go on." She smiled. "And please, tell her anything she wishes to take to the Dower House is hers."

"You're too good to me," Nev said, and meant it.

She looked down and blushed. She was so easy to please. Nev wished his mother at Jericho.

"You can't talk to Penelope that way, Mama," he said.

"Oh, I see how it is. Just because she is willing to allow you liberties that any self-respecting young *lady* would scorn, you'll take her side against your own mother!"

"If being kissed by her husband is a liberty any self-respecting young lady would scorn, I am glad Penelope is a Cit!"

"At the breakfast table, Nate? Where do you get it from? Your father would never have dreamed of doing such a thing!"

He would never have dreamed of doing such a thing with you, Nev thought. "Penelope has done us all a very great favor, Mama. I wish you could be civil to her."

"Oh, civil I shall certainly be—I would not dream of stooping to her level with vulgar scenes and catty remarks," Lady Bedlow said, with a sort of unhealthy agitation. "But you cannot expect me to be *grateful* that she is lording it over me, in my home, turning my son against me, using my breakfast parlor as if it were a brothel—" Her face was white. Nev looked closer and saw the dark circles under her eyes.

"Come here, Mama," he said gently, and held out an arm.

She flew to him, with a muffled, "Oh, Nate! It's been so dreadful—"

He stroked her hair. "I know, Mama. I know you didn't mean it." And for the moment he believed it.

Nine

Penelope watched in disbelief as the dowager Lady Bedlow's servants carted away a sofa, an ormolu clock, a painting of two shepherdesses, a small table, and—well, most of the other furniture Penelope remembered seeing in the parlor. The morning room and the master bedrooms had already been despoiled the night before.

"How much furniture can she *fit* in the Dower House?" Nev asked, bemused. "I've been there, and it's just not that big."

Penelope couldn't help laughing. "Perhaps I shouldn't have said *anything* she wishes to take. Were you fond of those things?"

"Not particularly. But we can't afford to replace any of them, can we?"

"No, but we can't afford to entertain either, so who's to know?"

Nev grinned. "It's clear you've never lived in the country. The servants will tell everyone in the neighborhood by tonight."

Penelope felt a slight pang. She so wanted to make a good impression in the neighborhood. On the other hand, she reminded herself, people would hardly like her *more* for a show of vulgar wealth. "If those things make her happy, I don't mind. I've never liked Fragonard, anyway."

"Who?"

Penelope felt another, greater pang. Her mother would have recognized the name. So would Edward. "The man who painted those shepherdesses. I've always preferred Boucher."

She realized he wouldn't recognize that name either, and flushed.

"What are you doing today?" he asked.

"I'm going to visit the laborers." Penelope tried not to sound as nervous as she felt. "Isn't the lady of the manor supposed to do that? They always do in books."

Nev looked uneasy. "I suppose so—who are you taking with you?"

Penelope did not quite like the idea of venturing into those rough cottages. She couldn't shake the image of the lean, grim men in the fields. She had told herself not to be fanciful, that none of them would dare lay a finger on Lady Bedlow, but at Nev's evident concern her fears flooded back. "I thought I might take one of the grooms, to drive the cart."

"Take Jack."

She nodded. "Is there anything I should take with me, do you think? Or would that seem like charity and offend people?"

"I don't know. Shall we send to my mother and ask her?"

Penelope hesitated. In a moment, she knew, she would say yes, because it was the sensible thing to do. But a tiny, foolish part of her did not want Lady Bedlow to know how unequipped Penelope was to be a countess.

"Here, how's this? We won't take anything with us this time, but we'll note what people need and go back in a few days. That is—would you like me to go with you?"

She looked up, unable to keep the relief off her face. "Yes, but not if you have other things to attend to."

"Nothing that can't wait." His slight hesitation told her he hadn't had any plans at all.

Penelope realized quickly enough that even if she had filled every corner of the cart with food, it would not have made up what these people lacked. The cottages were tiny, ramshackle, and threadbare. A straw pallet, a kettle, and perhaps a table with a chair or two were the usual furnishings; fuel for a fire at which to boil the kettle was a rare luxury.

Some of the laborers seemed embarrassed by their poverty; others sat with an air of grim satisfaction, seeming to say, *Look, and see how I live!* Penelope did not know what to say or what to ask; she tried not to look too obviously at the privation. Nev seemed able to make polite conversation—to ask about children and histories and employment, and get, sometimes, something more than respectful monosyllables. Penelope tried to at least commit names to memory, but each lean, prematurely weathered face seemed to blend into the next.

One, however, stood out: Aggie Cusher. She was a young woman, even rather pretty, despite straggly blonde hair, a lined face, and a few missing teeth. She wore a bright satin ribbon in her hair, and it looked as out of place in that cottage as a golden saltcellar would have. A skinny blonde girl of eight or nine, in a dress several sizes too small for her, pounded oats at the table; an unhealthy-looking child, perhaps two-and-a-half years old, played in the corner.

"Welcome, my lady, my lord, Mrs. Joe Cusher at your service—that is, I'm Agnes," the young woman said softly enough, and bobbed a curtsy, but there was an indefinable air of hostility about her.

"What a lovely ribbon," Penelope offered.

"Thank you." Agnes almost smiled, glancing at the little girl.

The girl paused in her pounding. "I gave it to her. I earned the money myself."

"I'm sure your mother is very proud of your hard work." To Penelope's surprise, a shadow passed across Agnes's face at these unexceptionable words.

"I work for Mr. Kedge," the little girl said.

"And does Joe work for Mr. Kedge too?" Penelope asked. It was a rhetorical question, to fill the strangely awkward silence; they were on land leased to Tom Kedge.

"He did." Agnes's gaze flicked to Nev for a moment.

"Oh, I'm sorry—are you a widow?" Penelope asked.

"Joe ain't dead," Agnes flashed.

The boy in the corner looked up. "Papa went to 'Stralia," he said, very clearly.

I should have seen that coming, Penelope thought, angry with herself. "Do you do all right on your own?" It was a foolish question. Agnes was alive, but for any other definition of "all right" she very clearly wasn't. And there was no answer that wasn't humiliating.

Nev went into the corner and sat down across from the sallow little boy. He pulled something from his pocket and spoke to him in a low tone. Penelope forced herself not to strain to hear what he was saying and listen to Agnes.

"I do all right," Agnes said. "I have help from friends in the village. My brother sends me money from America when he can, and my daughter, Josie—" Tears glimmered in Agnes's eyes. "I'd like to keep her at home"—Josie rolled her eyes—"but we used to spin for the woolen manufacturers in Norwich, and since the mill opened up there's no more of that work."

"Are you able to get help from the parish?" Penelope asked.

Agnes's face twisted. "No, my lady. I've lived here ten years, but Mr. Snively says I haven't got a settlement. Mr. Snively says I'd have to go home to Harwich and go on the parish there."

"We'd have a settlement if you married Aaron," Josie said.

Agnes turned bright red. "Don't make me slap you, Josie Cusher! I'm already married to your father, in case you'd forgotten."

"Aaron—" the little girl began to insist.

"Does Mr. Snively decide who gets poor relief?" Penelope broke in.

Agnes looked at once relieved and disgusted. "He's the head of the Poor Authority, isn't he?"

Penelope's eyebrows rose. Mr. Snively hadn't mentioned that. "I'm sorry. I'm new here, and there are a lot of things I don't know. I hope you will be patient with me. I mean to help you and the other people here, if I can."

Agnes's gaze dwelt almost insultingly on Penelope's fine clothes and smooth hands. Penelope's gown was plain, but it was neat and clean and new. Agnes's dress was none of those things; it was ragged and threadbare and dirty—not even patched, because the fabric was too thin to hold stitches.

"If you wished to go to Harwich, I daresay we could pay your coach fare," Penelope tried.

"How would Joe find me then?"

"Couldn't you write to him?"

Agnes looked almost pitying. "I don't know how to write."

"I could write it for you," Penelope offered.

Agnes sighed. "Thank you, but I wouldn't know where to send it—he don't have a proper address, like." She paused. "'Tisn't like for you, your ladyship. Joe and I don't write to each other. Joe did send me word once or twice, at the beginning—but he had to pay someone to have it writ, and then he'd to pay to send it, and then I'd to pay to get it and find someone who could read it back to me. A year ago, a letter came, and I hadn't the sixpence to pay the postage."

Penelope's eyes widened. "But—"

Agnes shrugged, hard-faced, but Penelope saw real grief in her eyes. "The baby was sick."

Penelope wanted to ask more, to clamor *Wasn't there anything you could have done?* The thought of the unclaimed letter filled her with—it wasn't quite frustration, and it wasn't quite anger. It was more like a restless need to *do* something. Penelope had always believed that if you put your mind to it, worked hard, and didn't whine, there was no reason you shouldn't solve nearly any problem. She was beginning to realize that she had never had such huge, hopeless problems as this woman.

There was an unexpected sound in the tiny cottage—the little boy giggled. "Do it again!"

Nev reached forward and pulled a shining sixpence from behind the boy's ear. He clapped and reached for it, but Nev twirled his hand and it disappeared. Penelope's heart sank—but she had misjudged Nev. "Look in your pocket," he said.

The boy did—and there was the sixpence! His eyes went round—and then he closed his fist on it, and put it behind his back. "It's gone," he said, slyly.

"Kit, give Lord Bedlow back his sixpence," Agnes said in a low voice.

Nev looked startled. "He can keep it."

"I couldn't—" Agnes stopped herself. "Thank you." Penelope had always supposed that pride was the one thing that could not be taken from you; now she saw she had been wrong. "Say thank you, Kit," Agnes said, almost desperately.

But Kit could not say thank you. He could only stare at his fist, and then at Nev. Josie too was staring. Nev shifted awkwardly.

As she and Nev were leaving, Penelope heard Agnes say, with a catch in her voice, "Tomorrow we'll go into town and buy some real bread. Would you like that?"

"Can we buy some bacon too?" Kit asked.

"Not this time, sweetheart."

Penelope thought of her own generous helping of bacon at breakfast that morning. Nev must have been thinking the same thing. "Tell Cook to send them some bacon."

"Can we?" Penelope wanted to, but—"It wouldn't be fair, unless we sent them all bacon." She did not know how to talk about Agnes's indefinable anger. Would a gift of food trample the woman's pride too far?

"Then we'll send them all bacon."

"But we can't afford it. Not until New Year's, at least."

"It seems ridiculous to say we can't afford something, after seeing that home," Nev said stubbornly. "We'll stop eating bacon ourselves and send them that—"

She was touched—she hated being the parsimonious, logical one. But her accountant's mind could do no other. "Nev, we're two people; we don't eat much bacon to begin with. And the servants eat what we leave. If we don't eat bacon, they can't eat bacon. There must be other things we ought to spend the money on first. I don't know—plows, or something."

"Couldn't we—" Nev lapsed into frustrated silence, and Penelope would have given up a lot more than bacon to take that hopeless look off his face.

"Never mind. We'll send Kit some bacon."

One look at his buoyant grin, and Penelope went up in a blaze. So this was passion.

Did it mean she was common? Gentlemen felt passion, of course. But ladies weren't supposed to or weren't supposed to give in to it. Immoderate feeling of any sort was to be shunned. Just because one *enjoyed* eating cake, that didn't mean one should eat cake with every meal, or one became fat and slothful and a slave to one's desires. It was all too easy to see how it might happen—she would have let Nev do anything to her, anything at all, right there on the breakfast table.

Control, restraint, elegance—they were all synonymous with that indefinable something that made you gentry and not common. Excess was wearing bright colors and crying in public and talking too loud and eating in big bites and all the things that Penelope had trained herself never, ever to do, ever since her first day at Miss Mardling's. This was just one more thing to add to the list. *I am just as good as that stuck-up Lady Bedlow,* she told herself. *My parents are worth a hundred of her. I will not give her justification to sneer at me and call me common. I will be a lady if it kills me.*

"Penny for your thoughts?" Nev tilted his head, pondering. "There's a pun there, I'm sure of it." He flashed her another grin and her breath caught in her throat.

It might really kill her.

That evening Lady Bedlow and Louisa were expected at the Grange for dinner. *I would invite you to the Dower House, but I'm afraid I can't afford to provide the kind of fare that your bride must be accustomed to,* Lady Bedlow had said.

Nev watched his family walk in, feeling unexpectedly and uncomfortably as if he were ranged with Penelope against them.

"Are you settling in nicely at the Dower House?" Penelope asked.

"Oh, nicely enough," his mother said. "It's hard to make a new place home after so many years . . . and I'm afraid it's smaller than what Louisa is accustomed to, of course—"

"We're settling in wonderfully." But even Louisa spoke to Nev, not Penelope. "How are you doing, Nate? How are things here?"

Penelope, her attentive gaze still on his family, gave a tiny sigh and tried to look as if she hadn't noticed. Nev reached out and grabbed her hand. "*Penelope and I* are doing fine, Louisa. Things have been difficult here, but I daresay we shall come about soon enough."

Louisa looked hurt, though she still did not look at Penelope. But several minutes later, when they were seated at table, she asked Nev, "*Have* things been difficult? Is there—is there anything I can do?"

Lady Bedlow tsked. "Don't be silly, Louisa. What could

you possibly do? It is not a woman's place to deal with money matters outside her household accounts."

Louisa's face burned. "Men do not seem to manage the business so well that I could do much worse."

Penelope made a soft choking noise, as if she were trying not to laugh, and Nev felt a little more charitable toward Louisa. "I quite agree," he said. "I am all at sea when it comes to accounts. Thank God Penelope knows what she is about."

"Of course you are all at sea." Tears filled Lady Bedlow's eyes. "Your father always dealt with all that. If only he were here—"

Louisa visibly tensed with irritation, and Nev felt impatient himself. Did she not remember where Lord Bedlow's management had gotten them all? He handed his mother his handkerchief. "Please, Mama, don't take on so—"

"Thank you, Nev." She smiled mistily at him. "My children are so good to me. I know I'm a dreadful trial to Louisa." She waited.

There was a pause, and then Louisa said reluctantly, "Of course you aren't, Mama."

Nev, meeting Penelope's mirthful eyes across the table, had to smother a smile. But Lady Bedlow beamed.

Louisa turned to Nev. "Would it be terribly improper for us to have a house party?" She sounded rather as if the world depended on his answer. "It will be unbearable here all summer and winter, else."

Nev thought about feeding a dozen greedy mouths and entertaining a dozen jaded minds. "I don't think we can afford a house party, Louisa. Perhaps one of your friends will invite you." He tried to look apologetic.

"I'm sure I don't know who Nate would invite that would be suitable company for *you*, Louisa," Lady Bedlow said. "Of course it's only a matter of time before Mr. Garrett's son is lording it over me in my own home."

Nev didn't want to talk about it, not with his mother, but she was sure to find out eventually. "I won't be inviting Percy or Thirkell, Mama. I told them that now I had responsibilities, I couldn't—"

"Oh, Nate, you finally cut the connection!" His mother gave his hand a congratulatory pat; he held himself carefully still. "I'm so glad! That boy has always been a bad influence on you, ever since Bedlow hired his father."

Louisa tapped her fork irritably against the edge of her plate. "Lord, Mama, I don't know why you're so hard on Percy. I always thought it was Nate who was a bad influence on him!"

Lady Bedlow put her nose in the air. "Unequal friendships never end well. It gave poor Percy aspirations above his station. How could he help but go wild?"

"I didn't cut the connection, Mama. I just—" Nev stopped. He could protest that it hadn't *been* an unequal friendship. Percy hadn't been a bad influence on him, and he hadn't been a bad influence on Percy. They egged each other on, that was all. But what was the use? That was how everyone would see it. That was how everyone had always seen it: Lord Nevinstoke and his low friend. Nev knew he had done the right thing, but he felt ashamed anyway—especially when he caught Penelope's curious, sympathetic glance. "I wish Mr. Garrett were still alive," he confessed, as a sort of compromise. "I didn't much take to Captain Trelawney."

"Oh, I never liked him either," Lady Bedlow said. "There is something overfamiliar about him. He acted quite as if he were your father's equal and not his servant."

Nev sighed. "I'm not sure he realizes how bad things are for our people. Penelope and I visited some of the cottages today, and the families seemed really in distress. And so many men out of work or gone."

"Yes." It was nearly the first thing Penelope had said

all evening. "Do either of you know why Joe Cusher was transported?"

Louisa, reaching for a roll, drew her hand back. "Joe Cusher was one of the ringleaders in that riot three years ago," she said tightly. "The vandals fired the barn with Papa's threshing machine in it. We thought they would fire the house too. Sir Jasper and his friend sentenced him to transportation, of course. Agnes Cusher spat at my feet the next time I saw her. The way she looked at me—" She shivered.

"Louisa!" Lady Bedlow's curls trembled anxiously. "You know I don't like to talk about that time."

Louisa opened her mouth, then closed it again with a tiny, frustrated sigh. "Yes, Mama."

For perhaps another quarter of an hour, there was polite, strained conversation such as Nev never remembered when his father was alive. Then Lady Bedlow cleared her throat. "Penelope, dear, don't you think it's time we left Nate to his port?"

Penelope flushed. "Of course. How remiss of me." She stood.

Nev stood too. "Let's all go together. I've given up port."

"Why, Nate," Louisa said, laughing at him, "marriage has certainly changed you! Has Penelope converted you to Methodism too?"

Nev frowned. "Penelope isn't a Methodist, Louisa." The sudden, horrible thought struck him that perhaps she was, and he had just made a fool of himself. No—he would know, wouldn't he?

He looked at Penelope. She remained perfectly civil despite his family's rudeness; she would not say or do anything to make Nev feel her discomfort. And yet she could not feign ease or gaiety. She looked quiet and shut off. It inspired a curious tenderness in him.

Lady Bedlow led the way unthinkingly to the parlor, and

her look of consternation when she realized all the furniture was gone brought a glimmer of amusement back to Penelope's face. She met Nev's eyes, and the two of them were hard-pressed to stifle their laughter. The evening suddenly seemed much less dire.

Louisa looked embarrassed for all of them. "Let's go to the music room. Will you play for us, Nev?"

"Penelope plays better than I do," he told her.

"Oh, but I want you to sing us 'The Ballad of Captain Kidd'!"

"I—I know 'The Ballad of Captain Kidd,'" Penelope offered.

"Really?" Louisa didn't bother to hide her surprise, but at least she was looking at Penelope.

Penelope nodded shyly. Soon enough the young people were all singing "I'd a Bible in my hand / By my father's great command / And I sunk it in the sand / When I sailed!" Lady Bedlow watched them with affection and faint disapproval; she had learned long ago that nothing got between her children and Captain Kidd.

Nev tried to remember the last time he had spent a pleasant evening singing with his family, and couldn't. Louisa was glowing, and Nev felt guilty. He'd barely seen them these past few years since he left university. The last time he'd talked to Louisa, really talked to her about anything that mattered, she'd been in the schoolroom.

Her enthusiasm for pirates, however, seemed undiminished. And to Nev's surprise, Penelope sang with as much energy as any of them. Then it turned out that she knew "Mary Ambree" too, and Louisa was able to extract a promise to consider naming a daughter Mary (Louisa resented that her parents had callously deprived her of the chance to sing *And foremost in battle was Mary Ambree* and have it be about herself). By the time Penelope had sung several unfamiliar songs about girls joining the navy (Nev suspected they might be old broadsides), Louisa had mostly forgotten that she had sworn to detest her new sister-in-law eternally.

Lady Bedlow, however, had not forgotten. She kept up a steady stream of sighs and theatrical yawns, and after an hour, she said, "I'm very tired. Louisa, it's time to go home."

Nev was not at all tired. Singing always made him feel awake and alive and full of energy. When they were gone, he said, "Louisa was impressed. You know an awful lot of songs about sailor maids."

Penelope reseated herself on the piano bench and smiled. "She wanted to run away to sea when she was younger, didn't she?"

Nev laughed. "I think she still does. Did you ever? That is, you do know all the songs."

"Of course I did." There was a touch of self-mockery in Penelope's smile now. "I think every girl has dreams like that, until she realizes how foolish it is to rebel against something she cannot change."

"What do you mean?"

She traced a pattern on the smooth surface of the bench. "It's like wanting to be a soprano: I can want it all I like, but it won't make me anything other than a contralto. It's entirely more sensible to stop repining."

"You wanted to be a soprano?"

She flushed. "I know it's foolish, but . . . it always seemed so ordinary, being a contralto. So common. Just what a Miss Brown would be. I was very young; I got over it. It's the same with wishing for a man's freedom. When I was a girl I loved these songs." She paused, and glanced at him. "This one in particular." She struck up and sang,

> "A merchant did in Bristol dwell,
> As many people knew full well;
> He had a daughter of beauty bright
> In whom he placed his heart's delight.

He had no child but only she;
Her father loved her tenderly.
Many to court her thither came,
Gallants of worth, birth and fame.

Yet notwithstanding all their love,
A young ship's carpenter did prove
To be the master of her heart,
She often said, 'We'll never part'—"

She stopped abruptly, eyes fixed on her still hands. "There's about a hundred more verses. Her father sends the true love to sea. And the girl follows and becomes the surgeon's mate, and heroically nurses him through an illness, and the father regrets his unkindness, and everything turns out wonderfully."

She smiled crookedly and raised her eyes to his face. "It's about a merchant's daughter, you see, and she's brave and noble and saves her true love. My first year at school, I was very unhappy. I thought about running off and volunteering for the navy all the time."

None of which explained her remorseful look, but he could guess. She had imagined the ship's carpenter as Edward. He didn't know what to say; he only knew that he was sorry, and painfully, irrationally jealous. "Did you ever try it?"

She shook her head, smiling up at him. "Even as a silly little girl I knew enough to know that things like that only happen to *beautiful* merchants' daughters."

"Who told you you weren't beautiful?" The idea was absurd, and yet it made him feel obscurely triumphant. Surely Edward had deserved to lose her, if he hadn't even told her she was beautiful.

"Oh, please don't. I *have* got a mirror."

He supposed she *wasn't* beautiful, not like the women he

had had before. She was just a pretty girl; but Nev thought, suddenly, that those other women hadn't been any prettier. They had painted their lips crimson and done up their hair and swept into rooms knowing that men's heads would turn. That was all. Penelope was pretty and she had a sweet voice and the candlelight turned her skin an impossible gold, and Nev realized that he'd been wanting to kiss her all day.

He was just reassuring her, he told himself. Reassuring her, and making her forget about Edward. That was all; it would go no further than that. He sat on the bench beside her. "I think you're beautiful," he whispered, and kissed her.

She let him, and when he stopped she sighed softly and leaned against him. He could barely keep from deflowering her right there on the piano bench.

"I wasn't fishing for a compliment, though," she said. "You told me you would never feed me Spanish coin."

"I'm *not.*" If she looked at the front of his breeches, she would see just how English his coin was, but of course a gentleman couldn't say a thing like that to his wife.

She shrugged and went back to their previous conversation. "Besides, they have to press men for the navy; no one volunteers. So it seemed like I probably wouldn't enjoy it."

Nev wrapped his arms around her. "You were a very practical girl."

She stiffened, but before she could speak, he bent and kissed her neck. She sighed again, a resigned little sound, and gave up on whatever she had been going to say. He thought of Penelope as a girl, miserable and excluded at some fancy finishing school, weighing the pros and cons of running off to join the navy. She had probably made a list. He was abruptly, fiercely glad that she hadn't been practical about marrying him.

Penelope leaned back against her husband. His arms were warm around her. For a moment she wished she weren't so very practical and unfeminine, so she would know how to make him mean the things he had said, about her being beautiful. She wished, almost, that she were fool enough to take him at his word. But if he saw that she believed him, and it had been only a polite fiction—she shivered in humiliation at the mere thought.

"Penelope—I want—that is, I know I said I wouldn't touch you, and I won't, if you ask me not to." She could feel his breath on her neck. "I won't do anything that might hurt, not yet. But I want to make you feel good. Will you let me do that?"

It was like his proposal all over again. There was that note of wistfulness in his voice, and part of Penelope wanted to say yes to whatever he asked. "I—" she stammered.

If she said nothing, it would only be another kind of consent. She would forget herself when he touched her, and she would tell herself she had never *agreed*, he made her feel like that and there was nothing she could do—

If this was going to happen, Penelope intended to take responsibility. She pressed back against him. "Yes. I will." It felt like an echo of her marriage vows.

Nev's hands tightened on her arms. "Thank you. Come upstairs with me." She followed him up the stairs, the shivery knot in her stomach growing with every step.

At last they were in her room. "Change into your night things," Nev said. "I'll start a fire in my room."

"We don't need a fire. It's a waste of fuel, it's summer—"

"Just this once," he said, and left her.

Penelope could not help blushing the entire time Molly was helping her, as if Molly somehow knew what was about to happen. By the time she stepped into Nev's room in her night rail and dressing gown, she was so overheated that the fire he had lit in the grate made her begin to sweat. She could not look at Nev.

"Take off your robe and come here," he commanded gently.

Her hands trembled as she undid the knot and slid the dressing gown off her shoulders. She wished her night rail were more attractive.

It didn't matter for long. Nev reached down and grasped her hem. He pulled it up slowly, and every inch of flesh tingled as air hit it. Then she was standing naked, and Nev took a step back to look at her.

How many women had he looked at like this? What did he see? She was thin and drab and brown; her bosom was disappointingly small. She fought not to try to cover herself with her hands—it would only make her feel more foolish.

"Mm," Nev hummed, low in his throat. "Definitely worth the wait."

She flushed with pleasure. He put his hands on her hips—his hands on her bare skin burned her like a brand—and guided her to the bed. "Lie down."

She obeyed him. The soft down coverlet under her bare skin was the most hedonistic thing she had ever felt. A moment later Nev was hovering half over her, his leg between her thighs. Penelope felt herself tightening in response.

"Tell me if I do anything you don't like."

She nodded.

He settled down and kissed her. She followed his lead, more easily this time for having a small bit of practice. His hand, which had rested on her hip, began to move up. She closed her eyes and followed its progress desperately. Last time, he had touched her breast and—yes, there it was, his hand settling over the curve of her left breast. There was nothing between them, nothing at all. He squeezed gently a few times, and tiny waves of sensation ran all through her. He brushed her nipple with his thumb, and she almost jumped at the sharp shock of pleasure. She didn't, though. This time, she was going to stay in control. She was *not* a common, wanton trollop.

He moved down, following the line of her throat with his lips. *I can do this,* she thought, and then his mouth closed over her other nipple and she despaired. It was hot and wet and his hair was brushing her skin and suddenly he sucked, hard—she struggled not to cry out, not to buck under his mouth and hands.

He raised his head. "Is something wrong?"

She swallowed, opening her eyes. His blue eyes were fixed anxiously on her. What had she done? "Why—" Her voice cracked. Why wasn't he touching her anymore? "Why would something be wrong?"

"Well—did that feel good, when I did that?"

She flushed. "Yes."

"Then—you're just being awfully still and quiet."

"Aren't I supposed to be?"

He sat up. "Why on earth would you be supposed to be?"

"I—I don't know," she said, mortified. "I didn't want to give you a disgust of me. Ladies don't give in to their base urges."

"They don't?"

Despite her embarrassment, she wanted to laugh at his confounded expression. "I don't know. Do they?"

"I don't know either. I've never done this with a lady before." Nev thought for a moment. "Did you *feel* like moving, or making any noise?"

Penelope held herself very still. "Well . . . yes."

He sighed in relief. "I'd really rather you did then. It lets me know I'm doing it right. Otherwise I start to worry."

She wanted to make him happy. "All right."

He started over, and this time she tried to relax and trust him. He went slow, so slow, and the heat built and built. His mouth was back on her breast, and she was so distracted that she didn't notice his hand moving lower and lower—until he touched her, *there*, and she felt her whole body arch toward him. "Oh!"

He murmured against her breast in response, the hum doing very pleasant things to her nerve endings. His fingers moved over her, and his mouth teased her breast, hotter than she had ever thought anything could feel without scalding. It would have been hopeless to try to be still, anyway, not when she felt like this—she had never felt anything like this—had never known *anyone* could ever feel this good.

A thought came to her—*this is how a violin feels.* She was filled with sound, resonating to Nev's playing—trills and arpeggios, higher and higher, the tempo increasing until she vibrated under his hands—

Suddenly the pleasure was so strong she could hardly bear it. "Oh!" she cried out—she would break—she would die—and then the whole world rang with a crescendo of bright, pure pleasure.

Penelope shuddered, again and again—and then it was over and she was herself once more. She could hardly believe it. She lay there, trying to catch her breath, for a long moment. Finally she opened her eyes and turned to look at her husband. "Was that—was that supposed to happen?"

Nev grinned widely. "Yes." He looked proud of himself. "It was, in fact, my intention."

"Oh." She couldn't think of anything else to say. "Um . . . thank you."

"You're welcome," he said, that pleased note still in his voice.

"Can . . . can you feel that too?"

He nodded.

"Do you have to be inside me to feel it?"

"No. Hands and mouths work just fine."

"Do you—do you want me to—"

"You don't have to. This was for you. There'll be plenty of time for me."

Didn't he want her to? "May I?" she asked, surprised by her own boldness.

He was very still. "Are you sure you wish to?"

She nodded, his uncertainty giving her courage. "Take off your clothes."

He shuddered and fumbled at the tie to his dressing gown, looking nervous. He pulled off his nightshirt, and then he was naked. Penelope's first impulse was to glance modestly away, but she made herself look. He *did* look like a painting or a sculpture—a Greek athlete, or a Jacques-Louis David hero. But he was real, and if she put out her hand his warm flesh would yield under her palm. The cinnamon-colored hair on his chest and legs was a surprise, but oddly exciting—intimate, somehow. And, she thought, finally bringing her mind to what she hadn't had the courage to look at first, he wore no grape leaf. Between his legs, surrounded at its base by more cinnamon-colored hair, his erect male part bobbed.

It was larger than she had expected. She pushed the uncomfortable thought aside that one day soon that would have to fit inside her. Taking a deep breath, she reached out—

A sharp, crackling pop came from somewhere. Another followed it almost immediately.

Penelope met Nev's eyes, feeling suddenly cold and frightened. "That—that sounded like gunfire." She drew back her hand.

"That *was* gunfire." Nev swore. "Stay here, do you hear me?" He threw his dressing gown on over his nakedness and ran out, slamming the door behind him. "Lock it!" he called, his voice receding as he ran down the hall, his bare feet making hardly any noise at all.

Penelope sat there stupidly for a few moments, and then she pulled on her discarded nightclothes and ran after him.

Ten

When she reached the bottom of the stairs, Nev's back was to her and he was speaking to Captain Trelawney, who wore a large red nightcap. "'Is something *wrong*?'" Nev mimicked. "Are my wife and I the only ones who heard the repeated sounds of gunfire?"

"Oh, that." Trelawney smothered a yawn. "Don't worry about that. It's only the poachers and your gamekeepers."

"Shooting each other?" There was an edge in Nev's voice that Penelope had never heard. "And this is a common occurrence?"

"Well, not precisely *common*. Once or twice a month, maybe."

"Let me be sure I understand you. There are Englishmen shooting at each other out there, on *my* land, and you're telling me *not to worry about it.*"

"Usually they don't hit each other in the dark." Trelawney seemed oblivious to the dangerous note in Nev's voice. Penelope thought he might be drunk.

"How many gamekeepers do I employ?" Nev asked, quietly.

"Eleven, my lord. It takes that many to keep the buggers away."

"They do not seem to be keeping the buggers away at all."

"Well, many a man would rather poach than earn an honest living," Trelawney said philosophically. "Would you like me to install traps? Spring guns, maybe, like Sir Jasper has."

Penelope flinched.

"No, I would *not* like you to install traps," Nev said with cold fury. "Your effrontery is appalling. Loweston is in a disastrous state. I do not doubt that my father is chiefly responsible, but you have done nothing to help. You were content to sit in your office, drink, and keep shoddy records while everything fell to pieces around you. Tonight my wife and I are roused from our bed by *gunfire*, and you tell me not to worry, because it is only the unconscionable war you have launched against people who *cannot* make an honest living because of *our* mismanagement? How dare you?"

Trelawney sniggered. "So you finally managed to tear her away from those account books? No wonder you're so angry."

Nev seemed to grow another three inches. "I ought to have you horsewhipped for that. I want you gone by morning. Get out of my sight."

Trelawney opened his mouth, shut it, shrugged, and left.

Penelope stood at the bottom of the stairs. For the first time, she had seen the centuries of inherited power, the iron hand without the velvet glove. Of course, she had seen her father angry—she had seen him berate men under him at the brewery—but her father was a big man. Trelawney could have broken Nev over his knee, but Nev had never considered that. His instinctive authority was something else entirely. He had never doubted that he would be obeyed. It was intimidating and unfathomable—yet also, if she were honest, a little thrilling.

He turned around and saw her, and the aristocratic command crumbled. "I shouldn't have done that, should I? Now we haven't got a steward at all."

"He wasn't very good. We'll hire a new one."

"But he knew Loweston."

It was undeniable, but Penelope couldn't be sorry the man was gone. "We can inquire locally, and I'll send an advertisement to the London papers. We may find someone familiar with this part of the country, at least."

Nev went to the window and peered out toward where the shots had been fired. Then he looked around the room. Penelope followed his gaze, seeing the missing furniture and the discolored rectangles on the wall where paintings were missing. He did not look at her. "You're tired. Go to bed."

She couldn't move, for a moment. "Don't you—aren't you coming?"

"Evidently not," he said, a little bitterly. "I'll sleep in Trelawney's office. Wouldn't want him making off with half our records."

It was a good idea, and yet Penelope felt unreasonably disappointed. She thought of offering to go with him, but she couldn't quite find the courage. Only a few minutes ago, she had felt so close to him, but now he was a stranger again. Besides, Trelawney's sofa wasn't big enough for two. "All right," she said meekly, and went upstairs to sleep alone.

Nev awoke to sunlight in his eyes and a crick in his neck. He staggered upstairs to be shaved and dressed. He couldn't hear anything from Penelope's room.

Last night came flooding back, all that soft fair skin in the firelight. She had been so afraid of losing control. And yet she was formed for passion—she had responded to his lightest touch. She had been so sweetly amazed at her own pleasure. Nev began to see why some men liked virgins.

When he walked into the breakfast room, she was watching the door with sparkling eyes and a nervous smile—she must have heard his footsteps in the hall. She had bathed, and her still-damp hair was more elaborately arranged than usual. Parts were braided and parts were bound and it all somehow became a sleek brown knot at the crown of her head. He wanted to drag her upstairs and take down her hair and get her out of her gown.

"Good morning," he said.

"G—good morning." She met his eyes with a shy smile, blushing all over. "How—how did you sleep? Here—come and sit down, I'll pour you coffee."

She put the right amount of sugar in his coffee without having to ask, and Nev got a very uncomfortable feeling in the pit of his stomach.

She was radiant and happy because she had never experienced the peak of pleasure before. When Nev had discovered he could do it to himself the summer he turned twelve, he had spent nearly three days in his room with the door locked. But poor, innocent Penelope didn't realize that's all it was. She thought there was something special about *him*.

Nev knew perfectly well that there wasn't. If she had married Edward, she would be looking at *him* right now as if he had hung the moon. The thought made him queasy. He had taken everything from her and given her only this one thing she could get from any man who took her fancy, and she was smiling gratefully at him and doing her hair up pretty. Nev did not like virgins.

Her bright face dimmed. "Is—is everything all right?"

"Of course," he said hastily, and could think of nothing else to say. "What—what are you doing today?"

"I haven't quite decided." She looked at him hopefully. When he didn't reply, she sighed and said, "I suppose I'll write that advertisement for the papers. I'm writing to my parents as well. I'll ask my father for advice, and I made sketches of a few of the paintings in your family's collection for my mother, and—"

"Do you miss them very much?"

She looked away and nodded. "It's all right. I'm used to it. I went away to school, you know."

Nev suspected it was a deal worse than school. At school she must have had a few friends at least, and the security that she would be home on holiday soon enough. And she had been in London. "Would you like to go up to London next week to interview stewards? You could see your parents, and perhaps we could go to a concert . . ."

"Really?" Then her face fell. "But—*could* we? It's so far, and we've only been here a week and a half, and there's so much to do—"

"Of course. Unless we interview applicants in person, how can we know we aren't getting another Trelawney?"

She nodded. "You're right, it's only sense." She gave him a mischievous smile. "I'll book us a room in a hotel."

Nev swallowed hard.

Penelope fled the breakfast room for her bedchamber, knowing she had made an utter fool of herself. But the moment Nev had walked into the room and met her eyes, every inch of her skin had seemed to wake up.

She stood at her writing desk, gripping the edges of the account books, trying to ground herself in charges and discharges and debits, but it was no use. Even just his eyes on hers had felt so—so intimate, somehow. This, she knew now, was why she had married him. This pull he exercised on her body without her consent.

She closed her eyes and relived that startling explosion of pleasure. She wanted it again. It was making her foolish, and weak. She'd had Molly do her hair up nicely. The maid had probably known she was trying pitifully to impress her own husband. Penelope wanted to tear it down and redo it in her usual simple style, but she *refused* to be melodramatic about this. Besides, he would notice when he saw her again, and that would make it worse. Instead she went into her dressing room and splashed water on her face.

The Hogarth engravings hung in a neat row by the mirror. She wasn't sure why she'd put them there. To punish herself for what she'd done to Edward, she suspected. She looked at them now, slowly and carefully. It was like a toothache or a scab; poking at it was both painful and irresistible.

Yes, she told herself, she had married someone entirely unsuited to her because of her base urges. Yes, she was as much a slave to her own body as any slatternly shopgirl. Yes, Nev had seen it, and it *had* given him a disgust of her. How could he help it? He was a gentleman, through and through.

Worst of all, though, was that he had seen her happiness. He knew that she had thought—that she had allowed herself to hope that last night had meant as much to him as it had to her. Had meant *something*. His look of distaste and embarrassment was engraved on her memory.

It was a bitter pill, but Penelope had swallowed bitter pills before. There was nothing for it but to put a brave face on things and muddle along. Nev was trying to be kind. Next week she would see her mother. Nev was taking her to London.

She had better write to that hotel and book a room. Despite everything, Penelope couldn't help smiling.

"I heard you turned off Captain Trelawney," Mrs. Kedge said.

News traveled fast in the country. Nev sighed and looked instinctively for Penelope, but she was across the churchyard, talking to the Cushers. "Yes," he said. "I didn't like the way he was handling the poaching problem."

"Good for you," Mrs. Kedge said. "I always thought he was too soft by far. Poachers are like rats. The only way to get rid of 'em is to exterminate them all, or they'll be back. Trelawney never struck me as much of a terrier, and those gamekeepers he hired—I heard they even had one of the poachers caught in a trap, and yet his fellows managed to get him free and get all away, every last one of them! Bungling, I call it."

Nev drew back, disconcerted. "You are very bitter against the poachers."

"It's these men from London." The farmer's wife shuddered comfortably. "Murderers and thieves, all of them, who've made town too hot to hold them. Then they come up here, and they work on our boys with their promises of easy money . . ."

"Then—you don't think the men poach because they're hungry?"

"Not on your life, my lord!—meaning no disrespect. The folk here poach because they hate hard work. They'd rather take eight shillings for stealing your hare than for a week's honest labor."

Nev privately thought that was understandable. But he could not have armed men running about the home woods. "Do you know who they are?"

Mrs. Kedge looked discomfited for the first time. "Of course not! *No one* knows who they are." In her tone Nev heard clearly, *Everyone knows who they are*, and smothered a groan.

"The poachers aren't so bad, really," Josie told Penelope. "And they *are* hungry." She darted an angry glance at Mrs. Kedge, whose cheerily grim monologue could be heard all across the churchyard. "They've got *family* who are hungry!"

"Hush, Josie!" Agnes said.

Penelope got the distinct impression that Josie also knew exactly who the poachers were. But asking a little girl to tattle on her friends seemed monstrous. Penelope sighed. "I'm sure they do."

Josie eyed Penelope. "You've been to school, haven't you?" She nodded.

"Do *you* think God has chosen me to be lowly because he knew my soul needed the guidance of my betters?"

Agnes grabbed her daughter's hand. "We're going, Josie. Good day, my lady."

Penelope's heart went out to the little girl. "Please stay."

Josie was quoting directly from Mr. Snively's sermon, which had been on the text, *Be subject, not only for wrath, but also for conscience's sake.* Nev had rolled his eyes so much through Mr. Snively's many references to Nev's "wise gover-nance" and "benevolent authority" that Penelope had half feared they would stick.

And Agnes Cusher had no choice but to bring her child to church to be insulted, because Tom Kedge made all his people go. For the first time, Penelope wondered whether Loweston's people really would riot. They had reason to be angry. Even now Agnes was giving her a sullen, trapped glare.

Penelope did not know what would be the best answer to help Josie navigate her world. She did not know the best an-swer to prevent a breach with the vicar, who, though out of earshot, would very likely have her words repeated to him by a dozen eager tongues.

But she knew the only answer she could give. "No, I don't think so."

"Really?" Josie asked.

Penelope nodded. "My parents were as poor as yours when they were born, you know."

"*Really?*" Josie's eyes were wide as saucers. "You mean—you're the same as me?"

The other girls at school had thought they were better than she was. Penelope believed it too, in some small part of herself, and always had. For a moment a hot rebellious spark inside her almost *wanted* the laborers to rise up and demand what was theirs. "I don't know why God makes some people rich and some poor. We have to believe He knows best. But I'm sure of this: no one's *soul* is any higher."

Josie did not look as if she could quite bring herself to be-lieve this good news. "But Mr. Snively said that lords are the king's angels. Angels are higher than regular people, aren't they?"

Penelope bit her lip. Josie had been listening carefully. Pe-nelope was not sure *she* could quote that particular lengthy metaphor about the divinely granted rights of the peerage, and here this child had been brooding over it.

She looked across the churchyard at Nev. He did look like an angel to her—the sunlight cast a halo in his cinnamon hair. But how did he look to his people? Would they think he was pleased by Snively's groveling?

Was Nev in danger?

Someone, people Josie knew, had been prowling around the Grange a few nights ago, armed and desperate. Something had to be done; someone had to keep them all safe. Maybe a firm hand *was* the answer; Penelope did not know. But she looked Josie in the eye and said, "We are all the same on the inside."

"I hate that man," Nev said with suppressed fury, as they walked the short distance from church to the Grange. "How could he talk to them that way and expect me to be flattered?"

"Your father must have had a reason for giving him the living," Penelope said without conviction.

"It was supposed to be Percy's," Nev said bitterly. "My father always intended it for Percy."

"What happened?"

"Percy would have made a terrible parson. But my father thought Percy could just collect the money, give a sermon every now and again, and be set for life. He didn't understand that Percy couldn't do that." He sighed. "I suppose it's just as well now."

"And when Percy refused the living?"

"My father had a friend who had just married Snively's cousin, and Snively was willing to toady to him and make a fourth at whist. My father looked no further."

Penelope tried to remember if Nev had ever said anything good about the last Lord Bedlow. "Forgive me if this is impertinent, but—did you like your father?"

"Of course it's not impertinent," he flashed. "You're my wife!"

She shrank back a little, but it was clear that his anger wasn't directed at her.

"I don't want us to be like that, Penelope. That's how my parents always were. Like strangers who just happened to have spent twenty-five years together. If my mother ever asked what he had done when he was out, he told her that what a gentleman did when he was not at home had nothing to do with his wife."

Penelope thought of her own parents. If her father had ever told her mother that *anything* he did had nothing to do with her, Mrs. Brown would have thrown the teapot at his head. And it would have been a vulgar display and Penelope would have been mortified, but—it seemed like the right response, somehow.

"And then he spent her jointure," Nev said, "and he got himself shot. I daresay he would have thought *that* had nothing to do with her either."

"Do you miss him?"

Nev shrugged. "It was impossible not to like him. But— that's all he was: charming. Likable. You couldn't *rely* on him." He took his eyes off the road for a moment to meet her eyes. "I don't want to be like that, Penelope."

It was exactly how she had pegged him, from the first moment they met, but she found herself saying, "Nev, listen to me. No one trained you for this. Neither of us know what to do, and I wish to God one of us did, but—you're here. You haven't gone off to the Continent to live well on little money and left someone else to do the hard work." She smiled at him. "I plan to rely on you for a good long time."

He opened his mouth to answer her, and it began to rain— lightly at first, then harder. Within a minute it was pouring, and Penelope was half soaked. Nev stripped off his coat and put it around her. "I can't even keep you out of the rain."

"Yes, I blame you for the weather."

He smiled, finally.

"Is there anywhere nearby we can take shelter?"

"The folly isn't far off. Do you mind running for it?"

They pelted up a hill through the rain, Penelope holding up her skirts and hugging Nev's coat around her. When the folly came into view, she stopped running and stared. "Oh, my Lord."

It sat on an outcrop of rock at the top of the hill: a round, squat tower with the roof gone from the upper floor. A broken wall and a great arch sprouted out of its side and straggled down the hill. It was much larger than she had expected— thirty feet high, at least. It was absurd and enormous and the most adorable thing she had ever seen.

"Come on!" Nev urged, and they ran the rest of the way. He held open a wooden door in the side of the round tower for her, then followed her in and slammed the door.

Penelope felt breathless and alive. She couldn't remember the last time she had sprinted anywhere. She turned to look at Nev, knowing she was smiling idiotically, and her mouth went dry.

His hair was damp and curling over his forehead, and his shirt was plastered to his shoulders and arms. She could see the color of his skin through the white linen. She had always thought boxing and fencing were frivolous occupations for men with nothing better to do, but she would never criticize them again, because Nev's muscles were the most beautiful thing she had ever seen. An image of him naked flashed into her mind.

Feeling suddenly feverish, she took off his coat and set it on the flight of stairs that curved along the wall behind her. Her wet clothes clung to her like a firm caress and her corset pressed against her breasts.

"I always loved this tower," Nev said. "I wonder how much bread for his tenants my grandfather could have bought with the money."

"I don't care." Penelope felt not at all her usual sensible self. "I like it."

He turned and smiled at her. "Do you really?"

"I do." Her heart pounding, not knowing what demon possessed her, she sat on the end of a step, her legs dangling over the side of the staircase, and began stripping off her shoes and stockings. When she glanced up, he was watching her legs hungrily. Encouraged, she pulled the neckline of her dress away from her breasts and looked down it. "I think the black dye ran onto my shift. I hope it's not ruined."

Nev made a strangled noise.

She looked up. He was staring at her breasts, just as she had intended, but he hadn't taken one step toward her.

"Just how much encouragement do you need?" Her nerves were singing. She couldn't tell anymore what was fear and shame and what was her body waiting for his hands.

He started, as if he really hadn't realized that's what she was doing, and then he tugged her upright and his mouth was on hers and everything was perfect. When he pulled away she was dizzy and hot.

"You—you *minx*!"

No one had ever called Penelope anything even approaching a minx before. It was oddly gratifying. He ran his hands over her, proprietarily, and she arched to meet them, the curving stone of the staircase at the back of her thighs.

"You're shivering," he said against her neck. "I don't want you to catch cold in those wet clothes."

She was going to protest that she wasn't cold at all, until she realized what he meant. She helped him remove her gown, and then she was standing there in nothing but her shift, stays, and petticoat, with mud on her hem and wet hair straggling down her cheek. Penelope knew how she must look, but Nev didn't seem to mind and just then Penelope didn't care about anything that wasn't the look on Nev's face.

He traced a finger over her breast and stomach—only a few layers of damp linen between her skin and his. Penelope had read about flowers springing up under the feet of the goddess of Spring as the land awakened. That was how she felt—as if her body were awakening under Nev's trailing fingertip.

"What do you want?" he asked.

"I—" She couldn't say it. It was too forward.

"Yes?" Nev leaned down to nibble at her bare shoulder.

"I want you to make me a real wife to you," she said quickly, and blushed.

She was afraid he would not take her meaning, but he froze, his hands spasming on her shoulders. "Here? Now?"

She flushed all over, desire swamped in a wave of shame. "I'm sorry. I shouldn't have—"

He tilted up her chin and looked into her eyes. "I want to. Very much. But I don't want to you to think that—I want you to feel that I honor you. That I'm treating you as a lady of quality. I want your first time to be in a bed, not in an outbuilding with your clothes half on. I don't know how to behave properly, but I know you deserve—better."

Better than him, he meant. Somehow she knew it. She tilted her head, pressing her cheek against his hand. "I don't know how to behave properly either. But you asked me what I wanted and I told you."

He swallowed. "Penelope," he said in a very low voice, "I'm afraid I'll hurt you."

She was afraid he would hurt her too, but she was more afraid that he would never make her his. That he would lose interest. "We'll work it out. Millions of people have done it before us, and none died." She frowned. "At least, not that I've heard of." He laughed a little at that, and she laid her hand against his chest. "Please, Nev. I want to."

He drew in a shuddering breath. "Then we will." He fastened the latch on the door. Then he took off his cravat and waistcoat and sat down, tugging off his muddy boots.

She found her nerves returning. "No one is likely to pass this way, are they?" Why hadn't she asked that before?

He looked up at her. "I don't think so. If anyone else was caught in the rain nearby, they'd be here by now. But if you want to just put everything back on and wait, it's all right."

Her heart was in her throat, but she shook her head.

He took his coat from the stair she had put it on and spread it on a lower one, at about waist height, and lifted her up to sit on it. Then he kissed her. His hand slid down and cupped her through her damp petticoats. She opened her mouth under his and closed her eyes. "Tell me if you want me to stop," he whispered, and lifted the hem of her petticoat.

Cold air hit her wetness. She was exposed to Nev in broad daylight; it was shocking and Penelope felt her muscles tighten pleasurably just at the idea.

Nev slid his fingers over her opening. "I've hardly done anything and you're already wet."

"Is that bad?"

"No." She could hear him smiling. "It's very good." He pressed the tip of one wet finger to the spot that had proven so sensitive last time. "Just relax." He rubbed, and she let her legs fall open and tilted her head back and just *felt*.

She had known he would do it, but it still startled her when he pressed the tip of one finger to her opening and began to slide it inside. It hurt, and she sucked in her breath and tightened her muscles automatically.

Nev froze, breathing hard.

Penelope knew that he would stop if he thought he was hurting her. She breathed deeply, forcing herself to open to him as much as she could. "I'm fine."

Nev's finger inched its way in. It felt odd, and uncomfortable, and a little wrong, and very intimate. But his thumb moved on her sensitive spot, and soon the finger inside her felt almost—almost good.

Then he slid another finger inside. It would have felt good, it did feel good for a second or two at a time, but she could not help wincing. There was a point at the opening of her passage, it seemed to her, that was narrower than the rest.

"It's your maidenhead," he said after a moment. "There's nothing for it, Penelope. I'm going to break it, and it's going to hurt. But after today it will be better, I promise."

She opened her eyes and tried to sound confident. "All right."

"You're doing wonderfully," he said softly, and kissed her. She smiled at him, and he smiled back, and for a moment the pain and the discomfort and the embarrassment didn't matter at all.

He unbuttoned his breeches, taking hold of his hardness. "I don't want to be in you too long." She watched him pleasure himself, watched his hand jerk back and forth, and glanced at his face. He was looking at her spread legs and the neckline of her corset clinging to her breasts as if he couldn't get enough of them. Penelope arched lazily, just to see, and he groaned.

"Will you—will you touch your breasts?"

She stilled, embarrassed. "I—"

"It doesn't matter. I don't think I can wait any longer."

He pulled her forward until she was sitting right at the edge of the step. The tip of his hardness pressed against her. She had not known you could feel this physically close to another person.

"I'm sorry, sweetheart," he whispered, and pushed forward.

Pain shot through her. She gritted her teeth.

He froze.

"Please. Just get it over with."

He nodded and shoved forward hard.

She felt something tear, a little, and suddenly she was filled inside. It hurt, and it was uncomfortable, and she could see that when it didn't hurt it would be incredible. Nev thrust a few times, shallowly. Then he brought his hand down and began touching that spot again.

It wasn't that the pain went away, exactly—it was just that it was hard to concentrate on it when the pleasure was building and building, and even though she knew what was coming this time, it was still unbelievable when the explosion came. She felt herself convulsing around Nev, this time, drawing him deeper inside her, pressing up against him, not caring about the discomfort.

Nev thrust again, only a few more times, and relaxed all at once.

He pulled out immediately, his hand gentling on her hip. She was distantly conscious that it would hurt in a minute, although right now it just felt empty. "All right?"

She nodded. "Thank you, Nev."

"Thank *you*," he said, very seriously. Then he grinned. "I wonder how long before you'll be up to doing it again."

He still wanted to do it again. Penelope grinned back.

Eventually the rain stopped. Nev and Penelope walked back to the house. He had hold of Penelope's hand and went slowly in case she was sore. His own damp clothes were becoming uncomfortable, but soon they would be home and could order baths. He let himself dwell on that thought—Penelope in her bath, clean and wet and naked. It was too soon to be inside her again, but maybe he could teach her a few other things.

He had never dreamed they were things you could teach your wife, but then he had never dreamed that prim little Penelope would take her stockings off and look up at him under her eyelashes and ask him to undress her and deflower her in the Gothic folly in the middle of a rainstorm. She had been amazing, and—he had never realized how different it would be, knowing beyond a shadow of a doubt that she wanted him, that she wasn't expecting a diamond bracelet afterward. It was a heady drug.

She winced, stepping over a puddle. "Sore?" he asked.

She nodded. "It's all right. It just—just reminds me of—" She stopped, blushing.

He squeezed her hand, knowing he was grinning like an idiot and unable to stop. She met his eye and smiled back, sheepishly, and then they were giggling. Nev hadn't felt this good in months.

Penelope winced a little again, climbing the steps of the Grange, and Nev said, "Here—I didn't do it the first time you crossed the threshold, so—" She made a startled noise when he picked her up, but she nestled against him and put her arms around his neck, and it wasn't as awkward a position as he had always thought it would be.

He had to put her down for a moment to open the door, and then he almost dropped her getting through it, so they were laughing and tangled when Nev turned and saw, standing and watching them at the doorway of the Blue Salon, his mother, Louisa, and Sir Jasper.

Eleven

Nev knew just how they must look—damp, muddy, disheveled, lost to all sense of propriety. Too young and ramshackle to be the Earl and Countess of Bedlow. He felt as if what they had been doing was branded across their faces. He remembered what his mother had said when they were merely kissing in the breakfast room. He straightened. She wasn't going to say anything to Penelope. Not now.

But he should have known she wouldn't, not in front of Sir Jasper. She just gave a brittle laugh and said in a reasonable facsimile of indulgent motherhood, "Go on, get out of those wet things before you catch cold! I'll order up more tea."

They escaped gratefully up the stairs. "Newlyweds," Sir Jasper said with a chuckle.

Sir Jasper expected to be kept waiting for a good long while. It had been quite obvious what the new earl and his common little bride had been doing during the storm.

He could hardly pretend to be astonished. The late Lord Bedlow had had the same red-blooded rakish streak—likable enough, but without his wife to keep him in check, he could easily have become unfit for polite society. The son had always had a taste for low company too; until a week ago Sir Jasper wasn't sure he'd ever seen him without the steward's boy at his shoulder. And in town, he'd taken his mistress everywhere. No sense of propriety.

In retrospect, it was predictable that the new earl would prefer whoring himself out to a Cit to accepting Sir Jasper's honorable offer for his sister. And he hadn't even the wits to make a decent settlement: Sir Jasper bribed at least one copy-clerk in every office with which he did business, and since the late Lord Bedlow—and by extension, the new one—used Sir Jasper's man of business, it had been simple enough to get a copy of the new marriage settlements and find out that most of the money was tied up until the new Lady Bedlow had produced an heir. It might seem sneaking, almost beneath him, but it had been Sir Jasper's duty. He needed to know how matters stood in his district—particularly as his future wife's family was involved.

Sir Jasper smiled at Lady Louisa, who was tugging absent-mindedly on a long red-brown curl as she gazed out the window. There was still plenty of time to get her brother's consent to their union, and plenty of other ways to try if he proved intractable.

He was surprised when the young couple came back after a mere twenty minutes, damp but otherwise presentable. The wife must be a businesslike little thing. She looked it now, cold and straight as a rail, as if she hadn't been giggling and spreading her legs half an hour before.

After he'd pretended to be delighted to meet her, Sir Jasper said, "I rode over to ask if there was any news of the poachers, but we ought not to bore the ladies—"

The countess stiffened even further. So that offended her, did it? She probably wasn't content until she'd stuck her freckled little nose into everything.

"It doesn't matter," Bedlow said. "I have no news."

"Have you been making inquiries among your people?"

"No." Bedlow sounded every bit as happy-go-lucky and negligent as his father. If only he proved as easy to influence! "When I hire a new steward, I'm sure he will do so."

Sir Jasper resigned himself to once again doing all the work of keeping the peace in the district. "I heard you had fired a number of your gamekeepers as well."

"They were an unconscionable expense," Bedlow said.

"They didn't seem to be solving the problem. And I dislike the idea of men shooting at each other in my woods."

Sir Jasper frowned. "You would prefer them to wander about with their guns, unhindered, making free with your game?"

Bedlow flushed, looking like a whipped schoolboy.

"Pardon me if I speak warmly, but it seems to me we must make these folk understand what is due a gentleman. Besides," Sir Jasper added, chuckling, "I know you are not a great sportsman, but Loweston has some of the thickest coveys of great bustards in the neighborhood."

Louisa, loyal girl, flew to her brother's defense. "Nate does not care for that! I do not like men wandering about with guns either, but they poach because they are *hungry!*"

Sir Jasper couldn't help smiling. She was so young and eager. "Perhaps that was once true," he explained. "An honest man may, in desperate straits, steal a bird or two to feed his children. But when a man paints his face black, takes up a gun, and joins with his drinking companions in a desperate gang, he is merely seeking to make easy money at his betters' expense."

"They form into gangs because they know if they are captured you will transport them," Lady Louisa said. She really was pretty when she was angry. He suspected she was passionate too; it would be a nice change from his first wife. Mary had been a dear girl, but she had never much enjoyed their conjugal intimacy.

"*Louisa,*" the young earl said. He needn't have worried. Sir Jasper had had his eye on Louisa for too long to be discouraged by a few wrongheaded notions.

"I only wish they were as afraid of me as you claim," he told her ruefully.

"You must admit, Sir Jasper, that corn is ruinously high," Bedlow said, putting a restraining hand on his sister's arm. "I spoke to the baker, and—"

"It is difficult, I know." Sir Jasper hoped his impatience didn't show in his voice. "But we all have to make sacrifices for the security of our great nation. Dependence on foreign corn would be far more ruinous than the present state of affairs."

The young countess looked surprised. "Why?"

"If we allowed the importation of cheap foreign corn to bring down prices, not only would we be turning our backs on English farmers, but in another war the French would have only to stop the grain supply to place us in the most difficult position."

"I've read that the real rivals in corn production are British companies in the colonies," Louisa said. "Not so patriotic after all, really."

Sir Jasper knew where he had heard that argument before. "My dear, I think you have been reading the radical newspapers," he said with some amusement.

Louisa tugged at her earlobe. She had always done that when she was embarrassed, ever since she was a child.

"Aaron Smith and some of the other men tell me," Bedlow said, "that our own corn cannot be sold advantageously because of the poor condition of the roads. I was hoping we might work with you to better them. God knows there are men who'd be glad of the work, and Jeb Tyler has some experience in that line—"

"Helen Spratt's husband too," the Cit said. "What was his name? Harry? He did something with roads on the Continent, during the War."

They knew the laborers' names already. Sir Jasper was startled. The late Lord Bedlow had never learned any of their names. "They exaggerate, I assure you. The idle wretches merely wish to be paid. Road crews are a breeding ground for sedition."

"You don't really think—" The girl cut herself off.

"You were not in Norfolk during the riots in '16," he reminded the couple. "I assure you, the men of this district showed themselves to be desperate characters, ready to murder us all in our beds if they could."

The dowager countess's gaze flicked to her children. "You think there is danger of a recurrence?"

"I would like to think there is not," Sir Jasper said. "I have no wish to alarm you, madam. I am perhaps overcautious, but I was in France in '89 and I remember all too well the atrocities that were committed."

The dowager's eyes widened. "But you couldn't have been more than a boy!"

"I was seven, madam. I watched from an upstairs window as an old man was dragged from his carriage and hanged from a lamppost." He could still feel the summer heat on his skin, the stink of the dirty river and unwashed humanity in his nostrils, the shouts of the mob echoing in his ears. Even the women had been ugly and furious, shrieking for blood like animals, their breasts dried up and sagging under their rags. The shadow of the jerking corpse had never entirely lifted from his face.

Did he catch a flash of sympathy in Louisa's eyes? He would never know what she would have said, because the little Cit exclaimed, "Oh, how dreadful for you!"

Sir Jasper shook his head, and everything faded but the heat. And that was only July in the country, the bright sun and the clean, earthy smell of grass and horses. "I beg your pardon, my lady. I see I have upset you. I promise you we should have warning of any disturbance in time for you to remove to London."

That did not seem to comfort her or Louisa; he was sorry he had spoken of it.

The moment he was gone, Lady Bedlow turned to her daughter. "Louisa, you were intolerably rude to Sir Jasper. He will think you pert."

"I do not care what he thinks me, so long as he stops ogling my bosom. Does he think I don't notice?"

"I hate it when they do that," Penelope commiserated. Nev jerked his eyes away from her neckline guiltily. As if she could feel it, she glanced at him and smiled, blushing.

"It is trying, I agree," Lady Bedlow said, "but it is a trial we women must bear. You could do a deal worse, and even if you do not marry him, his notice will do you a world of good in the neighborhood. Nev, tell her!"

Three pairs of eyes turned on Nev. This was part of responsibility, he told himself. "I'm not saying you should marry the fellow, Louisa, but it wouldn't hurt you to be civil. He's our nearest neighbor, and it won't do to start a feud."

Louisa stared at him.

In the old days, he would have laughed and told her he would shoot anyone who so much as glanced at her bosom, and they both knew it. But he had not known how important Sir Jasper was to the district then.

Nev and Penelope were off to London, feeling like boys cutting lecture. At least Nev did—it was that same mixture of guilt and conspiratorial triumph. They had left Davies and Penelope's maid at Loweston; it was just the two of them. Nev drove, and Penelope sat next to him in the box. It was sunny and bright and for a few days there would be no tenants or home farm or paupers.

He gave Bruenor and Gareth their head, faster and faster until the coach was flying down the road. Penelope laughed and took off her bonnet, throwing her head back, and Nev was distracted when he took a turn. They almost hit a cart.

At once Nev was swamped with guilt. Penelope could have been hurt. He slowed the carriage and told himself that her disappointed countenance just meant he was corrupting her.

* * *

Penelope sat behind her father's desk with Nev, interviewing would-be stewards. The first candidate was an idiot. The second seemed competent but thought "Thou Shalt Not Poach" was one of the Commandments.

The third was a tall, dark-haired young man who looked vaguely familiar. He entered the room, said, "Good morning," and stopped abruptly, turning a dull red. Penelope was beginning to really worry about where she had seen him before when she realized he was looking at Nev, not her. She glanced at her husband, and her eyes widened. His face was bloodless.

"Percy," he said, in a strangled voice. Everything slotted into place, and Penelope remembered where she had seen the young man before: next to Nev on the night they had met and again that night at Vauxhall.

"I'm sorry. I must have had the wrong address." Percy bowed and turned to leave.

Penelope watched Nev's face change. "Wait!" she cried out impulsively.

Percy turned slowly, pasting an expression of polite interest on his flushed face. "Yes?"

Penelope felt her ears turning red. It was what she deserved for meddling, but she forged ahead. "Mr. Garrett, isn't it? I'm Lady Bedlow." She came around the desk and held out her hand, so that he would be obliged to take it and it would be a few moments more before he could leave the room.

"Honored." His bow was graceful enough—and shallow to the point of rudeness. Penelope wasn't offended. She could feel his hand shaking under hers.

"Won't you sit down?"

"I don't think I ought." He glanced at Nev.

Penelope didn't dare look. "Please."

"I don't know what you think you're playing at," Percy said in a tightly controlled voice, "but—"

"Penelope, let him go." Nev sounded almost desperate.

There was no point pretending to be genteel any longer. She said sharply to Percy, "I'm not playing at anything. I'm interviewing an applicant for the position of steward at Loweston. I'm prepared to pay five hundred pounds per an-num—in advance. Can you walk away from an offer like that without at least sitting down?" She knew he couldn't. It was far too much money. It was what her father had always de-plored—financial recklessness.

"*Penelope*—"

"Loweston can't afford five hundred pounds per annum to a steward," Percy said. "Not with the lesser estates sold off and a jointure to pay."

Well, it was good to know the money wouldn't go entirely to waste. Percy knew what he was about. "It's my father's money."

Percy flashed her a look of intense dislike. "Then, no. I can't walk away from an offer like that." He pulled out a chair and sat down.

She wanted to protest that this wasn't her, that she wasn't the coarse, flashy Cit he thought her. But who would that fool? Of course she was.

"Penelope, don't." Nev's voice was like a lash.

Penelope finally turned to look at him. He looked angry and betrayed, and his eyes kept straying to Percy. "Come and talk to me in the hall," she said softly.

"No, I will not come and talk to you in the hall! He doesn't want the position, and we don't have the money, and I—let him *go!*"

Percy half rose from his chair, and Penelope remembered that crate from Paris and Edward's angry letter. Percy was an-gry too. No doubt poor Nev had cast him aside as clumsily and cruelly as Penelope had Edward.

She did not always understand Nev; she knew that. But in

his expression now, with blinding clarity, she recognized her own emotions as she had stared at the wreckage of her closest friendship.

No. Nev was *not* going to lose this, and there was no time—no time for gentleness or cajoling or anything that would have saved Nev's pride. "I have the money," she said. "And I don't intend to see Loweston ruined for your sensibilities, not after I pulled you out of the River Tick."

His face went blank with shock, and inwardly she shrank back—but there was no way out of this but forward. Her father had told her once that if you bullied a man into a deal, you'd better get the papers signed straightaway: give him time to think it over and he'd weasel out somehow.

He had also said that you should never expect to deal with that man again. Penelope didn't think about that. "Do you think he can't do it?"

"That's not the point!"

"What else *is* the point? Do you think he can't do it?"

"He can do it."

"Do you think he'll cheat us?" Penelope pressed him.

Percy sucked in his breath. She saw with surprise that he was not sure of Nev's answer.

Nev heard it too. "No. He'd never cheat us."

Penelope wanted to put her arms around him, but he would have pushed her away. "Then we have to hire him. It's the responsible thing to do."

Nev and Percy locked gazes. "Fine," Nev said.

"When can I get my money?" Percy asked in a strained voice, as if he couldn't wait to have this over with.

"If you stop by here tomorrow, my father will give you a bank draft," Penelope said. "How soon can you be at Loweston?"

"Within a few days. Where do you want me to stay?"

"You'll stay in the steward's room, of course," she said,

pretending there had never been any question. Nev said nothing.

Percy got up and walked out; Nev abruptly started forward and followed him into the hall.

"Are you all right?" she heard him say in a low tone. "I know you never wanted to be a steward. If you need help—" His concern was clear through the stiffness, and Penelope was violently, nauseatingly jealous.

"You're my employer, but that doesn't give you the right to pry into my affairs," Percy said.

"I'm *not* your employer. She is."

Percy spoke so low she almost didn't hear it. "Indeed. You traded us in for *that?*"

Penelope sat at her father's desk, where she had once been so comfortable, and tried not to cry.

They still weren't speaking when the Browns picked them up for the promised evening at the theater. By tacit agreement, they pretended cordiality in front of her parents, but Penelope's laugh was brittle and her fingers were stiff on his arm. Nev had not realized how friendly, how almost comfortable he and Penelope had become together until now, when it was gone.

He thought she would have apologized given an opening, but he did not want to hear it. He did not understand what had happened that afternoon. He did not want to.

Of course it had been a shock to see Percy, a miserable shock, but oddly, it hadn't been that which had lingered with him throughout the day. Rather, it had been the harshness of Penelope's voice and the cold, insulting logic of her words.

He and Penelope didn't know each other well; they had had to struggle to get along together. But they had been patient with each other. She had been patient with him—with his mother's insults and his poor head for business and his ruined estate. And in that room, at that moment, it had seemed as if all at once she had lost patience, and all that had been left was someone who resented and despised him. *I don't intend to see Loweston ruined for your sensibilities, not after I pulled you out of the River Tick.* Nev did not know how he would live for the rest of his life if Penelope thought of him like that.

He was barely listening to the play when a very familiar voice echoed through the theater. He looked at Rosalind, and sure enough, the actress was Amy.

His first anxious thought was whether the Browns would recognize her. They had seen her with him at Vauxhall—at least Penelope had. Would they say anything? Of course a lady or a gentleman wouldn't, but the Browns might. Would Penelope think he had arranged this?

Nev was so tired of worrying. He looked at Amy, standing in the footlights reciting in her clear voice, and thought, *A year ago I would have been here with Percy and Thirkell.* Now there would be no celebration with Amy and his friends after the show. Instead, there would be more awkward small talk with his mother- and father-in-law, and then he and Penelope would go back to their hotel room and not speak to each other. Tomorrow he would go back to Loweston and not speak to Percy and watch people who depended on him starve by inches, and Penelope would watch it too and hate him. He stared at Amy, and was seized with such a violent longing for his old friends, his old *life*, that it almost choked him.

Penelope could barely believe it. She ought to have known, she ought to have prevented this somehow—but how could she have? She hadn't even known the girl's name (Amy Wray, her program told her). She looked at Nev. He was staring at Miss Wray with an expression of hopeless yearning. Penelope's stomach twisted viciously.

She darted a glance at her parents; she could not bear it if they saw her humiliation. But her mother was absorbed in the play, and her father had settled in for a nap. Penelope was fiercely relieved that she hadn't pointed out Nev and his mistress that night in Vauxhall. That night had seemed so far away the day before; now it was apparent that nothing had changed.

Every minute of the play was a torment. Penelope longed for it to end, and yet she could not bear to think that it would end, and she and Nev would go back to their room and not speak and not make love, and Nev would be silently longing for Miss Wray. Then, as if Hell felt it necessary to devise yet another torment for her, Miss Wray opened her mouth and a pure, lovely soprano came forth. Penelope thought she would cry. Penelope had told Nev she had got over wanting to be a soprano; it had been a lie.

After a moment, Penelope admitted that Miss Wray's voice was not well trained, nor powerful enough to fill the house. The girl had an unfortunate tendency to embellish the melody, and she did it without real taste. In fact, Penelope noted with mean satisfaction, as the song went on, the actress's voice lost body and she began to pause awkwardly to draw breath.

Penelope started forward—this was more than poor singing. The actress's voice trilled high on the last line—and cut off abruptly. Miss Wray fell to the ground in a dead faint.

Nev shot to his feet, leaning over the balcony and craning his head out to try to see closer. Fortunately, people all over the theater were doing the same thing. Penelope hoped her mother had not heard him cry "Amy!" in tones of shock and fear as he rose.

"Can you see anything?" She was sorry for how cold she sounded—the result of trying too hard not to sound jealous.

He struggled gamely for nonchalance. "They're carrying her offstage. I don't think she's woken up."

"Then it should be a while before the performance starts again. Do you think you might fetch me some lemonade?"

His gaze shot to hers. Penelope nodded once. Gratitude flooded Nev's face. She pressed her lips together. She would not cry. She blinked, and he was gone.

Mrs. Brown turned to her. "Well? What's the matter?"

"Nothing's the matter." Penelope tried to sound surprised. Onstage, someone was announcing an intermission.

"What are you and he quarreling about? You've barely spoken a word to each other all evening, and just now you took the first opportunity to send him away. Lord knows he looked happy enough to take it."

"How do you know I didn't just want lemonade?" Thank God her mother had no idea Nev had rushed off to his mistress's side.

"Because I'm your mother. You can't fake a smile and expect me to think everything's roses, even if that works on that boy you married. Now tell me what's wrong."

Penelope could not talk about Nev and Miss Wray, and she did not want to talk about Mr. Garrett, so she began to tell her mother about Loweston. When she had got to the end of it all, had tried to explain about the Poor Authority and enclosures and Agnes Cusher and What Happened In '16, she watched her mother, hoping that Mrs. Brown could tell her what to do.

"Oh, *Penelope*." Her mother looked aghast. "I wish we could do something. I'm sure your father and I could pay to start a school for those poor children, if you'd like."

Penelope stared. It seemed like such a tiny answer to such an enormous problem. "Mama, they cannot afford to send their children to school. They need the money the children earn."

"But surely they could not be so selfish as to value a few pence a day over their children's welfare!"

Penelope was not even sure anymore that a school would

be in the children's best interests. Would education bring them more than learning young how to bind wheat into sheaves or find the best grass seed? Their people needed jobs, not a school. But Penelope knew without saying it that her mother would never believe or understand that. Mrs. Brown's greatest regret was that she had never been to school.

Being a landowner, Penelope realized, was different from being rich in the city. True, her mother felt herself in some way responsible for Mr. Brown's employees; she was well-known at the brewery for her soft heart and willingness to help if one of the workers had family trouble or an expensive illness. But in London, Mrs. Brown could found a free day at the British Museum and trust that someone else would found a pauper's kitchen, that if Mr. Brown did not give someone a job, they could find one elsewhere—and if they couldn't, it was not her fault.

At Loweston, if a man who had lived there all his life could not find work, it was because Nev had not hired him. If a child starved it was because Nev and Penelope had not given her food. At Loweston, they were answerable for all those people.

Her mother didn't understand, and Penelope would have to work things out on her own. She was a grown-up now.

Then Nev walked back in, and Penelope forgot all about Loweston. He looked pale and unhappy, but he had remembered to bring her a lemonade.

She wanted to ask after Miss Wray but was afraid she could not do it with sufficient nonchalance to fool her mother. Fortunately, it was the obvious question, so Mrs. Brown asked it for her. "Did you hear anything about that poor girl? How is she? Is she going to come back on?"

"She said—I heard that she told the manager she is fine." Nev didn't look at Penelope. "It was just the heat of the lime-lights, and she hadn't eaten dinner, is the story that's going about. They should recommence the play in a few minutes."

Mrs. Brown clucked in concern. "Poor girl. She ought to take better care of herself. She looks familiar—where have I seen her before?"

Nev blinked, looking cornered and guilty. Penelope knew he was thinking the same thing she was—*had* her mother seen Miss Wray with Nev, that evening in Vauxhall?

"She was in that production of *Twelfth Night* we went to, Mama, you remember," Penelope said.

"Oh, yes, of course. I do hope I'm not entering my dotage. It's funny, though—I remember thinking at the time that I'd seen her somewhere before."

The curtain went up and the play continued, but Penelope did not enjoy a moment of it. She could do nothing but watch Miss Wray for signs of a relapse and speculate as if by compulsion on what the actress had said to Nev, and what he had said to her.

They were silent on the carriage ride to the hotel, and though Nev wished it were a more comfortable silence he was glad of it.

He was sure that Amy was not fine. She hadn't wanted him backstage, that much had been plain. He thought the only reason he had not been barred the door was because it had never occurred to her he might turn up. "I'm fine, Nev, truly." She had frowned at herself in the mirror, repairing her thick stage makeup. "I didn't eat dinner, that's all, and the lights were hot. Please, go back to your father-in-law's box. You wouldn't want Lady Bedlow to think you're breaking your promise."

Despite his worry, the unfairness of that smote him. "Penelope said I might come and see how you did. And you shouldn't have fainted just from missing dinner."

"That was very generous of Penelope," Amy had said viciously. "If you must know, I have a hangover. I was up late last night with my new protector."

It wasn't like Amy to drink the night before a performance. Nev had been opening his mouth to say so when some rakehell had burst in, a man Nev recognized as one of Percy's pigeons in piquet. Amy had turned to him with a warm, reassuring smile—"Lord Bedlow was just leaving, Jack. I promise you, I'm quite all right"—and Nev had had no choice but to go.

She had talked to Jack just as she had always talked to Nev; he saw now that it was false. She had not felt warm or reassuring. He realized he had not seen Amy out of temper above once or twice, in the whole year he had kept her. She had never let him see anything she thought he might find unattractive. Probably she had not dared, for fear he would tire of her and stop paying her rent. And now something was wrong, very wrong, and he had not the slightest idea what it could be.

Instead of staying and shaking her and insisting on the truth, he'd had to go back to the Browns' box and pretend that everything was fine, because to do anything else would have been scandalous and awkward, and humiliating for Penelope, and besides they needed to borrow money from the Browns.

He was still worrying as they pulled up at the hotel and went silently up the stairs.

He turned around to put down his gloves and his hat, and when he turned back Penelope was standing with her back to him. She was hugging herself, and her shoulders were shaking.

He knew what he would see even before he walked around to look at her face. She was crying—silent little heaves that she was trying desperately to control. Her lips were pressed tightly together and her eyes were screwed shut, but tears were leaking down her face nevertheless.

It shocked Nev deeply. He knew Penelope disliked displays

of strong emotion, and it was so evident that she hated doing it that she must be miserable indeed to succumb.

"Penelope, what's the matter?" He didn't know if he should go to her. She hated that he was seeing her like this, he was sure of it.

Her eyes were dark and wet when she opened them. "I'm so sorry, Nev." Her voice was rough with tears. "I'm all right— just tired. I tried not to—I didn't want you to have to deal with a hysterical wife on top of everything."

He thought of Amy saying she was all right and him not knowing how to tell if she were lying, and panic shot through him. "Penelope, please. Tell me what's wrong."

"I'll be fine, truly." Her tears were slowing now. "I'm just being foolish." She sniffled and began searching her reticule for a handkerchief.

He gave her his, and thought about what to say while she was blowing her nose.

She spoke before he could, however. "Nev, I'm so sorry about this morning. I don't know what came over me."

Nev found that he wasn't angry about it anymore. He didn't understand what had happened, but it wasn't important just then. "It's all right."

"It's not all right. I shouldn't have spoken to you that way." She reached up and began taking her hair down, as if she were just tired of the whole evening and wanted it to be over. He reached out idly and pulled out a pin, and she jerked away. "Don't."

Nev was appalled. She didn't want him to touch her? "Penelope?"

She turned her face away. "I'm sorry. Just—not tonight. I'll feel better tomorrow, but—not tonight. Just help me get my things off and let's go to sleep. Please, Nev."

He wanted to insist on an explanation, but he was terrified that she would say it was nothing to do with him. "Of course. Only—" He did not know how to say what he wanted to. "You know I want you to be happy, don't you? You know that if you needed me to do anything, I would?"

She gave him a tired smile and nodded. "Thank you, Nev."

So he changed into his night things while she unpinned her hair and took off her jewelry and her slippers and stockings. He unbuttoned her dress and unlaced her corset and didn't let his hands stray even an inch, as much as he wanted to. They got into bed, and Penelope blew out the candle, and then she turned away from him and pulled the covers up to her chin.

Nev lay there in the dark. He didn't wish Penelope were gone, and that he had his old life back. He just wished he knew why she was unhappy and that he could fix it.

It took Penelope a long time to fall asleep. She hated how unreasonable she was being. She hated that she had hurt Nev's feelings—because they had been hurt, when she had asked him not to touch her. She *wanted* him to touch her. But she had found she couldn't bear it, not then, not after he had been talking to Miss Wray, not when he was thinking about his former mistress.

It would have been the height of melodrama for Penelope to suppose herself the forsaken lover; she was still his wife, after all, and she had no reason to suppose he had been madly in love with Miss Wray. But that, somehow, was what stung; that probably Miss Wray had meant to Nev exactly what Penelope did. Nev had desired Miss Wray, and liked her. He was kind and did not want anyone to be unhappy. That was very likely all.

It would have been irrational to expect him to feel more for her after a fortnight of marriage, and Penelope knew it. It was irrational to ever expect him to feel more; she was hardly the sort to inspire a grand passion in anyone. She was ordinary—common. She had known it from the start. She thought grand passions were ridiculous, anyway. She hated that she wanted him to feel more, that she could not help wanting to be special.

And yet when he touched her, it felt so—*affectionate*. It felt like it meant something. And tonight she could not bear that it didn't, and there was nothing to be done about it.

Twelve

The next morning she let him touch her again, and Nev seemed to feel as relieved and happy about that as she did. But relations between them, instead of easing, became more and more strained. To Penelope, traveling back to Loweston resembled nothing so much as returning to Miss Mardling's boarding school after vacation. There was the same feeling of putting back on a heavy cloak of dullness and misery. She did not know whether Nev felt the same or if his silence was due to worry about something else—Miss Wray's health, for example.

Neither of them spoke of Mr. Garrett, but as the days passed, Penelope sensed a growing unease in Nev. Their one substantive conversation (on how best to help Jack Bailey, a laborer who had gone to help his mother rethatch her roof the week before and returned with a broken leg) quickly disintegrated into bickering about which was better for invalids, chicken broth or French onion soup. Finally, on Thursday, Penelope looked out the window and saw a solitary figure trudging up the drive carrying a valise.

Nev was nowhere to be found, so when Mr. Garrett arrived there was only herself to greet him. "Welcome back to Loweston, Mr. Garrett," Penelope said, remembering how badly she had conducted herself at their last meeting and ashamed for herself and her husband. "I know I had to bribe you shamelessly, but allow me to tell you anyway how glad I am that you agreed to come and work for us."

He bowed. "Thank you, Lady Bedlow."

"Martin will be here shortly to conduct you to your room. Take this evening to settle in. Tomorrow morning after breakfast, I should like you to meet me in your office so that I may show you the work I have done on the books and ask you a number of questions about the estate that I have been unable to find the answers to."

He bowed again. "Certainly, my lady. I hope I can answer them to your satisfaction. My experience here is all years old. I did, however, take the liberty of purchasing several books and journals on the latest farming techniques, especially those popularized in Norfolk by Coke." Halfway through this speech Penelope heard the door behind her open. It would have been rude to turn round, and so she saw Mr. Garrett's eyes fly to the door and saw his shoulders sag a little in disappointment. Evidently it was not Nev who had walked in.

She glanced at his valise. If there were a number of farming books in there, there was not room for much else. "That was very thoughtful of you. I meant to do as much when we were in London, but somehow I did not find the time. If you will let me know how much you were obliged to spend, I should be happy to reimburse you."

He inclined his head. "Your ladyship is very kind."

She looked round to see one of the footman waiting by the door. "Martin will escort you to your room. Will you be joining us for supper? You are welcome, if you'd like . . ." She did not know how to continue.

He smiled ironically. "Thank you, but I am quite content to take my meals in the steward's room." Her distress must have shown on her face because his smile grew a little warmer, and he said, quietly enough that Martin would not hear, "It will be a deal kinder to Lord Bedlow and to myself."

She nodded, but her heart sank. What on earth was the point of going to all this trouble to reconcile them if they were both going to be so wretchedly stubborn?

"Now, if your ladyship will excuse me," Mr. Garrett said, "I should be glad to rid myself of the dirt of the road."

"Oh, certainly!"

He followed Martin out. She heard their voices in the hall a moment, talking familiarly together. It surprised her, though it should not have.

She had not forgotten that he had grown up at the Grange; it was more that she had never considered what that meant. How would he be treated in the steward's room? Would he be welcomed by the upper servants as one of their own? He must have dined with the family on his most recent visits to the Grange; would he be resented? Would he be taunted for his fall from grace?

The first thing Nev heard from the butler Hathick when he returned to the house was, "Good afternoon, my lord. Mr. Garrett has arrived safely."

He did not know what to say. Soon enough it would be clear to everyone how matters stood between himself and Percy. "I am glad to hear it," he said at last, awkwardly. "Will he be joining myself and Lady Bedlow for supper?" He didn't know what he wanted the answer to be.

"I believe he will be taking his meals in the steward's room, my lord." Not by a flicker of an eyelid did Hathick indicate that he remembered the dozens of times Percy had eaten at the master's table. But perhaps it had not been so very often; when they were boys they ate in the nursery, and when they were home from school Percy had generally dined with his own family—which must have meant, Nev realized, in the steward's room. It was only since Mr. Garrett's death that Percy had eaten in the dining room with Thirkell and the Ambreys. Nev had always suspected that Percy was uncomfortable there—he barely spoke, and Lady Bedlow would roll her eyes at what she termed his excessive politeness to the servants. Perhaps Percy would be happier in the steward's room, after all.

Nev had almost succeeded in banishing the matter from his mind by the time he sat down to supper. But Penelope seemed preoccupied and excused herself directly after the plates were carried away.

When he went to her room that night, she was sitting on her bed brushing her hair. Each stroke was very slow, as if she could not quite remember what she was doing. When she saw him she put the brush down and smiled with an effort.

"What is it, Penelope?"

"Mr. Garrett arrived today."

"I know."

"I invited him to eat with us, and he refused."

"I know," Nev said again, ignoring his hurt at the reminder.

"I wish you could at least be polite to him, Nev. It's not going to be easy for him here."

"What do you mean?"

"I talked to Molly just now and asked what the talk about him was below stairs. She says people weren't very kind to him at supper."

Nev stiffened. "It's not very clever of them to insult a man who is, for all practical purposes, their employer."

"You're their employer, Nev. And somehow they all know the two of you have quarreled."

"I certainly shall not impede him in the discharge of his duties," he said sharply. "If he wants to sack the lot of them, he will have nothing but my approval."

She smiled at him. "It would not be a very auspicious beginning. Apparently the elder Mr. Garrett was very much beloved, and the talk is that Mr. Garrett broke his parents' heart, running wild and never coming home, making a living at cards, and corrupting you in the process." She toyed with her brush. "*Was* he a bad influence, like they all say?

Like your mother said? Is that why you don't wish to speak to him? You said he wouldn't cheat us, that he could do the job—"

He could have said yes, and Penelope might even have approved of his fortitude and firmness of purpose. But he couldn't do it. "My mother was talking rot. He wasn't a bad influence. And he can do the job, and he won't cheat us."

"But then *why*—"

"Because I have to be respectable now, Penelope! Because I have to be a responsible landlord and a responsible guardian to Louisa! And I don't know how to do that, but I sure as fire can't do it by idling away my time with my disreputable friends. You asked me to promise not to leave you here while I went gallivanting about, remember? You asked me to promise not to be a spendthrift. I've never spent five minutes in Percy and Thirkell's company without being tempted to gallivant off somewhere and buy something. My friends and I did nothing but drink, gamble, and—" *Attend the theater. Fence. Talk.* They had done everything together.

"But Mr. Garrett is not a professional gambler anymore," she protested. "He is your steward."

He looked at Penelope's worried face and his resolve hardened. "My father was always out with his friends—drinking, gaming, whoring. 'At my club,' he always said. 'I'll be at my club.' We all knew what that meant." Nev remembered his mother with tears in her eyes, saying, *I didn't want to marry him, but after twenty-five years*—She had been a wreck, mourning a man she had never loved and who had never been there when she needed him.

"I don't want to be like that," he said. "Percy and Thirkell have good hearts, but they aren't suitable friends for me now. I mean to take care of my family, not spend my time in idle pursuits."

She smiled at him uncertainly and pressed his hand.

* * *

The next morning after breakfast, Penelope went to Captain Trelawney's office, attended by Molly. How different it looked now! Trelawney, she realized, must have forbidden the maids the room, because the dust, clutter, and smell of spilled claret had disappeared along with his pipe, pictures, and other effects. The windows were clean. Molly went to one and sat down with her pile of mending.

Mr. Garrett had cleared the desk and was occupied in organizing the shelves. A neat pile of new books lay beside him, evidently those he had brought with him from London; but it was an older, much-used book that engaged his attention. He stood turning it over in his hands, regarding it with an expression in which wonder and resignation were curiously mingled. When he heard Penelope enter, however, his face went blank. "Good morning, Lady Bedlow. How do you do?"

"Very well, thank you. And yourself?"

"It is kind of you to inquire," he said. She did not think he meant it. "I am in excellent health."

"What—what book is that?"

He looked at it impatiently, as if he wished he had put it down before she could see it. "It is Mr. Young's *Farmer's Tour through the East of England*. It was my father's."

"Was he fond of it?"

"Very. He revered Arthur Young second only to Mr. Coke."

"You must take the book, if you wish—do you wish?" Penelope hoped he wouldn't take offense. But he had looked at it so intently.

"Not particularly. But I suppose that, like this office, it is mine now." He looked around at the neat little room as though surveying a prison.

"Sometimes I think that is how Nev feels about Loweston." At once she wished she had not mentioned Nev. It was bound to make things awkward—more awkward.

He regarded her sharply. "And how do you feel about Loweston, Lady Bedlow?"

She was startled. "I—I don't know. I suppose the same, but—I did not inherit it. It is not my home. I think I would feel differently about my father's business." *Never say 'brewery.'* She had drilled that into herself for years.

"Of course, the brewery makes more money."

She was silent, trying not to let him see the sting. It was no more than she deserved.

"I beg your pardon," he said. "You said you had some questions about the estate?"

He only raised his eyebrows a little when he saw her list, and answered all her questions patiently. At times, explaining something that interested them both, he even seemed to forget that he disliked her. Emboldened, she brought forth her list of possible economies. He agreed with the first few items—cheaper and fewer candles, less beef and pork and more game, hot bricks and water bottles instead of fires.

"I don't wish to let anyone go who might have trouble finding another position," she said, "but our French chef is talented enough to find another position with ease. If we hired an ordinary cook to replace him, that would save us at least a hundred pounds a year."

He glanced at her uneasily. "You are certainly correct. But Lord Bedlow is very fond of Gaston. We used to practice our French with him. And Gaston told me last night at supper that Lady Louisa had been by to beg some brioche from him and hear how he did."

"Oh!" Penelope was abashed. "Then of course we shall keep him. Thank you for informing me."

He laid down the paper then. "I thought you did not intend to see Loweston ruined for Lord Bedlow's sensibilities."

She felt herself flushing. "I am deeply ashamed of my behavior on the occasion of your interview," she began firmly—

and then started to babble. "The truth is that I had quarreled with a—friend of my own on the occasion of my marriage, and it was a source of much pain to me. I thought—it little matters what I thought. I do not make excuses. I have landed us all in an exceedingly awkward situation. I can only apologize for the insults you have suffered—I did not expect—"

He was looking at her in astonishment, as well he might after such a confused speech. "Do you mean to tell me that you carried on like that because you wanted to make it up between me and Nev?"

She nodded, conscious of how foolish she must look.

"Does Nev know that?"

She shook her head. "He would only say I had no right to act as I did. It would seem like asking to be thanked for a piece of impertinence."

Mr. Garrett seemed bereft of speech.

"I really am sorry for your part in this. I did not think he would be so"—she searched for a word that would not be disloyal—"constant in his determination."

Mr. Garrett sighed. "When Nev does a thing, he does it with his whole heart. He does not know a middle road between Spartan restraint and hedonism."

"But moderation in all things is the most rational mode of existence."

He said something in a language she did not recognize, and laughed rather unhappily. "I studied Greek, and I agree with you. But Nev prefers Latin, and besides, one cannot always be rational." After that they were more in charity.

In the weeks that followed, Penelope found herself spending more and more time in the little office going through the books and drawing up budgets and plans. Things seemed manageable there. They were making progress, and there were no tenants or hungry children or husbands around to confuse her. One day she and Mr. Garrett were in the middle of reading about Coke's introduction of Southdown sheep when it was time for dinner. Penelope could not quite bear to exchange the comfortable amity of business for sitting awkwardly with Nev, wondering what he was thinking and if his hand would brush hers when he reached for the salt. Mr. Garrett raised his eyebrows when she rang for a tray, but he didn't send her away.

Nev did not say anything that night about missing her at dinner; she was drearily conscious that she had partly stayed away in hopes that he would, and that she had got what she deserved. She worked through dinner a second time, and a third; once Lady Louisa joined her and Mr. Garrett. Penelope was glad of it; she did not think Nev's sister was happy to be always in Lady Bedlow's company. And Penelope liked hearing Mr. Garrett and her sister-in-law talk of their childhoods. Nev, it was plain, had been a charming child and a devoted brother.

Nev was bored. Penelope never had time for him anymore now that Percy was here. The woman he had married to save Loweston and the friend he had given up for the same reason were closeted in that office at all hours, going over figures and making lists and doing all the things that came so naturally to them and only gave him a headache. He could not help feeling that his noble sacrifices in the name of duty were not appreciated and was well aware of how petty that was.

He missed her, but it did not occur to him to be jealous until his mother dropped in one morning. After she had eaten a large quantity of brioche, complained about the inferior quality of her current cook, and boasted that Sir Jasper had called no less than twice last week and paid Louisa a flattering amount of attention, she finally thought to ask after Penelope.

"She is doing very well," Nev said. "I'll ask her to join us if you like. She is probably with Percy in his office; they are always working. I never see her anymore."

Lady Bedlow smiled at him. "No, it is nice to have you all to myself."

He smiled back, warmed that there was *someone* who was glad of his company, and that was when she said it:

"I suppose it is only natural that Penelope should feel more comfortable with Percy—he is a gentleman, of course, but still he is so much nearer her own class."

Nev had told himself that Penelope stayed away from dinner because she was busy. He had not thought—had not allowed himself to think—that perhaps she had stayed away because she preferred Percy's company to his. Was his mother right? He remembered all the awkwardness and difficulties and compromises that had plagued his and Percy's friendship; did Penelope feel free of all that with Percy? Did she share an instinctive understanding with him that she could never have with Nev?

He did not think for a moment that Penelope would betray him. She was too honest—and, he admitted, too puritanical— for that. He did not even think she would be consciously disloyal in her thoughts. But she'd never been in love, he was sure; if she had loved Edward she would never have married Nev. And she had been so ignorant of passion and surprised by her own desire. It was plain enough that Nev himself was not the sort of man she could wholeheartedly admire. She might not recognize the symptoms.

"Is something wrong, Nate?" Lady Bedlow asked. "You look as if you just swallowed a toad."

"No, no, I'm fine." He took a hasty gulp of tea and choked.

She smiled mischievously. "Of course, I know exactly what you look like when you've swallowed a toad. Do you remember? You were six, and it was a very small toad . . ."

* * *

When his mother had taken her leave, Nev rode to the home farm and spent the rest of the day working in the fields alongside the men. After eight hours of hard labor in the hot sun, he felt sore but sated, drained of anger and jealousy by exhaustion. He was almost content—although his satisfaction was marred by the sight of the men's dinner. A little oat bread and water was all most of them had. Nev, eating bread and bacon and beer with the foreman, had felt positively decadent.

Still, they had seemed friendlier than before. He knew their names now, and the harvest, while not abundant, was respectable.

Nev was so tired that he hardly even missed Penelope. So tired that when he came home, he was able to take off his clothes and fall into bed without looking at the door between their rooms more than, oh, two or three hundred times.

So tired that he thought for certain she would be in Percy's office for hours already by the time he made it to the breakfast room in the morning, wincing all the way down the stairs and so hungry he hadn't even bothered to bathe first. Evidently fencing and boxing took a different, lesser, set of muscles than laboring with heavy tools all day.

But there she was, looking fresh and anxious and maybe as if she'd lingered in the breakfast room in the hopes of seeing him. His heart clenched. "Good morning."

"Good morning. Did—did you sleep well?" She didn't look at him when she asked, and he felt suddenly guilty about not going to her room last night.

"Like the dead. And you?"

Her face fell; perhaps that hadn't been the most tactful response. "Oh, tolerably well. You look sunburned. Does it hurt?"

He shrugged, realizing why his face felt hot as fire. Wonderful. She looked fresh as a daisy and he was lobster red and smelled like manure.

She smiled weakly. "I've some good news. My mother's offered to buy us new furniture."

So that was why she'd been waiting for him. She needed to talk business, and her parents wanted to give them something.

Nev had felt low enough, borrowing money from his father-in-law two weeks after the wedding. Worse, Penelope had done the asking; Nev had only been able to thank Mr. Brown inarticulately later and had felt the full force of his father-in-law's disapproval. And now this—Penelope might be kind and not reproach him, but the Browns must know damn well what a poor bargain she had made. He wanted so badly to make a go of this, to make a home for Penelope out of his own money, rents he had collected and corn he had sold. He wanted to be what she needed, and he wasn't.

She saw his face. "We needn't accept it if you'd rather not! I assure you, I never asked them—I only told Mama how Lady Bedlow had taken a deal of the furniture with her—"

Nev closed his eyes.

"Oh, Nev," Penelope sighed. "I'm sorry. I wasn't trying to make your family look bad—I knew Mama would think it was funny, that's all. And when I got her reply, I thought you might like to have a new dressing table. Here, if you don't want to, I'll write back this instant and tell her no." She stood up as if to suit actions to words.

Nev looked around the breakfast room; he remembered it from when Lady Bedlow had first redecorated it, when he'd been a little boy. It had been elegant and feminine and lovely, his mother's touch evident in every inch of it. Now the furniture was a jumble of light and dark wood, baroque and rococo and heavy Elizabethan—whatever Penelope could take from the guest rooms. There were darker patches on the walls where she hadn't found a picture the right size to replace the ones that were missing. He looked at Penelope, who wanted to be a lady. Who knew when they would be able to spare the few hundred pounds for new furniture? "Of course I don't mind. Thank your parents for me."

She smiled gratefully at him. "I will. What kind of furniture would you like to have?"

"I don't know." On impulse he put an arm around her waist and pulled her to lean against him. "The Chinese style is all the rage now, isn't it? We could have everything with gilt and dragons and bamboo."

Penelope laughed, and he felt it where she curved against his side. "No one would believe that you picked it. They'd all say it must have been your vulgar Cit wife."

"You'd look splendid in a dark blue kimono embroidered all over with golden dragons, and chrysanthemums in your hair."

"Kimonos are Japanese." But there was a smile in her voice, and she turned her head and let him kiss her.

He was already wondering whether she would let him make up for last night when she pulled away. "Nev, is that— have you been in the stables?"

Oh, Lord, he must be disgusting. "I—I'd better go and bathe," he said hastily.

"All right. Oh, and Nev, one more thing—Mama asks a favor, and we really can say no—there's a woman who works at the brewery, whom Mama knew when she was younger, and the woman's daughter has—" Penelope looked away uncomfortably; Nev was bemused at how charming he had begun to find prudery. "Well, she was with child, and she didn't want it, so she took something. And now she's very ill, and her mother is desperate. The doctors are saying that clean air might save her. And Mama doesn't know anyone else with a place in the country—she wants to know if we have an empty cottage, or if we can board her with someone. She says she'll pay for it. I know it's a lot to ask, Nev, but I can't help feeling it's our Christian duty."

Nev nodded. "Poor girl. By all means have them send her

up, if she can travel. I'm sure we can find someone who'd jump at the chance to make a little extra money by looking after her."

"Thank you, Nev," she said, as if he were doing her a favor, when it was her parents who were showering him with largesse.

The next three days passed by in a blur. The Baileys were eager to help Mrs. Brown's charity case; Mr. Bailey's broken leg was taking its time in mending, and the family desperately needed the money. They could spare a bed, and their children were old enough not to trouble an invalid. Penelope gave them a small advance to clean the cottage and wash the sheets and buy enough fuel so that they could heat water and make tea for the sick girl whenever they liked, instead of paying a ha'penny to a neighbor for the use of their fire, as Penelope had noticed the Cushers did.

On the fourth day the girl arrived from town, accompanied by a nurse who had made the journey with her and would be going back to London as soon as she had entrusted her patient to Mrs. Bailey's care. Penelope and Nev went to see her settled in and to make sure that the Baileys had everything they needed. Penelope didn't expect it to take long.

She stepped onto the freshly swept dirt floor just ahead of Nev. Unlike many of the laborers, the Baileys had two rooms. Since the Baileys' little bedroom had been given up to the invalid, the children's bed in the corner of the main room was now to house Mr. and Mrs. Bailey. The children were to sleep on blankets by the hearth. A table and a few rush-bottomed chairs comprised the whole of the furnishings, apart from the kettle, a pot or two, and the poker. But at least it was well-tended, the family's clothes were not too ragged, and the room smelled fresh and clean.

"Mr. Garrett was kind enough to give us some fresh straw, to change out the mattresses," Mrs. Bailey said in explanation.

Penelope thought of the furniture her mother was probably even now spending hundreds of pounds on, and her conscience smote her. But she smiled and tried not to look self-conscious as Mrs. Bailey exclaimed over the basket Penelope had brought, with real tea, a chicken for broth, and milk and butter for gruel.

"I tried to bring enough so that Mr. Bailey could have some too," Penelope said. "How is your leg, Jack? I mean to ask the nurse to look at it before she goes."

"It's very kind of you, your ladyship, but I'm sure there's no need for that," Mr. Bailey said. "It's doing very well. I'll be on my feet in no time."

Penelope did not think that could be true; he had been injured three weeks ago and still could barely rise from his chair. "Well, we'll see. How did the girl take the journey?"

"She's sleeping," Mrs. Bailey said. "I don't think she's quite in her right mind just yet—feverish, of course. She had trouble swallowing water when she was brought in. But I've opened the window; the Norfolk air should do her good."

Penelope and Nev went into the second, smaller room. It held nothing but a bed and a chair; the sick girl was in the bed, and the chair was occupied by the nurse, a stout woman who was bathing her patient's forehead with a cool cloth and encouraging her to drink some water. Penelope stepped forward, and for the first time she saw the sick girl's face.

The sudden buzzing in her ears drowned out the Baileys' fierce whispered conversation from the room beyond. The girl's blonde hair was dirty and tangled, and her elfin face was too thin and flushed with fever. But Penelope recognized her instantly.

It was Amy Wray.

Thirteen

Penelope wished her head would swim, that she would faint, anything—anything to make the present recede just a little from her consciousness. Anything to draw Nev's attention away from the pitiful wreck of his former mistress. But she did not. She could not. She was not built that way. She stood there, cold in the afternoon sun, and watched her life unravel around her in perfect, precise detail.

In an instant Nev was at the bedside. "Oh, God," he said in a low, terrible voice. "Is she—will she—?"

Penelope felt the knot climb in her throat—high enough to make her bite the inside of her lip to keep from screaming, not high enough to inconvenience anyone.

"I think she'll pull through, my lord." The nurse rose from her chair and bobbed a perfunctory curtsy. "But I couldn't say for sure. She's been sick an awful long time, more'n a week; don't seem to know where she is half the time and burning up with fever. She really shouldn't have traveled, but the air in London is so close this time of year, it might have killed her all on its lonesome. She's lost too much blood." The nurse made a clucking sound in the back of her throat. "That's what comes of opposing nature."

That was when the worst of it hit Penelope. Miss Wray was here because she had aborted an unwanted child. Nev's unwanted child. She was seized with a horrifying thought— had Nev known? Had Miss Wray told him, that night at the theater? Had Nev concealed this from her? For the first time since they had entered the room, Penelope looked at Nev's face. She could only see part of his crooked profile, because he was turned away from her to look down at Miss Wray. His face was gray.

Miss Wray shifted restlessly. "Nev," she moaned.

Penelope froze, her eyes darting to the nurse.

The woman frowned. "She keeps saying 'never.' Who knows what's going on in her head? I hope she isn't scared, poor thing."

The danger was over for the moment, but Penelope could not enjoy the reprieve. Of course the nurse had no idea. But the Baileys would surely recognize the name. Someone would, anyway. Soon everyone at Loweston would know that the new Lord Bedlow had had his mistress brought to Loweston under his wife's nose. Then the neighbors would find out, and everyone would know; everyone would look at her with pity or thinly veiled contempt. It would be confirmation of everything—that Nev didn't care about her, that the new Lady Bedlow was a citified fool who couldn't see what was before her eyes.

Miss Wray tried to push away her blanket. "Nev." Nev swallowed convulsively and balled his hands into fists.

Penelope blinked; the horror receded a little. "I'm sorry, I didn't catch your name," she said to the nurse.

"Oh, begging your pardon, your ladyship, it's Rawley."

"We appreciate your coming all this way, Rawley. I hope you will explain to the Baileys what is required for Miss Wr—" Penelope stopped, panicking a little.

"Miss Raeburn," the nurse prompted her.

"Yes, of course," she said gratefully. "Miss Raeburn's care. And I hope you will oblige us by looking at Jack Bailey's leg before you go. Lord Bedlow can sit with the patient for a few minutes, if you will step into the other room."

"Certainly, your ladyship." Rawley stepped back to let Penelope leave the room ahead of her. "Just call me if you see any change, my lord."

Penelope didn't look back; she couldn't and still keep her

wits about her sufficiently to get them all through the next ten minutes without a scandal.

Mr. Bailey was still grumbling that his leg was fine, but Mrs. Bailey, face set, said to Rawley, "Please, if you could look—"

"It's what her ladyship was just asking me to do. Sit down, Mr. Bailey."

Mr. Bailey sat reluctantly on one of the rush-bottomed chairs. Penelope sank down on the other and tried to think what to do. They could hardly send the girl away, not when she was so ill; to be moved again might kill her. Nor could they ask someone else to nurse her who might not recognize Nev's nickname or whom Penelope could trust; the secret the disappointed Baileys and their friends would create in explanation would no doubt be worse than the truth.

She could find no solution but to try to brazen it out, and take the scandal and humiliation with grace when it came. Penelope had lived with pitying, contemptuous glances all her life. She could do it again. Since Miss Wray—Penelope was still thinking of her by her stage name—was so sick, at least there could be no suggestion that Nev was carrying on with her in his home, which might have injured Louisa's reputation.

It was not Nev's fault. Even if he had known his mistress was carrying his child and had kept it from her, it was certainly because he had thought it would hurt her. It was painfully evident from his reaction that he had not known their invalid would be Miss Wray. Nev was sorry and worried for his mistress, and when he had had time to compose himself he would be sorry and worried for Penelope. She could not add to his burden by unreasonable complaints or recriminations. She could not even wish that Nev cared less for Miss Wray's danger; it would make him a lesser man.

No, there was no use blaming anyone. It was no one's fault that Penelope was miserable, and so no one but her should suffer because of it. There was no use being angry, no use crying, no use doing anything but making the best of it.

Penelope felt robbed: cheated of her anger and her sorrow.

A low groan made her look up. Rawley had unwrapped Jack Bailey's leg. It looked awful—red and swollen and raw, and not entirely straight. There were two ghastly holes near the knee, as well: one on each side. Penelope could not imagine what they might be. Rawley must have been equally puzzled, because Jack was saying, "I fell on the pitchfork, don't you know." Penelope swallowed and didn't let herself look away. *You have little enough to complain of,* she told herself.

"Mrs. Bailey," Penelope said when the leg was wrapped up again, a nauseating eternity later.

Mrs. Bailey turned to look at her, looking drawn and apprehensive. "Yes, Lady Bedlow?"

"I—please take good care of Miss Raeburn."

Mrs. Bailey nodded. "Her mother knew yours, is that right? Was she a friend of your'n?"

Penelope recoiled inwardly at the suggestion—at the idea that someone might look at a piece of Covent Garden ware and think she was Penelope's friend, that she was like Penelope. "No, but—" She did not know what to say. She only knew that she could not bear it if Miss Wray died; it would be, somehow, too much injustice all at once, and Nev would be so miserable. "And take care of Jack's leg, please. If you need anything at all—if anyone needs anything—please let us know. I—I couldn't bear it if anyone died, and I might have prevented it." She felt near tears.

Mrs. Bailey laughed a little. "I wish we'd had *you* when my Rosie took sick."

Penelope's throat closed. She had met the Bailey children, and none of them were named Rosie. There was so much pain, everywhere, and there was nothing to do to fight back, there was nothing anyone could do but bear it.

"Here now," Mrs. Bailey said, "don't take on so. Let's get Lord Bedlow to take you home."

Nev drove silently, without looking at her, his hands white-knuckled on the reins. Penelope did not quite trust herself to speak anyway. They arrived at the house, and Nev handed the cart over to a groom. He offered Penelope his arm to climb the steps and opened the door for her, and all that time he did not turn to her. There was a tension to him that Penelope didn't understand. He took her hand and pulled her up the stairs after him and into her room. Shutting the door behind him, he finally, finally turned to look at her.

Before she could even catch a glimpse of his face he was crushing her to him, his arms around her. Despite all her misgivings and her fears, she relaxed against him. Her sense of hopelessness receded, melting into his warmth. A small, petty part of her could not help a fierce joy that whatever he might feel for Miss Wray, it was she, Penelope, who was his wife, and she to whom he turned for comfort.

"Oh, God, Penelope," he said against her hair in a broken voice. "If that were you—if—"

She pulled away a little, surprised, and he kissed her fiercely and did not stop. She let everything burn away, all the bitterness and worries—they were consumed in a great rush of fire. She kissed him back with everything that was in her, her hands gripping his shoulders hard enough to hurt; she was his wife, she was his, she wanted him, that was all that mattered.

He pressed hot, urgent kisses on her neck and shoulders. "I need to see you."

Shaking, she turned around and let him unbutton her gown with hasty, fumbling fingers. She did not think, at that moment, that she would have cared if he ripped the gown apart; damn the expense, damn the embarrassment of lying to the dressmaker about what had happened.

She was wearing her most intricate set of stays, with a double row of laces down the back. He cursed, low in his throat, and Penelope said, barely able to get the words out, "Penknife—my desk—"

He paused for a moment, and then he snatched up the knife and cut the laces. Her corset fell away in three panels, she tore off her shift, and she was naked.

She remembered the first time she had stood before him naked. She'd been nervous, and he had looked her up and down and smiled and touched her, oh so gently. This was nothing like that. He swept her with his gaze, once, and then he bent and took one of her breasts in his mouth, sucking hard. She cried out—she couldn't help it—and he bore her back until she fetched up against the bed. Taking hold of her waist, he pushed her down so that she sat on the edge of the mattress and he knelt between her spread legs, his hands firm around her buttocks. There was nothing else, no warning, no gentleness, before he dipped his head between her legs and sucked her center of sensation into his mouth.

She had never imagined anything so shocking. It felt—it felt hot and urgent and indescribable. Nev's cinnamon hair brushed the inside of her thighs and his tongue teased her *there* and it was faster and hotter than anything she had ever felt. Then Nev jerked her forward with his hands and thrust his tongue *inside* her.

Penelope braced herself on the bed and let her head fall back. Nothing existed but white-hot pleasure. She moaned and pleaded and said words she had barely been aware she knew. And then, faster than she had thought possible, she was racked with waves of pleasure so intense they were almost painful.

For a minute afterward, she simply sat there with her eyes closed, feeling Nev's grip on her loosen. She did not quite want to look at him. What had happened was too intense— it seemed wrong to look and speak as if everything were ordinary. She was afraid he would look unchanged. But finally she opened her eyes and looked down.

Nev met her gaze for a long moment; she did not know how to read his expression, but the tension of earlier was eased. Then he closed his eyes and leaned his head against her thigh, his thumbs tracing small circles on her skin. "Penelope," he murmured.

Tears pricked Penelope's eyes. She put a hand on his head, running her fingers through his hair. He tilted his head against her palm like a tired puppy. "I love your hair," she said softly.

He smiled with his eyes closed, his same familiar small pleased smile.

"Let me—you didn't take your pleasure."

"It doesn't matter."

He meant to be considerate, but it stung her. He had turned the world over for her, and he did not want her to give him anything in return. He had possessed her—branded her as his with his mouth and his hands. All he had to do was touch her, and tiny fires sprang up under his fingers. She wanted to do that for him. She wanted to render him incapable of chivalrous consideration. "It matters to *me*. Teach me to do something new for you. Please. There must be something—something like what you just did for me."

"That—" He sounded as if he were having difficulty speaking. "That isn't something you ask a lady to do."

That would have stopped her, once; but now she rebelled. "I'm not a lady." She felt the familiar sting of it—but she felt something else too. She wasn't a lady; she could not control her base urges when Nev touched her, she could not keep herself from moaning and writhing and spreading her legs. But Nev liked her pleasure, and there was something he wanted that he could not have asked a lady for.

"Penelope—"

"I'm *not*. Nev—please, when it comes out that Miss Wray is here, everyone will know—everyone will say that I—that you—that I can't satisfy you. I don't want it to be true, I want—"

"Penelope, please, don't ever do anything for me because you think you have to. I—" He reached up and cupped her breast. "You satisfy me," he said intently.

She smiled, but she persisted. "Would it feel as good if I did it for you? Used my—my mouth—?"

He swallowed. Penelope saw sudden heat in his eyes before he closed them, trying to hide it from her. He nodded, once.

"Then let me—please—"

He pressed his lips together and nodded again. "Penelope—" His voice was thick. "Promise me that if you find it distasteful at all, you won't do it again."

"I promise."

Nev stood. Penelope could see his masculinity straining against his breeches. "Kneel down."

Nev watched Penelope get up off the bed and kneel in front of him, her expression triumphant but nervous. This was a bad idea, too intense, too much to ask, too *much*—but there was nothing to be done about it, because Penelope on her knees in front of him was the most irresistibly erotic thing he had ever seen. Her hair was still in its neat coil, and the bright sun that came through the gap in the curtains made a stripe across her stomach and thighs, and Penelope, proper Penelope, was going to suck him in the middle of the afternoon. Nev could no more have stopped this than he could have stopped an avalanche.

Amy, pale and wasted, flashed through his mind. Guilt smote him, that he was teaching his wife new sexual tricks while Amy might be dying a mile off. And yet the thought seemed far away. It could not begin to drown his utter focus on Penelope's kneeling form. When had familiar, comfortable desire become this furious hunger?

He wondered if he should have undressed to make this easier for her. That didn't matter either; he couldn't wait. "Unbutton my breeches. Er, please." She gave him an amused glance and reached for the flap of his breeches, and with every slide of button through buttonhole Nev's arousal built. He watched her small, capable hands as she unbuttoned his breeches and his drawers as if she had done it a hundred times, although she never had—always before they had been in their nightclothes, with the exception of that first time in the folly, and then he had dealt with his clothing himself. Then, her hand casually resting at the base of his cock, she looked up at him for further guidance. She looked nervous, but Nev thought she was a little eager too.

He licked his lips. "Take the tip into your mouth." It came out as a hoarse whisper. She obeyed him. Her hot, wet mouth that he had kissed so many times closed around him, and he almost came just from that. She didn't move, her tongue pressed patiently against the underside of his cock, and finally the thought pierced Nev's pleasure-shrouded mind that she was waiting for further instructions. He cleared his throat. "Just—just take it further in and then out, and keep your mouth tight around it." He wasn't going to last long enough for her to need more instructions than that.

Penelope gripped him tighter with her hand, took him in deep—and promptly pulled off, gagging.

He winced. "Sorry, I should have said—"

"I suppose it will take practice." She gave him an impish grin, and then her mouth closed back around him. Nev grabbed the bedpost to keep his knees from buckling.

This time she didn't try to take in more than a few inches; she moved slowly and carefully up and down him, her mouth and hand hot and close. After a few passes like that, she increased her tempo slightly. Nev watched her in fascination, still barely able to believe this was happening. Soon she tried swirling her tongue, awkwardly; he moaned, and he didn't know how but he could feel her attention sharpen. He could feel her making mental notes on his reactions. *It will take practice.* The idea of her practicing *this* with the same thoroughness and devotion she had given to ledgers and the piano pushed him to the edge.

"Penelope!" He had meant it as a warning, but it sounded instead like a plea, or a declaration, and by the time he realized she wasn't pulling off he could no longer form words. He gripped the bedpost hard enough to hurt and spent himself in Penelope's mouth. Pleasure rolled over him, so intense he thought he might black out. She stopped moving, but she didn't draw back. Instead, she struggled to swallow. Not until his muscles relaxed did she pull off, coughing a little, some of his seed dripping down her chin.

Nev had never, not once, seen Penelope let anything drip down her chin. If she ate a peach she cut it up first. "Get up here."

She stood, weaving a little. He kissed her gently, amazed by the taste of himself on her tongue, and then pulled out a handkerchief and began cleaning her mouth and chin.

She flushed. "I can do it."

"I know. Let me." She sighed and tilted up her face. He felt a flash of something—Penelope seemed haloed for an instant in perfect beauty, and he felt a sharp, unsettling pang as if someone had plucked one of his heartstrings, hard, and found it out of tune. It wasn't like affection or lust—those he knew; it was something entirely unfamiliar.

"Is something wrong?"

He realized he had stopped moving, his thumb at the corner of her mouth. "Not at all." He tried to smile. The feeling was gone now, but it had left something in its wake—a sort of lifting up, a yearning toward something undefined. He had sometimes felt like this when he heard the opening chords of a favorite piece of music. He had read a poem, once, that almost described it: *a shaping and a sense of things beyond us.*

That was how he felt when he looked at Penelope just now. As if something were happening to the two of them, just beyond the reach of his understanding. "Thank you. I think that was the most marvelous thing that's ever happened to me."

She looked away. "No Spanish coin." She spoke low enough he hardly heard it.

His hand dropped away from her face. "It's not. It never has been. Why don't you believe me?"

"Perhaps because I've seen your mistress," Penelope said dryly, and then looked as if she wanted to cut her tongue out.

How had he forgotten Amy?

"What did you mean?" she asked. "When you said, 'If that had been you—'"

It took him a moment to remember what she meant, and a moment longer to frame an answer that made any sense. He started refastening his clothes. "I just—you know how one gets the strangest thoughts when someone is sick, and I thought—her mother knew your mother when they were children. What if you were the actress and she were the heiress? Then you would be lying there—" The idea was too unthinkable even to say.

"I'm fine, Nev, I'm right here." Penelope leaned her face against his shoulder, and the idea that someday he might not be able to reach out and touch her was almost a physical pain. "I'm so sorry about Miss Wray."

"She didn't tell me. She must have thought I wouldn't be any use."

There was a pause; Nev wondered if Penelope was silently agreeing with Amy. "There's no use blaming yourself," she said. "We won't know why she didn't tell you until she's well enough to talk."

If she's ever well enough to talk. He knew they were both thinking it. "I never realized how much she didn't tell me. I was with her for a year, I saw her every day—I even told myself we were friends. And I never troubled to find out." Now he might never have the chance to ask. Everything that Amy had felt and thought and never told him might be gone forever. He looked down at Penelope's closed expression. "And you—there's so much you don't tell me. I never know what's going on in there. I don't know how to reach you."

That, he thought, was why he had needed to pleasure her, to see her gasping and flushed and hear her prayers and curses—to prove to himself that in that way at least he could get to her, in that way she opened herself to him completely.

A minute passed, and she hadn't answered him; he could tell she was thinking over what he had said and that she wouldn't voice her thoughts aloud.

"See, you're doing it right now," he said with something like despair. "Damn pennies; I'd give a hundred pounds for your thoughts right now."

"A hundred pounds is a lot of money."

"I know that." He did, and it was a hard-won knowledge. A hundred pounds was plows and horses and seed and food for his people's children. He would still give it, to hear Penelope's thoughts.

"I—" she began, and stopped. "I'm not keeping secrets. I just don't see why you should have to listen to my complaints when none of this is your fault."

It *was* all his fault; Penelope was too generous, as always. As she had been at the Baileys'. "You left me alone with her." He had been so grateful to be left alone to promise Amy that now, finally, he would take care of her. So grateful that Penelope was there to shoulder part of the burden. So weakly, selfishly grateful.

"You were hardly going to ravish her in the state she was in. Besides, I didn't want a scandal, and you would have created one if you were in that nurse's presence one moment longer."

In anyone else, he would have said they were trying to be cruel, trying to give him a set-down. With Penelope—well, perhaps it was partly that. But not all. "You just won't admit you did it to be kind," he said. "You don't want anyone to know how softhearted you are, but it's in everything you do. Penelope—"

"Please don't. Do you think a compliment from you can give me any pleasure when your mistress is here? It's cruel of you to say it, when you know I want it to be true."

"It *is* true! What do I have to do to convince you?"

"*Don't.* You said it yourself; if things were different, I would be lying there and Miss Wray would be here, and you would be saying these things to her. There's nothing special about me, nothing at all."

She seemed so sure, and she was cleverer than he. But he said, "You're wrong." He knew it. "Penelope, you're—"

She ignored him. "And then when the Baileys work out she's saying 'Nev,' and not 'never,' everyone will know she's here, and that she lost your child, and they'll pity me—God! Do you think a single one of them will believe that you find anything *special* about me? That *I* gave you the most marvelous experience of your life?"

Nev felt sick. He had wanted her thoughts; now he had them, and he did not know what to do. He had been too distraught to think about the consequences of Amy's delirium, but now he realized that Penelope was right. They were about to be the subject of a major scandal. And Penelope was right too, about what her role in it would be—the dull wife, losing her husband's interest after a month of marriage and too stupid to know it. The thought of it made Nev furious, the thought of people looking at Penelope like they knew her. Of people not realizing how wonderful she was.

He ignored his pang of disappointment that Penelope was worried because of the scandal; of course she wasn't jealous, it had nothing to do with him. It was unjust for him to want anything else, not now. Even insisting that she believe him, trying to tell her how much he had missed her these last few weeks, seemed suddenly selfish, a plea for a forgiveness he didn't deserve.

There was nothing he could say except, "I'm sorry, Penelope. I'm so sorry."

Penelope thought they were going to make it out of church without having to talk to Mr. Snively, but at the last moment he appeared from behind the pillar at the end of the family pew. "So I hear you have become as ministering angels and adopted a sick woman as your own charge."

"Her mother works for my father," she said, still startled by how fast news traveled in the country. "The poor woman was at her wits' end. The London air, you know, is quite harmful to invalids."

" 'The greatest of these is charity,' " said Mr. Snively. "And yet I fear that, as the guardian of your souls, it is my duty to remind you that the young woman in question is ill because she opposed God's plan to make her a mother. Perhaps the danger to her body is but a shadow of the danger to her immortal soul, and so one may question whether in such a case—"

Penelope stared.

"Perhaps it would be more *Christian* to let her die, is that what you're saying?" Nev demanded.

Mr. Snively shrank back. "No, no. I suppose your generous hearts have the right of it. Tell me, how is Jack Bailey?"

Nev did not answer, so Penelope said, "His leg looked

dreadful to me. I do not see how he can work for at least a
month if he wishes to be really healed. Do you think the parish might add to his allotment for that time?"

Mr. Snively frowned. "Alas, the parish is groaning under the relief that is already needed. His leg is very bad, you
say?"

Penelope shuddered, remembering. "He not only broke
the leg in falling from the ladder, he also fell on the pitchfork
he was using to thatch the roof. His leg is quite frightening,
with a gaping hole straight through—"

"There, there." Mr. Snively smiled and patted her arm. Penelope hated his smile; it was like a snake's. "Your ladyship
must not distress herself. I consider it very ill-advised to have
allowed you to see the wound at all. Your husband, I presume,
did not condone such a thing."

Nev had been with Miss Wray. "I assure you, I was not
nearly so distressed as Mrs. Bailey!" Penelope instantly regretted her words. Whether they liked it or not, Mr. Snively
would be their minister for a good many years. *Unless someone brains him*, she added to herself.

"We're almost there," Nev said. "Mama, try not to embarrass
us in front of Sir Jasper. Nothing is more terrifying to a gentleman than a matchmaking mama."

Lady Bedlow huffed indignantly. "Of course I wouldn't
have the ill breeding to—"

"And Louisa, try to be civil. Sir Jasper is our nearest
neighbor."

"Yes, my lord," Louisa muttered.

The carriage rounded a corner, and Penelope gasped. At
the top of a rolling hill, Greygloss lay enthroned in pastoral
splendor. It was the largest house Penelope had ever seen: a
Palladian manor with enormous symmetrical wings that
stretched out from the gleaming white columns of the por-

tico. She had thought the Grange gigantic, but the Grange would fit easily in one-half of Sir Jasper's house. She leaned across Nev to get a closer look, and felt him sigh.

"It's amazing, isn't it?" he said.

Penelope thought quickly. "One of my father's friends built himself a seat in Essex. He told me that these Neoclassical homes are almost impossible to get water to because they're all at the top of a hill."

Lady Bedlow sniffed. "What a very *practical* consideration."

"Don't provoke me, Mama," Nev said mildly. "I can still cut down the Loweston oaks, you know. We could use the money."

The ceiling of Sir Jasper's entrance hall was impossibly lofty, comprising as it did two stories. The tiled marble floor gleamed, and the furnishings shone richly. It was beautiful and in exquisite taste, but Penelope thought the antiquated, Jacobean Grange was friendlier.

"Good afternoon." Sir Jasper hurried toward them. "Welcome to my home." Penelope thought he looked at Louisa when he said it. Certainly he held her hand in his a fraction longer than he should have.

Of course, he was obliged to escort Penelope in to dinner, but Lady Bedlow quickly sat on Penelope's other side, hoping to leave Sir Jasper's left for Louisa. Instead, Nev took that chair, talking to the baronet about hunting and looking so very unaware that his choice of seat had any implications whatsoever that Penelope knew he had done it on purpose. She was hard-pressed not to laugh at the look on Lady Bedlow's face.

The food laid out for them was aggressively English—not a cream sauce or ragout in sight. "Forgive the simplicity of my table," Sir Jasper said. "I find English cooking more healthful than French, but it must appear sadly plain compared with the efforts of your splendid chef."

Penelope was unpleasantly reminded of one of her father's friends, a Methodist who had given up all forms of meat. His elaborate explanation that no, he didn't judge those who dined on animal flesh, only he found the mind was so much less clouded by carnality when fed on purely vegetable sustenance, had been delivered in precisely the same tone. "Not at all," she said, smiling. "My father disliked French cooking. It will be quite like home to have some plain beef again."

Until Sir Jasper's face went blank, it did not even occur to her that he might not like to hear that Greygloss was quite like home to Penelope Bedlow, née Brown. She wasn't usually so tactless. And she hadn't even meant it. Greygloss was far too elegant to be anything like home. God, she wanted to be home. She wanted her mother's horrible purple tablecloth and people who liked her.

"Your mother's cook was splendid!" Just the sound of Nev's voice made Penelope feel better. "I meant to ask her for the receipt for that calves' feet jelly." He tasted Sir Jasper's jelly. "This is very good, but that had something *extra* in it—I'm terrible at guessing ingredients, but perhaps a spice of some sort?"

"I believe she uses oranges and limes instead of lemon juice," Penelope said.

"Oh, is that all? We should ask Gaston to make it that way."

"Won't he be offended?" Penelope had not dared to ask Gaston to alter any of his recipes, both for fear that Nev liked them the way they were and because she had heard so very much about temperamental French chefs.

Louisa laughed. "Oh, no, not at all. He was forever altering receipts according to our preferences when we were younger. He even used to make me baked cheese in brioche with cheddar, though I know it went sore against the grain. Indeed," she added, "I have always been so used to French cooking that I do not know how I could feel at home with any other kind." She did not look at Sir Jasper when she said it, but a defiant note crept into her voice that made her meaning clear to everyone.

Lady Bedlow looked stricken, and Nev's lips thinned. Penelope sighed inwardly and cast about for some small talk.

Sir Jasper blinked. Then he smiled. "You may find out differently someday. When I was your age I thought I should never feel at home without my collection of model frigates."

Louisa's face set rebelliously. Penelope found the image of Sir Jasper making model frigates rather charming; she wondered what Nev's hobbies had been at seventeen. But she could have told Sir Jasper that it was the worst possible thing to say. No seventeen-year-old girl wanted to be told she was a child.

Lady Bedlow, evidently afraid that Louisa would say something unforgivable, rushed into speech. "Ah yes, being young can be such a trial, can't it, Sir Jasper? Poor Louisa has been so dull in the country that I'm afraid it's wearing on her nerves."

Louisa audibly ground her teeth.

"She's been begging her brother to host a house party, but—" Lady Bedlow stopped, probably not wanting to come out and say that Nev could not afford it. She gave a trilling laugh. "Well, I doubt his friends would be appropriate company for Louisa anyway."

Nev set his jaw and didn't say anything.

"There is nothing wrong with Nate's friends, Mama!"

Penelope, who had been wanting to slap the dowager countess, was seized with a sudden affection for Louisa.

Nev looked taken aback. "Thank you, but—"

"Anyway, I don't care about the house party anymore," the

girl said, still flushed. "I know that it's an unnecessary expense. And it's—it's nice to simply do as I like. There'll be plenty of time to see my friends in the autumn."

Penelope was once again agreeably surprised. She had assumed, when Louisa had stopped complaining about the house party, that the girl had simply given up the cause as lost. It hadn't occurred to her that Louisa might genuinely understand why it was impossible.

"That is very mature of you, Lady Louisa." Sir Jasper looked even more pleased than Penelope felt. "However, there is no need to be so Spartan. I have been thinking of hosting a house party in a fortnight, and if you provide me with the names of a few of your friends I would be happy to invite them."

Penelope smothered a groan; she would have wagered that Sir Jasper had had no such intention at all, and now there would be a house party, and she and Nev would have to go and pretend to like Sir Jasper's friends.

Louisa did not even seem pleased; of course, there was nothing worse than a gift from someone you didn't wish to be beholden to. "That is very kind of you," she said, "but it really isn't necessary."

Sir Jasper smiled at her. "Oh, no, I insist."

Despite Nev changing the subject to threshing machines (a heroic sacrifice), dinner dragged on interminably. Finally, the ladies left the gentlemen alone. Penelope did not know whether to long for Nev's return or dread Sir Jasper's, especially since the dowager countess spent the interim scolding Louisa for her treatment of the baronet.

"And you ought to be more careful to get enough sleep," Lady Bedlow concluded her speech. "There are circles under your eyes."

"Mama, there are not. Anyway, I sleep a good deal. It was only last night I couldn't sleep. I'm sorry I woke you, but—"

"Oh, and you've spilled something on your sleeve!" Lady

Bedlow spit into her handkerchief and rubbed at an invisible spot of food on the muslin. "You know what a light sleeper I am. If you *must* read in the middle of the night, you might at least bring your book to your room with you. I can see how you thought that Mr. Young's book would help you sleep, however. How a daughter of mine ever turned out so clever, I do not know. I suppose it's just as well; Sir Jasper told me he prefers a well-read girl."

Louisa jerked her arm away. "I do not give—I do not care what Sir Jasper prefers!"

Penelope could not help thinking that her own vulgar family had never made such an awkward display. She thought of her mother's endless matchmaking. It had irked her, of course, but—why hadn't it bothered her the way Lady Bedlow's bothered Louisa? The girl looked like a cornered fox. And there *were* shadows under her eyes.

When the gentlemen finally did return, Nev came at once to Penelope—Penelope took resigned note of how her heart jumped when he did—but his first words were, "Louisa looks miserable. What's my mother been saying?"

"She *is* miserable," Penelope whispered. "You had better go to her, or Sir Jasper will do it first, and I can't answer for the consequences."

It struck Penelope again, with a pang, how many more social graces Nev possessed than herself. Within two minutes he had maneuvered things so that Louisa was playing the harpsichord and she and Nev were singing a version of "No John No" that was a good deal less scandalous than the version Penelope had learned from her mother.

Sir Jasper came and sat by Penelope. "I have been hearing great things about your work to improve Loweston."

Never had Penelope felt so undeserving of praise. She flushed. "I wish I could do ten times more. Our people have suffered from the conditions there far more than we ever could."

"I saw your invalid today. It was very kind of you to take her in. Her mother is friends with yours, I collect?"

As afraid as Penelope was of what Sir Jasper might have guessed, her first thought was still to deny the more plausible explanation, the friendship between her mother and poor Mrs. Raeburn. She despised herself even as she said, "They knew each other a little growing up. Miss Raeburn's mother works for my father now." *Never say 'brewery.'*

"Miss Raeburn must have worked very hard to rise from such a background to be one of the lights of the London stage."

Penelope felt cold. "I am sure she did. I quite admired her in *Twelfth Night.*"

Sir Jasper frowned. He leaned toward her. "I should not say this, but I have been touched by your efforts for the district. I do not like to see you play the fool. Miss Raeburn's name has been linked with your husband's. I am morally certain they have been intimately connected."

Penelope stared at him, wishing she had worn long sleeves and faintly wondering at his bringing up such a subject with her at all. *I know,* she wanted to scream. *I know. What kind of idiot do you take me for?* Of course, that would have been shocking; she had to pretend to have no knowledge of any such thing. She had to pray that Sir Jasper would be discreet. Yet she was damned if she would thank him for his officiousness. "What a gentleman does when he is not at home is nothing to do with his wife."

Where had that sprung from? She sounded like an obedient little aristocratic wife, conniving at her own humiliation. What would she have said, if she had really not known? Probably the same thing. She was like that: a steady girl. The thought goaded her into an almost sarcastic, "But it was so very kind of you to pay her a visit. Did you know her in London too?"

"Oh, I wasn't there to see *her*," Sir Jasper said. "I must seem a regular old woman to you! No, that was my pretext, but I was there on quite another account. I had received word from your vicar that Jack Bailey's injury matched that inflicted by a mantrap, and I wished to see if he might be any connection to your poaching gang before I called in the constable." He smiled at her. "I daresay he has been taken up by now."

Fourteen

Penelope really felt faint. She could not believe her own blindness. No wonder Bailey had not wanted to show the nurse. How worried Mrs. Bailey must have been about her husband, to insist! In the midst of her own troubles, the woman had found a kind word for Penelope, and Penelope, like the worst sort of fool, had betrayed her to that snake Snively—

"Pray excuse me," she said through numb lips. "I must—I must speak to my husband."

He made a fine show of remorse. "My dear Lady Bedlow, you look quite dreadful! It was wrong of me to tell you about Miss Raeburn. You are taking it much too hard."

"I am fine." As if she were expected to hear that one of her people was to be arrested on her information with perfect equanimity! And she must pretend that her shock was caused by the news of her husband's infidelity, because aiding poachers was surely a bigger scandal. She shuddered. "Please—my husband—"

Sir Jasper placed a restraining hand upon her arm. She nearly threw it off, like a restive mare. "I beg of you, Lady Bedlow, do not say what you may regret. Anyone can see that Lord Bedlow is very fond of you. You were right in your first reaction, though I suppose it does not come natural to you. In our set, keeping a mistress is really not uncommon, no matter how devoted the husband."

She bit her tongue to keep from laughing. Yes, there was something so bourgeois about a faithful husband! His sympathy was repulsive. And how dare he continue to talk to her of such things openly, as if she were a—a common trollop?

She realized she had borrowed that phrase from Lady Bedlow, that dreadful morning in the breakfast room. The thought filled her with a kind of disgust.

Penelope had wanted to be one of these people all her life, but now she thought, *Well, and I* am *common.* As common as Miss Raeburn and the Baileys. Let Sir Jasper despise her. It was better than his respect. She drew herself up. "I promise you I shall not cause a scene. Only I should like to go home."

She thought she caught a gleam in his eye, almost of satisfaction. At once she chided herself for indulging morbid fancies. Because Sir Jasper was offensive and a Tory, it did not follow that he was malicious. Indeed, he was everything that was tactful and solicitous in pulling Nev aside and telling him that she had been taken ill.

Nev was at once more solicitous and less tactful—in a moment he was at her side, asking what was wrong, did she have a fever, feeling her forehead when she said no, though she did not think he would be able to tell a fever by that method anyway.

"I'm fine," she repeated over and over. "I just want to lie down." She waited in a fever of impatience as they drove to the Dower House to let down Lady Bedlow and Louisa. Louisa was concerned for Penelope's health. Lady Bedlow pretended to be, but it was clear that she felt Penelope had been taken ill on purpose to deny Sir Jasper the chance to win over Louisa. Clear to Penelope, anyway. Nev wasn't listening to his mother; his eyes were fixed on Penelope's face, and every time the carriage jolted he cursed under his breath.

It was touching, and yet she knew it was because of Miss Wray. If Nev's mistress were not prostrate with fever, he would never be this concerned over a slight headache. Still, Penelope was weak-willed; she leaned into him and let him stroke her hair.

When they had let off Louisa and Lady Bedlow, he turned

to her, his arm tightening around her shoulders. "What's wrong? You aren't fine, don't tell me you're fine—"

That too, was because of Miss Wray, who had said she was fine and was dying. She shook him off. "I'm all right. We must go to the Baileys'. I've been a fool—the constable is coming for Jack, his leg is from a mantrap and I told Mr. Snively—"

"You! I felt sorry for you, I kept your secret—I didn't tell a soul about the girl calling for his lordship day and night—and you turned us in! What will become of my children?" Mrs. Bailey turned away from Penelope and sat down hard in one of the rush-bottomed chairs, burying her face in her hands. "What will become of my children?" The children in question stood in a little knot, silent and fearful.

"We're too late?" Penelope said stupidly, though she had known it from the moment she had seen Mrs. Bailey's white, wild face. "He's been taken?"

Mrs. Bailey burst out weeping. "They'll send him to Australia. I'll be all alone like Aggie Cusher."

Penelope was used to thinking herself good in a crisis, but she had never before been the cause of the crisis. She stood frozen, trying to think. To throw in their sympathies altogether with Mrs. Bailey was impossible; it would be all round the country in a moment that the Bedlows aided and abetted poachers. Nev would be a pariah, and was it illegal? But neither could they abandon the Baileys. Penelope tried to think of a middle course.

Nev sat in the other chair and offered Mrs. Bailey his handkerchief. "Penelope, why don't you make Mrs. Bailey some tea?" Penelope did not quite trust Nev to deal with this, and still she was grateful to give over thinking and begin the simple preparations, filling the ancient kettle and measuring out the tea leaves as best she could with a tin cup.

"Mrs. Bailey, you must calm yourself," Nev said. "You're frightening the children."

Mrs. Bailey blew her nose, took a few last gasping sobs, and made a pitiful attempt at a smile. The little Baileys did not look reassured. "Why don't you go into Miss Raeburn's room and join Annie?" she said hoarsely. "This is grown folk's business."

The children filed out, silently. Mrs. Bailey blew her nose again, saw the embroidered monogram, and started. She looked at Penelope, tending the kettle. "She oughtn't to be waiting on me, it isn't right."

"Don't worry about that now," Nev said. "A cup of tea will do you good, and we need your help if we're to find a way out of this for Jack."

"What do you care?" Mrs. Bailey didn't sound angry anymore, just confused. "It's her who turned Jack in."

"You may hate me for my stupidity," Penelope said quietly, "but I promise you it was that, not malice. I did not recognize—they don't have traps in town. I told Mr. Snively because I thought he might raise Jack's allowance."

Mrs. Bailey closed her eyes. "You meant well, anyway."

"Mrs. Bailey, you must be honest with me," Nev said. "Jack's leg *was* caught in a trap, was it not?"

Mrs. Bailey nodded. "No one who'd ever seen a trap could look at that leg and not know. I thought—the nurse was from town and she was going away and his leg was doing so bad, I didn't want him to lose it, I didn't want him to die. He *told* me not to show her, and I insisted—I sent him to his death—"

"You mustn't blame yourself. You did what you thought was best, because you love him and you were afraid."

Penelope marveled at the conviction and sympathy in Nev's voice. How did he always seem to know what to say? And how could Mrs. Bailey help but be comforted?

Mrs. Bailey couldn't. She nodded, looking a little calmer.

"Listen to me carefully." Nev took Mrs. Bailey's hand. "Think before you answer. Is it possible that Jack was caught in the trap while in the woods for some innocent purpose, in broad daylight, and was simply afraid to tell anyone?"

Penelope caught her breath. Nev had found the middle course she had not been able to hit.

For the first time, there was hope in Mrs. Bailey's eyes. "Yes," she said cautiously. "Yes—we thought suspicion might fall on him. He was only—only—"

"I am sure he was only going to visit a friend at Greygloss." He said it so very plausibly. Nev, Penelope realized with a shock, was a good liar. She had thought it so easy to read him at the start of their acquaintance—had he simply never bothered with concealment? Had he chosen to be honest with her?

Or, she thought with a sudden painful jolt, had *all* of it been a lie? The endearing candor, the kiss, *I still wouldn't offer for you if I didn't feel we could rub along tolerably well together*— had he been sweet-talking a plain, gullible heiress into doing exactly as he wished? Had he been surprised at how easy it was?

She pushed the thought away as unworthy of both of them, but it was too near her deepest anxieties to vanish entirely. She could feel it hovering at the back of her mind like a malevolent bat.

"Yes, that's it precisely." Mrs. Bailey's hands trembled with relief as she took the cup of tea Penelope offered her.

"Very well," Nev said. "I doubt I can get you in to see Jack today, but tomorrow morning we'll go to the jail and you can speak with him and tend to his leg. Mr. Garrett is sure to know of some legal colleague of his father's who'll take the case. With some luck we will see Jack out of this whole."

Mrs. Bailey grasped his hand and kissed it. "Thank you. Thank you!"

"I would do as much for any of my people who were in difficulties unjustly," Nev said. "You can thank me by keeping Jack out of trouble in future."

Mrs. Bailey would have kept them there half the night with tearful protestations of gratitude if Nev had not bundled them out the door by main force.

"You were splendid," Penelope said as they walked home. Credit where credit was due, even if her emotions were in a miserable whirl. "Really splendid. I couldn't think what to say, and you—"

"I had to do *something*. You were so upset."

It was so far from what she had expected him to say that for a moment she was speechless. "Surely—surely you would have helped her anyway."

Nev shrugged. "Jack Bailey knew the risks when he broke the law. I would have tried to help, but I doubt I would have gone so far."

Penelope felt at once guilty and pleased, and guilty for feeling pleased.

Sir Jasper watched the constable's deputies disperse like a pack of hounds in search of a scent. He smiled, thinking of the foxes they would be bringing back with them. He had been too pessimistic; the district was not spiraling out of his control at all.

He was so pleased that when he heard the clatter of an approaching cart and saw that it was the Bedlows with Mrs. Bailey in tow, he even greeted them with enthusiasm. "This is the biggest breakthrough we've had in years! You should be very proud, Lady Bedlow."

"What—what do you mean?" the countess asked.

"The beggar's talked! He's given us names, places—we'll have the whole gang!" It hadn't even been that difficult. Sir Jasper had merely explained the situation to Bailey: on the one hand, languishing in jail with room-and-board fees piling up, then being sent to the Assizes and a quick hanging, with his wife and children left to fend for themselves in a cruel world; on the other, going home to his fond family that very afternoon.

The Bedlows did not seem to realize what great news this was. Bedlow actually laughed. "Come now, Sir Jasper, you've frightened the poor man into giving false information! His wife assures me that he was merely passing through the woods on an ill-advised shortcut to the home of one of your laborers, and when he was injured, was afraid to speak for fear of being suspected."

"And you believe her?" Sir Jasper listened incredulously as the man rambled on, assuring him of Bailey's long history of loyal labor and honesty. The new earl was even more gullible than his father.

He looked at the Cit countess to see how she was taking her husband's idiocy, but she simply looked white and miserable. Still sulking about her husband's actress, then. Sir Jasper smiled. At this rate they'd be separated by Michaelmas, and without his father-in-law's pocketbook to back him, Lord Bedlow would be begging Sir Jasper to take Loweston—and his sister—off his hands by the New Year.

"I'm sorry, Lord Bedlow," he interrupted, "but he was honest enough about where to find their store of arms, nets and snares, and the pitch they used to blacken their faces. I'm afraid there is no question of his guilt."

Mrs. Bailey's hand flew to her mouth. "Oh, he didn't peach! He wouldn't!"

The look on Bedlow's face was extremely gratifying. "I suppose you had the right of it, Sir Jasper," he said finally. "I ought not to be so credulous, yet surely it is better to err on the side of caution in these cases. The penalties are so harsh, and the crime—"

"The crime is black," Sir Jasper said. "Good God, have you no thought for your wife and family? You would give armed men license to roam the countryside?"

"They would not need guns if being taken did not mean assured transportation."

"The thieving blackguards must be stopped somehow, or they will tear the foundations of English society up by its roots!" Sir Jasper had thought, at first, that it would be all right to let Lord Bedlow keep Loweston. But the young puppy had quickly proven to be dangerously susceptible to the histrionics and sedition of his laborers. They wanted to see it all go up in flames, everything Sir Jasper had worked for his whole life—

He closed his eyes for a moment and breathed deeply, clearing the scent of the dirty Seine from his nostrils. It was all right. He had things well in hand.

"We will never agree on that point," Bedlow said. "In the meantime, I will arrange for a barrister to represent my people. I know you will treat them with fairness. Do you think you might tell me who has been accused?"

"I prefer to keep that information private until I am assured they are in custody," Sir Jasper said. "Mrs. Bailey, you won't mind waiting here? It should only be an hour or two, and then I shall be happy to return your husband to you."

The Bedlows waited too, arranging themselves on a low wall near the jail. Sir Jasper couldn't think why; they both looked dull and anxious, and barely spoke to each other.

Sir Jasper's interference was probably unnecessary. They would have drifted apart on their own, and as for heirs—he found it hard to imagine that governessy countess even allowing her husband his conjugal rights, although the memory of them giggling and glowing in the doorway, that day after the rainstorm, gave Sir Jasper a touch of unease. He comforted himself with the thought that she was so thin and pale, she was more than likely barren. Mary had had that same fragile look, after the last miscarriage.

At length all seven members of the Loweston gang were brought to the little jail. The last one, Sir Jasper saw with annoyance, provoked an absolute firestorm of misplaced sentiment in the Bedlows.

"Sir Jasper, please, she's only a girl!" The countess's distress made her common little face even more unattractive.

"A girl who is evidently hell-bent on following in her radical father's footsteps," Sir Jasper said as Josie Cusher was led past them, fighting and glaring and generally behaving like the disagreeably pert piece of trash that she was. "Do you wish me to circumvent the law? Perhaps her fate will persuade back to the path of righteousness other children whose feet have begun to stray."

He signaled the constable to release Jack Bailey. The man came out on his crutch, his head bent and his shoulders sagging. Sir Jasper didn't blame him; a gentleman would never have betrayed his word in that fashion, and although Jack Bailey was not a gentleman, he seemed instinctively to feel that he had done something shameful.

Mrs. Bailey hastened forward to help him. "Oh, Jack! It was wrong to do it, but the children will be glad to see you."

Aaron Smith opened the Cushers' door as soon as they knocked. "Your lordship, your ladyship." He nodded his head respectfully. "Is there news?"

"Good morning, Aaron," Nev said. "Not yet. Is Agnes home?"

"Aaron, is that Lord Bedlow?" Agnes Cusher rushed to the door with red, swollen eyes. She clutched at Nev's arm, and Penelope saw that she had been twisting her lavender satin ribbon, Josie's gift, in her hands. It was ragged. "Please, your lordship, you won't let them send my girl away? My little Josie—" Her voice broke. She did not look at Penelope.

"We are doing what we can," Nev said. "But I don't know that it will do any good if she is really guilty. Agnes, tell me— *was* she part of the gang?"

"She helped them with little things—making nets, carrying messages to the men who work for the butchers in London. She—she went into the woods once or twice, because she's small and handy. I didn't want her to do it, but how could I stop her? Joe was gone and we would have starved—

the baby would have died—" She twined the strip of satin around her palm until her hand turned white.

"It wasn't your fault, Aggie." Aaron reached out and covered her hands with his. "It's not your fault."

Penelope looked for Kit. The boy had been crying too—he was sitting in the corner now, staring. She went over to kneel by him. "Good morning, Kit."

"Kit, don't bother her ladyship," Agnes said.

Penelope looked up, surprised. "He isn't bothering me. I just—"

"Kit, come here." And Kit went past Penelope to his mother, who picked him up and held him tight.

Penelope stood, brushing the dirt from her gown. They all knew that Jack Bailey was arrested on her information then. They all hated her.

"*Aggie*," Aaron said in a low tone. "She's overset, your ladyship. Don't hold it against Josie."

"I wouldn't," Penelope said, more sharply than she meant to. "Of course I won't."

He looked at her carefully. "Good."

She bristled, but—he seemed to believe her, at least.

"As I said," Nev told them evenly, "*we* will do everything we can for Josie. Are you doing all right for money?"

Aaron's eyes were on Agnes. "I'll take care of them."

It was at Harry Spratt's house that the worst blow was struck. Young Helen Spratt opened the door dry-eyed and seemingly collected, but it took only a few sentences for her fevered state of mind to become clear. "I'd like to kill Jack Bailey," she raged. Penelope remembered the taciturn laborers of their early visits, and marveled at how stress stripped away the discretion and reverence. "I'd like to murder that old son-of-a-bitch. You were coming to free him, and he couldn't be a man for another hour? My Harry would never have peached on *him*. They all risked everything to save the bugger from that trap. It was Jack Bailey that recruited the half of them, anyway! We were always hungry after the commons were enclosed, but Harry thought we'd get by honest until Jack told him how easy it was, how safe, how sure! And there didn't seem to be no harm—there's plenty of game for us all, and if rich folk in London want to pay us for a few rabbits, who does it hurt? When the baby was sick, we could buy him some milk! It seemed so little to take, when we had to get rid of our cow—"

It was inane, but Penelope grasped on the one thing she didn't understand, just as an excuse to not hear the horrible sound of Helen Spratt's misery and anger for a few seconds. "Why did you have to get rid of your cow?"

Helen stared at Penelope as if she'd been dropped on her head as a baby. "You can't go on the parish if you've got a cow. We had a pig too, and some geese."

"But if you were doing so well, why did you want to go on the parish?" Penelope asked.

"You can't get a job around here if you aren't on the parish. That's how it works. Mr. Snively gives us our dole, and Tom Kedge pays him for the men's work. Mr. Kedge won't hire you if you aren't on the parish. It's cheaper for him, see, so he gives Snively a little something to grease the wheels, and it's all sunshine and daisies for everyone."

Penelope rocked backwards. Why hadn't anyone told her this before? How many of the farmers had had to give up what little they had, just to keep their jobs?

"Is this true?" Nev said. "Why didn't anyone tell us?"

Helen nodded. "It's God's own truth." She didn't answer the second question. Penelope supposed she thought the answer was obvious. Why *would* anyone tell them?

"We will certainly investigate this further," Nev said. "Thank you for bringing it to our attention. But we came to tell you that we're doing everything we can for Harry, and in the meantime you must stay strong and not lose hope."

Helen just shook her head. "Harry's never coming home again."

Nev was hiding in the library. He had been reassuring and masterful all morning, and he could not do it one moment longer. His boots were discarded on the floor, he was using his folded coat as a cushion from the stone embrasure of the window seat, his waistcoat was unbuttoned, and he was a third of the way through the first volume of *Chronicles of an Illustrious House; or the Peer, the Lawyer, and the Hunchback*.

So of course Penelope must walk in and find him. He swung his feet onto the floor hastily, trying to smooth his hair and hide the book at the same time, and she actually smiled. It was the first time he'd seen her smile in days, he realized with a shock.

"What are you reading?" She was still standing in the doorway with her hand on the frame.

There was no point in lying. He held up the book. "Minerva Press. I lied about it being Louisa who reads them."

Her eyebrows flew up and her mouth opened with a sort of incredulous amusement, as if she could not wait to begin mocking him. He was conscious of an overwhelming desire to kiss her, coupled with a despairing conviction that he would always look the fool in front of her. "I read *Farmer's Tour through the East of England* last week. I just—I can't be serious *all* the time, Penelope."

She flinched away. "Am I such a killjoy?"

"*No.*" Why must he always make things worse? And she *wasn't*. There had been very little of joy between them in recent days, it seemed, but he was sure it wasn't because of her. She was—sweet and sly, and she surprised him with how happy she could be, over the smallest things. "No, Penny, come here."

Her mouth had folded sadly in on itself, but she came, and she let him pull her down till they were both stretched along the window seat, her back to his chest and her head on his shoulder. He ignored the hard wall at his back and breathed in the scent of her. "I never meant that. I only meant—I know I could never do what you and Percy do. I get restless, trying to read and make plans and manage money. I—"

He could feel her turn thoughtful. "What have you been doing instead?"

"Well . . ." He felt suddenly embarrassed. "I got bored, so I've been visiting Tom Kedge and the laborers. And—"

"That day you came home sunburned. Where were you?"

He felt silly and caught-out, like a little boy trying on his father's clothes. "I helped harvest the wheat on the home farm."

"I hate doing all that." He could hear the smile in her voice. "I hate trying to be friendly to people and standing outside in the hot sun. I'd rather stay in an office all day looking at books and talking with a friend."

Nev was startled by this view of things.

Penelope tilted her head. "You did well in school. Didn't you study?"

"I never did very well in mathematics. Percy coached me for the Tripos—that's the Cambridge mathematics examination—and I barely passed even so. I did much better in Latin and music. I like books so long as there are things happening. Farming equipment—"

"—is dull." But she didn't sound disapproving, just amused. "Didn't you ever tag along when Percy helped his father in his office?"

"Of course. At first. I wanted to do whatever Percy did. And Mr. Garrett was always willing to explain things to me. Even farming equipment doesn't seem so dull to an eight-year-old boy." He shrugged. "My father found me there one day, entering receipts into one of the ledgers, and explained that gentlemen didn't interest themselves in petty financial details."

Penelope swallowed. "I never know what to say to things like that." She tried to laugh. "Because on the one hand, that leads to bankruptcy, and on the other, it's true, and I'm not a lady."

"Why does it bother you so much? You spend so much time trying to be a lady, and—"

She tensed in his arms. "And failing?"

"*No.* And missing chances to be happy."

She was silent for a few moments, and he wondered if he had gone too far. Then she pushed out of his arms. He froze, but she didn't storm off—she just sat on the edge of the window seat and didn't look at him or touch him, as if—as if she had to have her defenses about her, to say this. "I can't even imagine what it would be like, not to try to be a lady," she said. "I've been trying ever since my first day of school. You— you might not understand this because you've always been a gentleman. But my mother scrubbed floors for a living, once. I would meet people who had been her friends, and they had no teeth. They didn't know how to read. I was a fat, freckled little girl, and I sounded like any street urchin in London when I opened my mouth. You've no notion how it feels, to go to the opera with your mother in your prettiest dresses, and a beautiful thin blonde girl sweeps by on the arm of a man you're sure must be a lord, and she says in the most perfect English, 'La, look at those people! What mushrooms!'" Penelope sighed, and made a hopeless gesture, as if what she was trying to explain was too basic to put into words. "Oh, I don't know, Nev. I know those sound like a child's reasons. They *are* a child's reasons, but I don't—I don't know how not to care."

He didn't know what to say to that, but he wanted suddenly to tell her something else. "I missed you, when you didn't come to dinner these past weeks."

"Did you really?" A pleased, uncertain smile spread over her face.

"Desperately."

She beamed at him. "I'm so sorry. I never imagined you would care in the least." There it was, that sudden simple joy he never expected from her. It was in every line of her face, and affection burst through his veins like drunkenness. "Nev?" she asked, and he would have given her anything. "Will you read to me?"

He blinked. "You want me to read to you?"

She nodded. "You—you're good at it."

She had only heard him read aloud once—Byron, at her parents' house. She didn't even like Byron. He had supposed she was thinking him the most frivolous fellow alive, and instead she had liked it. For the first time in days, Nev felt that life was full of pleasant surprises. He grinned at her. "Let me dig up our copy of Malory."

When he had found it, he returned to the window seat. He glanced at her to see where she wanted to sit; to his surprise she crawled between his legs again and settled there. So he rested the book on her lap and his chin on her shoulder and began to read. She was soft and warm and laughed in all the right places, and when he bent and kissed her hair she made a contented humming sound in the back of her throat.

When Penelope asked for Tom Kedge's books and the Poor Law Authority's, they were given over to her with a blithe confidence that made her half suspect the whole story was an ugly rumor concocted by the laborers. But it only took her and Mr. Garrett an hour or two to see that it was true, or mostly true. Kedge's salary payments were made exclusively to the Poor Authority, which confirmed that he hired only Authority workers. That was bad enough, but Mr. Snively recorded those same payments in the Authority ledgers as rather smaller, which meant either that he was indeed receiving bribes or that he was embezzling.

But they could not accuse Kedge of graft without proof. Penelope and Mr. Garrett calculated that it would cost Kedge an extra two hundred pounds a year to pay a fair wage. Surely if they lowered his rent by a hundred and fifty pounds to compensate, that would be more than fair.

Mr. Garrett agreed to discuss the matter with Kedge first; perhaps that way, he would not feel threatened.

Nev was surprised but not too concerned when a servant came to tell him that he was wanted in Mr. Garrett's office. But when he neared the office and heard raised voices, he started to worry.

"Then you had better tell Lord Bedlow at once," Percy was saying, "because I will certainly not—"

"You weaselly rascal! Don't take that high-and-mighty tone with me!"

They both stopped talking when Nev entered the room, but Percy's white face and the vindictive malice in Kedge's eyes were impossible to hide.

"Lord Bedlow," Percy began, "Mr. Kedge has flatly refused to consider your proposal. When I persisted, he tried to blackmail me—"

Kedge interrupted him again. "Your lordship, you cannot be serious about this plan to raise wages so high! Your father would never have asked it of me."

"My father was an excellent man," Nev said, "but he would never have asked economy of anyone, least of all himself. That is partly why the district has been brought so low."

Mr. Kedge drew himself up, all twenty stone of him. "Your father was a great man, and he deserves more respect from you. *I* deserve more from you. *I* kept this place going in '16, *I* bought up the land and planted the hedgerows when no one else would! I have lived here, boy and man, for nigh on fifty years. And now you've a mind to tell me how to run my farm, when you've bothered about Loweston for less than two months!"

Perhaps at another time Nev would have felt the justice of that. Now he felt nothing but rage. He opened his mouth to remind Kedge just who was tenant and who was lord.

Percy was before him. "Mr. Kedge, you forget yourself! I asked his lordship to step in so that we might have done with this melodrama, not so that you could insult him. If Lord Bedlow had come into the title years ago, we would not be in this mess now."

Nev stared at Percy.

Kedge took a step back. "Indeed, my lord, I am sorry. Forgive me my impertinence. I've been loyal to the Bedlows for fifty years, and I ain't fixing to change."

"That is very good of you," Nev said without much sincerity. "Perhaps now you can tell me what the devil is going on."

But Kedge was warming to his theme. "There's some in this district as think their bread is buttered on the other side. Some as seem to have forgotten their lord and begun looking to Sir Jasper. That rat Snively, for instance, running to Sir Jasper with every bit of gossip he hears. I'm not that type. You know what I mean, don't you, Mr. Garrett?"

Percy didn't look at Kedge. His eyes were fixed on Nev. "Nev, I'm so sorry—"

"Mr. Garrett makes a fine show of loyalty. But he isn't so very loyal when you aren't watching. Everyone knows Sir Jasper is sweet on Lady Louisa. Well, he'd hardly be so eager to make a match of it if he knew what she'd been up to with the steward, would he?"

"You had better come out and say what you mean," Percy said.

"If you please. I saw the two of them at your grandfather's

ruin, my lord, kissing and sighing. But I kept my mouth shut, because I'm a Loweston man."

"Forgive me if I am not more grateful that instead of coming to me, you chose to try to blackmail my steward into working against my interests," Nev said coldly. His thoughts seemed to come from far away. "Get out. We will resume this discussion at a later date."

Kedge got up smugly and began moving toward the door. "And we *will* resume it."

"Just remember. As long as I'm a Loweston man, Sir Jasper doesn't know. If I stop being one . . ."

"For God's sake, get out!" Percy said.

When Kedge was gone they stood there, staring at one another. "Is it true?" Nev barely recognized his own voice.

"Yes," Percy said, and Nev barely recognized his voice either. "I'm sorry, Nev, I am, but I love her—"

"Oh, Christ." Nev wondered if there had ever been a time when this news would have made him happy. Even in the midst of his horror and disbelief, he was obscurely ashamed to think that there might not have been. "Here I've been worrying about you and Penelope, and all the time you've been sneaking around with Louisa—"

Percy stared. "Me and Penelope? Nev, Penelope is your *wife!*"

"Louisa's my baby sister. You had no problem seducing *her.*"

"I didn't *seduce* her. I wouldn't have—it was only a few kisses."

That was a relief, at any rate. Nev did not feel relieved. "One would be enough to ruin her."

"I know." Percy looked away. "Christ, I know. I never meant for this to happen, but she was so unhappy. So very unhappy. I thought there could be no harm in spending time with her, and then—I want to marry her, Nev. I *will* marry her, if you'll agree to it. I may not be what she deserves, but I'm what she wants, and that's good enough for me."

Nev felt a stab of guilt that he had not found time to deal with Louisa's unhappiness, and then sharp unreasonable anger that Percy had. "It's not good enough for *me*, damn it! She's *seventeen*, Percy. Seventeen. She hasn't got the foggiest notion of what she wants or what it will mean to be married to you. She's just a kid, and if it comes out she's been meeting with you alone, she'll be ruined! She doesn't understand what that means, but *you* do! What were you thinking?"

"I wasn't thinking. I just knew—she was the one for me. She always has been, I think. I couldn't say no."

"Are you suggesting that my sister was the instigator in this?" Nev said in a low, dangerous voice.

Percy almost smiled. "Come off it, Nev, of course she was. Louisa's been waiting her whole life to plot an assignation."

Of course she had. Poor irrepressible Louisa. Unlike Penelope, she had never learned not to rebel against things she could not change. Nev had wanted so badly to keep it that way, but now—"And you were right on the spot to take advantage of it, weren't you? How do you propose to keep her, Percy? I know you never wanted to be a steward. Were you planning to take her to your lodgings and feed her off what you could win at piquet? I daresay Louisa would think it a grand adventure—at first."

Percy flushed, a sure sign he was about to lose his temper. "Nev, please. Of course not. I never did want to be a steward, but—I'll be honest. I'm here because when you left, I didn't get invited so many places. People started to look at me askance. The whole thing was a house of cards, and it fell apart. But I've tried stewarding now, and I like it all right. We're not kids anymore. I'm willing to settle down. I've been doing some translations, and that's bringing in some money. I'd never spend a penny of Louisa's principal, and the interest would make sure we did all right—"

"You want Louisa to live on two or three hundred a year? Why do you think I fought so hard to save Loweston and her dowry, if not so that she could make a good match and never have to worry about money again?" Nev remembered those few weeks before Penelope agreed to marry him—his grim visions of Louisa in shabby lodgings and a made-over dress, cajoling duns and hoarding tallow candle-ends, all her happy glow and piratical daydreams and enormous cherry-trimmed bonnets brushed away like the bloom on a butterfly's wing. That was why he had worked so hard to save Loweston, for her and his mother.

And now through his own fault it was all for nothing. He should never have been such friends with Percy; he should never have let Penelope hire him. He should have seen Louisa was unhappy so she wouldn't seize on this; he should have been paying attention and found out what was going on before Kedge. "That money was to find her a husband who could take care of her, not to go to some damn fortune hunter who—"

But that was the limit of Percy's forbearance. "How dare you? You canting *hypocrite!*" he said through clenched teeth. "When a month before your marriage you were gossiping about your bride-to-be's dowry with your *mistress!*"

Nev opened his mouth to make a hot retort—and saw Penelope standing in the doorway. If he lived to be a hundred, he would never forget the frozen, humiliated look on her face.

"I—" she began, and stopped. "I heard that Mr. Kedge was gone and I wanted to know how it went. I—I'll just be going—" Her voice broke, and she turned and fled down the corridor.

Nev ran to the doorway. "Penelope!" he shouted after her retreating back. "Penelope, wait!"

"Oh, God," Percy said, aghast. "I didn't see her, I never would have—I know the two of you—"

Nev turned back and looked at his best friend of almost

fifteen years. "Get out of my house. Tonight. And don't ever go near my sister again." Then he ran after Penelope. He could hear her footsteps on the marble floor of the entrance hall a ways off. Then they stopped. He sprinted after her and stopped short in the doorway of the great hall.

She was wrapped up in the arms of a greatcoated stranger. He walked towards them more slowly. "Penelope?"

She turned but didn't quite disentangle herself from the stranger. Her face was streaked with tears, but underneath it was glowing. She smiled at him as if she couldn't stop. "Lord Bedlow, may I present Edward Macaulay."

Fifteen

Edward Macaulay had a broad, sensible, Scottish face, and broad, sensible, Scottish shoulders. His sandy hair was kept unfashionably short and brushed carefully back from his forehead, even though it was clear that had he allowed it to grow, it would have curled riotously in the best modern style without any prompting. He looked like a steady, dependable man, and Nev hated him on sight.

"How do you do?" Nev's hand was more tanned and callused than it had ever been in his life; it looked like an indolent child's clasped in Macaulay's sturdy, ink-stained fingers.

"Very well, thank you." Macaulay sounded downright hostile. "Yourself?" He looked Nev up and down with a scrutiny that was almost insolent.

"I'm well. Are you planning on staying long?" Wonderful. A minute into the conversation and he already sounded petty and childish.

"You're staying at least a day or two, Edward, aren't you?" Penelope's eyes were fixed anxiously on Macaulay's face.

Macaulay smiled familiarly down at her. "Since you ask me to, I am. I've brought your furniture too. It's outside. There's four carts of it. Penny, whatever did you want a great ugly *chinoiserie* settee for?"

"It was a joke," Penelope muttered, glancing at Nev, and he remembered his suggestion that they get everything in gilt and bamboo. She had done something sweet and funny for him, and now that was spoiled too.

"Wonderful. Thank you," Nev said, not meaning it in the

slightest. "Then perhaps the housekeeper can show you to your room while I have a word with my wife."

Edward didn't move. Instead, he looked to Penelope for guidance. Nev gritted his teeth.

"Yes, Edward, do go," she said. "You're covered in dust, and you must be dying to wash and change. When you're feeling more the thing, we can have a much more comfortable coze."

"Dear Penelope," Edward said fondly. "Always sensible."

Nev knew he must have imagined the flash of annoyance that crossed Penelope's face.

When Edward had been escorted from the room by the housekeeper, Penelope turned to Nev. She didn't meet his eyes. "Well, what did Kedge say?"

"Penelope, please. What Percy said—"

"It's quite all right. It's natural that you should have—"

"It was that night at Vauxhall. Your name only came up because I couldn't stop staring at you."

"Nev, please don't."

"Damn it, no. Not this time. You were crying, you can't tell me—"

"I can tell you whatever I please. Was crying not enough? Or won't you be satisfied until I've also admitted that I'm a silly girl who is ashamed to be caught out daydreaming? Don't tell me pretty lies just because I've made it obvious that I want to hear them. Being sensible and facing the truth is all I *have*."

"Penelope, I wouldn't lie to you. I didn't realize it at the time, but from the moment I saw you, you made me want to see you again. Sometimes I think I could talk to you forever and never get tired of it. You're all I have anymore, and somehow it's enough—"

"Stop," she said, and she sounded frightened.

"You wouldn't leave me, Penelope, would you?" He regretted the words as soon as they were out of his mouth; they were plaintive and selfish. And yet he waited for her answer without breathing.

"Leave you?" She looked really taken aback. "Why on earth would I leave you? Have you done something?"

"Nothing new. I just—Macaulay—"

Her face grew very cold. "So that's what this is all about. You're afraid I'll leave you for Edward. Given that your most recent mistress is currently living a mile off, I'm inclined to say that Mr. Garrett was right and you are a hypocrite. Now tell me what the two of you were quarreling over *this* time."

It all came flooding back, and Nev could not understand how he had forgotten. "He's been meeting secretly with Louisa. Kedge knows, and he's blackmailing us with it. Percy wants to marry her."

To Nev's relief, Penelope saw at once all the horror of their situation. She put a hand on the wall to steady herself. "Oh, God, how can Mr. Garrett have been so indiscreet? Do you plan to allow the match?"

"Certainly not. Louisa is seventeen. She's too young to know her own mind."

Penelope nodded doubtfully, and he remembered that she was nineteen and that her parents had let her make her own choice. Well, it had been unpardonably foolish of them— only see what had come of it. Only see how miserable she was. If he had had the keeping of her, Penelope would never have got within fifty feet of a wastrel like him.

"Then what are we going to do?" she asked. "If we don't do something to scotch the scandal, Kedge will have the upper hand of us forever."

"I don't know. But I'm not going to sacrifice Louisa, not even for every laborer at Loweston."

Unexpectedly, she smiled at him. "Well, we've got six months to work something out before the lease is up. I'll think about it while I'm talking to Edward, and maybe tonight we can discuss it some more."

"You're going to tell Edward—"

She stared at him. "Of course I wouldn't tell Edward about your sister."

He pulled her to him and kissed her, hard. She was breathless when he pulled away, and he rejoiced in it. "Just remember, you will find me harder to give back than I was to buy."

"I didn't *buy* you," she said. But her cheeks were flushed.

Penelope's mind was in a whirl; she found it difficult to concentrate on her conversation with Edward. Everything was so muddled and awful: those men in jail, the laborers under Kedge's thumb, her marriage a shambles—and Nev's sister, poised on the brink of ruin. How could Louisa have done this to her family? How could she have done this to Nev?

But Penelope, if she admitted it, envied Louisa too. Louisa who was madly in love, Louisa whom Mr. Garrett loved madly enough to throw caution to the winds.

Penelope had tried her whole life to be rational and sensible, to never make a scene, to accept the world as it was. And it had never got her respect or admiration or anything she wanted. It had only got her ignored, or worse, taken for granted.

Nev had been afraid, just now, that she might do something stupid and leave him for Edward. If Nev had ever met Edward, he would have known there was no danger of him doing anything so shocking, but that was beside the point. The point was that Nev might say he wanted to talk to her forever or such rot, but really, it was just as he said: she was all he had. She was a good partner for him, and he was afraid to lose her.

Just then Penelope didn't want a rational, amicable marriage of equals. She wanted Nev to tell her he couldn't live without her; that her eyes were like stars and her hands were like a flock of wild birds and a hundred other improbable similes; that his pulse quickened at the very sight of her; that he would die without her . . . and he never would. Not honestly. Because he liked her but he didn't love her, because he had married her for her money and that was all there was for girls like Penelope.

A thought struck Penelope like a blow. Mr. Garrett was here at Penelope's insistence. Why had she meddled? It seemed as if every time she followed her heart instead of her head, she made things worse.

Edward's voice broke through her reverie. "Penelope, is everything all right? I just asked you four times how you found the weather in Norfolk."

"I'm sorry. It's been a difficult week."

"Poor Penny! Do you want to talk about it?"

"No. I want to hear about you. What brings you to this part of England?"

He looked at her in surprise. "I came to see you. Why else would I be here?"

Her face heated. She felt thoughtless, and guilty. "I thought perhaps—on business—you did not write to say you were coming—"

He looked down, fidgeting. "Penelope—"

"Yes?"

"I was passing through on business, it's true, but I might have gone a shorter way. I convinced your father to let me oversee the transport of the furniture. I didn't write because—I wasn't sure of my welcome when I came here tonight. I hoped you would see me—Heavens, how I hoped—but I thought if I came in person there would be less chance to turn me away. Those engravings—how can you ever forgive me?"

She had forgotten them in the joy of seeing him. And now—in the rush of relief at the knowledge that he had been as afraid to lose her friendship as she was to lose his, in the heady sensation of being *wanted*, just for herself—she had already forgiven him. It was weak of her, but there it was. "If I didn't forgive you, I couldn't talk to you, and I've been wanting so to talk to you."

He smiled at her, a sad smile. "I must have been mad. I *was* mad—all those years, all our plans. I couldn't bear it. I wanted to hurt you as you had hurt me. It was not the act of a gentleman."

"I'm so very sorry, Edward," she said around the lump in her throat. "It is I who am to blame, I who should beg forgiveness. I broke my word to you. And then I did not know how to tell you—it made my letters short and cold, when they should have been so much more. You've been so much to me, all my life."

He reached out and took her hands in his. They were warm, capable, well-shaped hands, nearly as familiar to her as her own. Affection welled up within her at the sight, dear affection and a thousand memories. And yet there was no spark, no sense of physical recognition when he touched her. There never had been, and she had never known what was missing.

Penelope tried to imagine being married to him, sharing a bed with him. It did not repulse her; it only left her feeling blank. Would she ever have realized that something vital was absent? Or would she have gone her whole life believing that anything more—flame, fire, passion—was a lie dreamt up by horrid novelists?

"Penelope, I could forgive everything, if I believed you were happy. But you aren't. You look like you used to on school vacations."

She was surprised that he'd noticed how miserable and thin she had been those years at school. He had never said a word about it. God, how she wanted to tell him everything! But he would hate Nev. "I *am* happy, Edward." Her voice sounded false to her own ears; could Edward hear it? "It's only that there have been troubles with the tenants, and I'm tired."

He nodded seriously. "All over the country, there's been disquiet. That's why—" He flushed and smiled. "That's why I'm to be director of Mr. Meath's woolen mill in Norwich."

"Oh, Edward, how wonderful for you!"

His smile broadened. "I'm young for it, but Mr. Meath assures me he has every confidence in me."

"Edward, that's wonderful!" Penelope repeated. "But what's that to do with the disquiet in the countryside?"

"Well, it's not entirely an honor. They've been having some trouble with trade unionists. The old director stepped down because his wife was afraid for their children, and all the other candidates were family men too."

So Edward was getting promoted because she had not married him. She wasn't sure what to feel about that. She wished she knew what Edward felt about it. "Will it be safe?"

He smiled at her. "I'll be all right. But will you? What has happened?"

She settled for part of the truth. "It's only—Nev's father did not do well by the estate, and everyone is so poor and has suffered so much here. And so much of my dowry went to pay old debts or into settlements that we haven't the funds to do everything we need. And Edward, you should see the books—they use a sort of simple double-entry system!"

He stared. "But then how do you know when you've wasted money on a project, or when—"

"You can't!" His horror made her laugh. "I knew you would understand. Here, I've got to show you, you'll die—Molly, come with us, I want to show Mr. Macaulay the books."

He put on his spectacles to read them and was properly horrified. For half an hour it was quite like old times. She found herself telling him all about Captain Trelawney, and that first night she and Nev had heard the poachers. "He didn't seem bothered by it at all. And then he said, 'Well, usually they don't hit each other in the dark!'" she told him, giggling. She waited for him to laugh too, but he didn't.

He stared at her with a faintly shocked expression, pushing his glasses down his nose to look at her over them in a motion so familiar she shivered. "You mean there are men running around here *shooting* each other for game? That's hardly a laughing matter, Penelope."

Penelope had forgotten how low Edward could make her feel, when he looked at her in that way. "Well, I know that. It was the *way* he said it that was funny . . ." She knew she sounded like a chastened schoolgirl and hated it. "Actually, you're right, it isn't funny. They've caught most of the poachers now, and they'll transport them all if we can't stop it. You should see their wives and children. And mothers: one of the villains is a nine-year-old girl. It's dreadful. They're half mad with grief and rage." It all rushed back, and Penelope felt very cold. She wished Nev were here.

"Is that why you were crying when I came in?"

She looked away.

"We used to tell each other everything," he said sadly.

And Penelope realized something else. She had never told Edward everything. There were a million things she had never told him, ways she had felt, things she had dreamed. She had never told him about wanting to run off to be a sailor. It wasn't even that she had been afraid he would condemn her, though he would have. It was that she had condemned herself. She had never told anyone those things, until Nev. She had tried to show Edward, along with everyone else, the person she had wanted to be.

They were the same, she and Edward; they had wanted the same things, respected the same things. If she had married Edward, she would have gone on being drab, practical Penelope forever. And she would have thought that she was living her best, truest self. Never joking or crying or making love in the middle of the day. Speaking seriously on serious subjects. And the part of her that had sobbed and beaten the pillow and wanted to be a sailor at Miss Mardling's would have grown smaller and smaller until it faded away entirely.

Penelope found that she couldn't quite bear the thought. She did not want to be ashamed of her feelings anymore.

Edward leaned closer to her and spoke quietly. "Penelope, I—I know that this is very improper, and if you never wish to speak of it again we shall not. But I want you to know that if you wished to leave him, you would always have a home with me."

She stared. It was the last thing she would ever have expected him to say. "L—leave him?" she said, louder than she meant. She glanced at Molly, bent over her sewing at the far end of the room, as she had sat through all Penelope's tête-à-têtes with Edward for years. The girl hadn't looked up. "But Edward, he's my husband!"

He flushed and took his glasses off with an abrupt gesture. "I know it's wrong. But any fool can see he doesn't deserve you. He's making you miserable."

She wanted to defend Nev, but she was still too shocked by Edward's shocking proposal. It was so very unlike him. "But Edward, I would be ruined. Think of the scandal! Think of what Mr. Meath would say!"

"I have thought of it," he said grimly. "I have been thinking of it ever since I walked into this house and saw you crying. But I would face it for you, Penelope. I love you. I always have. You shall always have a place to go as long as I am breathing."

Was it possible that all the things she had never felt for Edward, he felt for her? Or did he love her like a sister? It didn't matter; he had just offered to sacrifice everything he believed and everything he wanted for her. He was her oldest friend and—she found herself crying again.

His hands tightened on hers. "Penny! Give me the word: we'll go now, this moment—"

She yanked her hands away just as Nev walked into the room. She saw his stunned expression, saw the blazoning of guilt on Edward's face, and began to laugh through her tears. "Oh, Nev. What a Gothic novel our life has become!"

He just stared at her. So did Edward. She was becoming a madwoman. Perhaps Nev would lock her in the attic and hire Agnes Cusher as her keeper.

"Penelope," Nev said. "May I speak to you a moment?"

"Of course." She wondered what she would tell him. Would she tell him what Edward had said? "Edward, if you'll excuse us a moment." She followed him into the steward's sitting room.

"Amy's woken up," he said. "They think—they think she might be all right."

A mingled pang of relief and fear smote her. She did not know what to say. This, then, was the source of his dazed look. Like everything else, it had nothing to do with her.

"She's asked for me. I—I have to go. But—"

"Of course you must go," she said, numbly. She wished he *would* go, and leave her in peace.

But he didn't. He stood there, his cinnamon hair falling into his downcast eyes, his hands knotting together. "Penelope—I know I've no right to ask, especially tonight. But I can't go without you. It wouldn't be proper."

"What exactly is proper about taking your wife to visit your mistress?" Penelope snapped.

Nev looked stricken. And he was right, of course. She could not understand why she hadn't seen it at once. He could not visit Miss Wray alone without scandal.

Miss Wray had been Nev's constant companion for a year and she had almost died.

Penelope passed a hand over her eyes. "I'm sorry. It's been a long evening. Of course you must go. Let me get my cloak and my boots."

"Thank you, Penelope." The gratitude in his voice brought fresh tears to her eyes. "I—thank you."

Amy was awake. Amy would very likely live.

Nev knew he should be overjoyed. He should not be re-playing in his mind, over and over, the moment he had walked into the steward's room and seen Penelope crying, seen that bastard Macaulay leaning toward her and holding her perfect hands in his. Of course they'd been in the damn steward's room: the room that inevitably made him feel like a dullard, the one room in his own house where he did not be-long and never would.

Edward belonged there; anyone could see that. What if Edward belonged with Penelope? She let him see her cry. She had never let Nev see that, not willingly.

And now he had driven a deeper wedge between himself and his wife by asking her to go with him to see Amy. It was hardly a request calculated to endear to her either him or Loweston. But Amy had asked for him. She would be fright-ened and alone, and he could not fail this responsibility too.

He did not know what to say, so he said nothing, only watched his wife's face and tried to trace the tear tracks in the moonlight. He couldn't.

Amy was thin and pale and dirty, and her eyes were full of unhappiness. She had always seemed so happy before.

But she smiled a little when she saw him. "Nev." It was her, her voice—raspy and weak, yes, but not that strange restless mumble it had been this past week. Something eased inside Nev.

He smiled back. "Amy. I'm so glad you're all right."

"Why am I here? Did you—?"

He shook his head, ashamed. "Your mother asked Mrs. Brown to help her remove you to the country, and Mrs.

Brown asked Penelope to take you in. Neither of us had any idea it was you until you arrived. You gave me the fright of my life, Amy—we all thought you were done for."

"Did I make a lot of trouble for you with your wife?" Amy asked in a small voice.

"Not really." Nev was fairly certain it was a lie. "Penelope's been very good about the whole thing."

Amy shrugged a little. He could see the bones in her shoulders. "Doesn't love you."

"That's not fair." Nev knew he shouldn't upset Amy when she was still so weak, but he found he was quite incapable of letting such an insult to Penelope pass. That is—of course she didn't love him. But that wasn't why she had been so kind about Amy—was it? "She's been good about it because she's a kind, principled girl. It would be a dreadful scandal for her if it got about you were here, and she hasn't breathed a word of reproach to me, only sent you chickens and fuel. She agreed to escort me here tonight, even though she was visiting with an old friend. She's better than I deserve."

Amy's lips twisted. "You're very happy, then?"

That gave him pause. "I don't know. I hope—I hope I will be."

Her gaze sharpened, but she said, "That's good, Nev, I'm glad."

"Oh, Amy. I'm so sorry. You should have told me what was wrong, that night at the theater. You should have known I would help you."

Tears glittered in her eyes. "Should I have?"

He took her hand. "I'll always help you, Amy." Finally he said what had to be said. "It was mine, the baby, wasn't it."

"Who else's should it be?" She turned her face to the wall, a very un-Amy-like tremor in her voice, and Nev felt worse than ever. "Are you very angry with me?"

How could he be angry? "No. What do you want to do now?"

"Oh, I don't know, Nev. Gain back some of this weight, first of all. I just don't know, I'm so tired."

"Go to sleep."

"Will you come and see me tomorrow?"

He felt a flash of irritation and resentment at the request—Penelope would be hurt and angry again, and he had so much to do already—and then guilt at his own selfishness. "If I can. Of course."

"I'd like that. Stay with me till I'm sleeping, won't you?"

He nodded.

When she was asleep, he went out into the other room. Penelope sat at the table in earnest conversation with Mrs. Bailey. She looked up at Nev, her face grave. "I think perhaps we ought to find another place for Miss Raeburn."

"Certainly, if it's too much trouble for Mrs. Bailey," Nev said, puzzled.

Mrs. Bailey gave him a pleading look. "That ain't it, your lordship. Everyone hates us now on account of Jack peaching. And Sir Jasper's been to visit her, and that doesn't help none. People have been—a rock came through the window in there and almost hit Miss Raeburn on the head, this morning."

Nev rocked back on his heels. "Oh. Well, then. Certainly. And—I'll find someone to guard the house. The children ought to be safe."

Penelope was unsurprised when she woke up the next morning with her stomach in knots. She barely made it to the basin in her dressing room before casting up her accounts. Thank God Nev hadn't slept in her bed last night.

Her stomach rolled again. He hadn't touched her, not after talking to Miss Wray. It was too much, all of it—the poachers and Edward and Miss Wray. She wasn't strong enough. She had never been strong enough, not at school and not now. She was a weak, silly, nervous girl and she felt like crying.

She wiped her mouth and looked at the Hogarth engravings. Edward's anger didn't trouble her anymore, and yet the sharpest sting of the engravings remained: the unequal marriage that ended in disaster. Had Hogarth and Edward and Lady Bedlow been right after all?

Miss Wray had been moved to Agnes Cusher's house. Penelope brought them some soft white bread, soft enough for Miss Wray.

"Thank you, my lady." Agnes's face was closed and lined. She took the basket and didn't move from the doorway.

"I'd like to talk to Miss Raeburn. I'm writing to my parents, and I thought she might want to include a message for her mother." It was the truth; Mrs. Brown had asked Penelope to do it. But Penelope wasn't entirely sorry. She was perversely curious, she admitted to herself. She wanted to see what kind of a woman Nev had chosen when he was choosing for himself.

"That's very kind of you," Agnes said, in a voice that said she wasn't impressed, and moved aside.

Miss Wray lay on a cot in the corner of the room. She looked at Penelope with interest, fighting for breath as she tried to sit up. Agnes was at her side in a moment, arranging pillows behind her with gentle hands.

"Thank you, Agnes." Miss Wray smiled, and Agnes smiled back, with a malicious glance at Penelope to see how she took it.

Penelope raised her chin. So. Agnes knew this was Nev's mistress and had taken to her out of spite against Penelope. It didn't matter. It couldn't hurt her.

If only Penelope believed that.

"I'm going to fetch water. I'll be back in a few minutes. Come along, Kit." And Agnes bustled them out the door as if she couldn't wait to get away from Penelope.

"Lady Bedlow," Miss Wray said with some constraint. "Allow me to thank you for—"

"Oh, don't." Penelope felt as if she were choking. "It was no hardship, and your mother has worked for my father for so long, and—" She did not know how to break through the polite lies, so she was grateful when Miss Wray did it for her.

"Nev says—" She twisted a golden curl round her finger in a nervous gesture that Penelope could see would be bewitchingly flirtatious when she was a stone heavier and clean and well-dressed. "Nev says you know how things used to be between us. So thanks for not tossing me out or having me quietly poisoned or anything."

Penelope was surprised into a laugh. "I—it bothers me. But Nev's been so worried about you and felt so guilty. I wanted you to get well."

"He oughtn't to feel guilty. It wasn't his fault, none of it."

Penelope could not bring herself to say the obvious, that it had been his child. "He thinks—he thinks you must have wanted for money, to go without proper care. And that he could have helped you, in that way at least."

"I didn't want for money," Amy said wryly, "only sense. My mum didn't know where the money was, that's all. And I didn't tell any of my friends I was in trouble because I felt so stupid. Then I knew it hadn't gone right, and I was bleeding too much and getting sick. But I was so miserable and angry with myself I just soldiered on, and then it was too late."

Penelope listened to this speech with a growing and uncomfortable sense of recognition. "I've done that. When I was fourteen, I decided to run away from school and tried to climb the fence. But I fell and broke a tooth, and I was too ashamed to tell anyone. I went on like that for weeks until I could barely eat, and one of the teachers noticed my face was red and swollen. I've never seen my mother so angry."

Miss Wray plucked at the blanket. "My mum must be out

of her head with worry. You *will* tell her I'm all right, won't you?"

"Of course I will. I—listen, I know we're supposed to be at each other's throats, hissing like spiteful cats, but none of this is your fault. I don't see why we can't be friendly."

Miss Wray smiled at her, a charming smile that dimpled her cheeks, and Penelope thought of several reasons; but she tamped them down.

"I don't see why either, though I never expected to be friendly with one of my gentlemen's *wives*. But you seem nice enough, and there's no reason practical girls like us can't get along." Miss Wray made a moue, her voice turning a little bitter at the end.

Penelope couldn't help it, the instinctive recoil at being told by an actress that they were two of a kind, and yet she felt abruptly that they *were*. They were both London girls who wanted to be something they were not, something glamorous and genteel; they were both girls Nev did not love.

"It gets tiresome being practical, doesn't it?" Penelope said. "You just want to do something stupid, like smash the china, even though you'd feel foolish the next moment, and it wouldn't help. You *know* it wouldn't make you happy but you can't help wondering if it—would make you different, somehow."

Miss Wray nodded ruefully. "They want someone who will give them thrills, and I only know how to make them comfortable. We just aren't the sort men fall in love with."

Penelope knew that was true, had always known it; but she thought of Edward. "I don't know—"

Miss Wray's eyes brightened. "So there is someone? That old friend Nev was so jealous of?"

"We were engaged, before," Penelope confessed.

"Is it Ed Macaulay? My mum always said the two of you would make a match of it for sure. Half the girls in the plant were green with envy."

Penelope was startled for a moment. But of course the Raeburns would have known Edward. "Yes."

"You gave him up for a title, and you're sorry."

"I—it wasn't the title. I gave him up for Nev, because Nev needed me and he was so—" She searched for the word that would describe Nev and why she had wanted him, and could not find it.

"Nev has a way about him, doesn't he?" Miss Wray asked wistfully. "He gave me money when we split up, you know. He told me he knew it would be more useful than a pretty diamond bracelet, and he was right—but from him I would rather have had the bracelet."

Penelope felt a pang, thinking of Nev learning to be practical. "Did you—" It was a terribly personal question, but she needed to know. "Why didn't you want the baby?"

Miss Wray stared at her wasted hands. "I—" She swallowed. "I shouldn't tell you."

Penelope felt cold. Perhaps she didn't need to know after all. What secret did Miss Wray have to share about Nev? "I—" Her lips had gone dry. "I don't mean to intrude upon personal confidences."

Miss Wray's mouth twisted. "Such a good girl. No. You deserve to know, only—I suppose you won't let me stay, and—"

"You can stay," Penelope said before she knew she was going to. "Until you're well, I promise you that."

Miss Wray looked back at her hands, her mouth a tight line. "I don't know if was his."

Penelope stared. "What?"

"I don't know if it was his. Nev's friend Thirkell—Nev threw him over too, and he came by to see how I was doing. I was so grateful, and we had too much to drink, and—it was such a *stupid* thing to do. And I couldn't tell Nev. I ought to have, none of this is his responsibility, either of yours, but I—I was afraid that you would toss me out." She licked her cracked lips. "And I was angry."

"He thinks you didn't tell him you were in trouble because you didn't trust him to help." He'd be so relieved to learn that it wasn't that at all—wouldn't he? Or would he be jealous?

"Poor Nev. I suppose you'll tell him."

"I think I have to." And yet—she understood so clearly why Miss Wray would not want Nev to know.

"Wait till I'm gone, won't you? Until I'm back in London?"

Penelope nodded.

The next day was the first day of Sir Jasper's house party. All the Ambreys were invited to pick strawberries with the guests, and Nev didn't see how they could get out of it with any grace. Since Macaulay was still at the Grange, he came along.

The moment the party from the Dower House climbed into the carriage, it was clear that Louisa knew that Nev knew about her indiscretion. She sat silently in the corner, flushed and sullen. That meant, Nev realized with dismay, that she had a means of communicating secretly with Percy.

It was equally clear that their mother had not the slightest idea of what was going on. While Penelope and Macaulay conversed quietly about mutual acquaintances, Lady Bedlow spent the drive to Greygloss instructing Louisa on how to attract Sir Jasper. "And be polite to him this time!" she repeated for the tenth time.

"Mother, stop it," Nev said.

"Yes, we all know if *you* had your way she'd be running around behaving in whatever hoydenish way she likes!"

Nev raised his eyebrows. "That is not in the least true. I am frequently disappointed in Louisa's behavior."

Louisa flushed.

Upon their arrival they were shown into the parlor, where Sir Jasper and most of the houseguests were already assembled in their most summery clothes. The Ambreys, still in full mourning, stood out painfully. Nev looked around the room for familiar faces—

He froze. In the corner were Thirkell's aunt and his cousin Harriet. Beside them, Thirkell gazed at him uneasily. And next to him stood Percy, pale but defiant.

What the *devil?*

Sixteen

"I'm so very glad you could all make it." Sir Jasper bent over the ladies' hands gracefully—lingering over Louisa's—and turned to Nev. "Your friend Lord Thirkell is here with his aunt and cousin," he said. "I thought you might like to see him."

Nev just stared at him.

Sir Jasper leaned forward and spoke more quietly. "You look displeased. I hope I haven't done wrong by allowing your steward to stay here. I gathered he had left his position, but I had no reason to think it was on bad terms. Lord Thirkell asked me to invite him."

Did Sir Jasper expect him to swallow that? "I—"

"Of course you haven't done anything wrong." Louisa smiled brightly at Sir Jasper. "Mr. Garrett is one of Nev's oldest friends. What could there possibly be to object to?"

Nev wanted to wring his sister's neck.

Sir Jasper's whole face softened as he smiled back at her. "I'm glad to hear it."

After introductions were made, the party was led out to a shady, hilly area covered in strawberry plants and given baskets. "Won't you sit by me, Lady Bedlow?" Thirkell's cousin Harriet said.

Nev could feel Penelope's sudden uncertainty. "I—I—" She looked at him.

"Of course you must." Nev attempted to smile. "I'll see Louisa settled and be back directly, shall I?"

He deftly detached his sister from their mother and led

her a short distance away. He opened his mouth to let her know exactly what he thought of her, but she didn't wait.

"I'm sorry, Nev, I'm so sorry. I knew I was doing wrong, but I *love* him! I want to be with him forever. I'll die without him."

"You're seventeen! You're not going to die without him. I assure you, after a few months of remade gowns you'd find that forever seemed a very long time."

The black lace at her shoulders trembled with rage. "You think I'm shallow, don't you? You think I'm a frivolous, silly little girl who doesn't care for anything but her bonnets."

"Of course not, Louisa, but—"

"I was willing to do my part and marry well when the family needed it. I was willing to sacrifice everything. I would have done it for you and Mama. But you wouldn't let me. And now—now that we have enough money for me to marry where I love, now that I've found love and know what I would be sacrificing—*now* you ask me to give up everything. Well, I won't."

He wanted to slap her right across her tragic, noble mouth. "I'm not asking you to give up everything, Louisa. Don't dramatize."

"I hate you! I hate you for speaking to me that way. I love him, Nate, can't you understand that?"

"No, dash it all," he said through gritted teeth. "I can't understand it. I can't understand how a clever girl like you could have been so *stupid* as to risk *everything* for a few stolen kisses. Tom Kedge saw you, did you know that? He's threatening to tell Sir Jasper. The bastard's been skimming from the Poor Authority funds and underpaying his employees, and I'm going to have to renew his lease to save you from the consequences of your own folly. Think about what you've done, Louisa."

Louisa turned pale. "I'm sorry," she said in a choked voice.

"I'm *sorry*. But you don't have to renew his lease. You just have to let me marry Percy, and then everything will be fine."

"You can't think five minutes ahead, Louisa. How do you expect me to believe you can think ahead to forever?"

"I love him, damn you!"

"No, you don't," he said brutally.

"I *do*. And I'm sorry that *you* couldn't have that with your wife, I am, but don't try to take it away from me!"

He thought he had been angry before, but that had been nothing to his furious rage now. It filled his lungs, choking him. "You willful, irresponsible, insufferable little brat! How *dare* you? You think love is just—just—something out of a damn Minerva Press novel! You think that because you happen to feel, right now, that you'll die without someone, that you love him? That you can marry him? Love isn't a game. Living with someone, being married to her—that's *work*, Louisa. It's trying to be what she needs even if it doesn't come naturally, and struggling to understand her, and working together to make a life! It's accepting that sometimes things aren't perfect. It's understanding that sometimes one of you has responsibilities that have to come first, and knowing that she understands that too! So don't dare tell me that because I haven't behaved like an idiot and brought a host of troubles down around my family's head, that I don't love Penelope."

She stared at him for a long moment, conflicting emotions chasing each other around her face—affection, anger, regret. At last she said, quietly, "I'm not the one who reads Minerva Press novels, Nate. You are. And you're right, love is work. But it's also something more. And if you don't know that, then you *don't* love Penelope." And she turned on her heel and walked away.

Nev breathed deeply, fighting for calm. It didn't help that when he looked over at his wife, she was laughing and picking strawberries, her bare, juice-stained hands brushing those of her childhood sweetheart. She couldn't see Edward's face, because she was turned toward Harriet, but Nev could.

Edward was looking at Penelope as if he would die without her.

To Penelope, it all had a dreamlike unreality. The dappled sunlight, the sweet taste of the berries, the charming straw baskets, the ladies and gentlemen in their fine country clothes—the pastoral loveliness of the whole scene—it all seemed so unconnected to the past weeks, to dust and sweat and hunger and Poor Authorities and Agnes Cusher's desperate eyes. She could not help thinking of fiddles and burning Italian cities.

"What do you think, Lady Bedlow?" a girl asked. Penelope remembered her from school; Lucy Hopper, her name was.

There was a respectful silence as everyone waited for her opinion. And she had no idea what they had been speaking of—talk about a massive upcoming demonstration in Manchester had been mixed with gossip and clothes and Mr. Scott's latest novel, which was not selling very well. "I'm sorry, I'm afraid I was woolgathering."

"Do you think a riot in Manchester could set off violence in the countryside?" Miss Hopper repeated.

"I don't know. But I hardly think a riot in Manchester is likely. From what I've heard, the organizers are going to great lengths to keep the gathering peaceful." She realized she was repeating something Louisa had said at dinner a few days ago.

"I hope you are right," said a young man whose name Penelope could not remember. "But surely the presence of the yeomanry and so many Hussars indicates that the authorities have reason to be worried."

"I think the presence of the yeomanry is indeed a good reason for the authorities to worry," Edward said. "I recently made the acquaintance of several members of the Manchester yeomanry, among them the son of a leading manufacturer and friend of my own employer. I was dismayed by the vitriolic hatred they felt for the local trade unionists and reformers. They mentioned a number of them by name and expressed in the most violent language their desire to deal with these men. Moreover they seemed rather intemperate in their habits. I would not trust them very far with a saber myself."

A hush greeted this speech. Most simply seemed stunned that anyone would admit, in polite conversation, to being employed by a manufacturer. Penelope felt a sudden fierce, protective pride in poor verbose Edward, who worked for his living and had a million kinds of knowledge these society folk would never understand. But his picture of a demonstration presided over by, in effect, hundreds of armed Sir Jaspers horrified her so that she could not think of anything to fill the silence.

"That is not very encouraging," Miss Lovelace said gamely.

"No," Edward said. "But surely such divisiveness does not exist here. Factories and manufacturing towns, as concentrating a large number of men who are not always of the best character in one place, are breeding grounds for factionalism and resentment. Here, where you know your workers personally, things must be different. And surely it is better to be poor in the country: it is so clean here, and on my way I saw several kitchen gardens, and even chickens. There is nothing like that in the towns."

Penelope almost laughed, but it was a bitter amusement; at once there were a dozen voices all eager to assure Edward that the poor thirsted for the blood of the rich every bit as much in the country. So much for Edward's superior understanding.

She felt pulled this way and that. Who was she now? A brewer's daughter? Or a landowner's wife? Lucy Hopper, who had laughed at her accent at school, had asked her opinion and listened deferentially to her answer. She had wanted so badly for that girl—all those girls—to respect her; yet she found none of the expected pleasure in her sudden elevation.

Her life had been so much simpler when she was just a Cit. She had known who she was and what she ought to be doing.

Edward leaned down, so close she could feel his breath warm against her ear. It did not affect her in the slightest. "Your sister-in-law is about to create a scene."

She started and followed the direction of his eyes. A little ways off, Louisa was clinging to Mr. Garrett's arm. His face was dead white, and he seemed to be trying to detach her. Louisa looked almost in tears. Penelope looked for Nev and felt her face heating. Nev did not see Louisa; he was looking at her and Edward with a distinctly murderous expression.

Penelope smiled at Miss Lovelace. "Please excuse me. I had better make sure the strawberries have not made Lady Louisa ill."

As she drew near she heard Louisa saying, in a furious undertone, "You men! You're all the same—you think that because I'm a girl, you must know better than I what will make me happy!"

Penelope felt an unwanted pang of sympathy, remembering how her parents had refused, all those years, to let her marry Edward. Now it seemed they had been right—although she was not sure that in permitting her to marry Nev, they had not made a far greater mistake. "Louisa, Mr. Garrett." She had made no effort to approach quietly, but they both started as if she had leapt out from behind a tree and screamed. "Please," she said, "Louisa, won't you come away? People are staring."

"Let them stare," Louisa said.

"Louisa," Mr. Garrett remonstrated under his breath.

Penelope tried to stand so that she was blocking Louisa's

white, wild face from the view of most of the guests. "Louisa, please, we'll have this all out later, I promise. But in the meantime wouldn't it be better not to do anything irrevocable?"

"I want to do something irrevocable," Louisa said in a low, thick voice. "I can't be a good girl like you. I can't pretend that I'm happy living the way everyone else wants me to. Living without scandal and noise isn't enough for me, I want to *live*—"

"This isn't the time or the place to discuss this! Mr. Garrett, tell her—"

Louisa turned to her lover. "Yes, Percy, tell me. Tell me to be bloodless and cold and think three tricks ahead before I discard."

"I might tell you to have more consideration for the feelings of others," Mr. Garrett said. "It is not merely yourself that will suffer if you make yourself miserable, Louisa."

Her mouth trembled, almost smiling. "I'll only be miserable without you." He gave her a small, fond, helpless smile back.

Penelope smothered an impatient sigh. "We will all be miserable if your mother catches wind of this."

Louisa's eyes widened. "Nate isn't going to tell her, is he?"

"I haven't the least idea," Penelope said honestly. "But he certainly isn't going to tell her here, if you don't do it for him by making a scene."

Louise fixed her with an urgent stare. "You don't understand. You don't understand what she's like. She'll probably suggest I marry Sir Jasper and take Percy as a lover."

Penelope couldn't help a small sputter of laughter.

For some reason, that seemed to calm Louisa. She took a deep breath and eyed Penelope. "You aren't going to do that, are you?"

Penelope started. "What?"

"Take a lover." Louisa leaned forward impatiently. "Nate just told me he loves you."

Mr. Garrett gave her a small shove. "Louisa!"

Penelope's heart stuttered in her chest. "No, you must have misheard him—"

"I didn't mishear him," Louisa said. "I don't know if I believe it either, but he believes it. And I don't care what kind of bloodless bargain you made with Nate when you married him, if you think you can do as you like as long as you pretend nothing's happening and the neighbors don't find out, think again. Because if you hurt my brother, I will kill you."

"Lady Louisa," Sir Jasper said from right behind Penelope, and she started. Oh, God, how much had he heard? "You're missing all the strawberries." He held out his arm. "And I know how fond you are of them. Your father used to buy up half my strawberries sometimes to make you happy. Come, there is a patch over there that no one has found yet."

For a moment Penelope was afraid Louisa really would do something irrevocable. Instead, the girl hesitated, glanced in her mother's direction—and placed her hand on Sir Jasper's arm.

Penelope smiled at her. "Did your father really?"

Louisa rolled her eyes. "He never remembered. Not once. But Nate always ate mine, so it was all right."

"Strawberries make Louisa ill," Penelope explained.

For several seconds, Sir Jasper could only blink. "Oh, my dear. How very unfortunate. I assure you, I had no idea."

"Neither did my father," Louisa said impatiently. "So I can hardly claim to be greatly offended by your ignorance."

"I hope you will forgive me enough to come with your family to a dance at Greygloss tomorrow night. I know you are in mourning, but it is to be an informal affair, and I thought it might prove a welcome diversion from recent distressing events in the district."

Penelope, remembering the way Sir Jasper had looked at Josie Cusher, wanted to strike him across the face.

"Mr. Garrett will naturally be attending." He looked at Penelope significantly; his tone of voice suggested that he thought this would be an inducement to her to come.

She stared at him, puzzled. But she did not want to be unsociable, and in the normal course of things she would have accepted his invitation anyway. It was not as if they had a prior engagement. "We shall certainly be there, if Nev thinks it is proper. We are nearly in half mourning, anyway."

As the baronet was leading Louisa away, he leaned in toward Penelope. "We are not all as puritanical as Louisa. Pardon her; she is very protective of her brother and very young."

Penelope flushed crimson. So. He'd heard at least the last part of their conversation. Did he mean—did he think she was having an affair with—*Mr. Garrett*? And that that was why Nev had tossed him out? Then why invite him to stay? Did he *want* her to have an affair? Why? She shook her head, trying to clear it. Nothing made sense anymore. Edward was reckless, Sir Jasper was a pander, and Nev—Nev had said he *loved* her?

"I'm sorry," Mr. Garrett said once Louisa and Sir Jasper were out of earshot. "She isn't usually so—so intractable. She's having a hard time, and she feels trapped, and it makes her say things she wouldn't otherwise. But she shouldn't be so careless, or speak to you that way."

"Don't apologize to *me*," Penelope said tiredly. "You've put Nev through Hell, the pair of you."

"I know," Mr. Garrett said miserably. "But I love her." He and Louisa said it the same way, as if it excused everything, as if it were the one unanswerable argument in the world. Maybe it did, and maybe it was.

"Mr. Garrett, listen to me. Nev loves both of you, he does. He only wants to protect Louisa."

"Louisa is wretched. I don't think Nev knows it, but Louisa has been wretched for a long time. It isn't—it isn't a happy home, and never was; without Lord Bedlow, it's a hundred times worse. Nev always spent as little time there as possible, as soon as he was old enough to choose. Louisa can't do that."

Penelope sighed. She wouldn't like to live with Lady Bedlow either, but how bad could it really be? Perhaps, though, that didn't matter, especially not at seventeen. She wished she had done more to befriend Louisa, so that she might have some influence now. "Nev only wants to protect her," she repeated. "She's so young. But I'll talk to him. I think if Louisa can behave herself and be patient and prove this is not merely a fleeting ungovernable passion, he will agree to an engagement. Perhaps a lengthy one, but I suppose you will be willing to wait."

"I would wait an eternity, but he will never agree," Mr. Garrett said with finality. "You did not hear him last night. Nev does not compromise. He never has."

"He was angry." She felt unreasonably angry herself. "You must admit that neither your behavior nor Louisa's has been the sort to inspire confidence."

"I do admit it. I have sacrificed every claim to his good opinion. He has a right to be angry." He looked at her. "You are very generous not to be. My words last night were not those of a gentleman."

She had hoped he would not bring it up. *A month before your marriage you were gossiping about your bride-to-be's dowry with your mistress.* What had Nev said? *Your name only came up because I couldn't stop staring at you.* With a sudden flash of inspiration she could imagine it all—poor Miss Wray, trying to be practical and pretend she didn't mind, and Nev believing it. *He doesn't believe you when you pretend,* she thought suddenly and wondered what that meant.

"No," she said, a chill in her voice. "I should thank you for reminding me of a truth I had almost let myself forget."

Mr. Garrett bit his lip. "Lady Bedlow, I've known Nev a long time. I don't know what he said to Louisa, but I do know he is very fond of you. I really thought he would hit me last night."

Nev was very fond of her. She knew it was true. She ought to be grateful; she ought to be satisfied. And she wasn't. "I know."

"He hates Mr. Macaulay."

It was childish, but she smiled. "I know."

It was a horrid, hot day. As Penelope walked home from a visit to the dressmaker's, everything seemed malevolent and too bright. She went by a wheat field and saw workers standing in tight knots, talking in low voices. When she passed, they quieted and watched her, their faces blank and sullen. She thought of Sir Jasper and his fears of revolution. These men had rioted before. Penelope hugged her packages to her chest and walked faster.

In the entrance hall at the Grange, she found Nev by the silver salver of mail, staring at the newspaper. Her heart leapt into her throat without her quite knowing why. "What is it? What's happened?"

"There's been a massacre at Manchester." Nev's face twisted. "Listen to this: 'The local troops, it is said, behaved with great alacrity. The consternation and dismay which spread among the immense crowd collected cannot be conceived. The multitude was composed of a large proportion of females. The prancing of cavalry, and the active use of the saber among them, created a dreadful sense of confusion, and we may add of carnage. By the accounts received through the mail, no less than eighty or a hundred persons are wounded, and eight killed—'" He broke off. "There's hardly anything else. They hadn't got their correspondent's article yet when the paper went to press. God knows what really happened."

Penelope skimmed the brief article. Edward had been right; the yeomanry had begun the bloodshed.

She tried not to think about it as she dressed for Sir Jasper's party. She tried to think about her hair and her jewels; she had to be a credit to Nev. But as she clasped the jet around her neck, she saw only Agnes Cusher's exhausted scowl and Sir Jasper's frightened, furious face.

She came down the stairs still brooding. Nev and Edward were waiting, each looking preoccupied and uncomfortable. They both moved forward, and then Edward hesitated and fell back, letting Nev take her hand.

"What's wrong, sweet? You look fagged to death."

She tried to glare at him, but really she just wished Edward weren't there and that they didn't have to go to the party, so she could curl against his side and tell him everything. She opened her mouth to at least tell him about Sir Jasper's strange behavior the day before.

"Don't listen to him," Edward said loyally. "You look perfectly elegant."

She pulled herself together with an effort. "Thank you, Edward. I'm all right, Nev, truly. It's just been a difficult week."

Penelope was dreading seeing Louisa, and it was clear from Nev's expression that he was too. What new histrionics would they be subjected to this time? But they were pleasantly surprised by the reality; when Louisa climbed into the carriage, she looked radiant. "Thank you so much for the new dress, Nate. I hadn't realized how tired I was of black!"

Penelope wondered, blinking, if that could really be all. She had never seen Louisa in any color but black; the girl was striking even so, but there was no doubt mourning had subdued her, washing out her already pale complexion. Now, in white with gray ribbons, she glowed. At Penelope's suggestion, Nev had hinted to his mother that perhaps Louisa needed some diversion, and that she could not dance with Sir Jasper if she were kept in full mourning.

"Mama says I can even dance two or three dances!" Louisa said. Penelope did not know what Nev would do if she danced them all with Mr. Garrett.

However, no one was dancing when they arrived. Instead they were talking in tight knots, looking worried and angry. Penelope was reminded of the laborers at Loweston.

Sir Jasper rushed over as soon as they entered, barely even looking at Louisa. "Bedlow, we've got to talk. The people in this district are on the verge of a riot, and we have no yeomanry here we can call out. The two of us must do something to maintain order. Perhaps if we were to shut down the tavern for a few weeks and—"

"Yes," Louisa broke in, her voice rising, "it really is a shame we can't have drunken louts with sabers ride down our tenants and kill them! How can you—"

"Louisa." Nev put a hand on his sister's arm. "I believe Sir Jasper was speaking to me. However, I must agree with my sister, Sir Jasper, that I hardly find it a matter for regret that we are in no danger of the sort of atrocity that occurred in Manchester. Perhaps if you were to consider granting bail for the men accused of poaching, our laborers would feel less wronged and—"

Sir Jasper was vibrating with anger. "I can be silent no longer. Lord Bedlow, you are allowing your judgment to be suborned by a woman. I understand that given her background, your wife may feel a natural sympathy for these lowly folk, but now is not the time to allow sentiment to—"

Penelope could not even feel very affronted; she was too amazed by Sir Jasper's breach of good manners.

Nev blinked. "Sir Jasper," he said amiably, "though I hardly like to draw such a strong conclusion on my own, I think you just insulted my wife."

Penelope felt at once mortified and ridiculously grateful.

"I'm sure he didn't mean to, Nev," she said—the party would be awful enough without out-and-out violence—but she couldn't help favoring Sir Jasper with a triumphantly gracious smile.

Nev smiled too, a silly-ass smile that didn't reach his eyes. "Well, there you go. You know, Sir Jasper, I think you may have the right of it; my wife is far too softhearted. Revenge is so much more satisfying than mercy, don't you know. But perhaps justice is somewhere in between."

Sir Jasper nodded stiffly. "My apologies. I do not know what came over me."

"Being a complete bastard?" Louisa whispered in her ear, and Penelope had to choke back a nervous giggle.

Sir Jasper strode away, and a few moments later the band struck up. Penelope remembered her earlier fears that Louisa would make a fool of herself with Mr. Garrett, but she was soon forced to admit that her suspicions had been unjust. Far from trying to talk alone with Mr. Garrett, Louisa danced attendance on Lady Bedlow, showing none of her usual impatience when Lady Bedlow sent her running back and forth to the refreshments table for lobster patties, and then a glass of punch when the patties turned out to be distressingly salty, and some tartlets, and another glass of punch because the tartlets were too dry. In between, the girl was very hot on the subject of the confrontation at St. Peter's Fields, but Penelope could hardly blame her for that.

However, a party of young gentry could not be distracted by politics forever. Soon Penelope found herself sitting between Nev and Edward and watching couples turn about the floor.

Conversation lagged; she realized she was exhausted. "I don't think I've eaten anything today," she said, surprised.

Edward frowned, but it was Nev who burst out crossly, "No wonder you look so awful! For heaven's sake, Penelope, you've got to take care of yourself."

Her apologetic smile turned into an embarrassed grimace as her stomach rumbled. "I don't know how it happened. But I don't imagine I'll starve from going without food for one day."

"I don't intend to find out," he growled, and stalked off toward the buffet.

"But Nev, I don't—" It was too late; he was gone. Penelope groaned inwardly. She hated eating from buffets, holding a plate in her lap and trying not to get crumbs everywhere. It was impossible to cut things into bite-sized pieces. At their first meeting, she had worried about how she would eat the hors d'oeuvres Nev gave her.

"He shouldn't talk to you that way," Edward said.

She sighed. "He's just worried about me."

"So am I, but you don't catch me—" He stopped and drew in a deep breath. "I'm sorry, Penelope, I oughtn't to let my temper get the better of me."

It was hard to believe she had once considered making a snappish remark "letting her temper get the better of her." Now she spent half her time afraid she would start screaming and not know how to stop. She thought of those vicious Hogarth engravings and the cold little note that came with them. Edward might be happier if he did let his temper get the better of him once in a while. It would be like the relief valves on the great boiling tanks at the brewery that let out air and steam so the tanks didn't explode. "It's all right. I know you're worried about me too."

He took her hand, and she didn't know how to take it back. He leaned closer. "What I said, two nights ago. You never gave me an answer. Penelope, I—"

"Here," Nev's voice said furiously, and a plate of food appeared in front of her. "Take it." Edward let go of her hand, and she took the plate. Nev handed a glass to Edward. "Here's her punch. Make sure she eats." He turned on his heel and walked away.

Penelope's heart sank. Then she looked at the plate and almost couldn't bear it. He had cut everything into bite-sized pieces for her.

She wanted to get up and go after him—but everyone would stare, and she would have to abandon Edward, and there was already so much gossip. She picked up a fork and speared a tiny piece of pie, but when she brought it to her mouth she almost gagged. She loved nutmeg, but somehow today the smell repulsed her. She set the plate down and took the glass of punch from Edward.

Nev stood by the window, watching the sun go down and hating Edward Macaulay. How dare he hold Penelope's hands and speak into Penelope's ear that way? Penelope was Nev's wife, and Macaulay had no right.

Nev snorted at his own self-righteousness. He forced himself to dwell on Penelope's life if she had married Edward. She would be respected; her mother-in-law and neighbors would not be always turning up their noses at her behind her back. She would not be worrying about money. She would not be fretting herself into an early grave over poachers and blackmailers and riots and snobbish neighbors and indiscreet sisters-in-law.

She looked so *tired*. He looked over to see if she was eating. She was sitting alone, fanning her heated face. It really was very close in the room. He could see that her plate lay nearly untouched in her lap, and he almost went to her; but Macaulay appeared with another glass of punch, and Nev stayed by the window.

At least Louisa seemed to be trying to put her Cheltenham tragedy behind her. She was laughing and dancing with one of Sir Jasper's friends, looking not at all as if the day before she had been on the verge of a hysterical scene at a picnic. She had been so good all evening. Nev felt something loosen in his chest; Louisa was the darling little sister he remembered again. She didn't hate him. All that had been wrong with her was a touch of the blue devils. He could still fix this.

If Percy left the neighborhood, she would forget him quick enough. If only Sir Jasper had not clumsily tried to be generous and invited Thirkell.

Thirkell was talking to his cousin across the room, and it occurred to Nev that he could still appeal to Thirkell for help. Thirkell might be angry with him, but surely he would see reason for Louisa's sake.

He made his way around the dance floor. "Thirkell, Miss Lovelace." He bowed over Cousin Harriet's hand. "I hope I'm not intruding."

Thirkell became very preoccupied with his fob. "Evening, Nev." Nev's heart sank.

Harriet smiled at him. "Of course you're not intruding. I was about to take myself off anyway. I'm engaged to Mr. Avery for the next dance and I want to get a glass of punch first."

"Try the lemonade instead," Thirkell told her.

"But I like punch."

"It's not very good punch."

Nev wasn't listening. He remembered, suddenly, the last time he had spoken to Harriet. The three of them had been supposed to lend Harriet countenance, and instead he had engaged her for two dances and then run off without dancing them. "Miss Lovelace, I—I just wanted to tell you that I'm very sorry for my shabby behavior, when we met. I am ashamed to remember it."

She blushed and smiled at him. "I was very angry at the time, but I assure you I'd quite forgotten. That was the night you met Lady Bedlow, wasn't it? I was glad just to be there. We all thought it was so romantic, how you picked her out of the crowd without knowing who she was and then married her so soon afterward."

Nev was aware that this was the most charitable interpretation possible of his and Penelope's abbreviated courtship. He wished even more that he had not been so thoughtless. "I wish I could dance, so that I might make it up to you tonight."

She had a very sweet smile. "All my dances are taken."

He nodded and watched her go. "She's not a wallflower now."

"No," Thirkell said. "I knew she just needed a little boost."

"Thirkell, the last time I saw you—"

"Didn't think you'd mind if I was just staying in the neighborhood," Thirkell said, an edge in his voice. "I wanted to see Percy."

It hurt, though Nev knew he had no right to feel that way. "That wasn't what I wanted to say. I've missed you. I—I was an ass. I'm sorry." He could no longer remember what all the fuss had been. He had been afraid they would drag him into expensive dares and brandy and cards and horse races. When had he thought he would find the time? It was easy to be frugal. It would be beyond him, now, to spend a hundred pounds on a wager, knowing what it would buy. No, he had failed in other ways, bigger ways, ways he could not even have imagined then. His grand gesture seemed childish and small.

He wondered, if he had been less absolute—if he had not been so harsh to Percy—if Percy would have been more reluctant to carry on with Louisa.

To Nev's surprise, his apology rendered Thirkell even more uncomfortable. "I—er—don't give it another thought." But it was several seconds before he raised his head and met Nev's eyes. "I've missed you too, Nev. I wish it could be the three of us again, like it's always been. I don't see why it can't be."

"God, so do I. But—Thirkell, did Percy tell you why I dismissed him?"

"Percy's been your best friend since you were eight," Thirkell said, not answering, by which Nev assumed that he had. "You ought to patch it up with him."

"I'd like to. But my sister has to come first. Come on, Thirkell, you know Louisa and her enthusiasms."

"They generally seem to last. How long has she been mad for pirates, now?"

That was true, and yet . . . "Louisa could never bear an unkind word from anybody," Nev said, low and intent. "How will she feel when she's ostracized by *everyone?*"

Thirkell bit his lip. Nev was about to follow up his advantage when Macaulay appeared at his elbow, frowning. "I think Lady Bedlow may be ill. She's acting feverish."

Seventeen

"*What?*" Nev didn't wait for an answer. He crossed the room and knelt beside Penelope. "How do you feel, sweetheart?"

She smiled mistily at him. "Nev. You came back."

Definitely not typical Penelope. He drew in a deep breath and tried to think. Leaning forward, he pressed a kiss on her forehead like his mother used to do when he was a child. Her skin didn't feel hot. "Do you feel sick?"

"Not anymore. Please don't be cross with me, Nev. I tried to eat, I just couldn't. Thank you for cutting my food for me." She smiled at him again and reached for his hand. It took her a couple of tries to grab it.

Nev was so relieved he almost laughed out loud. If it had been anyone but Penelope, he would have realized instantly. "How many glasses of punch did you have, Penny?"

She blinked several times. "Just two."

Nev frowned. That shouldn't have been enough to get her foxed, even on an empty stomach. Just then Louisa tapped his shoulder, looking worried. "Mama's falling asleep on her feet, Nev. Do you think she's coming down with something?"

Nev picked up Penelope's near-empty glass and drained it. Sure enough, it tasted faintly of brandy. "Someone's spiked the punch," he said disgustedly, getting to his feet. "You know Mama always falls straight asleep if she has more than half a glass of wine."

"Am I foxed, Nev?" Penelope asked.

"I think you are. Who on earth would—" Nev groaned; Thirkell had told Harriet to drink lemonade. Thirkell had followed him to the couch where Penelope was sitting; Nev turned to him. "Did the two of you *really* spike the punch?"

Thirkell tugged at his collar, an abject look of guilt on his face.

"*Why?*"

"Because we were bored," Percy said easily, walking up. "Now I'm unemployed I have to think of some way to amuse myself. Time was *you* would have thought it a great joke too."

"Mr. Garrett, I think I'm foxed," Penelope said. "I've never been foxed before. I think I like it."

Percy blinked. "Er. Sorry, Nev."

"And my *mother*, Percy? For God's sake, we're not fifteen anymore." Maybe he had been right about the pair of them all along.

"Please don't be cross, Nev." Penelope tugged at his waist-coat pocket.

He couldn't help smiling at her. Her answering smile was blinding and uncomplicated and he wanted to kiss her. "I'm not cross at *you*, sweet."

They had been standing in a knot for long enough to draw attention. Sir Jasper walked up. "Is everything all right?"

Nev didn't have time to hold a grudge against Sir Jasper at the moment. "*Someone* spiked the punch. You should probably make an announcement before all the dowagers are three sheets to the wind."

Sir Jasper looked rather amused. "Oh, dear. I suppose I'd better. I do apologize. I hope Lady Bedlow has not been too affected." His gaze slid to Penelope, who still had a hand in Nev's pocket.

"Yes, I'm drunk," she told him. "Perhaps you'd like to tell me how vulgar I am. Ah, how this must remind me of my childhood at the brewery!"

There was a stunned silence, during which Nev realized that if he didn't get Penelope out of there right away, she would never, ever forgive him.

He turned to Sir Jasper and was shocked by the intense dislike on their neighbor's face as he looked at Penelope.

Feeling cold, Nev covered Penelope's hand with his own and gave Sir Jasper his most charmingly apologetic smile. "Lady Bedlow forgot to eat dinner today, and I doubt she's ever had brandy before. I'm sure she doesn't have any idea what she's saying. My mother is very susceptible as well—Louisa tells me she's already falling asleep. We'd best be taking our leave."

"Of course," Sir Jasper said sympathetically, calling over a footman to summon their carriage, and Nev was left to wonder if he'd imagined the murderous gleam in his eye. "I'm sorry we did not get our dance," the baronet said to Louisa. "But I had the pleasure of watching you, and that must suffice. You look lovely in your new dress. I hope soon to give you another opportunity to wear it."

Oh, for the love of God. "Louisa, can you fetch Mama?"

"Whatever you say, Nev," Louisa said with poisonous sweetness. Nev glanced swiftly at her, but she had already turned away.

He turned back to Penelope. "Come on, love. We're going home."

She stood. "All right." She seemed steady enough on her feet, but Nev put an arm around her waist anyway. She swayed into him, and he closed his eyes, just letting himself feel the trusting length of her against his side.

"I've got her." Louisa's resigned voice was close by, and he opened his eyes. His mother was draped over Louisa. "Let's get out of here."

"Nev," Thirkell said. "Nev, I need to tell you something—"

"Ugh, her earring is caught on my dress." Louisa tried impatiently to untangle herself from Lady Bedlow's jewelry.

"Careful!" Lady Bedlow slurred. "That's your father's hair . . ."

"That is so very morbid, Mama." Louisa twisted her head around in a vain attempt to see what she was doing.

Sir Jasper stepped forward. "Allow me." In a moment he had disengaged the earring and was straightening Louisa's neckline. Louisa slapped his hand away.

"I'm sorry, Thirkell," Nev said, "but maybe now's not the best time. Why don't you come by for dinner tomorrow?"

The drive back to the Dower House passed mostly in silence. That was all right with Nev; he could have sat a million years with Penelope slumped against him, breathing quietly. It felt so natural and right, as if they had been formed just for this, just for each other.

At the Dower House, however, Lady Bedlow proved difficult to wake. "Come on, Mama," Louisa said. "Get up and put your arm over Nate's shoulders so he can help you down the steps."

"Nate, is that you?" Lady Bedlow asked.

"Yes, it's me." He put his hands on his mother's waist to steady her. "Come on, now."

"Always such a good boy."

Nev rolled his eyes. "I was never a good boy, Mama. Yes, that's right, hold on to the rail."

"You were always my favorite, Nate." There was still a smile in her voice.

Nev almost dropped her. Instead, he said, "Hush, Mama," and got her down the carriage steps. Louisa climbed down without waiting for his help.

"Louisa—" All summer he had ignored his mother's treatment of her. No wonder she was miserable at home and desperate to get away. No wonder she resented them all.

Louisa sighed. "Come, Nate, it's nothing we didn't all know before." Her smile was resigned. "It's all right. You were always *my* favorite too."

"You're coming to live with us," he said fiercely. "Start packing your things. You can move into the Grange tomorrow."

"I—you needn't—" She sniffled. "Oh, Nate!" She threw herself at him. He hugged her tightly with the arm that wasn't supporting their somnolent mother. "I'm so sorry for everything! I hope—I hope you can forgive me."

"Of course I can." He was surprised to find it was true. "You're my little sister, aren't you? Everything will come right, you'll see."

"I hope you still feel that way tomorrow."

"*I'm* not drunk. I know I haven't been a perfect brother, but I'm not so fickle as all that."

She hugged him again. "I *do* love you, Nate." There was a catch in her voice. "Come along, Mama," she said with weary affection, taking their mother's arm. "Let's get you inside." Nev watched to make sure they got safely through the door before climbing back into the carriage.

"Your family gives me a headache," Penelope said.

"Penelope!" Edward hissed.

"They give me a headache too." Nev took his seat again, feeling a moment's triumph when Penelope immediately leaned her head on his shoulder.

"Actually, maybe it's my hairpins that are giving me the headache."

"We'll be home soon."

Penelope shrugged, sat up, and began pulling out her hairpins.

If they had been alone he would have let her, but they weren't. Even so, it was several seconds before he could bring himself to speak. "Penny, sweetheart, don't." He reached for her hands.

She stopped, looking stricken. "Oh, God, am I acting vulgar? I can't tell anymore. I don't want to embarrass you, Nev."

"This is dreadful," Edward said in a low voice.

"This is your fault for not making her eat something like I told you to!" Nev turned back to Penelope. "You're not acting vulgar, sweetheart. You know I love your hair." He reached out and tugged on a sleek brown lock that had fallen over her ear. "But if you take all your hairpins out, you'll lose them."

Penelope smiled. "Do you really like my hair?"

"I adore it."

She sighed contentedly. "I love your hair too."

Nev swallowed hard. She had told him that once before, after he had pleasured her for the first time with his mouth. He remembered clearly the heat of her naked thigh against his cheek and her fingers in his hair, and he wished Macaulay at the devil.

"It's like cinnamon," she said dreamily.

Nev glanced at Macaulay and saw only his rigid profile as he stared out the window. Unexpectedly, he felt sorry for the man. It was impossible to be jealous when they were almost to the Grange, and then Macaulay would go to his room alone and Penelope would come with Nev. "Hush, Penny. You're making Edward blush."

"I'm sorry," she said at once, and was silent until they were standing in the hall at the Grange.

"Good night." Macaulay turned away.

"Good night, Edward." Penelope pulled away from Nev to stand on tiptoe and kiss Macaulay's cheek. "I'm sorry I embarrassed you. You're my very dearest friend and I don't want you to be angry with me."

He smiled sadly down at her. "I'm not angry with you, Penelope. You're my dearest friend too and—I hope you shall be very happy," he finished roughly. "Good night." He looked into her face for another moment, then hurried off.

Penelope turned and saw Nev watching her. "Edward is stuffy," she said, "but he loves me."

"I know." He hesitated. He had been waiting impatiently

for this moment, but it seemed crass to simply take her in his arms as soon as Macaulay was out of sight.

Then it didn't matter; Penelope stepped toward him and put her arms around his neck. "Kiss me."

He obeyed her. She tasted like brandy. He pulled her hairpins out by feel, her hair tumbling down around his fingers as he kissed her.

"Upstairs," she murmured against his mouth, and he picked her up so he could walk and hold her at the same time. "No Sir Jasper this time."

He remembered carrying her over the threshold, muddy and laughing, the day he had made her his. It seemed so long ago. They had been so uncertain and so easily cowed. "No. Not this time."

"Sir Jasper doesn't like me."

"No, he doesn't. I can't think why."

"He keeps talking to me about Miss Wray, and I think he thinks I'm having an affair with Mr. Garrett."

"He *what?*" Was *that* why Sir Jasper had let Percy stay at Greygloss? Why would he do that?

"Well, I might be wrong. But Louisa was telling me not to have an affair, and Sir Jasper heard her and he said—"

"*Louisa* told you not to have an affair?"

"She was suspicious of Edward," Penelope confided. "And I felt guilty because I hadn't told him no, and I made things worse. And then she told me what you said, and the truth is—" She looked at him with sudden decision. "The truth is that—"

She was going to tell him everything, just as he'd always wanted her to. And she was going to do it because she was drunk. "Penelope, stop. Tell me in the morning."

"I thought you wanted to know. I thought you wanted to know how I really felt."

"I do. I do, more than anything. But tell me in the morning."

"All right. I never knew being foxed was so pleasant. Why on earth did you give it up?"

Somehow it was easier to say it when Penelope was soft and slow and heavy in his arms and the house was dark. "My father was drunk. He was drunk and he got his brains blown out. I'm not going to do that to you."

"Oh, Nev," she said sadly. "You would never do that to me anyway."

"Before I met you I was drunk almost every night. I was a good-for-nothing. I don't want to be that person anymore."

She sighed. "Mr. Garrett said you could not compromise. Because you studied Latin. I told him it was stuff, but maybe I was wrong."

They were at his door. Nev opened it with his foot and set her down on the bed. "What do you mean?"

"You can drink a *little*." She smiled as if she were pointing out the obvious. "And play cards a little." She fell back on the bed, bouncing slightly. He watched her breasts and hips through the layers of muslin.

"I'm afraid. I'm afraid that if I start I won't be able to stop." Afraid was an understatement. He was terrified that the person he had become over the last few months was an illusion, who would vanish like words written in the sand when confronted with temptation. That his true self was the hard-drinking ne'er-do-well he'd been.

She frowned. "Let's try an experiment. You'll drink a glass of brandy, and then you'll stop."

"And if I don't?"

"Then you'll probably be too drunk to make love to me, and I'll cry." She smiled lazily up at him from where she sprawled on the bed.

He sat on the edge of the bed and ran a finger along her thigh. "I could make love to you now." He let his finger slide over the juncture of her thighs.

She tilted her hips up. "Mm. Brandy first."

"I don't know if I can wait that long." He slid his finger up and down and watched her back arch.

"If you hurry . . . you can be done by the time . . . Molly takes my clothes off." She closed her eyes.

"I like you just fine dressed like this."

She smiled and shook her head. "I have a surprise for you. I—I hope you don't laugh at me."

A surprise involving Penelope and nightclothes? "You win. One glass." Her smile was triumphant, but she sighed when he drew back his hand.

She stumbled getting to her feet, and he put out a hand to steady her. "It's not the punch," she said. "You make me dizzy."

When the door was shut, he drew in a deep breath and rang the bell.

"Davies, will you decant a bottle of brandy for me?"

Davies's eyes widened. Of course the entire household knew of his recent puritanism. Nev tried to look as if *he* did not see anything unusual about his request. What made it so odd was that Davies had decanted probably hundreds of bottles for him, over the years.

"Of course, my lord, at once." Davies didn't move. Then, abruptly—"My lord, is everything all right?"

Nev wanted to snap at him, but he was touched by the man's concern. "Everything is splendid. I am simply in the mood for some brandy."

Davies nodded, and in a few minutes he was back with a full decanter and a snifter. After the man had left the room, Nev poured himself a glass. He stared at it, turning it in his hand. This was it, then.

For a moment he was tempted to pour it in the grate and tell Penelope he had drunk it. But that would be ridiculous. He was a grown man, and he refused to be afraid of a damn glass of liquor. He took a small sip. It tasted just as good as he remembered.

The warmth spread down his throat, all the way to his stomach. But there was no time to savor it. Penelope must be ready by now. He smiled and gulped the brandy down.

Changing into his nightclothes, he already felt himself affected. His hands were clumsy on the ties of his dressing gown. He hadn't eaten in a few hours, and he had grown unaccustomed to liquor.

To his surprise, being drunk was not the seductive paradise he had created in his mind during these last few months of sobriety. He felt a little happier, that was all. He could still remember his problems but they seemed smaller, further away.

Penelope wasn't far away, though. She was in the next room. His smile grew. He had been afraid he would want another glass; at that moment he didn't want *anything* that would delay getting to Penelope.

He didn't bother to knock. Penelope was waiting; she was on him before he got two steps into the room. Her mouth was sweet and warm, and the heavy embroidered silk of her robe was smooth and sensuous under his hands. There was a heady floral scent in his nostrils.

"You did drink the brandy," she said happily when he finally pulled his mouth away from hers.

"You told me to, didn't you? I—" He got a good look at her and stopped talking. She was wearing a dressing gown made of the same fabric that covered the ridiculous new settee. In the candlelight the golden dragons glimmered and the contrast of the dark blue silk with her pale skin was shocking. The robe covered most of her; all he could see was her head and neck, her bare feet, and the ends of her fingers. It reminded him of that first night at Loweston, of Penelope swathed in her nightshirt. There were three great purple chrysanthemums curling in her loosely pinned hair. "You—you—where did you get chrysanthemums?"

She smiled. "My mother grows them in our back garden at

home. I asked her to send me a few plants. I didn't tell her why I wanted them."

Penelope had gone to all this trouble for him, because of a chance remark. "You're the best wife in the world." Pulling her forward by her wide yellow sash, he crushed her mouth beneath his. He felt for the ends of the sash and worked them free. His fingers told him the best part, but he didn't believe it until he pulled back and looked.

She was naked underneath.

Nev had died and gone to heaven. He raised one hand to her breast, filled with intoxicated wonder. "So beautiful. So damned beautiful . . . Sorry, dashed."

She hummed in satisfaction. "Come here." She tugged him over to the settee. He sat, reaching for her eagerly, but before he could kiss her she climbed on top of him, pushing him back against the cushions, and trailed openmouthed kisses down his neck. "Nev." Her breath was hot against his skin. "Mine."

"Yours," he gasped.

"I bought you. I bought you and you're mine."

He nodded, drunk on happiness and desire, and threaded his fingers in her hair. A chrysanthemum fell to the floor and filled the room with fragrance.

Penelope woke up feeling happy, although she didn't remember why. It was late, nearly ten o'clock. She ought to be up doing things, but somehow it was all right that she wasn't. She was wearing—she was wearing a Chinese silk dressing gown and sleeping in Nev's bed. His hand rested lightly on her waist. She smiled.

However, she also had to use the necessary. She sat up gingerly, trying not to wake Nev—abruptly nausea washed over her and her head ached. At the same time she remembered everything that had happened the night before.

Oh, God. She had exposed herself utterly. Figuratively *and* literally. She barely made it to the basin in her room before being sick. So this was a hangover.

But it was worse than that. She had wondered about love, she had wondered if Nev loved her and if she loved him, but it had been almost like a game; she had never quite believed in it. It was real now. She was in love, she loved him madly. She had always thought that grand passions were a myth created by fools to explain their own weak-willed behavior, and now their reality was blinding. Penelope felt as if she had turned a corner on an ordinary London street and seen a great dragon coiled there.

She took deep breaths and tried to be still; every movement made the nausea worse. She loved Nev. She would have told him so, last night. She was pitifully grateful that he hadn't let her.

Still, he must know. She had barely stopped touching him the whole evening. Everyone must know. Edward must know. Oh, God, had she really tried to take her hair down in the carriage? Had Nev really had to cajole her into propriety as if she were a spoiled child? Had she really told him his hair was like cinnamon? That he made her dizzy?

Her mouth tasted like acid and her head ached. She planted her hands on either side of the washstand and stared in the mirror, her chest still heaving. In the brutal light of morning she saw her plain face and slight form swathed in blue and gold and felt sicker than she had ever felt in her life. She looked like a sparrow borrowing a peacock's feathers, and she had let herself feel pretty. She had let herself feel *beautiful*, because Nev had said she was. Dear, sweet Nev who must have said that to a million girls. Who must have made a million girls believe it.

Nev cares about me, she reminded herself. *He respects me. Well, he did before last night.* That was what she had wanted, wasn't it? A marriage based on reason and compromise and mutual esteem?

Reason and compromise and mutual esteem were shadowy intellectual conceits. Her love for Nev was blood and bone and sinew. It was all true, all the poetry and the damn Minerva Press novels. She really did feel as though she would die without him.

But the idea of living *with* him, like this, knowing that she loved him, was far worse. God, her head ached! She wanted someone else to fix it, to comfort her, to smooth back her hair and give her cool water to drink. She wanted Nev.

She shied away from that, searching for something safe, and thought of her mother. What would Mrs. Brown say? She wouldn't understand, that was certain; she wouldn't see that it was complicated. She'd say, *What a lot of fuss over nothing, Penny. Just tell him how you feel!*

Penelope *could* tell him. Perhaps—perhaps he felt the same way. Perhaps she could be happy. He liked her, he cared about her, he'd told her again and again how much—

But she couldn't even *think* it without a sense of impending horror so strong she could not get round it. She couldn't tell him. She couldn't let herself believe that he might return her feelings. What if she were wrong?

Knowing that she burned for him while he thought her a very nice girl was bad enough. But if *he* knew it and pitied her and tried to be kind—and if he knew, moreover, that she had *hoped*—

She had to compromise. She would stay and see him every day and never tell him how she felt.

But she knew that she couldn't do that either. She couldn't compromise on this. Always before she had been in control of herself, the one thing she *could* have mastery over, and now she was come to the end of that control.

Nausea washed over her again in dizzying waves. She

needed time. Time to think, time to come to terms with herself. *Time to hide*, she told herself scornfully. And, *What of it?* she snapped right back. Her head felt like it was inside out; she just needed a little *time*—

Nev opened the door between their rooms. She turned, wiping her mouth with the back of her hand. She had never felt more unglamorous. He looked fresh and rumpled and happy and handsome beyond bearing, and she could not speak.

"Have a head, do you? You didn't drink much, it shouldn't be too bad. After you've drunk some tea and had breakfast, you'll feel right as rain."

The thought of breakfast made her gorge rise; he must have seen it, because he came forward and brushed her hair back from her face. She closed her eyes and leaned into his touch.

"I know it sounds all wrong," he said, and she thought how very dear his voice was, how it was the first thing she had loved, without knowing it, "but bacon and eggs are just the thing when you feel rotten the morning after drinking."

Breakfast with Nev. She remembered him licking honey off her fingers, and tears stung her eyes. She felt so sick, and she just wanted to lie down and have Nev read to her. Sing to her, maybe.

"What's wrong, sweet?"

If she went down to breakfast with him she would stay. "I'm going home." As soon as she blurted it out, she was choked with longing. Her mother might not understand, but she would hold her, she would stroke her hair, she would *love* her. And Penelope could lie in her familiar bed and eat familiar English food and feel *safe*.

There was a moment's pause; then Nev said, as though he must have misheard her, "What?"

"I need some time to think. We both do—Nev, you know

things have been awful. And I'm the one who got all your people arrested, it'll be easier without me. I'll go stay with my parents for a while. I can't think here, Nev, everyone *hates* me—" Oh, God, she sounded like a child. She sounded pathetic and she wanted to slap herself. But it was the *truth*.

"*I* don't hate you!"

She turned her face away.

"Surely this isn't necessary. Tell me what's wrong. Surely we can compromise—"

She flinched. "*No*," she said. "No. I've been compromising all my life."

"I just—I don't understand. Last night—" He didn't seem to know how to finish the sentence.

Last night I made it plain to the entire neighborhood that I worship you passionately? Is that what you were going to say? she wanted to shout, humiliated. Instead she said, "I'm very sorry for my behavior last night. I know I must have embarrassed you sorely."

"Penelope, what is going on? What happened? Are you really serious?"

"Yes, I'm serious!" she said angrily. "Why is it so hard to believe?" She knew the reason was her own foolish behavior. She couldn't meet his eyes. She couldn't even look at him, not when his disbelief and hurt were plain in his voice. *Take it back*, a voice whispered. *Apologize. You're being selfish and foolish and all kinds of irrational.* But she *wanted* to be selfish, damn it. She wanted to do what was right for *her*, just this once. "I can't stay, Nev. I need to think. I'll just go home, for a while, and then we'll see. We'll talk. Whatever happens, I'll make sure you keep the money, I promise—"

"Hang the money! This *is* your home!"

She stared. He stalked toward her, looking as if he would grab her by the shoulders and shake her. Backing hastily away, she trod on a wilted chrysanthemum. The smell made her gag.

"Just tell me one thing. Last night, if I had let you tell me how you felt, is this what you would have said?"

God, his eyes were blue.

"Are you telling me that—that was a goddamned good-bye present?"

She was against the wall now, trapped. She couldn't let me believe that, but—

The door opened and a white-faced Lady Bedlow flew in. "Louisa's eloped!" She took in the scene. "Penelope, dear, what on *earth* are you wearing?"

And so, for the second time in twelve hours, Nev found himself making the carriage ride to Greygloss. But this time, Louisa wasn't with them. How had everything gone so terribly wrong? It was worse, even, than those two weeks after his father had died, before he had proposed to Penelope. Then there had been hours of books and faulty arithmetic and a faint, persistent grief; now there was a jagged hole inside him. He had thought he had fixed everything. He had thought that with Penelope by his side, everything might come out all right in the end. Just last night, it had seemed as if, maybe, everything *was* all right.

But he had fixed nothing at all. Instead, he had failed in every way imaginable. His sister was gone. His best friend was gone. His wife was leaving.

Penelope was leaving. God.

What was he fighting for? *Who* was he fighting for? What was to be his reward when he had pulled Loweston out of the hole it was in? He might as well give up. He might as well go bankrupt tomorrow.

He might as well get drunk and find someone to blow his brains out.

The thought snapped him out of his stupor of self-pity. What would Penelope say if she knew how morbidly he was thinking?

He clung to the last hope he had. He would bring Louisa back. Percy was a faster driver than either of them, but if Nev and Thirkell spelled each other they could overtake him. And when Louisa was safe home, he would talk to Penelope. She was a sensible girl; she would see reason. She had to, because Nev could not imagine how he would live if she did not.

She said she might come back. She said she just needed a little time to think. But what was there for her to come back for? *Everyone hates me here,* she had said. And the only answer Nev could give her was that *he* didn't. If she didn't want him, then there was nothing for her at Loweston.

He had thought she did. Last night she had been so warm and sweet and she'd wanted him—hadn't she? She didn't seem to want him now.

He looked at his wife, leaning back against the seats with her eyes closed and her mouth set in lines of nausea and pain. She looked so pale and tired and unhappy. *I've compromised all my life,* she had said. All he had ever wanted from her— besides her money, he reminded himself bitterly—was for her to be herself. To do and say what she wanted, what she needed. Now she was, and if that meant leaving him, could he really ask her to stay?

They pulled up at Greygloss. Nev put his thoughts aside and ran up the steps. He banged on the door, but it was several minutes before the butler opened it. "I'm sorry to intrude so early, but I have urgent business with Lord Thirkell," Nev said, grabbing Penelope's hand and pushing past the startled butler. "If I might just take my family to the breakfast room first—"

"Nev," Penelope said. "Please—"

He dragged her into the breakfast room and flung her down in a chair. He poured tea and filled a plate with eggs and bacon and toast and set them in front of her. "Eat. It will make you feel better. I'll be back soon." He turned back to the butler. "Take me to Lord Thirkell's room."

He followed the man to Thirkell's door and banged on it, hard. There was no answer. Thirkell always slept like a log. Nev pounded harder. "Thirkell!"

"My lord," the butler said in pained accents, "people are sleeping."

"And I want them to bloody well stop, that's the point. *Thirkell!*"

His fist was raised to pound again when Thirkell opened the door, and Nev nearly hit him in the nose. Thirkell blinked bleary eyes at him. "Nev?"

"Thirkell, I need your help. I need to borrow your racing curricle."

Thirkell yawned. "You can't. Percy's got it." Then his eyes widened and he clapped a hand over his mouth.

Nev realized abruptly how very, very stupid he had been. He could not understand why he had not tumbled to it immediately—perhaps because he had been so distracted by Penelope's announcement. Of course Thirkell was in on it. The spiked punch, when Lady Bedlow was so susceptible; Thirkell's guilty face; *Nev, I need to tell you something.*

Nev had no one left now—no one to help him. He wanted Penelope so badly it hurt, physically hurt. He clenched his teeth.

"I almost told you, Nev." Thirkell's words tumbled over each other and meant absolutely nothing, because Thirkell had helped Louisa and Percy. "I wanted to tell you, but you know how Percy is, and you had been awfully rough on him, and I had promised silence faithfully—there's no help for it now, you know. Percy and my curricle, and such a head start—"

"It is very early in the morning to be talking of curricle racing," Sir Jasper said, appearing at Nev's elbow. Oh, God, Sir Jasper. Lord knew what he would do if he found out how matters lay. He might take his disappointment out on anybody—on Nev's people, on the poachers, on little Josie Cusher. It had to be hushed up as long as possible.

"Oh, we weren't—" Thirkell broke off with such obvious guilt that Nev very nearly laughed at the whole absurd situation.

"We weren't talking of curricle racing," he said. "Mr. Garrett's mother has been taken ill, and he borrowed Lord Thirkell's curricle to go see her. But he has left his luggage behind him, and we were wondering if it might catch up with him."

"I see," Sir Jasper said. "Is that what brings you here so early?"

"My mother lost an earring," Nev said. "She was so distressed that I offered to drive over directly."

Sir Jasper was too well-bred to inquire further into what Nev was all too aware was a paltry lie, and one he did not even trust his mother to corroborate. But he could think of no other way to explain the dowager countess's presence.

Though they had been the only people in the breakfast room when they arrived, by the time Nev, Thirkell, and Sir Jasper entered it again, it was full of guests and the bustle of conversation and silverware and morning papers. Nev's gaze instinctively turned to Penelope. She was eating, methodically, her color somewhat restored. But her drained, unhappy look was as pronounced as ever.

Sir Jasper greeted Penelope and Lady Bedlow graciously. "I will instruct the servants to search the ballroom and hallway for your earring at once. I know it is irreplaceable."

Lady Bedlow's startled gaze flew to Nev. He gave her the smallest nod he could manage, and to her credit she said, "Yes. It has my dear husband's hair in it, you know."

"But where is Miss Ambrey?" Sir Jasper asked. "Still abed, no doubt?"

Lady Bedlow's small store of subterfuge was used up. She

flushed crimson and stammered something in which, "Lou-isa," "a school friend," and "taken ill" were discernible, but not much more.

Nev looked at Sir Jasper to see how he took this. The man was no fool. Nev was prepared for skepticism, perhaps even anger. But he was shocked by the pure violence of the baron-et's emotion. His face was chalk white, his eyes dark furious slits.

Nev's heart sank. Louisa and Percy had made him and his people a powerful enemy in the neighborhood.

Penelope stood abruptly. "Nev, I'm going to be sick."

"You, fetch a basin," Nev snapped at a footman.

"No time," Penelope said in a tiny voice.

This, at least, was a crisis Nev felt equipped to deal with. Hurrying to the side table, he unceremoniously dumped the bacon in with the sausage and brought her the pan, cursing as it burned his fingers. The poor girl was promptly, violently sick; the breakfast hadn't had time to do her any good.

"I'm so sorry," she said miserably as he wiped her mouth with his handkerchief. "I'm so sorry about everything."

"It's all right. It's not your fault." He wanted to be angry with her, but she looked so very mortified. Sighing, he gath-ered her up in one arm and let her bury her face in his jacket. He signaled to the footman to take the soiled pan away and looked round at the assembled guests over Penelope's head, daring them to look even the smallest bit amused.

Several *were* hiding smiles, but Thirkell's aunt said com-fortably, "It *is* embarrassing, isn't it? I remember when I was expecting my third, I cast up my accounts on my husband's new Persian rug. Oh, he was furious!" Soon all the married ladies were swapping stories about their morning sickness.

Penelope, however, had gone rigid.

It would never have occurred to Nev, otherwise; she had been drunk the night before. There was nothing out of the way in her feeling sick. But he glanced down and met her eyes, her mouth a stunned O, and the word *expecting* echoed in his ears very loud.

He tried to remember when she had last had her month-lies, and could not recall. "Are you—?" he asked under his breath.

"I don't know."

He could not tell what she felt. He could not even tell what *he* felt. It would be a great difficulty, if Penelope really meant to be gone. And then, she might stay for the sake of the child, and the thought made him furious. But despite all these rational considerations, there was something very much like joy being born in his heart: a hopeful, infant joy.

He turned his head so that Penelope would not see him smiling, and spied Sir Jasper going out the door. He ignored his irrational flash of unease. "Here, sit down. I'll get you a cup of tea."

Penelope sat, a look of shock still on her face. Nev crossed to the tea service and was just adding the obscene amounts of honey he knew Penelope liked when Mr. Snively raced in, sweaty and gasping for breath.

For once in his life, the vicar didn't bother with polite greetings. "Where is Sir Jasper? He must come directly!"

"He just stepped out," Nev said. "What is the trouble?"

"He's needed to read the Riot Act. The folk are form-ing up here and at Loweston, and they mean to free the prisoners!"

Eighteen

Sir Jasper rode down the drive, the shade of the Montagu oaks heavy on his face like a corpse's shadow in the hot Paris summer. In the fields, his men's faces twisted with hatred as he passed. Fear grew within him, hot and thick.

It was all slipping away, everything he had worked so hard for. He had spent his life keeping the wretches in his district from revolting. He had spent countless hours on the bench and spent a fortune to discourage poaching and sedition, he had enclosed the commons, he had spent years painstakingly guiding the late Lord Bedlow in everything, he had built up contacts and relationships, he had *spent his life*. Other people were happy, but not he. He had worked so hard, always, to make sure that everyone was safe. To make sure his sons never had to hide in the attic and watch an old man hanged on their doorstep.

He laughed, a strangled, high sound he didn't recognize. What sons? His wife had been barren and was dead, and Louisa was gone, eloped with the steward because of Bedlow's mismanagement and that bitch Lady Bedlow, who had somehow tricked him into thinking it was her the steward had his eye on, and not beautiful Louisa, the pride of the neighborhood.

And now the Cit countess was breeding. Breeding! *She* would have a son, and all that money would be assured, and together that wretched family would lead the district straight to Hell. Loweston would be ruined and Greygloss with it, and then the whole country would go, slipping and sliding into bloody revolt like at St. Peter's Field.

As sudden and fierce and unstoppable as a revolution, something inside Sir Jasper rose up and said *No more*. It was all that bitch Lady Bedlow's fault. Bedlow would have seen things Sir Jasper's way easy enough if she hadn't always been there with her idiotic town notions. The district was up in arms, and she'd made Bedlow think he could stop it with a few hocks of ham.

Without her degenerate influence, Louisa would never have dreamed of running away.

Sir Jasper was going to stop this. He had tried to do it kindly, to see that no one was hurt. They had been too willful. It was too late for that now.

Amy felt herself waking up and fought against it. It was no use, but she didn't open her eyes. As long as she kept her eyes closed, she might still be in her charming, sumptuous bedroom in London and not a wretched, dirty hovel. Of course, even with her eyes closed, she could tell she was lying on a hard cot, not her huge featherbed. She had worked so hard not to live like this. She could not wait to be better and go back to London, away from sweet, handsome Nev and his likable wife who made her green with envy.

It took her a moment or two to realize she was hearing voices, and that they had woken her up. Agnes and—Sir Jasper, she realized. She tried to be pleased. The baronet had been visiting her regularly ever since she was well enough; she rather thought that was one reason the Baileys had wanted to get rid of her. She had quickly learned that Sir Jasper was not popular among the local people.

She didn't like him either, though she could not put her finger on why. He simply made her hackles rise. *Stop being fanciful*, she told herself. *Open your eyes and charm him.* The thought exhausted her. *In a moment*, she promised, and snuggled deeper into her blankets.

Sir Jasper broke off. "Is she awake?" Amy heard him coming closer and stooping down to look at her. "Amy," he said softly, his breath hot on her face.

She did not know what in his tone made her do it, but she shifted and sighed, as if still asleep, throwing an arm over her face. Feigning sleep was one of Amy's many professional skills.

Sir Jasper stood and walked back to Agnes, speaking to her in a low voice. Amy strained to hear. She caught "my house," "Lady Bedlow," something she thought was "get her alone" and "woods" but might not have been, and her own name. Everything else was a murmur whose sense she could not fully grasp but which somehow made her intensely uneasy. "Wait for me there," he finished.

"But sir—" Agnes said, audible and agitated.

Amy heard his next words very clearly. "Oh, come now, it's not as if you have any affection for the woman."

"No, sir, but—"

"If you care for your daughter at all, you will do it. I can see her saved, or I can send her to the Assizes."

There was a pause. "Yes, sir. I'll go at once."

Sir Jasper strode out.

Amy heard a rustling thud that might have been Agnes kneeling. "Kit," she said softly. "Mama has to go out now. Stay here, sweetie."

"Mama go where?"

"Mama is going to help Josie." Agnes's voice shook. "Stay here and watch the pretty lady. Don't go outside. There are angry people outside."

"Angry?"

"Because people like Sir Jasper think they own us," Agnes told him, sounding stronger for a moment. "But they don't, do they, Kit?"

"No," Kit said doubtfully.

"They don't own you on the inside, Kit. Always remember that." Agnes went out and shut the door behind her.

Something was very wrong. Amy did not know what; she only knew, deep in her bones, that something was wrong, and that Sir Jasper wanted to hurt Nev's wife.

Amy opened her eyes and considered, staring at the ancient thatch. Yesterday she had managed to walk from her bed to the door and back again without stumbling. Of course, she had leaned on the door frame for a minute or two in between. She did not know if she could make it to the Grange to warn the Bedlows. She did not even know where the Grange was. And Agnes had said there were angry people outside. Whatever that meant, it couldn't be good.

She could lie here and pretend she had heard nothing. Even if Penelope were hurt, what did it harm Amy? Nev might even take her back if his wife was out of the way.

Amy sighed and threw back the blankets. She sat up, slowly, and her head spun. Standing, she balanced herself with a hand laid flat against the wall.

"Kit? We need to go for a walk." The child would slow her down, but Amy could hardly leave him behind.

"No outside. Mama said."

"Mama told you to stay with me. And I'm going for a walk. Do you know where the big house is?"

"Grange," Kit said. "Sloship gave me sixpence."

That took her a moment. "His lordship gave you sixpence?"

Kit nodded.

"If we go there now, he'll give you a shilling," Amy promised. "Do you know how to get there from here?"

"Another riot?" Lady Bedlow was white and trembling, but Nev had no attention to spare.

"Is this true?" he asked. "How many are involved?"

"It's true," Mr. Snively said. "I saw them with my own eyes. Thirty at least and half of them drunk. They want an audience with Sir Jasper. They're on their way here now." There were gasps from a number of the guests. Nev distinctly heard his mother's sharp intake of breath; when he glanced down at Penelope, however, she looked merely intent, her brown eyes fixed on the vicar's face.

"Where in Heaven's name is the baronet?" Snively asked.

"He walked out just a minute ago." Remembering his earlier unease, Nev gestured to a footman. "Go find your master. Tell him it's urgent."

Ten excruciating minutes later, made worse by Snively's unbroken moralizing on the rebellious nature of the English peasant, the butler entered the room. "Sir Jasper is not in the house, my lord. Nor in the stables or any of the outbuildings. Shall I send to the home farm?"

"Send everywhere. Do it quickly." Nev did not know that he trusted Sir Jasper to deal with the crisis, but they must have a magistrate to read the Riot Act. Or the sheriff, but he was miles away, nearly to Bury St. Edmonds. Perhaps the people would simply disperse. *Or perhaps they will hang Sir Jasper to the nearest tree.*

"Very good, my lord." The butler bowed his way out.

Nev looked down and met Penelope's fearful, resigned eyes. She knew what he was about to say. "I've got to go talk to them."

She opened her mouth as if she were going to protest, then shut it tightly and nodded, once.

"Stay by Thirkell. He'll protect you if things get ugly."

She gave a little sobbing laugh. "Who'll protect *you?*"

Nev felt a rush of anger. He took his arm from around her. "What do you care? You'd be a deal freer as a widow than a separated wife."

Now she drew in a sharp, shocked breath.

He looked at her white face, and out of all the ruin of his life today, this was the only thing that mattered. He took a quick step away from her before he could do something stupid and selfish, like beg her to stay. "I'm going to see if I can reason with them," he said loudly. "All of you stay here. I doubt they will try to hurt you, but you will be safer together."

"I will go with you," Mr. Snively said. "Perhaps I can bring them to a sense of their insolence, their hubris if I may say so—"

"You may say nothing of the kind. I consider your hypocritical moralizing partly responsible for this disaster. You will stay here or by God, I will see you broken."

The vicar fell back, muttering to himself in a shocked undertone.

Several of the other men offered to come with him, but he didn't know any of them. He didn't know what they would do. "In a direct contest of strength, five of us will have no better chance than one," he said. "If it comes to that, we're already lost. Stay here and protect the women."

"Let me come with you at least," Thirkell said. "I know I'm useless, but I'd have your back."

"I had rather have you than anyone," Nev told him. Anyone but Percy. And Percy was gone. "But I need you here. Don't let anything happen to Penelope or my mother."

Thirkell drew himself up. "Never." He was going to say more, but Lady Bedlow threw herself on Nev, sobbing.

"Don't go. Barricade the doors, and when those wretched folk get here we'll shoot them all. Don't go, Nate! What will I do if something happens to you? I can't lose two of my children at once!"

He put her away from him gently. "You haven't lost Louisa. She'll be back in a few days. And I'll be back in a few hours."

"Come, Lady Bedlow." Penelope's face was still bloodless, but her voice was steady. "Come and sit by me. You heard Nev. He'll be back soon."

To Nev's surprise, Lady Bedlow allowed Penelope to put

her arm around her and lead her to a chair. Penelope looked back at him, once. "You had better be," she said. "I care."

Nev had not ridden as far as he would have liked—a mile, give or take—when he saw them ahead of him on the path, a crowd of laborers and their wives. He thought there were more than Mr. Snively had estimated, perhaps forty in all. As the vicar had said, some were drunk. Some held pitchforks and other potentially deadly farming tools, some held—Nev's heart sank—guns. More poachers, he supposed. When he drew closer, he recognized many of the faces: the Baileys, Aaron Smith, the families of some other of the poachers, more of his laborers. Helen Spratt was there, holding an old fowling piece. He thought for a moment of staying in the saddle, but he did not know how a display of aristocratic authority might strike them at the moment. He dismounted and walked toward them, leading Sir Jasper's horse.

The group stopped, clustering together. Whispers and murmurs blended together so that he could not hear what they were saying, except for his name. When Nev was ten feet away, Aaron came forward to meet him. "My lord," he said derisively. "Get out of our way."

"Where are you going?"

"We're going to talk to that buggering son-of-a-bitch Sir Jasper and tell him to free our folk."

"Sir Jasper isn't at the house. No one can find him. You'd better talk to me."

Aaron's brows drew together. "You aren't a magistrate. You can't release Josie."

"You should be glad Sir Jasper isn't at home. You know that once he reads the Riot Act, you have twenty minutes to disperse before he can take you all by force."

Aaron sneered. "No doubt he'd try to run us down and kill us like they did those poor folk at Manchester," he said, loud enough that the assembled mob could hear him. "Let him try. We're not going to stand like sods and take it the way they did." There were cheers, and a couple of men raised their guns.

The horse stamped and snorted nervously behind him. Nev quashed a tremor of fear and raised his voice. "This is madness. You cannot do this. For the love of God, go home."

"We can't do this?" Aaron asked. "Why? Because we're the dirt under your feet and we must be good little children? Because Mr. Snively says God says we can't? Because you're used to us taking orders and now you're scared?"

"No," Nev said, though he *was* scared. He heard the Oxbridge cadences of his voice project over the crowd and wondered how he sounded to them. "You can't do this because it *will not work*. What do you think will happen to you if you kill a baronet and justice of the peace? Do you think the Crown will simply let you walk away? They'll make you an example to all the countryside, and the poachers too. They'll hang you and send your children to the workhouse." He lowered his voice. "Help me stop this, Aaron. Do you think Agnes will be pleased to see you hang by her daughter's side? I see she had better sense than to come out here."

Aaron flushed. "I don't know where Aggie is. And I don't think she gives a damn whether I'm hanged. But I'm not about to let her little girl die without a fight."

"Even if Sir Jasper did release Josie and the men," Nev told the crowd, "he would only retake them all next day, when he could get troops to back him."

"We know," Aaron said. "We know you gentry's word can't be trusted. It happened to Downham in '16. We'd be gone before he could come after us."

Nev looked at them. Some had been here since before he was born. "Really? You're all going to pick up and leave your homes, every one of you? No, most of you will stay, and then you'll be arrested and you'll turn on one another. Don't you remember why your men are in jail to begin with?"

There was suddenly a ring of empty space around the Baileys. Mr. Bailey's face flushed. An uncertain mutter rose up among the men.

Nev began to hope he might be successful. "Go home. Go home peacefully before anyone else sees you. I promise I will do everything in my power to save your friends. I am already hiring the best lawyers I can find—"

"Hang lawyers!" someone yelled, and the mood of the mob shifted to violence. "Lawyers are lying, thieving buggers! Free the men now!"

"See how *you* like losing your family!"

"The only one who might identify us to the magistrate is *you*!"

A rock flew out of the crowd and struck Nev hard on the shoulder.

Penelope reflected that she and Lady Bedlow were very different women. Penelope wished only for peace to sit silently by the window and watch the drive for Nev's return. Lady Bedlow's fear, on the other hand, rendered her even more voluble than usual. She kept up a steady stream of anxious questions (whose answers she did not wait to hear), disjointed reminiscences about Nev's prowess in school as an orator, and vows of vengeance against any laborers who dared to so much as raise their voices in her son's presence. In this Mr. Snively encouraged her until Penelope could no longer tell where her hangover ended and her nerves began. Or, God, her morning sickness, what if she were really going to have a baby and something happened to Nev?

She wouldn't think about it. She couldn't. If he didn't come back, and she had told him she might leave him—

There was a brief silence. Penelope drew a grateful breath,

and then Lady Bedlow said softly, "Mr. Snively, if he doesn't come back—"

"You must be brave," Mr. Snively said. "The Lord giveth, and the Lord taketh away."

"For God's sake be silent!" Penelope's voice was half a shriek, and all the conversations in the room stopped abruptly. "Not another word! You're driving me mad!" Lady Bedlow's jaw dropped, hurt tears starting in her eyes. Everyone was staring. Penelope knew she ought to feel ashamed, but she didn't. She only wanted Nev.

A woman she did not know put a hand on her arm and began speaking in a low, sympathetic voice. Penelope shook her hand off. "Don't touch me!" She turned back to the window. There was someone coming up the drive, but it was a woman, so Penelope wasn't interested.

Whispers rose around the room in a wave. Penelope didn't care, so long as they left her alone. She felt someone coming up behind her, and tensed for a confrontation.

"Steady on," Thirkell said. "Nev's talked his way out of worse scrapes than this." He didn't say anything else, only stood solidly at her shoulder. Penelope felt comforted.

She watched the woman come slowly up the drive and realized it was Agnes Cusher. Her heart quickened. Had Agnes been at the riot? Did she bear news?

Agnes was almost at the door. Penelope glanced at Lady Bedlow, sobbing quietly into Mr. Snively's handkerchief. She had better hear what Agnes had to say herself first.

"I have to use the necessary," she told Thirkell, then slipped out of the room and half ran to the front door. The footmen must all be searching for Sir Jasper; no one saw her ease the door open and slip out.

Agnes started back, looking shaken. "B—bad news—"

Penelope closed her eyes and prayed she wouldn't faint. "What happened? Is he alive?"

"Who?"

Penelope was at once disappointed and transcendently relieved that the woman had no news of Nev.

"I've come about the girl. Miss Raeburn. She's taken bad, calling for you."

"Calling for *me*?"

"You've got to come and talk to her. I'm afraid she'll do herself a hurt. She liked you, that time you came to visit."

Penelope did not want to go. She wanted to stay here and wait for Nev. *Selfish*, she reprimanded herself. It did not hold the same weight it once had.

But what would Nev say if Penelope let his mistress suffer alone? What if Miss Wray were really to injure herself?

Agnes actually reached out as if she would take Penelope's arm, though she didn't quite dare. "Come on. I shouldn't even have left her alone for this long. Not with the men up in arms."

A fresh fear struck Penelope. She should not go out with only another woman, not today. It might prove dangerous. But she couldn't take Lord Thirkell with her; she had to leave him here to protect Nev's mother. And she could not ask for any other escort, because any gentleman present would be sure to recognize Nev's mistress, and it would be a scandal.

"Please, you *must*!"

The desperation in Agnes's voice decided Penelope. "Let's go." She started down the steps.

Amy, her eyes closed, leaned against one of the huge oaks that lined the long drive to the Grange. Sure enough, Kit had known the way, but it had seemed to take years to get even this far—years of putting one foot down in front of the other, sweating, and struggling for breath. She had spent the last month indoors, in rooms with tiny windows; the sun was blinding. The heat too was unbearable, even in the shade. It was at least another quarter mile to the house, and the world was already starting to wobble around the edges.

"Come 'long." Kit tugged at Amy's skirts. "Shilling."

Amy opened her eyes reluctantly, seeing the little boy through a wash of blue produced by too much sunlight.

Kit waddled a few feet toward the manor and stopped, staring at Amy insistently.

"Coming, Kit." Amy pushed herself upright and started forward. She made it three steps before she tumbled and fell, the flats of her arms hitting the gravel with a painful scraping. She lay with her cheek against the ground and stared at the rolling park that was Nev's birthright.

Something terrible was going to happen to Nev's wife because Amy was too weak to make it another quarter of a mile. Her last thought before she lost consciousness was that the heroine of a play would have managed it.

Nev's arm throbbed where the rock had hit it. "Think about what you are doing," he shouted, placing a calming hand on the restive horse. "Who is tending the harvest while you play at storming the Bastille?"

There was silence.

"I know my father didn't treat you well. I know you have no reason to trust me. But I'm trying, and I am going to save your friends. You aren't helping them by proving Sir Jasper right that you all wish to murder the gentry in their beds. Bring in the harvest and be patient—"

Aaron Smith looked uncertain.

Helen Spratt stepped out of the crowd. "We've been patient an awful long time." The coarse tones of her voice cut effortlessly through Nev's words. "I've been patient, and my mother was patient before me, and my grandmother. I ain't going to be patient anymore. I'm getting Harry back." She leveled her fowling piece at Nev's face from two feet away. "Get out of my way."

The crowd drew back, gasps and shocked whispers rising.

"Helen," Aaron said, real alarm in his voice.

Nev's heart pounded, and Sir Jasper's horse snorted behind him, pacing backward. *I can't die*, he thought. *I have responsibilities.* He had to stand aside. But if he did, they would march to Greygloss and do something unalterably foolish, and they would all be hanged, every last one.

Besides, Penelope and his mother were at Greygloss.

He straightened. "No. If you want to hang, the quickest way to it is by shooting me. Well, here I am."

"*Helen*," Aaron Smith hissed. "Don't."

She hesitated.

"Then stand down!" Nev roared. "If you want to change anything, we have to work together!"

"Work together my arse." She fired the gun.

"Are you sure we're on the right path?" Penelope followed Agnes down a little trail that skirted the edge of the Greygloss woods. Through gaps in the trees she caught glimpses of the Gothic ruin on its hill coming closer, so she supposed they must be going in the right direction. Still, she did not like being so near the spring guns. Of course the traps would hardly sneak out of the forest and ambush her on the path, but—Nev had told her never to wander the Greygloss grounds alone. She wished she had listened to him.

"I think I've lived here a little longer than you, my lady," Agnes threw back over her shoulder as she hurried along ten paces ahead.

"Agnes—" Penelope began warningly.

"Just be quiet. We're almost there." She went round a curve in the path and was out of Penelope's sight. Penelope hurried to catch up.

She almost ran straight into Sir Jasper. Agnes hovered anxiously at his elbow. He smiled at her, and her earlier nausea came crashing back. In his hand he held an elegant dueling pistol.

"Here, drink this."

Amy came back to the world in a haze of blissful shade and something cool sliding down her throat. She opened her eyes. A sandy-haired, tanned face hovered over her, and a strong arm supported her shoulders.

"Good, you're awake." There was a faint Scots burr in his voice. "Here, have some more water."

Amy sipped the water gratefully. She was reflexively calculating how to use her position in his arms to lay a groundwork for seduction, when everything that had happened came back to her. She sat up with a start, nearly knocking her forehead into his. They were in an elegant sitting room that seemed to be inexplicably missing half of its furniture. "Kit?" she called.

"Your little boy is fine. I sent him down to the kitchens for a snack." The man looked oddly familiar.

"He's not mine. How long have I been asleep? I have to see Nev—Lord Bedlow—at once!"

The man stiffened. "Lord and Lady Bedlow have gone out. I believe they went to Greygloss."

A hot spurt of frustration boiled up inside Amy. She didn't curse, she never cursed—but she *wanted* to. She shot to her feet, then regretted it when her knees refused to take her weight. Her rescuer sighed and snaked an arm around her waist, holding her up.

Amy clutched at his coat. "You've got to take me there. Lady Bedlow is in danger."

The man started. "Penelope in danger? What do you mean?"

"I don't know precisely. But I overheard Agnes Cusher talking to Sir Jasper. It sounded like they were plotting to hurt her. You must take me to her at once!"

The man frowned. "What exactly did you hear?"

Amy nearly ground her teeth together. She didn't have time for this! "They spoke so softly that I heard very little." She was painfully aware how thin that sounded. "But I distinctly heard Lady Bedlow's name, and I am morally certain they were planning some mischief."

He nodded as if she had confirmed something he already suspected. "You've been ill," he said gently. "You shouldn't be walking about alone. You might have suffered a serious setback."

"I am not delirious! I need to get to Greygloss!"

"Why would Sir Jasper want to hurt Penelope?" His voice was the embodiment of patience and reason. "You're sick, and anxious, that's all. Just lie down, and I'm sure—"

It was all for nothing. She had actually made it here and now it was all for nothing because she was a female and weak and had fainted, and why would such a capable-looking male believe a word she said? Amy reached out and overturned a bowl of fruit. Porcelain shattered and an apple rolled under a far table and it was the most satisfying thing she had ever seen. "Listen to me! Why won't you listen? I am *not delirious*! He'll hurt her!"

He looked really alarmed, and for a moment Amy thought she had won. Then he reached out and seized her wrists. "You'll injure yourself. Please, everything is all right. Sit down, and Lady Bedlow will be home directly. You can talk to her then."

Amy began to cry, childish tears of frustration and weakness. She knew she was only making it worse, but she couldn't stop.

"There, there." Handing her a handkerchief, the man gave her a reassuring pat on the shoulder. "Don't cry. It's all right."

"It's not all right," Amy sobbed.

*   *   *

Nev was never sure if Helen had meant merely to scare him or if she had terrible aim, but the shot flew harmlessly into the air over the horse's back.

The spirited Thoroughbred reared up, his hooves flashing dangerously close to Nev's face. Struggling to keep hold of the reins, Nev felt something give in his arm as the horse prepared to plunge directly into the mob.

Nev hung on to the reins as hard as he could, wishing desperately he had Palomides with him instead. "*Whoa!*" The horse reared again. Heart pounding, Nev threw himself in front of the horse, shoving Helen Spratt out of range of its hooves. He dodged a fierce kick and lunged, grabbing the bridle from the other side as well. When the horse next reared up, he hung on grimly, letting all his weight pull the gelding back toward earth. "Whoa!" he shouted again. "Calm down!"

He might not have managed it if Aaron Smith had not darted forward and jerked on the bridle with a casual strength that surprised Nev.

It seemed like an eternity but was probably only a few seconds before the horse stilled, nostrils flaring and eyes rolling. Nev, trembling with relief and anger, took a few precious moments to soothe the horse, running his hand over the beast's flanks and whispering to him. Only when he trusted his voice not to shake did he turn around.

"Sir Jasper." Penelope was pleased to hear that her voice did not shake. "I am glad to see you. There has been some trouble, and I believe you are needed to read the Riot Act. Mr. Snively is waiting for you at the house."

"Of course there is trouble," Sir Jasper said. "I warned you that you could not coddle these folk. I *warned* you what would come of it if you did not keep them on a tight rein. I hope you are satisfied when our houses are all burnt to the ground."

Penelope shrank back at the poison in his voice. "I doubt any homes will be burnt if you are quick," she said, trying to maintain her calm. "Please, do not let me detain you."

He laughed. "There will be time for that when I've dealt with you. You've meddled enough."

"What do you mean?" Afraid she knew, Penelope tried to look around without being too obvious about it. There was no one in sight but Agnes, and Agnes would not meet her eyes. *Miss Wray never had a relapse at all*, Penelope realized. That was when she began to be really frightened.

"I *mean*," Sir Jasper said with savage mockery, "that you are destroying everything I've worked for."

Penelope wanted to say something rational and soothing, something that would make Sir Jasper see—but the words died in her throat. There was no making Sir Jasper see anything. He was mad, and he hated her, and she was alone with him save for a girl who hated her too. "Sir Jasper." She hated the thready sound of her own voice. "Please, there's no need—"

"There is *every* need! Since Bedlow married you things have gone from bad to worse."

"Sir Jasper—"

But it was as if the sound of her voice was anathema to him. His face contorting, he raised the pistol. "You've done all the talking you're going to do."

Penelope stared down the gleaming barrel of the gun and, to her complete surprise, instinctively covered her stomach.

Unexpectedly, Agnes Cusher stepped forward. "Sir Jasper, surely you needn't—"

"Oh, yes," Sir Jasper said with sudden calm. "I'd forgotten about you. Don't think I'm going to let a Jacobin's wife like you ruin everything." The gun swung away from Penelope, and there was a report, unnaturally loud in Penelope's ears. Agnes cried out and toppled to the ground.

Penelope only had a moment to decide what to do. If she stayed where she was, Sir Jasper would use his second shot on her. She looked at Nev's grandfather's ruin, rising over the top of the Greygloss trees. She turned toward it, gathered up her skirts, and ran directly into the forest.

Nineteen

"Stay here," the man told Amy. "I'm going to see if I can find someone to take care of you."

She hurt all over and there was a pounding in her ears. "I don't need someone to take care of me. Lady Bedlow does."

"Lady Bedlow has a husband to take care of her!" The man left the room. Amy tried to think if there was anything else she could do, anyone else she could turn to.

She would try to send a message to Greygloss. Perhaps she could give it to a servant. There must be paper—there must—she tried to stand, the blood rushed to her head, and she fainted for the second time that day.

The crowd was obviously shaken. Mrs. Bailey had pushed her way to the front. "Are you all right, my lord?"

"I am fine," Nev said curtly. "Mrs. Spratt, are you injured?"

Helen looked subdued. "No. I didn't mean to spook the animal."

"No. You only meant to make me think you would shoot me in the face if I stood in your way. This has gone far enough. Go home, all of you, before you do something you will really be hanged for."

"She could be hanged just for firing at you, my lord," Aaron said with a spark of his old defiance. "What have we got to lose now?"

Nev raised his eyebrows. "I don't plan to tell anyone about this. Least of all Sir Jasper, when he comes to read the Riot Act. Go home. Bring in the harvest. The money from the corn will pay for lawyers for your men. I swear I will do everything I can to help them."

"And if you can't save them?"

"Then I can't. They broke the law. They knew the risks. I'm sorry. But if I can't help them, then you certainly cannot."

"And that is supposed to comfort us," Aaron said with quiet bitterness. "That there is nothing we can do. That we are not real men, that we're helpless to protect our families. The law is wrong. They were *hungry*."

Nev's heart clenched. "I know." Then he had an idea. A compromise. *It doesn't have to be all or nothing,* Penelope had said. "I know it has been hard for you at Loweston. For all of you. My wife and I are trying to make things better. Perhaps you would like to select one or two among yourselves to be . . . delegates. To come speak to us and our steward once a week. To tell us what you need."

Murmurs began in the crowd. Nev thought they sounded considering. And Helen Spratt looked completely non-plussed—as well she might, since if a similar arrangement existed anywhere in England, Nev had certainly never heard of it. "You—you'd do that?"

Nev wondered if he would regret this. But it seemed fair. "We can't promise to follow all your suggestions. Money will be tight, especially in the coming year. But we'll listen and do our best."

"Will you get rid of Tom Kedge?" someone shouted from the crowd.

The tension eased out of Nev so abruptly he found himself laughing, a little shakily. Louisa's elopement had one good consequence after all. "That I can promise you!"

That simply, it was over. He could feel it. There would be negotiations and perhaps a few more protestations of good faith to be made, but there would be no blood. Weak with relief, he was already planning the conversation he would have with Penelope upon his return, when rapid hoofbeats came clearly from the direction of the house.

The crowd froze, staring in the direction of the sound. Nev hoped to God it wasn't Sir Jasper. But when the horse came into view, and he recognized Thirkell in his most reckless hell-for-leather gallop, the shock of fear that went through him was worse than had an entire band of yeomen been riding down on his people. He could think of no reason for Thirkell to have left both their families that was not of the direst.

The horse drew closer. Nev ran to meet him.

Thirkell dismounted, gasping for breath. "Lady Bedlow—your wife—she's run off somewhere. I can't find her."

Nev stared, unable to take it in. Penelope was missing; she was somewhere on these unfamiliar grounds, laced with traps to catch poachers. Where could she have gone? *Why* would she have gone?

Then there was a gunshot, somewhere to the east and close. Nev took off running, not waiting to see who followed him.

He crested a hill, and his blood froze; the crumpled figure of a woman lay on the path skirting the Greygloss woods. He could not quite be ashamed of his relief when he recognized Agnes Cusher's faded gown and blonde hair. Someone raced past him, and he realized that he *was* followed—by the entire crowd. Thirkell caught up with him, panting.

"Aggie!" cried the man who had passed him. "Aggie!" He fell to his knees and turned her gently over, revealing a blood-soaked bodice that, thank God, still rose and fell. "She's breathing," Aaron said in relief as Nev reached them.

Agnes's eyes drifted open. "He shot me . . . Bastard looked right at me and shot me."

"Who?" Nev asked, crouching on her other side. "Who would do such a thing?"

"Sir Jasper. He made me bring her here. Don't blame Josie, please—"

Nev knew he ought to speak gently to a woman in pain, but he found himself saying fiercely, "Who? Bring who here?"

"Lady Bedlow. She ran into the forest. He ran after her. Know it sounds crazy."

Nev remembered that vicious gleam in Sir Jasper's eyes when he looked at Penelope. It did not sound crazy at all. "Which way?"

"Toward Loweston." Her hand fluttered. "Sorry—"

Nev didn't wait to hear it. He stood. "I'm going after her."

He tried to think how he would even begin to search for Penelope in Sir Jasper's woods, filled with traps for poachers that only Sir Jasper knew—then his thoughts caught up with themselves. *Traps for poachers.* There were men here to whom Greygloss land was not as unfamiliar as it was to Nev. In his mind the most reckless compromise he had ever made sprang into life. He turned to the crowd. "Sir Jasper has my wife somewhere on these grounds. Some of you know Greygloss better than I do. Please, come with me and help me save her!"

"Why should we risk our necks for your wife?" someone shouted, and although he was shushed by several voices, the crowd still waited for Nev's answer.

Nev fought down his rage and his terror, fought down the urge to shout at them that Penelope was worth a hundred of them and he would *make* them help. That could not serve Penelope now. He didn't think about what he was about to promise them. "Because if you do I will *personally* see those men freed from jail. Your families for mine. Do we have a bargain?"

"What about Aggie?" Aaron asked.

"Take her home. I'll pay for the doctor. Who's coming with me?"

Aaron reached for Agnes, but she flinched away. "Go with his lordship."

"Aggie, you're hurt, I can't leave you!"

A tear leaked out of the corner of her eye. "All my fault. If I'd married you, Josie would never have had to take to poaching—"

"Aggie, please," Aaron said, almost begging, "let me take you to a doctor!"

Nev's mind was filled with a hundred terrifying images of Penelope afraid, of Penelope in pain. The one thing he did not allow himself to think was that it might already be too late. "I don't have time for this. I'm going."

Aaron didn't look up. "You won't get far without help."

"Someone else will take me to a doctor," Agnes told him. "You have to save Lady Bedlow."

Aaron bowed his head. Then he picked Agnes up as gently as if she were a porcelain vase neither of them could ever afford and carried her to one of the other men. "Take care of her." Then he turned to the mob and roared, "Let's get this bastard! Who's with me?"

The mob roared back.

Nev's vision blurred. "Wonderful. Thirkell, go to the Loweston side and start a search there in case she got through."

"Of course," Thirkell said, dependable as always.

"Thirkell—" Nev put a hand on his arm. "If I don't come back—tell Percy to take good care of Loweston. And wish him and Louisa joy for me."

Thirkell didn't protest or try to make a comforting speech. He just nodded and got back on his still-winded horse, spurring her on toward the Grange.

Nev turned and saw that Aaron was organizing a contingent of men, most of them armed. "Give me a gun," he said.

"No," Aaron said, and continued on.

"I wasn't asking."

Aaron looked at him and laughed. "These aren't nice, re-liable weapons like yours, my lord. These guns belong to these men, and they know just how far to the left they fire and how hard they jump. You'd have trouble hitting the broad side of a barn. Have you got a knife?"

Nev reached into his pocket. His fist closed around his pocketknife. "Yes. Let's go."

Penelope was lost, and close behind her she could hear Sir Jasper crashing through the woods. She was winded, and weak from having barely eaten in two days. Any second now Sir Jasper would emerge from a stand of trees and find her a pathetically easy target, and she had no idea which direction led toward Loweston and safety.

Perhaps running wasn't the answer. She slipped behind a tree and prayed Sir Jasper would pass her by.

His footsteps came nearer and nearer. She held her breath and pressed herself against the tree until she could feel the knots digging into her back through her stays. She could hear him going past. Now if she could just inch her way round to the other side of the tree so he wouldn't see her if he glanced behind him . . .

He was nearly past when a slight breeze set her skirts billowing. She snatched them back; Sir Jasper had stopped moving. She held herself poised for flight—

An arm snaked round the tree and grabbed hold of her, and she screamed so loudly she would have been embarrassed if she weren't occupied in trying to get free. Thrashing wildly, she hurled herself backward so that his hand smashed into the rough bark of the tree. His grasp loosened, and she threw herself into headlong flight. He was close behind her— she could hear him. Afraid to look back, she put on a last burst of speed, and something came into abrupt focus ahead of her.

She skidded to a halt, her stomach an inch from a trip-wire. She backed up a step, turned, and saw another to her right. The two wires came together at a tree a foot away, and at their junction a gun was mounted on a swivel. She turned. Sir Jasper stood about five feet away, watching her.

"If you come near me—" She coughed; her throat had gone dry. Swallowing, she tried again. "If you come near me, I'm sure I can contrive to get us both shot."

"I'm afraid I shall have to risk it," Sir Jasper said with the wry smile she had once, briefly, thought charming. "I seem to have used up my ammunition."

"That wasn't very well-planned."

His mouth twisted irritably. "Perhaps not. But I shall enjoy strangling you."

He advanced on her. Penelope was preparing to dodge when she heard a noise to her left. She cut her eyes that way, and the absurdly loud pounding of her heart seemed to double in volume.

It was Nev, edging toward them, about thirty feet away.

Any second now Sir Jasper would hear him too, and the element of surprise would be lost.

Without conscious thought, Penelope began to cry. It was surprisingly easy. Years of crying silently with her face pressed into her pillow seemed to melt away; she sobbed and heaved and made horrible gasping noises. "Please! Sir Jasper, please, I'll do anything!"

Amazingly, he stopped. "Oh, for God's sake."

"I'm sorry, I can't help it!" It took all her willpower not to look toward Nev. She couldn't hear his footfalls over the noise of her own tears.

"You've got snot dripping down your chin," Sir Jasper said. "You're a disgusting little thing, aren't you?"

Even at that moment, it stung. She must look horrendous.

He took a step closer and repeated, louder, "*Aren't* you?"

"Yes!" She wiped at her nose with her sleeve. "Yes, I am. I know I am, but please—"

"Please what?" Sir Jasper was enjoying himself now. "Please don't snuff out your pathetic, vulgar little life? You ought to be thanking me for putting you out of your misery. If Bedlow's tired of you already, just think how he's going to feel when you're six months gone and fat as a sow."

Through her sobs, Penelope heard a twig crack. Sir Jasper blinked, and Penelope screeched like a fishwife, "Nev isn't tired of me!" A triumphant smile spread across Sir Jasper's face, and Penelope hated him, just hated him. She wiped her nose on her sleeve and glared.

"Oh, isn't he?" he said. "You're crazy about him, aren't you?"

The sobs froze in Penelope's throat. She stared at Sir Jasper, at Sir Jasper's horrible smile, and could not think, could not speak, could not make a sound. Sir Jasper's eyes flickered again, as if he were going to look away, and Penelope heard herself say loudly, her voice choked with tears and nearly unrecognizable, "Yes! Yes! I'm crazy about him! Are you happy now?"

"And how do you suppose he feels about you?" Sir Jasper asked.

Nev rolled under the tripwire and came up in a crouch, his knife out. "He feels pretty much the same." He lunged at Sir Jasper.

Within a very few moments, Penelope had more sympathy with Gothic heroines than she ever had before. There simply did not appear to be anything she could do to help Nev, or even anything she could do that wouldn't actively hinder him. So she stood like a particularly useless stone and watched as he and Sir Jasper lunged and feinted and were very, very careful not to step too far to the left or right, because the tripwires were close.

The one good thing was that Nev knew what he was doing. He was swift and focused, and Penelope saw quickly that he had the advantage over Sir Jasper in skill, speed, and condition. The problem was the enclosed space, and that his only weapon was a short pocketknife. Sir Jasper was soon bruised and bleeding from a dozen small cuts, but it was clear that Nev did not dare close with him for fear of toppling them all into a wire. He tried to drive Sir Jasper back, away from the deadly corner and Penelope, but Sir Jasper was no fool and refused to give ground.

But, Penelope realized, Nev did not seem desperate. He fought steadily and calmly, as if he did not have to win.

Then she thought she heard another rustle in the trees, and Nev tensed, ever so slightly.

Nev was waiting. Nev thought help was on the way.

Penelope remembered the Gothic heroine's weapon. She began to scream, as loudly as she could. Surely they would hear. Surely they would come. Her throat hurt and Nev was beginning to sweat, and she could not tell how near help might be because her screams drowned out their noise. But if she could not tell, then Sir Jasper couldn't either, and that was something.

"Tell your wife to shut the hell up!" Sir Jasper snarled, looking decidedly wild. On Nev's next lunge, Sir Jasper seized his wrist. Nev twisted easily out of his grasp, but somehow Sir Jasper used their contact to swing them round so he was between Nev and Penelope.

Nev's eyes widened, but whether he was looking at her or at something behind her, Penelope could not say; she saw him come to some sort of decision.

Nev charged forward, and Sir Jasper clocked him in the face. Nev fell like a stone.

The screams died in Penelope's throat. In the abrupt silence, she heard a rustle directly behind her, and thought she understood. Nev wasn't unconscious. He was making Sir Jasper a clear target.

Sir Jasper made to kneel beside Nev, and Penelope said past the pain and soreness in her throat, "I'll kill you if you touch him." Where was the help? Why weren't they shooting? Had she been wrong? Any second now Sir Jasper would kneel down and put his hands around Nev's throat. She began to count to three; if nothing had happened by then, surely she could run into Sir Jasper hard enough to knock the two of them into a tripwire. If she could twist them round so he was toward the tree, she might not even be hurt.

One.

Two.

There was a deafening noise and a flash of red, and Sir Jasper slumped to the ground on top of Nev.

Penelope's knees buckled, but she pushed herself forward in time to land on the ground at Nev's side instead of falling into the tripwires.

Nev opened his eyes and looked at her. There were leaves in his hair and Sir Jasper's blood was spattered across his face, and his smile was as sweet as ever. "I think I have a handkerchief in my pocket," he said. He sounded absolutely all right, but when Penelope gingerly reached a hand under Sir Jasper's shoulder to pull it out, her fingers came away wet with the baronet's blood.

She started to cry again, and Nev shoved Sir Jasper off him and gathered her up. She clung to him, pressed into his chest, ignoring the blood smeared across her face and the snot still dribbling down her chin and the horrible, sniveling picture she must make. She focused instead on Nev's heartbeat, steady under her ear. He held her and shushed her and stroked her hair and murmured, "It's all right, sweetheart, you're safe now, it's all right, he can't hurt you anymore, he can't hurt our people, we're safe." He knew just what to say and just how to hold her and he was perfect, perfect for her. How could she leave him? That had been death's chief terror too: leaving Nev.

Penelope got through the next half hour in a daze: thanking the men who had shot Sir Jasper, telling Edward and Lord Thirkell that she was all right, really, it wasn't her blood, it wasn't Nev's. Edward looked guilty and on edge. Penelope didn't know why and didn't have the energy to find out.

They were in the hall at the Grange. Nev was explaining for the tenth time what had happened, this time to the constable, inquiring how soon they could have an inquest and asking after Agnes Cusher and generally being a responsible landlord and a rational adult even though he was still gripping Penelope's hand hard enough to hurt. Penelope was tired and bloody and her feet ached. "I want a bath."

She was shocked at herself in the next instant, but Nev said, "Of course you do. I'm sorry, I'll ring for Molly."

She nodded. "C—come with me." The constable smirked, Lord Thirkell coughed, and poor Edward looked as if he might have a coronary at any moment. Penelope blushed and set her chin and looked at Nev.

He blinked. "Penelope, are you sure—?"

She nodded, and Nev turned to the other men and said in his most charmingly rueful tones, "My wife has had a very long and frightening day. Perhaps if you came back tomorrow morning, we could discuss the matter further. Thirkell, you can move your things into one of the guest rooms if you'd like. And thank you."

All too soon they were in her room, alone, waiting for the footmen to bring up the tub. Penelope did not know what to do. Reluctantly, she let go of Nev's hand and went to the mirror. Good God, she looked dreadful.

It didn't matter. Nev knew what she looked like.

Nev sighed behind her. "It's all right, Penelope. I know you were just trying to distract Sir Jasper. I know you didn't mean it. And I know you're upset now. You've been through a lot today, and you don't want to be alone. I understand. I won't—" He stopped for a moment, then said, very steadily, "I won't think it means more than it does. You don't have to say anything."

"No. No, I think I do. Nev, what I said this morning—"

"Can't we talk about it later, Penelope?" He looked at the floor, sounding so tired it broke her heart. "I know you want to go, at least—at least for a while, and I know that it complicates things that there might be a child, and I know we have to talk about it. But does it have to be right now? Can't we just take a damned bath because we're both filthy and covered in our nearest neighbor's blood and not talk about it?"

"*No.*"

His head jerked up at the unfamiliar edge in her voice.

"No, because you've got it all wrong. I don't want to leave. I never wanted to leave, except—" She still didn't know how to say it, she didn't know what she would do if Nev said he didn't love her, not like that, as a sister maybe, as a friend, but not like *that*.

"Except what?" The tiredness was gone from his voice.

"Oh, damn." She rubbed at her forehead; bits of blood flaked off under her fingers. "I wasn't lying to Sir Jasper, Nev."

"You—you weren't?" Nev sounded as if he were having difficulty speaking.

"No. I—that is, of course I was trying to distract him, but I was perfectly sincere. I *am* mad about you. I never thought love like this was real, but it is and it hurts and I can't bear the thought of going away, but I can't bear the thought of staying either—"

"Why on earth *not?*"

She could barely breathe, but the words kept coming anyway. "I told myself I was being strong, going; but I was being cowardly. I was frightened of telling you the truth. I didn't want to stand here like I am now and wait for you to tell me that you don't feel the same way. I know I told you I wanted a marriage based on comradeship and mutual esteem. I know we made a bargain. I know we made vows. And I'm sorry I'm not strong enough to keep them. I made that list, but none of them were the right things, the important things—you've *done* all that, you've been wonderful and I don't know what I'll do if you don't feel the same way, I can't bear it—"

Her nails were pressing into her palm until it hurt, until surely she was drawing blood, and then Nev was beside her and he was holding her hands in his and kissing her fingers. "Don't, Penny, don't, I love you too, I swear, don't cry again—"

She giggled at that, but her chest hurt too. "How do you love me?"

"I love you to distraction," he whispered in her ear. "My heart burns within me; I have no peace. I am so enamored I know not whether I am on horseback or on foot—"

He was quoting Malory. He was perfect. She laughed, her eyes stinging. "Do you mean it?"

He stepped back for a moment. "Have I ever lied to you, Penelope?"

She thought about it, and was surprised by the answer. "No. No, you never have."

"Have I ever paid you in Spanish coin?"

"No," she said again, giddy with it. He hadn't, Nev had never lied to her, he wouldn't, so all those things he had said to her, they must have been true—

"Will you stay?"

"Yes," she promised, "yes."

"Forever?"

"Well, you know what they say: a Penny saved is a Penny earned."

Nev whooped and crushed her to him, and Penelope was definitely about to cry again when the door opened and Lady Bedlow walked in.

Penelope tried to pull back, but Nev held her tight against his side and she gave up, smiling like a fool. "Lady Bedlow, what can I do for you?"

"It's Louisa," Lady Bedlow said. "And I couldn't wait downstairs, I had to see for myself that you were all right, oh, Nate, you scared me half to death! You look dreadful, are you sure you're not hurt?" She did look white and shaken, and Penelope tried again to pull away so that Nev could go to his mother.

His hand was firm and unmoving on her hip. "Yes, I'm sure. What about Louisa, Mama?"

"She's back," Lady Bedlow said. "She and Percy."

Nev groaned. "Oh, for God's sake. Where?"

They were waiting on the front steps. "We didn't want to go in; you *had* forbidden me the house—" Percy stopped short. "Good God, Nev, what's happened to you?"

"Don't worry, it's Sir Jasper's," Nev said.

Louisa turned quite pale. "Oh, Nate—"

"It had nothing to do with you, Louisa." Nev did think Louisa's elopement might have been the penultimate straw for Sir Jasper, but he could hardly blame her for their neighbor's insanity, and anyway he couldn't be angry with anyone at the moment. "I thought you would be halfway to Gretna by now. Did you throw a wheel?"

"I made him turn back after the first twenty miles. I couldn't do that to you, Nate, I couldn't—"

His heart, already overflowing, threatened to burst.

"Thank you, Louisa. Would you like to announce your engagement tomorrow?"

Louisa tensed, looking dubiously at his blood-spattered waistcoat. "To . . . ?"

He swallowed. "Sir Jasper's dead, Louisa. I know I haven't been the best of brothers, but how could you think I wanted you to marry him, anyway? He offered when we were still in London, and I turned him down."

"I *told* you," Percy said to Louisa in a superior tone.

Nev smiled at his friend. "Your engagement to Percy, naturally. But it will have to be a long one, Louisa. A year or two at least. You can live here in the meantime—"

He didn't get farther than that, because Louisa and her new white dress flew into his arms, heedless of dirt and blood.

Penelope and Nev smiled at each other over their eggs and toast. Penelope eyed the honey jar thoughtfully, reaching for it just as Edward walked in. She drew back her hand with a sigh.

Edward fidgeted with the brim of his hat. "I just—I just wanted to say good-bye."

Penelope glanced at Nev, who nodded. "All right," she said. "I'll see you out."

She followed him in silence to the door, where his trunk was already lashed to the coach. On the first stair he turned. "I'm glad you're safe, Penelope."

"I know. Thank you."

"Don't thank me," he said bitterly. "If you had had to rely on me, I suppose you would be dead."

She gave Edward a crooked smile. "Well, it's true I was rather irked when I heard Miss Raeburn's story, but you thought you were acting for the best. I don't blame you, truly—"

"Of course not. You're far too good-natured for that."

Penelope thought again how little Edward really knew her.

"But I blame myself," he said in a low, troubled voice. "I can't help wondering—did I really believe she was delirious? I was angry with you, I think. I was angry that you didn't love me. I told her you had a husband to take care of you, and I felt so spiteful—what if I knew? What if I knew you were in danger and I didn't help you because I was angry?" His knuckles were white on the handle of his valise.

Penelope reached out and touched his arm. "You didn't. I know you didn't. Edward—I didn't know this either until recently, but it's all right to be angry. It really is. If you're afraid of your emotions, it only makes them more dangerous. You have to—you have to let yourself feel." She put her hand over his heart. "I know you, Edward. There's nothing in here that you have to be afraid of."

He looked down at her hand. "I wish I could be as sure."

Even though she had been half wishing he would go for days now, she said, "Stay another few days, Edward. I don't want you to leave like this."

He smiled at her. "I'd only be in the way. I know that."

"You're still my best friend. Nothing will ever change that." A thought struck her. The doctor had said that Amy's exertions had weakened her greatly, and recommended she not be moved from the Grange. Penelope was surprised at how little she minded; and Amy's pleasure at being back in a feather bed had been hard to resist. "Besides, Miss Raeburn is going mad from boredom, and if you'd sit with her a little it would be doing me the greatest favor."

He hesitated, and then—Penelope hid a grin—blushed. "Are you sure?"

She nodded.

"I suppose I could read to her . . ."

Amy must be used to Nev's reading. "Just talk to her. I don't think—I don't think people have really listened to her enough in her life."

"I certainly didn't," Edward muttered, and asked the coachman to take down his trunk and send back the carriage.

The door opened, and Penelope slipped back into the breakfast room. "Now, where was I?" she asked, reaching for the honey.

Nev hastily swallowed his bite of muffin and put his napkin on the table, in case Penelope should decide to sit in his lap.

Louisa and Percy walked in; Nev devoutly hoped they had met on the stairs. Penelope picked up the jar of honey and began to demurely drizzle it onto a slice of toast, blushing only a little.

Nev stifled a sigh. He supposed he had better get used to having company at the breakfast table; Louisa would be living with them, after all, and Percy would start eating with the family again. Nev wondered for a moment where Thirkell was, since he'd moved his things in last night, then remembered that he never woke early enough for breakfast.

"Brioche!" Louisa exclaimed rapturously, and fell upon the spread. "Oh, Nate," she said around a mouthful of brioche, "if you're planning a daring raid on the jail to free the poachers, I want to come."

Nev closed his eyes.

"*Louisa*," Percy said.

"Nev?" Penelope asked. "What is she talking about?"

"Nate told the poachers that if they helped him save you from Sir Jasper, he would free their families," Louisa explained. "Thirkell told Percy."

"Sorry," Percy said, shamefaced. This was going to be odd, knowing that everything he said to Percy might get back to his sister. But it also meant, Nev realized suddenly, that Percy would be family. Percy would be his brother. He had been so worried for Louisa that it hadn't even occurred to him before. He grinned at Percy.

Percy smiled back, looking startled but relieved.

Nev looked around the table, at his wife and sister and best friend, and the happiness of the future that he hadn't been able to imagine burst on him all at once, with interest. Ever since his father's death it had seemed that if he did not fix things quickly enough, disaster would strike. Well, it had struck, and they had come out of it whole. He could see now that there was plenty of time. He wasn't going to get himself shot. There were years and years, and he would learn how to be a big brother to Louisa again, a friend to Percy and Thirkell, a landlord to his people. A husband to Penelope. He was learning already.

There was plenty of time to fix Loweston. It would be beautiful and prosperous and safe when he handed it over to his son.

He would learn how to be a father. Penelope might already be carrying his child. Well, there was plenty of time to find that out too. Nev beamed.

Penelope looked at him uncertainly, flushing. "You didn't."

It took him a moment to remember what they were talking about. Right, his promise to the poachers. "Of course I did."

"Are you planning anything very rash?"

"Something very rash indeed," he told her. "There's nothing for it. I shall have to become a justice of the peace and drop the charges. They should be out and back to their families in a couple of months at the latest." True, he'd originally been planning something more in line with Louisa's suggestion, but with Sir Jasper safely dead, this was a better way.

"Oh, Nev, you'll hate it." Penelope's eyes were bright.

He smiled at her. "I expect I will. It will be dull and dreary and quite a lot of sitting around indoors doing paperwork. But I made a promise, and I don't do things halfway."

She catapulted into his lap after all. "You reckless fool," she said, and kissed him right there in front of everyone.

INTERACT WITH DORCHESTER ONLINE!

Want to learn more about your favorite books and authors?
Want to talk with other readers that like to read the same books as you?
Want to see up-to-the-minute Dorchester news?

VISIT DORCHESTER AT:

DorchesterPub.com
Twitter.com/DorchesterPub
Facebook.com (Search Pages)

DISCUSS DORCHESTER'S NOVELS AT:

Dorchester Forums at DorchesterPub.com
GoodReads.com
LibraryThing.com
Myspace.com/books
Shelfari.com
WeRead.com

CPSIA information can be obtained at www.ICGtesting.com
Printed in the USA
269888BV00001B/9/P